THE BERLIN GIRL

Mandy Robotham saw herself as an aspiring author since the age of nine, but was waylaid by journalism and later enticed by birth. She's now a former midwife, who writes about birth, death, love and anything else in between. She graduated with an MA in Creative Writing from Oxford Brookes University. This is her third novel – her previous two have both been *Globe and Mail* and *USA Today* bestsellers.

By the same author:

A Woman of War (published as *The German Midwife*
in North America, Australia and New Zealand)
The Secret Messenger

The Berlin Girl

Mandy Robotham

avon.

Published by AVON
A division of HarperCollins*Publishers* Ltd
1 London Bridge Street
London SE1 9GF

www.harpercollins.co.uk

This paperback edition 2020
1

First published in Great Britain by HarperCollins*Publishers* 2020

A catalogue copy of this book is available from the British Library.

ISBN: 978-0-00-841863-2

Typeset in Bembo Std by Palimpsest Book Production Limited, Falkirk, Stirlingshire
Printed and bound in UK by CPI Group (UK) Ltd, Croydon CR0 4YY

MIX
Paper from
responsible sources
FSC
www.fsc.org
FSC™ C007454

To Hayley — a good friend.
Thanks for many words spilled over coffee.

Author's note

Hindsight is a wonderful thing, so the saying goes. Never more so than with World War Two, when no prophet could have foretold the atrocities that were witnessed and subsequently woven into the tainted fabric of history.

It was that time *before* that I wanted to capture in *The Berlin Girl* – a time when humanity had plumbed certain depths throughout the centuries, but never to quite the same degree as with the Holocaust. So that time has become divided into before and after Auschwitz and Dachau – and Sachsenhausen; before and after we knew what Man's potential could sink to.

The degree of inhumanity might not have been predicted, but there were those who both saw and warned of Hitler's hunger for domination, those who were there in the eye of the early storm; in my research, from diaries and biographies, it was the journalists centred around Berlin who warned repeatedly of the conflict to come – among them, the highly respected William L. Shirer from CBS, in his *Berlin Diary*. Sadly, it was a world not prepared to listen closely enough – politicians especially.

Among the press pack in the 1930s – and throughout the war – were a good many women, beautifully depicted in Nancy Caldwell Sorel's *Women Who Wrote the War*: Sigrid Schultz, a shrewd Jewish reporter for a US newspaper, who managed to be both friend and foe to the Nazi elite, and Clare Hollingworth, who scooped everyone with her exposé on the Nazis' final move into Poland. Martha Gellhorn – the reluctant 'Mrs Hemingway' – was not in Berlin circles, but remains a hero of mine, and her excellent biography by Caroline Moorehead was both an avenue into the mind of a correspondent, and yet almost a fairy tale of adventure too. Having been a journalist in my days before midwifery and writing (though a very unexciting local hack), I can only imagine the courage of such women in times when they were constrained by their sex, and often by ridiculous etiquette. They broke through many barriers for women as a whole, not least in print.

In a time before social media, readers hung onto those opinions from newsprint and radio – it was their window to the world before the luxuries of mainstream television, Twitter and Facebook.

Like the fictional Georgie, I also wanted to explore the personal side of impending war – what it meant for families like the Amsels to live life on a knife edge, for months and years, never knowing if your world would be tipped upside down in a split second, by a slighted neighbour, or a careless word to the Gestapo – feelings recalled by Irene Matthews's memoir, *Out of Nazi Germany and Trying to Find My Way*. As I edited this book in unprecedented times of the UK Coronavirus lockdown, loss took on a new meaning; it was weeks and months for us, separated temporarily for the most part, but for a lifetime? Forever? Not based on a quirk of science or nature, but on the whim of just one man. It still beggars belief for me.

I can't pretend that including the Amsels wasn't something of a personal journey too – my family history is fairly disjointed, but I did discover late in life that my paternal grandfather was Jewish; likely in North London before the war. My own father knew very little of him and was not raised as a practising Jew, but I can't help wondering what circumstances brought my grandfather to England – whether he and his family were pushed from a European homeland in the brutal sweep of fascism.

The research journey was, again, a fascinating one; not only the recollections of apt and quick minds in the foreign press, but trawling through the hundreds of pages of old newspapers. The *News Chronicle* was upbeat and a darned good read – fierce and brave in the articles it produced – and the adverts for 'Bile Beans' were in there too, I promise.

And of course, any reader that's familiar with my work knows that I am hopelessly enticed by any hint of a newsroom; the feverish rush on press day, furious tap-tapping, even in post-typewriter times. I remember so fondly the camaraderie of local newspaper offices as we pushed towards a deadline, and the vast, open space buzz of the *Evening Standard* offices, where I worked for a short time. It's tomorrow's chip paper, as they say, but something we still can't seem to do without – thankfully. Long live print journalism.

Prologue

Plans

Berlin, 23rd July 1938

Leaving the clang of cell doors behind him and the ebbing sounds of agony within, Major Hugo Schenk holstered his pistol and climbed the stairs from the gloom of the basement with renewed energy.

As the light of the upper floors lifted his mood further, he spied the tiny crimson droplet out of the corner of his eye, unable to ignore it soiling the cuff of his otherwise spotless and pressed uniform. Despite its minuscule size, it moved like a virtual beacon in his line of vision. He scratched at it, irritation rising when it remained embedded in the fine, grey weave. These days, he rarely got his hands dirty, but today's quarry for vital information had proved intensely frustrating – the target foolishly stubborn – and he'd acted in haste. Hence the spatter. He was relieved, though, to have left the majority of the red slick several floors down, a congealing pool across the filthy tiles of the cells. Doubtless, it was being mopped as he attended to his business above ground, its donor limp within the bowels of the building, unburdened of bodily fluid and what information he and his colleagues had managed to extract before his patience ran out. Even so, the tiny fleck sprayed upon him during the event was unfortunate, particularly as he had an appointment with Himmler later in the afternoon. Despite the day's intense heat, the Gestapo chief would expect him in full uniform, collar and shirt tightly fastened.

Back at his desk, he looked with satisfaction at the neat stack of files to his side, meticulously categorised and all ready for Himmler's approval. They were in size order; the fat folder labelled 'Jew' on the bottom, topped with 'Romani', 'Sinti' and 'Jehovah's Witness'. Uppermost sat a slimmer folder marked 'Undesirables'. With a self-satisfied nod, he scanned the full-scale plans for expansion spread across his desk – yes, much more capacity. More *creativity*. They were on target. Himmler would be pleased.

He scratched again at the blood spot as the phone trilled beside him.

'Yes?'

'Major Schenk, sorry to disturb you. But we've just had word on your attaché. I'm afraid to report he was killed this morning in a motoring accident. Both he and the woman in the car.'

The first emotion to rise was annoyance, sparked initially by that blood spot, but also by the inconvenience. Dammit, it was unfortunate to lose a good attaché, someone proficient at smoothing his sometimes rough edges, a worthy diplomat. He'd been efficient and obedient. A good Nazi. Schenk was aware, though, of the need to conjure up some semblance of sympathy. It wouldn't do to appear callous.

'Ah, that's unfortunate. He had children, I believe. Do we know if they will be cared for by others in the family?'

The voice on the other end coughed with embarrassment. 'Erm, the woman in the car wasn't his wife, sir.'

'Oh, I see. Well, send his wife condolences and flowers. And make sure we pay for the funeral.'

'Yes, sir.'

'Have we got a replacement lined up?'

'Yes, Major, I have someone in mind. Young, but very keen. I'll sort the necessary paperwork; make sure you are able to meet him for approval.'

'Good work. Heil Hitler.'

He replaced the receiver, and the red speck flashed across his vision, a spark to his temper within. Fucking Jews. Why did they have to bleed so copiously?

1

Heat and Dust

London, 23rd July 1938

Georgie sat with her eyes fixed on the ceiling, tracking the light glinting off the chandelier and noting several cobwebs that hadn't been dismissed by the cleaning staff prior to this evening's ball. The glory of the London Ritz held fast in its reputation, but in its pockets and corners the renowned hotel might have been fading just a little – clearly dirt and dust soiled even the rich. And yet the thought made Georgie feel oddly comforted; if this glamorous venue – a place she could have only dreamt about in her childhood – was hiding behind a façade, then there must be others who sported such a veneer. Maybe even a good portion of this well-populated ballroom. It made her feel less of a fraud.

She shifted on her bar stool in an effort to bat away the waves of unending heat. The barman caught her eye and she smiled meekly, trying not to give the impression of being either stood up or lonely, when she was neither. Still, he looked back with sympathy. Others in the room might not have noticed Georgie's awkwardness, the way the strap of her dress cut into her shoulder, lent to her by a cousin who was clearly half a size smaller. Or the shoes pinching at each little toe, biting into her flesh as she was forced to endure a dance with the office lothario and his two left feet.

She'd managed to excuse herself after one long and painful tune, retreating to the bar, where she now sat, nursing a Martini. The dance floor was full again, as correspondents mingled with reporters and photographers, watching editors and their wives twirling amid the heady table chatter of wordsmiths putting the world to rights. The summer media ball was where hardened London hacks let their hair down for just one night and forgot about the simmering rivalry of Fleet Street – who was first to the story, who bagged an exclusive, and who splashed the biggest headline. For Georgie it was intoxicating, though not nearly as effective as the very strong cocktail mixed by the barman who, in his pity, had added a second shot of vodka. The music and the heat were making her head swim, but she was enjoying the spectacle too much to leave.

'Sitting this one out?'

Georgie swivelled her head in the direction of the voice, her short, blonde curls swaying with the sharp movement. For a brief second she wondered if it was the lothario come to hound her for a second dance, but the tone was unfamiliar. When her eyes fell on its owner, she noted there was barely a smile to accompany it.

She nodded at her feet perched on the bar stool. 'I might be willing but my shoes are working against me.'

'Oh,' he said, and leaned his elbow on the bar, one flick of his finger signalling to the barman. Either her reply had come across as tart or he was simply making small talk, and Georgie returned to her people-watching.

Still, something about him forced a sideways glance; he was tall, lean and appeared surprisingly cool in his full evening suit.

Noting her glimpse, he grasped at his own cocktail and turned to face her.

'Are you here as a guest of someone?' He clearly didn't absorb the sharpness of his own tone. Any other woman might have supposed it rude, but it merely bounced off Georgie's well-constructed shell. *Does he think I'm an imposter, some kind of gate-crasher?* she thought. Her irritation rose, and then fell as her sense of humour bubbled upwards. There was always fun to be had with such men.

'No, I'm here with my boss,' she replied. 'I work at the *Chronicle*.'

'Oh.' More of an enquiring air this time. 'Whose secretary are you?'

Georgie dragged a smile out of her deep and varied supply bag, the type of expression that hid her contempt well. 'I work with Henry Peters.'

Whoever this young man was, he couldn't fail to recognise the name of one of Fleet Street's most revered men on the *Chronicle*'s foreign desk.

'Oh,' the man said again.

Is this his entire vocabulary? Georgie mused. *He can't possibly be a journalist, with such a poor grasp on language.* 'And you?' she asked, eyeing her Martini as if it held more interest. She wasn't in a mood to feed his ego, but the alcohol was making her playful.

'I'm with the *Telegraph*,' he shot back, turning and puffing out his chest. 'Foreign desk.' His voice was pure public school, his stature and dress reflecting the same.

'Oh,' Georgie responded. *Two can play at that game.*

They both looked out onto the dance floor again, the silence between them hovering like a thick winter fog.

'Strange to see so many newspapermen with their wives,' Georgie said at last, when the fog began to feel cloying. 'I've never seen this many on their best behaviour. Or smiling.' And she peered at him, assessing if he'd caught her humour. His gruff cough signalled not. Still, he didn't seem inclined to walk away either.

'Not tempted to tie the knot yourself?' she pressed, noting the absence of a wedding ring. It was like prodding at a roasting spit of pork, and Georgie felt slightly guilty at how much she delighted in it.

He looked at her quizzically. 'Me? Oh no,' he said decisively. 'I don't know how any serious reporter could contemplate it. Not the way the world is right now. A foreign posting is no place for a wife. Or any woman, in fact.' His hard, blue eyes relayed complete conviction in his statement.

'Really?' Now Georgie wanted to prod some more. With force. And a sharp object. 'Are you not a fan of Martha Gellhorn then?' she added.

'You mean the future Mrs Hemingway?' he shot back. His assumptive pairing would have been a red rag to the celebrated correspondent herself. Likewise to Georgie.

'I feel sure *Miss Gellhorn* would take you to task for assuming she is writing in Ernest's shadow,' she fizzed through gritted teeth. 'I'm inclined to think her dispatches from the Spanish frontline are just as good, if not better, than those of her lover.'

Now he looked at her again, his eyebrows knitting together in confusion. *What on earth would a mere secretary know about that?* they seemed to be saying.

'Well, that's a matter of opinion,' he said at last. 'It's dangerous out there. You need your wits about you. And besides, marriage isn't for me.'

'Oh,' Georgie said again. And she withdrew the toasting fork. *He's not worth the wit,* she thought and turned her eyes to the dance floor again, transformed to a kaleidoscope of activity and colour, music flooding the entire room, the chandelier teardrops swaying from thermals of cigarette smoke and human heat.

He swigged suddenly at his cocktail, perhaps gaining courage from the action and the alcohol combined.

'Care to dance?' he said, and held out his hand for her acceptance.

Georgie gestured towards her feet and scrunched up her nose. 'Thank you, but my feet are telling me it's way too dangerous out there.'

Those very blue eyes bored into hers for a second. Realising he'd been snubbed, the man turned tail without a word, striding up to the first lone woman teetering on the edge of the floor and almost yanking her into the dancing fray.

Georgie drained her own glass and signalled for one more. Despite her sore toes and her undersized dress, it really had been a very entertaining evening.

2

Paranoia

His pace quickened as he hastened down the busy street, breath squeezing at his ribs. Sweat ran in rivulets between his shoulder blades, causing his shirt to stick to his skin as he darted forward under the late, low sun nudging at the Berlin skyline. His brain seesawed while his legs scissored in a motion of their own making – paranoia and fear were an effective fuel. Should he look backwards to check if he had a tail? Could he shake them off if he did? Only one purpose dominated his mind and body: he had to get home.

At the last corner before his own street, he stopped at one of the rounded pillars pasted with political posters, pretending to read but inching his way around so that he looked back along the street from where he'd come. In his heart, he knew this sudden, consuming fear was irrational, but he couldn't shake it off until he reached home. Thankfully, no one appeared to be loitering in the steady stream of human traffic going to and fro, least of all Gestapo. But then, what did the Gestapo look like? No tell-tale leather coats for months now in this lengthy, hot summer, and they didn't tend to favour formal announcements. Turning towards his own street, he launched once again in the direction of his own front door.

'Rubin! What are you doing home so early?' Sara swung out of the kitchen, drying her hands on a cloth. 'Has your work been cancelled?' His wife looked suddenly alarmed at the prospect of vital funds no longer dropping into her purse. Any job the Amsels secured these days was crucial to their survival.

'No, no, it's fine, Sara,' he lied. 'I was just nearby. How's Elias?'

'He's all right,' she replied. 'More settled today, dozing right now.'

'Good,' Rubin breathed with relief. 'No callers? No one asking after him?'

'No . . . why? What's all this about?' she quizzed with rising unease. 'Have you come home simply to ask after my brother's health?' Rubin was almost always out from early until late, touting for business – driving, interpreting, moving groceries – any job he could find.

'No,' he admitted, his face pinched with worry. 'But I do need to talk to you about him. Come into the kitchen.'

'But I don't understand,' Sara said, clutching a cup of the hot coffee she'd brewed them both. 'You mean they would take him away, just because he can't work? Put him in a prison for that? He's sick, Rubin, not a criminal.'

Her husband poured out more of the weak, tan-coloured liquid. Sara was not naive to the lengths the Reich would go to, not in the Berlin of the day, but she was a naturally forgiving soul. 'They don't call it a prison,' he explained. 'It's a camp, they say, for "protective custody".'

'Protection from what?' Sara said, her already furrowed face

11

creased deeper with misunderstanding. 'We've looked after Elias since his accident. He's a burden to no one, least of all this wretched government.'

'I know, my darling, but that's not what the Nazi Party think. And he is a Jew. Two marks against his name.'

'Are you sure?' she said, horrified. 'This isn't simply a rumour?'

'No, I'm not entirely sure, but I don't think we can take the risk, do you? We have to protect Elias, as much as we can.'

'So what do we do?' She was genuinely empty of ideas. 'There's no one who can look after him, not like us. Where would he go?'

Rubin cast his eyes towards the ceiling, to the attic above their third-floor apartment, the space beyond the wooden hatch currently daubed in cobwebs, the roof slats allowing slivers of daylight and a stiff breeze to come through in winter.

'Rubin – no!' Sara said, incredulous again. 'This is my brother – we can't shut him in the attic. Not in this heat. Not ever. His life is bad enough as it is.'

Rubin didn't dare voice his thoughts in that moment: it might be no life at all if what he had heard was right.

Sitting in a bar only days previously, he'd overhead two men talking of their neighbour's son, a teenage lad who'd always been considered a 'bit slow', one man said. The boy had been plucked suddenly from his house by soldiers from the Wehrmacht with no explanation, his parents left distraught and with little idea where or why he'd been taken. At the time, Rubin thought little of the conversation beyond a general sadness that accompanied life in Nazi-led Germany for anyone of Jewish blood.

But this morning, he'd eavesdropped on a different kind of conversation, one that had caused bile to rise rapidly in this throat; two SS officers outside the Hotel Kaiserhof, a favourite haunt of Hitler and his inner circle. They were smoking nonchalantly, clearly unaware of Rubin's presence. One mentioned a 'sweeping up' operation, part of a much larger 'clean-up'. At first, it had been hard to work out who or what he meant, but Rubin ran with a chill as it became apparent: 'They'll start with the retarded,' the officer said, 'then the sick – the incurables – and those who can't work will be swept up finally. Who knows, they might just use a large enough broom for all Jews, eh?' The two sniggered and blew smoke into the air while Rubin hardly dared release his own breath. Tossing aside their cigarettes, they moved inside, leaving Rubin to sprint from the shadows and head swiftly towards home and his wife.

In his own kitchen, Sara looked at him with disbelief and dread. 'Is there no other way?' she said.

'I'll get up in the attic as soon as I can,' Rubin said in reply. 'Make it the best I can without drawing too much attention.'

3

The Penny Drops

Croydon Aerodrome, 2nd August 1938

She was bent over pulling at a wrinkle in her stockings when they came into her vision – tan brogues that were well worn and polished, but expensive enough not to show their wear and tear. This particular pair she didn't so much as recognise, but it wasn't hard to marry them with the voice directed at the back of her head: 'Hello, fancy seeing you here.'

Georgie pulled herself to standing and adopted the same expression she'd engineered at their meeting at the Ritz, a forced but well-versed half-smile. His was warmer, though also contrived, his eyes roaming into the distance of the airport lounge.

'Your feet are not still playing up, are they?' he said indifferently.

'Just my stockings misbehaving this time,' she replied, prickling with irritation that etiquette demand she wear them on such a hot day.

'Are you off on your holidays?' he went on.

'No, no,' she stammered. 'A business trip.'

'Oh,' he said, his attention on small clumps of travellers milling around the gate.

For Georgie, it was too much of a coincidence; the penny had begun to drop, with the force of an anvil plunging into a deep, dark ocean. The man in front of her, however, had not put two and two together. His face was alight with blissful ignorance as he continued to skim the airport lounge. She prayed her thinking was wildly off track, or else this was a cruel irony that life – and her editor – was playing on her.

'I'm off on business too,' he said. 'Supposed to be meeting someone here, only I don't know what he looks like. He's one of your lot, from the *Chronicle*, I mean. You probably know him, don't you? George Young?'

It's now or never, she thought. Better put him out of his misery or we'll be here until our flight's called. She extended a hand, in a 'pleased to meet you' gesture. 'Georgina Young – most people call me Georgie . . .'

His eyes were at least on her, but he seemed to have been struck dumb by her introduction. Pupils wide and disbelieving, jaw sinking towards the floor, his hand falling away from hers in surprise.

'Or George,' she went on, to fill the yawning chasm of embarrassment between them.

'Oh,' he managed.

Is this really all he can say? Will he always be so inarticulate?

Finally, his fish-pout of a mouth closed and he was able to form some other words. 'I . . . I just imagined . . .'

'Yes, so do most people,' Georgie said quickly. 'You're not the first, and I suppose you won't be the last. I am quite used to it.'

He looked at her face-on. There was no apology, though no detectable malice either. More like a deep-seated disappointment that she recognised all too well. She suspected from their last meeting that his thinking aligned with the majority of male Fleet Street journalists, harbouring a long-held belief that women were incapable of being serious reporters, bar the tittle-tattle of the fashion or society pages. She might have quoted a long line of celebrated women who were both icons and heroines, but doing so was increasingly tiresome.

She squared her shoulders and stood tall – Georgie Young had served her apprenticeship and earned her place on this posting. She just had to prove it. Starting now, it seemed.

In time, he swallowed down his shock and pulled himself up, as a gentleman would. Manners overcame prejudice, and he held out his hand, searching for hers to shake.

'Max Spender,' he said, and she noted his cool, lean fingers, mindful hers were clammy with anticipation as the time of their flight approached. He hesitated, mid-shake. She watched a shadow move across his face, perhaps prodding at a dusty corner of his memory.

'Wasn't it you who secured the exclusive with Diana Mosley?' His features clouded, with suspicion rather than admiration.

'Yes.' At the time, Georgie had been thrilled at being the first to probe the aristocratic wife of Britain's foremost fascist, though she also knew it caused consternation among the other papers who missed out – rumours circulated of her using underhand means to gain access. 'I had good contacts,' she qualified, which was entirely true.

Max Spender's expression said otherwise. Disbelief and accusation lodged firmly on his brow, and it took all her resolve to match his firm stare. Who would crack first?

'So we're to buddy up together, I hear,' he said at last, in a tone that said he was trying hard to make the best of a bad job. He wasn't forgiving, just brushing it aside – for now. 'You've been to Berlin before, my boss says, on assignment? And you speak German?'

'Yes,' Georgie replied. 'I was there in '36, for the Olympics. Of course I wasn't based directly in the city centre, but I saw a little of it, plus I've got a map. I daresay we'll find our way around.'

'I'm sure we'll each be casting out on our own in no time at all,' he came back quickly, not bothering to even manufacture a smile. She took it as a heavy hint – he really was planning to have as little to do with her as possible, she being tainted and untrustworthy. *Well done, Georgie, off to a great start.*

'How's your German?' she pitched with genuine curiosity. His features stiffened then – this time, he could not feign any semblance of control.

'Passable,' he countered.

'Fairly non-existent then?' Georgie followed up with her own false grin, tinged with a smugness she couldn't resist. If it was bordering on cruel, it was only payback for his own reactions. And for all those jibes she and every other female correspondent had been forced to endure with their lipstick smiles.

This time Max bared his straight, white teeth and a sigh fought its way through. 'I've spent the last week holed up with a German dictionary but I'm not much beyond saying hello and asking for a beer.'

'Well, that might get you further than you think,' she said. 'Never mind, mine's a little rusty too. But I think I can at least order us dinner, so stick with me and at least we won't starve.'

For a second, Georgie imagined he might have softened a little – spotted the hint of a slight, appreciative nod in Max Spender.

'Perhaps we should get a drink before take-off?' he suggested.

'Yes, definitely,' she said, grasping the opportunity. She wasn't much of a drinker, never had any real need of it, but the thought of her first ever flight in a heavy metal tube that lifted several thousand feet off the ground was more intimidating than their final destination. A drink might just settle the herd of elephants in her stomach.

Georgie downed her whisky in three gulps, the ice chill causing her to gasp and swallow hard.

'Steady!' said Max. 'Are you nervous by any chance?'

There was no denying her anxiety – it was his turn to enjoy the upper hand when she admitted to being a virgin flyer against his veteran status. Still, he didn't dwell on it, and this time he was magnanimous in his advice.

'Just keep yourself distracted during take-off and landing,' he said. 'Have you got a book?'

She nodded.

'Good. And if you have a wobbly moment, just remember the pilots. They're not nervous, and they have to fly the bloody thing! That's what my mother always told me.' He smiled only briefly, eyes cutting away and staring into his glass wistfully.

'Thanks. I'll remember that,' Georgie said.

But as they walked out onto the tarmac, her anxiety reared again. The aircraft was little more than a corrugated metal crate; beads of perspiration collected at the nape of her neck. She looked suspiciously at the three extremely small propellers charged with hoisting such a great mass into the sky, a weight that would soon include her. The other passengers boarding appeared relaxed enough, and she had to remind herself of Max's advice, that thousands of people flew every day – and survived. As the engine sputtered into life and growled towards take-off, she opened her book and steadied her breathing, hoping she reflected a picture of calm. Inside was another matter.

★

Once in the air, the whisky nicely stroking at her angst, Georgie pushed her nose further into the pages. Her choice of *The Trouble I've Seen* by her hero Martha Gellhorn was not a deliberate irritant to Max Spender, but nicely fortuitous. She held it high in front of her face, partly as a distraction, but mostly as a way of nailing her colours firmly to the female mast.

Max, by contrast, was reading the morning's *Daily Express* – she noted his eyebrows twitching at reports from the new Austria, still in its infancy, the Nazis having simply trooped into their neighbouring country in March and declared it to be henceforth part of Germany. Buoyed by this, native Germans living in the Czech Sudetenland were agitating for their own alliance with the Fatherland and looked to be gaining strength. Few in the world, it seemed, had issued much of a protest, least of all Britain's politicians, with the British and American government officially refusing to accept any more Jewish refugees.

And so, even without the summer swelter, Berlin promised to be a cauldron. Yet, to the population in England, Chancellor Hitler was merely a strange little man with a moustache who liked to stalk around in shorts and bark into a microphone at huge gatherings of idol worshippers. It was the correspondents – writers and analysts tracking Hitler's meteoric rise and his harsh, legal restraints directed at Jews especially – who recognised the real threat. To Georgie, Herr Hitler was both strange and dangerous, and somehow, she needed to get that across in her writing. Objectively and professionally.

Already, she felt that familiar mix of trepidation and excitement at being the one to report on Germany's political tableaux. It wasn't simply seeing her name next to the print – though that still gave her a lift – more that her words might actually inform someone's thinking. To have that responsibility for representing the truth gave her a buzz like no other – that she was shaping the tiniest part of history. And no, she wasn't naive to that old argument about journalistic bias, but she still believed passionately in a free press. It was why she had become a reporter, after all. And if there was ever a need for a free press, it was in a country under the dictatorship of a small man with big ideas.

Throughout the three-hour flight, broken only with a jerky descent and a brief refuelling in Paris, they continued to defy the laws of gravity in their glorified crate, bumping through the cloud film as Georgie peered at the carpet of sea and land barely visible beneath them.

Coming in to land, her nerves and excitement reared again in equal measure. The patchwork green of rural fields gave way to granite lines of runways as they circled above their final destination, the window beside her stippled with cloud dust. She pushed her nose against the pane, eager to pick out more, and it was then that – through the white mist – it came into view: a beacon of red pulsing through the opaque sky, a vast line that seemed to sway in a rhythm. As they taxied and puttered to a halt, everything drew into focus behind the warp of noonday heat – the line *was* moving, huge flags of crimson fluttering above the airport terminal, each with their own, iconic black and white centre. The sight was stark and impressive – no doubt designed for its impact, and perhaps as a welcome to newcomers, although that remained debatable, given what she already knew. The sun's glare formed a dazzling backdrop, and yet – in Georgie's own mind – the dominant red swathe against the building's sandy façade created a brooding, leaden cloud: a tempest of swastikas. And she was just about to enter into the eye of that storm. By choice.

The tinny speaker aboard the plane crackled into life. 'Thank you for flying Lufthansa today, ladies and gentlemen,' the stewardess said in her native, crisp tone. 'Welcome to Germany's great capital – Berlin.'

Towards the back of the plane, a voice rang out in response, distinct and audible: 'Heil Hitler!'

4

A Simmering City

Berlin, 2nd August 1938

Georgie stepped onto German soil for only the second time in her life and sensed a change in the air, dense with heat and politics. Glancing back at the plane, she noted the Lufthansa tailfin was painted entirely in a large swastika and felt a pinch in her gut that she had been unwittingly flying inside a large advert for a party she already viewed with a great deal of suspicion.

The small line of passengers made their way towards the terminal, which – though dressed in Nazi regalia – was undoubtedly impressive: commanding yet stylish, the sleek art-deco lines of its tall, slim windows cut into fawn limestone brick, glowing against the sun's rays.

Civilian staff along the way smiled and said how welcome the passengers were, how much they hoped she and Max would enjoy their stay. And yet the atmosphere was thick with mistrust. A uniformed border guard thrust out his hand for Georgie's passport, his eyes boring into the print for some secret missive between the lines. He caught her eye and held it defiantly, perhaps as a way of injecting a clear message: *You may be welcome, foreigner. But you are watched.* If she didn't know otherwise, Georgie might have imagined Germany was already at war.

A good deal of Tempelhof Airport was still under construction, with builders milling about amid the staff. Georgie also felt a definite presence of Stormtroopers and army personnel, their red or white Nazi armbands easily picked out against the dull granite of construction and the ghost grey of SS troops, eyes narrowed under their caps. She stared almost open-mouthed at the spectacle, while Max the seasoned traveller strode confidently into the building, casting about for signs of the driver who was due to meet and transport them both into the city centre. Seeing no obvious driver, he stood awkwardly, shuffling his feet.

Georgie, for her part, was marvelling at the inside of the terminal, the great height of its ceiling and its coolness, sleek desks of chrome and muted beige, airport staff in crisp attire, plus a bustle and excitement that she only ever felt when travel and change were imminent. It felt a world away from her routine life in London. It was wonderfully cosmopolitan.

'Coffee while we wait?' Max said finally, gesturing at a small bar to the side.

Again, the answer was a resounding yes. It was one of the things about the continent Georgie missed most – like the French, Germans knew how to brew thick, strong coffee, unlike the distinctly weaker version back home. It was stout and uncompromising, and not unlike its politics at present. She was thirsty but coffee was needed most.

The bartender raised his eyebrows in anticipation, but Max's eyes shifted uncomfortably. He turned to her instead. 'What will you have?' He'd lost his air of confidence – and authority – in an instant.

Georgie took up the mantle. '*Zwei Milchkaffee bitte,*' she said, surprising herself at how easily it tripped off her tongue. Max pulled a wad of Reichsmarks out of his pocket before she had a chance to delve into her own bag, but she let this one go – for now. She would pay her way.

Balancing on bar stools, they sipped at the hot, strong liquid, the caffeine giving an instant thrust to their senses.

'So, *George*, how did you get this posting?' Max asked.

'Not how you probably imagine,' she said smartly. It was a common query from other journalists, almost always male.

'And how would that be?'

Georgie looked at him squarely, trying to work him out; even if they were to have little to do with each other in Berlin, it irritated her that he already swayed in her estimation, minute by minute. She liked to get the measure of people quickly – her survival in this world depended on it. But so far she could make neither head nor tail of Max Spender; arrogance in abundance, yes, but there was something else. That large chip on his shoulder aside, she also tasted something nearing fear.

'Well,' she said, 'either you imagine I've had some romantic liaison with an editor or publisher, someone who's able to arrange a job like this, more as a way of keeping me out of the way of his wife, or that my daddy is someone rich in the city and has used his influence.' She sipped again, keeping a firm look upon his face. Did she catch a split-second wince around his eyes? Maybe.

He was soon back to teasing, except she couldn't decide if it was out of humour or conceit. 'So which is it?' he said.

'Could you ever contemplate that's it's neither of those?'

'Try me.' His confidence was rising again in line with the caffeine consumption.

'All right,' she said. 'I got my degree in English at university. I worked on a local newspaper first and then climbed my way up at the *Chronicle*. From the bottom.'

24

'Don't tell me you started as the tea lady?' His eyes sparkled at his own joke.

But Georgie wasn't laughing. 'Pretty much. You'd be surprised at how many pots of tea you have to make to get an editor to notice your work.'

He noted her vexation and heeded the warning. 'So, was it in regional news that you earned your stripes?'

Now, her eyes dropped away – Georgie's turn for her confidence to take a knock. She wasn't ashamed of it, but she surprised herself at how hard it was to admit which department was responsible for her promotion to foreign news.

She flicked up her head, drew in a breath. 'I started in fashion actually,' she said. Her tone was tart, daring him to respond with incredulity.

He took a second to absorb the meaning of what she'd said. 'You were here, at the Olympics, as a *fashion* correspondent?' He was barely keeping his laughter under wraps.

'Yes,' she said. *Steady, Georgie,* she chanted to herself, *don't let them get to you.* It had been her mantra almost since entering the *Chronicle*'s office just two years previously, principally when she was handed a sheaf of typing and told to 'make it snappy'. Handing it back and voicing – calmly – that she was a reporter rather than one of the typing pool had taken a good deal of resolve. Good training for any journalist.

'And we uncovered a good many stories that the news hacks did not,' she added with pride. 'It does well to be invited to plenty of social events and mingle among the gossips. It's where tongues are loosened by too much champagne. In the end, it was the news boys who came to us for the goods.' It was also where she had nurtured her contact for the Diana Mosley exclusive, but she held back on revealing that little nugget.

It was clear from Max's face that he didn't quite know what to do with this unexpected piece of information – his deep frown signalled it was worse than he could possibly imagine: stuck with a woman, and one who reports on tweed versus linen instead of hard news. Georgie, though, was unapologetic. Better she admit it now, rather than risk being 'outed' at some gathering of the press corps, when the drinks and the secrets flowed freely. She knew her resolve wouldn't hold so well in a crowd.

Despite the office prejudice of some, Georgie truly loved the *Chronicle*. It was a people's paper, filled with a diverse mix of news, features and stories; alongside the adverts for Bile Beans, Bird's Custard and lawnmowers, there were endless articles on home management and 'The best way with a cauliflower'. But the *Chronicle* was also keen to publish editorial on women's career achievements, and not afraid to call 'Jew-baiters' to task. Its politics were firmly on the side of humanity.

'I know I have plenty to learn, and plenty to prove,' she said to Max, filling in the awkward silence.

'You and me both,' she thought she heard him mutter into his cup. But by then he'd leapt off his stool and was yards down the concourse, chasing after a man with a welcome sign. Their driver had finally arrived.

The journey north from Tempelhof took them through residential streets and then into the heart of bustling Berlin. Max rode in the taxi's front seat, talking with the driver who had a decent grasp of English, while Georgie was happily alone in the back, tasting the air through the open window and enjoying the breeze on her cheeks. A chance to absorb, to take in the extraordinary sights.

Extraordinary it was, in overshadowing Georgie's last view of the city in August 1936, when the world's athletes had descended upon the unlikely choice of Berlin as host of the Olympic Games. Back then, the pomp and ceremony had been enough of an eye-opener. Streets around the city and the specially built stadium – designed to seat 100,000 spectators – were swamped with Nazi insignia, clean lines of flags that seemed programmed to flutter by order. Everything was precise and in its place. Pristine. The world was watching as the Nazis orchestrated their best show at the opening ceremony – a Wagnerian display of music and procession under the silver cloud of the imposing master airship, the *Hindenburg*, which hovered above, a tense build-up to when Hitler himself arrived in the arena with all the kudos of an emperor and strode up to his viewing box.

Even when African-American athlete Jesse Owens won four gold medals, threatening to soil the whiter than white showing of Aryan strength, the Nazis did not falter. Georgie heard foreign visitors with her own ears, muttering that perhaps France and Britain, even the US, had been wrong in judging the National Socialists too harshly. Germany – and with it, Berlin – seemed a place where you could feel safe. The Nazi propaganda machine had triumphed. What the visitors hadn't seen, but the journalists were party to, was more telling; those Jewish athletes 'persuaded' not to take part, or the visitors who'd stood naively by during a Nazi parade without offering the Hitler salute, being shuffled off the pavement by Stormtroopers and given a firm, sometimes physical reprimand. Those were the stories that made it to Georgie's ears, via the whirl of social parties and 'trivial' fashion journalism. The same stories that occasionally made it into the paper, buried as a few lines in the back pages, always overshadowed by the pseudo-fiction of the German Minister for Propaganda, Joseph Goebbels, and his army of crack publicists.

Two years on, the sheen was gone and the Berlin in front of Georgie's eyes was astonishing in a different vein; it was still ordered, the wide impressive streets designed in distinct, neat lines and the buildings grandiose and imposing. But there was no mask anymore, no need to hide what the National Socialist German Workers' Party – the Nazis – were about. Their determination to dominate was unabashed; that much was clear from the imposing columns that came into view as the taxi approached and then turned into the capital's most prominent thoroughfare, the Unter den Linden. Scores of white pillars, four abreast, swept down the entire length of the boulevard, many topped with the eagle emblem of the Nazi insignia, some white, some gold, blinding in the midday glare. It was no accident that Georgie needed to look upwards at these towering symbols of power, like the pictures of ancient Rome she remembered from her history books – the phrase 'delusions of grandeur' came immediately to her mind. It was an uneasy feeling, and one she would be keeping to herself.

The driver parked at the far end of Unter den Linden, on the Pariser Platz, unmistakable with the city's iconic gateway directly opposite: the impressive Brandenburg Gate, with its six vast columns leading towards the Tiergarten, the city's equivalent to Hyde Park. The gate was topped with the statuesque goddess of peace on her chariot and four horses, embellished nowadays with the Nazi emblem. Another supreme irony, Georgie mused, given the storm clouds of war looming in the nearby embassies and scores of government offices.

'I think my hotel's a bit further down this road,' Georgie said. They were parked directly outside the renowned Hotel Adlon, and although the *Chronicle* had been generous in its first week's allowance of a decent hotel, she definitely wouldn't be housed in Berlin's centrepiece of style.

'Seems there's a little bit of a post-lunch welcome party arranged for us in here,' Max said from the front. 'The driver says he'll take our luggage on.'

She felt like royalty as the doors were opened by staff in

neat blue livery, and then immediately underdressed in her tailored but worn everyday skirt and blouse.

'Welcome, madam,' the doorman said in perfect English, and she replied her thanks in German. Walking into the lobby was like entering a labyrinth of sheer opulence; her eyes combed over the vaulted and painted ceilings in Baroque style, feet stepping on intricate Turkey carpets, with statues alongside dripping in gilt, silent staff gliding to bring glasses that chinked with good cheer and echoed money. Somewhere in the background, the gentle trickle of water fountains calmed a total assault on the senses. Neither needed a journalist's nose to locate the welcome party, following a general hum of conversation rising above the splendid aura of the Adlon.

'This looks like us,' Max said as he led them eagerly towards the bar.

'Here they are, another couple of lambs for the slaughter,' one loud voice boomed with good cheer, as his long arms extended and his imposing form scooped them into the fray. 'What'll you have?'

The drinks – Georgie opting for a soda water, while Max craved a cold German beer – seemed to appear magically and before long they were deep in conversation. The group was mostly made up of print journalists from the British, American and French papers, with a smattering of radio hacks too. *Was this their first assignment?* they quizzed. *What was the feeling back in Britain? Was there much talk on the streets about Germany, Hitler or war?*

The gathering of ten or so clustered around the bar introduced themselves, though the names swam around Georgie's tired brain. She was glad to see two women on the edges of the group, heads together, and for a minute she didn't feel quite so alone. She longed to approach them and ask how it was, being a woman on the job – how they were treated and viewed

29

– but the two seemed preoccupied, perhaps a little aloof, so she didn't dare intrude. *There's plenty of time,* she told herself.

Max appeared very much at home, and as if he half knew some of the personalities. Certainly, his father was mentioned more than once, but he replied only briefly, steering the conversation promptly back to the Berlin of the moment.

'I'm supposed to hook up with my bureau man today. Cliff Sutton?' Max queried, draining his beer. As perhaps the longest serving of the resident correspondents attached to the overseas newspaper offices – or bureaux – Cliff was distinctly absent. Looks were exchanged across the group. Georgie noted several sets of eyes making contact with the floor.

'Ah well, you've missed him for today,' said Rod Faber, the *New York Times'* veteran correspondent and he of the long arms, copious beard and resonant voice. 'He's usually here until about midday, but probably at home by now. I'd give him 'til at least six before you make contact.'

Max's face dropped. Reading between the lines was essential for a journalist and, whatever his background, he was no exception. Anyone who propped up a bar until midday and then needed a rest was clearly a slave to the bottle – no wonder the London office had wanted a fit and mobile apprentice in Berlin. Someone who could focus.

'And my contact – Paul Adamson? Will he be coming?' Georgie asked. Surely they couldn't be so unlucky in having two hacks married to the schnapps?

'Hmm, Paul's suffering from a touch of confusion,' a man behind her pitched in. Georgie cocked her head with interest.

'He's fallen head over heels for a German actress,' the man went on, then paused. 'And his wife's just about to have a baby in England, meaning you might not see a great deal of him, either before or after the birth.' He placed his empty glass on the bar. 'Still, you've always got us to guide you through, eh guys?' There was a small cheer as they all raised glasses at the suggestion.

Georgie failed to dredge even a weak smile out of her supply bag, despite the friendship on offer. Instead, she glanced at an equally apprehensive Max. She had expected to think on her feet, even relished the challenge. But guidance in a foreign city was essential. She had no contacts and finding them would be almost impossible in the dark. These men and women of the press, they seemed nice enough, generous too, but everyone guarded a good story when they had one. That was just the name of the game. She cast around the Adlon and its luxury, the beautiful people of Berlin sipping coffee and cocktails, and it all seemed so perfect. But it wasn't, was it? This was real life now, not a soiree or a socialites' party designed to produce critical copy on whether lace or organza was more suited to the occasion. This would be hard, and she'd better grow up swiftly, or Berlin might swallow her whole.

As the hour wore on, one or two of the group left to send over their stories to newsrooms worldwide and the bar began to empty. Georgie and Max made their excuses and left together; the Hotel Bristol was a short walk along the Unter den Linden, and Georgie especially was keen not to waste the day, eager to map the city in her mind. They walked in silence, Max clearly deep in thought, and – for the first time – a despondency in his step. Georgie's eyes couldn't help but be drawn upwards, at yet more of the red swathe draping each and every stone monolith – scores of Nazi flags rippling in a minor breeze, like vast ceiling-to-floor curtains upon a stage. The same thought crept into her mind from two years previously: never mind the strong rumours of Hitler's rearmament, using Germany's heavy industry to stockpile weapons and tanks, all in breach of worldwide conventions, Georgie Young wondered how many factories and women were now employed in making

31

Nazi insignia, weaving and stitching the symbol of their Führer into cloth? And how many really believed in its power? Or his, for that matter?

Such lightweight notions she kept to herself, while Max closely guarded his own thoughts, his face a cloud compared to its animation at the Adlon bar. They neared the grand edifice of the Hotel Bristol, embroidered with its layers of ornate stone lacing. As with every other building, it flew the colours of its Nazi allegiance at the entrance.

'So, would you like to look around and find some dinner, after we've had a rest?' Georgie asked her reluctant companion as they checked in. Presumably, it was why they'd been booked into the same hotel by rival papers, as a way of orientating themselves, together. Truthfully, she preferred to explore alone but in the interests of diplomacy – and her command of the language – she felt obliged to offer.

'Hmm, think I'll grab something at the bar or in my room,' Max replied. 'I'm not very hungry, and I'm quite tired.' He turned away and headed towards the stairs without another word. *Suit yourself,* Georgie thought. One part of her registered relief, the other felt slighted for offering an olive branch and being so quickly rebuffed. What *was* his issue? *Still, if this is how it's meant to be,* she thought, *I'd better get used to being on my own, hadn't I?*

Inside the hotel room that was at least twice the size of her poky bedsit in North London, she unpacked quickly and pinned her hair up and off her neck, changed her shoes to flat, walking brogues and stepped down into the lobby, which was slightly less grand than the Adlon but still of the luxurious 'pinch me' variety. Like every life challenge that she could remember in her twenty-six years, she took a deep breath and uttered under her breath: *Come on, George, you can do this.* Then she walked through the doors and entered an early evening Berlin that was exciting and infamously debauched, cosmopolitan and yet ultimately German – and now a city cloaked with the cloth and under the pressing heel of Adolf Hitler.

Map in hand, Georgie strode east, away from the Adlon, over the two channels of the River Spree and the 'island' housing some of Berlin's grandest museums, her eyes scanning left and right, absorbing every detail. She reached the huge, rectangular Alexanderplatz and stood marvelling at the tram interchange, criss-crossing its centre like a turntable on a toy train set, Berlin's huge six-wheeled buses trundling the outskirts, their prominent metal snouts pushing out a heavy engine throb. It was a metropolis like London, and yet the drapery of the flags seemed in some way to muffle the raw city sounds.

Hungry for more – and also craving something to eat – Georgie walked on, veering north, peering into shop windows, delighted when she could make out the German signs and odd snatches of conversations. She forged on, so enchanted she almost didn't realise the landscape changing with each step; block by block the buildings became less ornate, ordinary and then distinctly shabbier. The people, too, slowed their step and had begun to stare, their eyes gaping as she walked past. She noted they looked different from those on the Unter den Linden – darker features, less Germanic – and she found herself tucking her own blonde hair further under her cap. Each lengthy gaze seemed to track her, though whether they were clouded by fear or suspicion it was hard to tell. Perhaps both.

Flattening herself against a wall, she consulted her map. How far had she come, and where was she? Dusk was fast approaching, the atmosphere murkier, and she was beginning to regret her enthusiastic wanderlust.

'Fraulein?' Georgie's head snapped up at a gruff interruption. Two Stormtroopers looked down on her – in more ways than one, expressions as muddy as the brown of their shirts. 'Are you lost? You shouldn't be in this part of the city.' It was irritation and not concern. 'This is where . . . where Jews live. Do *you* live here?'

'N-no,' she stammered, tongue twisting around the language. 'I've just arrived . . . from England.' She smiled widely, in the hope of some return.

'Papers?' They were not in the mood for diplomacy, twin sets of beady eyes boring into her.

'I . . . I haven't got my press papers yet . . . only this.' She scrabbled in her bag for her passport.

'English press?' one sneered. 'You definitely shouldn't be here.'

Did he mean Berlin as a whole, or this particular street? And why – was it a crime or simply an affront to them? 'I suppose, I've wandered too far,' she offered. 'Can you point me in the right direction, the Hotel Bristol?'

The other grunted to signal his distaste – she as a British alien, sullied in the same way they viewed Jews as dirty. And rich enough to lodge at the Bristol. Short of physically turning and pushing her down the street, they pointed her firmly in the other direction. 'Down there, keep going. And we would advise you not to come here again.' It wasn't an order, but neither was it an option.

Georgie's steps were fast and furious, breath rising as she saw the lights and safety of Alexanderplatz again, then she puffed out her cheeks in relief on reaching the Bristol and its comforting lobby. There was her taste of the new Germany. Bittersweet at best.

'Welcome to Berlin, Georgie Young,' she sighed to herself. 'Round one to the Reich.'

5

Hiding

Berlin, 2nd August 1938

Rubin Amsel emerged from the attic with tell-tale cobwebs in his hair, skin smudged with the dirt of neglect.

'Well?' Sara was standing at the bottom of the makeshift steps Rubin had fashioned with the help of his twelve-year-old son, Leon, nailing together the struts as quietly as any hammer would allow. No one – not even their trusted neighbours – should know what they were planning; better to be naive for their own sakes.

'I've closed over the roof holes as best I can,' he said, 'and I've made a little area for a bed and a pee-pot. It's cleaner at least. He'll have to have an oil lamp for light.' Still, he puffed out his cheeks in defeat. 'But you're right, Sara, he can't live up there – it's like a hothouse now, and he'll freeze in winter. You wouldn't keep a dog like that.'

'So what do we do?' she said in earnest. 'You know Elias can't move quickly these days, even if he has to. It would take at least two of us to help him up, and you're so often out.'

Rubin pictured Sara's once-vibrant, fit younger brother, now slumped in their tiny living room, his mind still active but his body broken by a heavy fall the year previously. His badly fractured hip and leg had been pieced together at the time by an elderly, out-of-practice doctor and it was a poor job, the nerve damage beyond repair. Elias would still be able to work, in an office perhaps, were it not for the Nazi decree banning him and all other Jews from work in public offices. The fit, healthy ones scrabbled for any job they could find, but Elias rarely left the apartment. In this tragic journey, he had lost the spark that made him such a lively spirit, and which Rubin suspected had lost him his health in the first place – he'd never admitted why he was on a high wall very near to the Berlin home of Heinrich Himmler, the unimposing but much feared overseer of Hitler's secret police. The Amsels rarely spoke of the night when Elias was brought limp and bleeding to their home, his skin bearing the scrape of a bullet so close to his scalp. They both sensed that attending the state hospital would arouse a dangerous suspicion, yet never dared to question him about the cause. It was often safer not to know.

Rubin thought hard. 'I suppose we just have to be extra vigilant,' he told Sara. 'Any knock at the door, we have to delay and get him up to the attic temporarily, with the children's help if we have to.'

'And will you tell him why we're doing it?' Sara said. 'The consequences if we don't?'

'I don't think we'll have to,' Rubin answered. 'There's nothing wrong with Elias's imagination when it comes to Nazi capabilities.'

6

Welcome to the Ministry

5th August 1938

The following days lived up to expectations for the newest additions to the press pack: long and hard, with a steep learning curve. Georgie finally met her bureau chief after several attempts at pinning him down at their office. According to the Adlon crowd that she met with several times in those first few days, Paul Adamson was a competent journalist who'd become hopelessly distracted. He was certainly no film star himself, resembling more of an insurance broker, and so Georgie had to wonder at his charms to attract a German starlet.

'I think perhaps the temptation is his British passport,' someone at the Adlon had muttered, and Georgie felt sorry for both the actress and his heavily pregnant wife back home. Each was being strung along in blissful hope of a promised future.

Paul wasn't offhand, only preoccupied. He didn't so much show her the ropes as point Georgie towards buying a better map, and making a solitary phone call to request her press accreditation card – vital if she were to access any of the numerous news conferences hosted by the Nazi publicity machine.

'So, if you can cover what's in the diary,' Paul said, pointing to a lengthy list of invitations, 'that will free me up to do the rest.'

'And what's that?' Georgie couldn't help asking pointedly. It was abundantly clear he'd every intention of leaving her to do the donkey work.

'Oh, just a story I've been working on a while. Can't say too much right now,' he replied, at which point the office phone rang and his voice softened in an instant, clearly placating the actress, whose flouncy tone Georgie could hear at the end of the line. *An engaging story indeed*, she thought.

Max appeared on the third day at breakfast, edging towards her table in the Bristol's dining room, though only when it was clear he'd been spotted and couldn't easily escape. She saw him pocket a small German dictionary as he sat.

'How are you? Managing all right?' Georgie said, gesturing towards the book slipped into his jacket.

'Oh, that. Yes, fine,' he said with obvious bravado. 'Coming along nicely.' His sheepish smile said otherwise.

'Have you hooked up with your bureau man yet?'

This time, Max couldn't attempt a convincing cover-up, puffing out his cheeks in despair. 'I'm afraid they weren't wrong at the Adlon – Cliff's a nice chap, and a bit of a hero of mine as a writer, but he's seen too much German beer. No wonder there weren't many takers for this posting. Quite stupidly, it never occurred to me to wonder why. I thought I'd struck lucky.'

He smiled meekly into his teacup, and Georgie felt a pang of sorrow for his situation, despite his general offhandedness. His appearance was tall and commanding, but suddenly he seemed a little boy lost, and she wondered what portion of his outer confidence amounted to bravado.

'Same here,' Georgie attempted to reassure him. 'Several in

my office back home did ask why I'd volunteered for the "snake pit", and I thought they were either jealous or joking.'

'I suppose only time will tell,' he said. 'We'll just have to make the best of it. Along with seeking out that award-winning story, sure to make our names as crack correspondents. Let's not forget that.' This time he did smile at his own sarcasm, following it up with a deep sigh as he bit into a slice of heavy German bread.

'Have you got your press card yet?' Georgie asked.

'Off to get it this morning.'

'Me too – shall we go together?' she shot back, then hoped it didn't sound too eager or needy. While she was anxious to understand the Nazi machine, the Ministry of Propaganda, and the control it exerted over journalists, was something to be wary of.

'Um . . . I have to pick something up on the way, so I'll be a while,' Max stammered, putting down his napkin. It was an obvious excuse, and Georgie sat for a moment as his frame disappeared from the breakfast room. *It could be that I'm a woman,* she said to herself, *or that he doesn't like me, or trust me. Perhaps all three.* Whatever the reason, she was on her own again.

As it happened, she wasn't alone for long. Georgie ascended the steps to the ministry building and the bear-like form of Rod Faber – he of the welcoming arms and *New York Times* – was on his way out. He greeted her like an old friend, and hearing it was her first trip inside, and not surprised to learn Paul Adamson hadn't come to guide her, he took up the mantle. At first, Georgie resisted – she didn't want any kind of special treatment as a woman, and wasn't afraid to say so, in the politest way she could manage.

'Hell no, it's not because you're a woman!' Rod said in his

distinctive American twang. 'It's because you have to know who to talk to, who to bribe and who to suck up to. I would have been eaten alive if I hadn't had my own guide way back when.'

Rod's wisdom was proven almost on stepping through the grand entrance, SS guards on each side of twin granite statues – all four stony-faced. They climbed the sweeping stairway and were faced by a large, dark and intimidating doorway, the first in a succession of hoops Georgie was required to leap through.

'Papers,' the military man inside barked, looking hard at her photograph, passport and letter from the *Chronicle* asserting her role, and then at her face, his steely eyes crawling over her loose hair and stopping short of her shoulders. The assessment was meticulous.

'What on earth was he looking for?' she whispered to Rod as they moved down the corridor and towards the next hoop. 'I felt as if he was trying to stare into my soul.'

'Checking to see if you have any Jewish features,' Rod replied. 'And I think your blonde hair did you a great favour there.'

She was genuinely shocked. Georgie knew of the Nazi decree since 1934 banning German Jews from working in newspapers and publishing, amongst a whole host of other professions, including practising as doctors, lawyers and teachers. 'Surely, that hasn't extended to the foreign press?'

'Not officially,' Rod said, 'but since when have the Nazis worried about officialdom when it suits them? If he didn't like the look of you, he could simply refuse your press pass. He doesn't need a valid reason. He has the Reich on his side.'

Georgie looked aghast, though Rod only nudged playfully at her shoulder. 'Welcome to Hitler's paradise.'

The wait between successive doors seemed an age, though ample time for her guide to provide a running commentary of each department and its occupants.

'Watch out, the mini-Führer approaches,' Rod whispered, standing as a man in a dark double-breasted suit approached, not quite clicking his heels to signal his arrival, but almost. He was wider and smaller, but his attempts to mimic his obvious hero in Adolf Hitler made him look faintly comical, like some sort of tragic lookalike in a sideshow act. His brush of a moustache stood almost to attention as he tried – and failed – to smile with conviction.

'Herr Faber,' he said briskly to Rod. 'How nice to see you here.' His expression, however, told another story.

'You too, Herr Bauer.' Also a falsehood. 'May I introduce a new addition to the press corps, Miss Georgie Young? She's part of the London *News Chronicle* staff.'

'Ah,' said Herr Bauer, 'welcome to Berlin, Fraulein Young. I expect you are finding the city engaging?'

'Very much so,' Georgie said. 'It's very . . . pristine. And enticing.'

He took it as a compliment, no doubt to the wonders of Nazism, briefly flashing his tiny, crooked teeth before quickly regaining a serious composure, as if his humour – all humour – was necessarily on ration. 'Not too enticing, I hope,' he went on. 'Not so it will keep you from us. I trust we'll see more of you at our press calls than your colleague, Herr Adamson. He's been rather absent of late.' His eyes were the black, shiny beads of a crow.

'Don't worry, we'll keep her on the straight and narrow,' Rod cut in to soften the discourse. 'Make sure she's in all the right places.'

Herr Bauer smiled once more, his teeth on ration this time, nodded curtly, turned and marched away.

Rod sighed. 'That,' he said, 'was Bruno Bauer. A toady little man but he does manage the foreign press corps, which means he has a certain power over us. It's as well to keep on his right side, or you'll find yourself frozen out. Don't worry, though, I think he liked you.'

'And are they all like that . . .' It wasn't often that Georgie was lost for words, particularly of the descriptive type. 'I mean, creepy?' By 'they' she wasn't alluding to Germans or even German men, but devoted, dyed-in-the-wool Nazis.

Rod laughed under his breath. 'Oh, he's not the worst by far,' he said. 'Though he is an obsequious chump. And yes, they are a fairly horrible bunch. But it is good fun trying to get one over on them from time to time.'

Three hours, several offices and one grilling later, they emerged onto the ministry steps. Georgie was emotionally battered, though relieved: she clutched the all-important press card, signed and stamped with the eagle icon. It was a strange feeling to be accredited by the Third Reich, and yet she was now part of the pack. Officially.

'Time for lunch?' Rod pitched. Georgie's stomach reminded her it was midday, but she hesitated, aware of the *Chronicle*'s diary entry for one p.m. in the Tiergarten – some middling Nazi official reviewing troops of the League of German Girls showing off their gymnastic skills. Paul had marked it clearly for her attendance.

'That?' Rod scoffed. 'I can tell you now your paper won't touch a few girls leapfrogging as a news item – too trivial. Much better I show you the best café sights of Berlin, places where you might pick up some real contacts.'

The gripe of hunger and the promise of coffee, plus Rod's easy company, persuaded her. She was unlikely to see Paul to have to make any excuses.

They walked up the Wilhelmstrasse and back onto Unter den Linden, where the crimson banners were in full flight. Rod piloted her to Café Kranzler, a grand corner restaurant with small, potted trees marking the sitting area outside, its lantern lights on stalks and neatly aligned with the Reich columns stretching into the distance. They sat at one of the street-side tables, Georgie instantly seduced by the vibrant café culture. Berliners, she thought, knew how to socialise both day and night. The chink of teacups and hum of easy conversation between well-dressed women might lead anyone to believe that everything in the city – in the world, in fact – was fine. Unoppressed. Free.

'I won't say a thing if you choose to have cake for lunch,' Rod said, lighting a cigarette and blowing the smoke plume up into the awning. 'The strudel is famously good here.' He patted the middle-aged paunch under his shirt. 'My daughter is constantly warning me against it.'

'And how old is she, your daughter? Is she here in Berlin?'

'No, no, she's back home in New York, with my son and both my ex-wives.' His face expressed not sadness, only something like resignation at the personal life of a veteran reporter. 'She's nineteen. In fact, she wants to become a journalist herself. She's at college right now.' His face couldn't muster any enthusiasm.

'And you're not happy about that?' *Perhaps Rod sees me like so many others,* Georgie mused, *a woman abroad who's not up to the job, and never will be.*

'Oh, it's not that she's female,' he added swiftly. 'More that she's my daughter. I dare say your father might think the same?'

He was more than likely right. Georgie thought back to where she grew up – a small, provincial town in the Cotswolds, with her schoolteacher father and her housewife mother. Moving to London had seemed bad enough in their eyes but she wouldn't easily forget the drained look on their faces after announcing her posting to Berlin, the worry she'd caused them. It was as much for them that she felt driven to prove herself now – to survive and succeed in unison.

'I suppose,' she said, swallowing back guilt with a spoonful of the strudel. He was right – it was divine, the pastry light and airy. Unlike the mood of Berlin.

They lingered for some time, and Georgie held fast to Rod's conversation – he'd been in Berlin for ten years, on and off, and he was a fountain of knowledge on survival; time much better spent than watching Hitler's young maidens practise their hula-hooping in the park.

Finally, one of the waiters approached them – tall, his dark hair slicked and with intense brown eyes. 'Anything else, sir?' he asked.

Rod barely looked up or acknowledged the man. 'Ah, Karl, no thank you,' he said in a low voice while looking aimlessly at the menu. 'But my new friend here – Fraulein Young – might want something else.'

Georgie looked on, a little confused. She was full to the brim with strudel and coffee and couldn't stomach another morsel. And yet the air between the two men, the tone, suggested it wasn't the menu under discussion.

'Not just for the minute,' she said weakly. She looked directly at him, but he didn't flinch. 'Perhaps later.'

'Very good, Fraulein,' he said in a virtual monotone and glided away.

Georgie leaned into Rod with a spy-like whisper. 'What just happened there?'

'You've made your first underground contact,' he said with satisfaction. 'Look around you. There are scores of Nazi, SS and Wehrmacht officers through here every day. It's among their favourite female hunting grounds.'

Georgie scanned the Kranzler's customers – clutches of grey and green uniforms were entertaining women at the tables, both inside and out, laughing, smoking and flirting.

'Free with their Reichsmarks and conversation to impress

the ladies,' Rod went on. 'And Karl has excellent hearing. If I were you, I'd become a regular here, once or twice a week, sit in the same place if you can, alone. If he likes the look of you Karl offers a little extra cream with your coffee.' His eyes sparkled at the game.

'Rod, how can I thank you?'

'You don't have to,' he said jovially. 'It amuses me to stick two fingers up to Hitler and his bully boys at every opportunity. Just use your contacts wisely.'

They ambled back along the Unter den Linden, the sun slicing between the sheer walls of the Baroque buildings. Georgie's stomach was heavy with pastry and, despite the strong coffee, she felt weary. Still, she needed to justify her existence to her employers, to at least feed some copy back to her London editor. She followed as Rod ducked down a side street, guiding towards their offices, just a few streets apart.

They were a barely a few yards along when Georgie sensed a scuffle in a nearby alleyway, assuming at first it was a pair of scrapping cats. There was a yowl again – undoubtedly not feline. She slowed her step, peering into a narrow, gloomy gap between tall buildings. The moving forms were too big to be animals, and she could hear muffled voices, words barked with particular venom: 'Kike! Dirty Jew!'

A dull shout followed, an unmistakable sound of someone – a person – in pain. At the hands of another. 'No, no, I beg you,' someone pleaded. 'I'm sorry, I won't . . .' The voice trailed off to a thud, a shrill cry of pain. Power and pain inflicted.

'Rod?' she said. He stopped and turned, his jovial face immediately sad and dejected. He'd heard it too.

'Leave it, Georgie,' he said. 'You can't stop it.'

'But, but . . . someone needs help,' she urged.

'There are thousands in this city who need help,' he came

back gravely. 'You have to pick the battles you might win, and know when to walk on.'

She stood, utterly helpless, the sounds of violence ongoing. Painful to her ears. More so to its unfortunate recipient.

'Georgie, please,' Rod said. 'Intervene and it's your ticket back home, instantly. I promise you'll do more good by staying.'

Her feet were lead, body pushing through a sludge of shame. But she did it. Georgie walked away, until the sounds receded to nothing, to be replaced by an uncomfortable clamouring in her ears.

No wonder they called it the snake pit.

In the *Chronicle*'s small office on nearby Taubenstrasse – empty as expected – she found a note from Paul Adamson: *Gone to Munich for three days. Please attend to the diary.* There was no indication whether it was for work or a last-gasp holiday before his impending fatherhood, and Georgie didn't really care. She was quickly becoming resigned rather than angry about being left in the lurch. Suddenly Rod and the Adlon crowd seemed even more like family. She had to look on it positively: a chance to show her enterprise, and the London office she could do the job as well as anyone. But what did she have so far?

Georgie fed a sheet of paper into the typewriter, a shiny new Deutscher Mechaniker model, the Gothic type 'DM' embossed high on the roller, as if to purposely remind her she was within and overlooked by the Reich at all times. She glanced up at the window and caught the eye of a woman on the second floor of the building opposite, whose gaze cut away briskly. Her dark cap of hair seemed familiar. Had Georgie seen her at the Bristol, or Kranzler's? *No, stop being silly,* she told herself. It was just a woman doing a job. Yet she couldn't shake the sense of being watched; the implied threat of the airport guard and those two Stormtroopers with their menace.

She shook her head to rid herself of the feeling – *come on, George, focus* – pushing her fingers pointedly into the keypads.

Postcard from Berlin, Georgie typed at last. She had nothing of substance to report on – no news, but just before leaving England, she'd persuaded the *Chronicle*'s features editor to consider a piece from time to time. The paper often ran pull-out pieces – musings and opinion – from their correspondents. Weren't her first impressions the best opportunity to offer a bird's eye view? This was not the Berlin of 1936, all sparkly and on its best behaviour for foreign dignitaries and tourists, with the Nazi Party sporting the reasonable face of politics to pull Germany out of its lengthy economic slump. Now, even three days in, the air seemed grubbier, despite Berlin's display of opulence. Already, it felt tainted.

Georgie had never been short of words – sometimes in her actions she was reticent, but always free on the keyboard; the blank page did not faze her. Finally, her fingers set to work.

Postcard from Berlin

Dear News Chronicle readers,

Recently, I became a foreigner in a strange and possibly alien land, a shiny city of old that is now entirely cloaked in the deep crimson standards of Herr Hitler's Nazi Party – only a sea of military green and grey uniforms dilutes the blood-red palette of the Führer's future vision. In towns across England we are familiar with newspaper criers touting the news from their stands, but here Berliners stop randomly at lampposts, eyes on the metal speakers hoisted high, ears tuned to their tinny barking of rhetoric, inescapable to everyone's consciousness. By comparison, Berlin's citizens appear to gloss over the prejudice of park benches clearly marked 'No Jews', unashamedly stepping past – and stamping on – one person's right to sit alongside another. The Third Reich, it seems, is everywhere. And no one is allowed to forget it.

Auf Wiedersehen

Georgie sat back and read the words. She looked up casually, and a shiver from nowhere zig-zagged up her spine and pricked painfully at the base of her neck – the woman's gaze again from across the street. She wished the blinds were drawn, to blot out the eyes focused on her, and with an added paranoia, her page too. In a swift move, Georgie pulled out the sheet from the roller, scrunched it up and tossed it in the bin. Then, she plucked it back out, rifling through the desk drawers for some matches and setting light to the paper in an ashtray. As it crimped and burned to nothing, she positioned her back to the window, hiding the orange flame amid the darkened office that might act as a flare to unwelcome interest.

She sighed heavily. This was deep distrust, three days in.

Welcome to Berlin indeed.

7

Into the Fold

6th August 1938

There was no sign of Max at breakfast, and Georgie wondered if he had checked out of the Bristol and moved elsewhere. Fairly soon, she would have to do the same, and it was part of her day's work to go searching for a bedsit. First, though, another trip to the Ministry of Propaganda, this time as an accredited reporter.

The Ministry of Enlightenment and Propaganda, to give its full and official title, was a sharp, square building just off the Wilhelmplatz, a short walk from Hitler's seat of power, the Reich Chancellery. This time, Georgie passed with ease through the checkpoints and guards with rigid features, joining the thirty or so journalists who were seated in rows in a large room, in front of a slightly raised flooring and a lectern.

'Morning,' Rod mouthed, and motioned her to a seat next to him. Georgie found herself sandwiched between her new American friend and another familiar face from the Adlon, all red hair and spectacular moustache, who introduced himself with a brisk handshake as 'Bill Porter, *Chicago Herald Tribune*, for my sins.' In the opposite corner, Max was deep in conversation with a woman sitting alongside him.

'Looks like we're to be treated to the man himself today,' Rod whispered over the expectant hum. Georgie's pencil twitched with apprehension.

'Oh, here we go, Joey boy's approaching,' hissed Bill Porter. 'Ears on standby, everyone, for "limping Larry" himself.' All eyes swivelled to the open door – the man who stepped through triggered an automatic hush.

It may not have been the Führer himself, but arguably the next in line when it came to wielding power within the Reich; Joseph Goebbels was no military man, had no army under his command, but the skill with which he twisted words and information – fed to the German people and seemingly ingested by the bucket-load – made him equally dangerous, and cemented his place among Hitler's closest allies. His fashionable wife, Magda, was a darling of the society pages and regularly graced *Die Dame* magazine with her perfect crown of blonde hair and her tips on being the perfect mother to seven Aryan children. 'Joey' – as the press scathingly called him – possessed nothing like her charm or her looks. His loathing of the foreign press was also well documented.

He limped onto the plinth, wiry in his brown, fitted suit, with deeply sunken cheeks and ebony slicked-back hair, a creature halfway between a weasel and a shrew. His eyes were as black as his hair, darting around the room and settling momentarily on one body, before sliding to another. Despite his lack of allure, he held sway and power in his small frame, and Georgie hoped she wouldn't fall under his gaze just yet. Perhaps ever.

Finally, Herr Goebbels coughed and drew himself up to full height, launching into his speech with few niceties – how the Nazi Government had reduced unemployment during its four years in office, helping good German families to flourish; a nation fervently committed to peace in Europe, proven by their signing of various non-aggression agreements with neighbouring states. The reporters scribbled furiously, though even as a newcomer Georgie doubted any one person present believed the truth of what this man spouted in his terse delivery. After all, wasn't it the Ministry of Propaganda? And hadn't Goebbels famously broadcast that good propaganda need not lie – it was only necessary to present the right idea in the appropriate way? So blatant and yet effective: coat the stark truth in a convincing way and the nation swallows it whole.

'He doesn't mention how they've massaged the unemployment figures by creating spurious labour programmes, or the families that are left out in the cold if they don't join the party,' Rod whispered.

'Something of a magician with the truth then?' Georgie murmured in response.

'Catching on fast, kiddo.'

After a good twenty minutes of rapid-fire lecturing, and with no questions permitted, Doctor Goebbels – as he insisted on being addressed – picked up his notes and limped away. At his leaving, a hum of conversation sprung up.

'Well, what are you going to make of that in print?' Bill pitched to Rod. 'I think my paper will have a good laugh if I file that verbatim.'

'A little analysis and a good pinch of salt will be my approach,' Rod said. He patted his stomach. 'But first, some lunch.'

Georgie joined a portion of the press pack in a nearby café, where they chewed over the details and unpicked the truth behind the good Doctor Goebbels and his rhetoric. Why, when it seemed so transparent to everyone in the room, did the German people believe it?

'Fear,' said the *Daily Express* correspondent swiftly. 'Maybe your average German doesn't believe it, but they wouldn't dare express it. Not even to their neighbours. It masquerades nicely as belief when you've got no one telling you you're wrong.'

Still deep in thought, Georgie unlocked the door to the *Chronicle* office and noticed immediately the air seemed different, disturbed. Had someone been in, checking up on her? Paul was still away. . . Her heart jumped. Could it be that woman opposite? The ashtray was cleared of the burnt paper from the day before. The bin was also emptied, and the small toilet cabinet in the corner smelled fresher. Of course! The cleaner had been in – Georgie breathed hard at her own stupidity, imagining her nerves might give out long before the lead in her pencil. With the blinds drawn low, she crafted her report of the press conference several times, each version toning down a cynicism that crept towards sarcasm. It wouldn't do for her first dispatch to be inflammatory, and she settled on a tone alluding to uncertainty instead.

It was only four p.m., and there were still two tasks to tackle before she rejoined the Adlon crowd, who had promised to introduce her to a new venue later that evening. She needed somewhere to live after her week's grace at the Hotel Bristol was up, and a means of transport – the press gang suggested a driver was essential if she were to reach some of the events in the Berlin suburbs, especially if things were to flare up suddenly; likely an unofficial show of strength from the Reich's Stormtroopers, usually with Jews or other 'undesirables' in their sights.

Rod had offered to pass on some names, but Georgie determined not to rely wholly on his generosity. She rifled through her dog-eared notebook, recalling the driver her paper had used during the Olympics. He'd been reliable and a mine of local information; it was a long shot, but he might still be in Berlin and available. The telephone number filed was out of order, so she wrote out a short note and ran to catch the last post. One job half done.

On the way back to the hotel, she bought a copy of the daily *Berliner Tageblatt*, and crawled over its pages in the lobby of the Bristol, her heart sinking as even the rent on small apartments seemed too expensive for her wage. She was resigned to settling on a room in a flat, though Georgie didn't relish it. Would any German be willing to share with her? In their shoes, and with relations between Germany and the rest of Europe in sensitive limbo, a British newspaperwoman was far from an ideal tenant.

Deflated, she stood up and sighed. Out of the corner of her eye, she glimpsed Max walking through the lobby, sure their eyes met for a split second – either they didn't, or he pretended not to notice. Possibly because he was accompanied by the same dark-haired woman almost glued to him at the press conference. Was she a reporter? She didn't look like one – too timid. And she seemed to be following in his wake, rather than alongside. Had he found himself a woman already? If their meeting at the Ritz was any indication, it wouldn't be a surprise.

For a second, Georgie thought of saying hello, pushing herself in front of him to test his reactions, prod at him a little. Would he be embarrassed by his avoidance of her? But she thought better of it. After they each checked out of the Bristol, she and Max would see little of each other, perhaps only crossing paths at press conferences. Or she might simply read his reports in the *Telegraph* from time to time. That would suit her fine.

Stepping into La Taverne restaurant alongside Rod later that evening was a delight. It felt immediately like a homecoming to Georgie, a thin cigarette haze hovering at ceiling height instead of the swirling fog of a London pub. Some of the Adlon crowd had simply upped sticks and transported themselves into a much less salubrious, but essentially relaxed, venue, clustered around a large table in the corner of one room that led into two others, all three full of diners and a steady hubbub of conversation. The smell and the theme were unmistakably Italian and yet it was a very rounded, moustached man who greeted them – only in full lederhosen could he have looked more German.

'*Hallo*, Herr Faber,' he bellowed as they eased in around the table. 'The usual?'

'*Danke*, Herr Lehmann,' he said, 'and the same for my friend.' That was the choice tonight, it seemed – beer or beer. Georgie made a note to check her alcohol consumption and take it slowly.

While the Adlon was a regular haunt of the foreign press, this was clearly their daily respite – a real home from home. The owner kept back the same large table every night, certain of one or two desiring a bolthole, sometimes a whole posse of reporters late into the night – depending on their press deadlines back home – chewing over the day's news or frustrations about Bruno Bauer and his PR fortress.

The florid red hair and sizeable moustache of Bill Porter were instantly familiar, alongside a few whose names were not yet fully registered in her memory.

'The booze here is fine,' Bill said in a low voice as Georgie edged into a seat beside him, 'but the pasta is even better. I recommend it.' As if on cue, a painfully thin woman placed a steaming bowl of spaghetti in front of him and smiled at Bill.

'*Danke*.' His bright green eyes signalled a total love of her cooking. 'If she wasn't already married to the owner, she'd be my dream woman,' he whispered with pure mischief.

'Then I promise I won't tell your wife.' Georgie felt relaxed, among friends and, perhaps for the first time since arriving in Berlin, truly at home.

The conversation was animated, with a great deal of caustic humour about the Nazi high command, and not merely centred on Adolf Hitler. The crowd's descriptions of Heinrich Himmler – the bespectacled Gestapo chief – and larger-than-life Hermann Göring were puppet caricatures painted with their wit.

'Last night I was sitting behind old Hermann at a concert and I heard one old dear say he possessed the "hind end of an elephant",' said the *Daily Herald* reporter, to peals of laughter. 'She practically shouted it. I desperately wanted to use it in my copy – then I thought about the Gestapo knocking on my door and marching me off to the bowels of their HQ.'

'Perhaps it's best to keep that observation under wraps,' Bill said, between mouthfuls of pasta. 'We like having you around for now.'

A woman's voice travelled across the table: 'Just watch your back, and your own bottom, if you get anywhere within pinching distance of fat Hermann. He may be a portly old so-and-so, but he's got very quick hands.'

It was one of the two women Georgie had noted at the far end of the table on arriving, the same two on that first day at the Adlon in their very private huddle. Now, they were part of the relaxed crowd, laughing and smoking.

'Frida Borken,' she said in a light German accent, extending a long, thin hand. 'Freelance. And this is Simone Doucette – French free press.'

Georgie muttered something out of politeness but could really only gawp in wonder. They were stunning, each in their own way, the epitome of everything she had admired in her journey to being a female correspondent, oozing confidence and certainty.

Frida's face was that of a pixie, her enormous doll-like eyes emphasised with ebony kohl and mascara, tiny bow lips stark red with lipstick. She wore a tweed, tailored jacket, a cream shirt and a bright red tie, as if she were just off to a shooting party. Topping it all off was a shocking and sharp blonde bob, cut bluntly to her jawline; a darling who'd just leapt off the fashion pages.

Simone, by comparison, presented as a pre-Raphaelite painting; long, wavy reddish hair pulled into a loose tie, pinned in some way to the top of her head and cascading like a waterfall, strands falling either side of her pale oval face, her grey irises outlined with a thick, black rim. It gave her a ghostly, ethereal quality. The spectre in her was intensified by a cloud of grey cigarette smoke and a shimmering scarf swirling around her neck.

When they both smiled broadly, however, the complete awe that Georgie felt melted a little.

'Welcome to our little group,' Frida said, shuffling in and causing the fluid table dynamic to shift again. Georgie moulded as part of their little cluster, more so when the two discovered she'd been part of the fashion press, pumping her for the latest gossip from Paris and London, though she had little of recent value to tell.

'So, where are you staying?' Frida said, picking at Bill's left-over pasta. With her near-skeletal wrists, Georgie wondered if scraps were the only eating she ever ate.

'The Hotel Bristol for now, though I only have two days left. I'm looking for a flat-share.'

The two women stopped and looked at each other; something passed silently between them and Frida's eyes grew even wider. Her red bow lips spread.

'Well, it just so happens we have a spare room in our flat,' she said. 'Clare Howard moved off to report from the Spanish Front yesterday. It's fated, surely?'

The rent, fortunately, was within Georgie's budget and she didn't doubt it to be stylish, with Frida and Simone's influence.

And it was only a short tram ride from the centre of Berlin and the *Chronicle* office.

'Then it's a yes!' Georgie said. 'When can I move in?'

The glow surrounding Georgie was partly down to the beer, but also the company and her day's exploits – she had bagged herself a contact and a flat in the space of a week. Yes, by a combination of coincidence and assistance, but it was done. Now, all she needed was a driver, and a clutch of stories to make her name. She was allowing herself a virtual hug of congratulation when the door opened and Max Spender walked in with a youngish man, the dour *Manchester Guardian* reporter.

There was a slight thud to her heart, perhaps nudging at her very round bubble of happiness, and she struggled to understand why. She neither understood nor matched Max's dislike of her, but his presence then was a smudge on her otherwise perfect evening. One saving grace: the bird-like woman was absent. The two men were absorbed onto the table with Herr Lehmann bringing more chairs and beer, and Max eased swiftly into being 'one of the boys'. She wondered how he gained such skills so quickly, and although she hated herself for it, there was a stab of envy directed at him. Why did it take her time to trust and join in the general bonhomie of the newspaper world, when everyone else managed it so effortlessly?

In surveying this new realm, Georgie caught Max looking intently in her direction, though only because his gaze was set firmly at the body next to hers, unable to hide his overt admiration. Simone Doucette, in turn, had those grey, ghostly eyes returning his look of fascination.

8

Old Face, New Friend

Frida's place wasn't a flat by London standards, those poky dwellings teetering on top of one another, with balsa wood walls masquerading as bricks and mortar. The apartment – owned by her grandmother – was on the leafy Herderstrasse, west of the Tiergarten, and a palace by comparison: a vast, modern edifice cut by clean lines into apartments with high ceilings and tall, sleek windows stretching almost floor to ceiling. The white walls inside were enhanced by an eccentric array of furniture and ephemera, quirks and curiosities provided by Frida, with flowing ostrich feathers draped over lamps, presumably Simone's contribution to the décor.

Georgie's attempts to play it cool worked for a time, keeping her mouth from falling open in wonder, but only until she reached her new bedroom and shut the door, jumping on the bed and trying to suppress a fit of giggles at her own good fortune.

The rest of the day was spent unpacking and appreciating the space and the roll-top bath, her first full day off since arrival.

★

Despite Paul Adamson's continued absence, she felt more at ease setting off for work the next morning. The office was cool and in shadow, but empty, and she made a mental note to at least buy a pot plant, something to talk to in her bureau chief's absences. Relief, too, at seeing the window opposite devoid of faces. There was an envelope in the pile of post – the first addressed to her personally – and she was pleased to find it was a reply from Herr Amsel, the driver whom she met in 1936. Yes, he would come to the office at two p.m., and would be delighted to discuss her needs and terms.

Since the diary stipulated nothing of importance, the meeting with Herr Amsel became her most pressing engagement. In the meantime, she needed to generate something aside from press conference reports, eager to prove herself. Already, she had several ideas for news features to tempt the desk in London, starting with a focus on the young women behind the BDM – the female German Youth League – since she had little hope of being allowed access to the male equivalent, the Jungvolk and Hitler Youth, now a compulsory activity for all German boys aged ten and above.

The second was to highlight preparations for the Nuremberg rally in early September, the Nazi Party's annual showcase for its might and the adoration of its leader. Georgie, by contrast, would not be showing the Führer in a glowing light, or giving credence to his politics, highlighting instead the pomp and expense for what it was – a grotesque extravagance for a nation that was still struggling to pull itself out of a deep economic depression. That was her thinking, anyway.

The planning of both demanded a lone trip to the Propaganda Ministry – without Rod Faber to act as guardian this time – and a direct request to Bruno Bauer. *No time like the present, Georgie.*

Approaching the building's entrance, she mentally checked

her supply bag of sweet smiles for each checkpoint; it turned her stomach to employ it, but feminine charm would be necessary in this case, and it certainly helped. She was surprised to be granted an immediate audience with Herr Bauer, quickly composing herself as she was led into his office, easily twice the size of that of the *Chronicle*'s Editor-in-Chief back home.

'Fraulein Young, how nice to see you,' he began in English, and when Georgie replied in German, he allowed a portion of his crooked teeth to show a near pleasure. 'What can I do for you?' He sat back behind his vast desk, the marbled eagle icon at its helm almost obscuring his tiny head.

When she explained her idea for an article – though perhaps a little short on detail – Herr Bauer became animated, reaching for his telephone immediately and ordering the stables – where the mounted divisions were busy polishing every equine decoration before the move to Nuremberg – to be on full alert for a visit that same afternoon. A second call was to the uniforms and insignia section, with similar requests.

'You understand I can't permit a . . .' the word 'woman' was clearly on the tip of his tongue '. . . reporter to access the armaments section, but I think we can give you a good representation of how the Reich rightly celebrates the belief in our future.'

'Please, Herr Bauer, don't arrange anything special on my account – I want to see each place at its most natural, a behind-the-scenes account if you like.' She used up another supply smile.

He stopped short and looked perplexed, as if the cogs of his brain had ground down a gear in processing this latest request. In turn, it dawned on Georgie that the Nazi regime did not understand the concept of 'natural' or at ease. The starch in his brilliant white collar was proof enough. Every newsreel of the Führer 'at home' or mingling with children to show his softer side was clearly scripted and orchestrated, frame by frame.

Herr Bauer snapped out of his thought process. 'As you wish, Fraulein Young,' he said and stood to show their meeting was at an end. 'I look forward to seeing your article.' He let loose with his teeth again, just the top set this time, and held out his hand. It was warm – too warm – and Georgie squirmed inside. She skipped down the steps of the ministry, partly from relief, and bought a sandwich on her way back to the office. From an empty diary, she now had a tight deadline imposed upon herself. But it's what she thrived on, and it began a slow drip of adrenalin she so badly needed.

Herr Amsel rapped on the glass window of the office door at precisely two o'clock. His otherwise drawn face spread into a smile when he clearly recognised Georgie from their previous work together. He had been a solid man, but his big frame was a good deal leaner than she remembered, his greying hair thinned to sparse strands – except for his same affable manner, she might not have known him.

'Fraulein Young! I didn't recognise the name, but I remember your face very well,' he said, pumping her hand in greeting. 'How are you? And what are doing back in Berlin?'

When she explained her request for a retained driver, with a regular monthly fee, Herr Amsel's face lit up. 'Of course, of course,' he went on. 'I would be delighted. Much like during the Olympics, I have use of a car whenever I need.'

'You no longer have your own?'

Very few Jews now owned a vehicle, he explained plainly and without bitterness, though Georgie burned with her own naivety. 'But I have a very good arrangement with a garage owner, and I won't let you down,' he went on quickly. 'In fact, I have the car with me now, if you'd like a tour of the city.'

It was exactly what she'd hoped for – but there was to be no tour, since she was due at the military stables, and then on to the uniforms section. A quick call to the *Chicago Tribune* office had secured the use of a freelance photographer, and she hoped not to have blown the entire office budget in her first week. Since Paul Adamson wasn't there to tell her otherwise, she'd simply employed her own initiative.

They set off almost immediately so as to take a long route around several of the suburbs, with the aim of introducing Georgie to the different neighbourhoods; Herr Amsel pointed out each government building, the prominent streets, cafés populated by ordinary Germans, film starlets or SS personnel. And Jews. In other words, where it was appropriate to be seen and where to avoid. How to stay safe. Both his words and his tone spoke volumes: the Berlin of 1938 was a world away from the open city of 1936 and the Nazi-contrived zeitgeist of moderation and tolerance.

Both sessions at the stables and the uniforms were, as expected, played out like a Reich PR exercise, with the best horses and the most decorated soldiers laid out for Georgie to inspect, almost as the Führer would in less than a month's time. With 100,000 loyal subjects marching and 350,000 spectators expected to fill the field-cum-stadium – Herr Bauer had reeled off the figures with pride – preparations began early. Fortunately, the photographer seemed to gauge Georgie's desire to dig a little deeper, instinctively snapping close-ups of the skin-and-bone stable boy and his visible rack of ribs as he worked to beautify the cossetted, well-fed animals.

Whenever she could escape the minder following her every move, Georgie snuck into corners and talked with anyone she could find, engaging the woman whose brow was wet with sweat as she pressed each uniform, thanking the Führer for the chance to participate in his glory, on top of her full-time job as a cleaner. Georgie felt there would be little need to inject even a mild irony into her written piece – it was all there for any intelligent reader to see.

Herr Amsel drove her back to the office and she worked late in typing up her piece, the images still fresh in her mind. There was a post train leaving from the central Zoo station the next afternoon, and the photographer promised to meet her on the platform with his prints, all to arrive in London in the next few days, leaving no possibility for the editorial team to make excuses over lack of page space in the time she had allowed. As the light began to fade within the office, though, she pulled down the blinds that had become her shield, turning on the lamps. If not safe from prying eyes, it made her feel cocooned at least.

The piece flowed easily for Georgie – her style was naturally more suited to the lengthier news features than to hard fact stories. Inevitably, editors would be more brutal with their red cutting pen over the coming months, so this was her chance to really play with words.

As if by some spooky coincidence, the phone trilled loudly as she pulled the last sheet from the roller, the sudden intrusion causing it almost to rip. Her eyes shot to the cracks between the blinds. Who knew she was here?

'Hello,' she said, guarded.

'Georgie! I was hoping to catch you,' said the crackled but familiar voice of the *Chronicle*'s foreign editor, Henry Peters.

'Why are you working so late?'

'Because Berlin never sleeps, didn't you know, Henry?'

He laughed and coughed cigarette smoke down the phone. 'How is everything? Is Adamson there? Helping you to settle in?'

'Hmm . . . Paul's in Munich. He has been for . . . a while.'

'Munich? What the hell's he doing there? I didn't send him.'

Henry sounded slightly irritated. 'Are you all right, though, finding your way about?'

'I'm fine, Henry – the press pack here are very helpful.'

'Good, good,' he mumbled. 'Press men anywhere are usually a nice bunch. And how's that *Telegraph* man we sent you with – are you sorting each other out?'

'Yes, we're muddling through,' Georgie lied. Henry – a true mother hen despite his reputation – might have been on the phone to the *Telegraph* offices if he'd known the truth about Max's chilliness. And gaining a reputation as a whining female was the last thing she needed.

'The diary's pretty run of the mill at the moment, Henry,' she told him. 'But I've secured a contact and I'm just about to dispatch a words and pictures piece, a preview to Nuremberg. The word this year is that Hitler will use it to assert his strength.'

'Great,' he said. 'Can't promise anything, but I'll give it a look. Stay in touch, Georgie. Keep safe.'

He rang off, and Georgie sighed at the finished piece in her hand. Was it all worth it? Along with every other journalist under Henry's wing, she was now vying for column inches on the page, and with the rise of fascism across Europe nudging for space – Franco's war in Spain hotting up and demanding attention – she had to come up with fresh angles to bid for the reader's interest.

'Come on, George,' she breathed to herself. 'Just get on with it.'

9

Hope and Fear

'Sara, Sara!' Rubin came barrelling through the door of their apartment in haste, only to be met with his wife's ghostly pallor.

'Oh, it's you!' she said, grasping at her throat in relief.

'Who did you think it would be?'

'Your footsteps were like a stampede – I imagined it was the Gestapo,' she said, her chest still rising and falling with effort. 'I thought I was going to have to get Elias into the attic by myself.'

'I'm so sorry, my love,' Rubin said, though he could barely contain himself, desperate to reveal the good news. 'I'm just so relieved! She said yes, Sara. That reporter, from the Olympics, she hired me! A regular monthly fee – a very generous one at that. We'll be fine, for the time being at least.'

Sara smiled her pleasure, though she couldn't match Rubin's feverish optimism. It would mean paying the arrears at the local grocery store, with possibly something left over. No one admitted it, but all their friends were squirrelling away every spare pfennig, and not for a family holiday on the lakes, as in the old days. The stockpiled Reichsmarks were for escape – enough to bribe for a visa, more for a safe route, with the rumours circling that soon all borders would be closed to Jews. Imprisoned in their own country, one that had recently been robbed from them.

An idea brewed within Sara Amsel's mind as she began scraping together their meagre evening meal, and she chanced on asking while Rubin was in a good mood. He'd already pulled out the chessboard and was preparing for his evening match with Elias.

'Rubin?'

'Yes, my love?'

'Do you think she can help with anything else, this reporter?' She looked at her husband, her eyes wide and serious. 'I mean, she'll have some influence, surely – at the embassy? She'll know people. She might be able to help Elias and the children? It doesn't matter about us, but . . .'

Rubin stepped quickly across the tiny kitchen, put one hand on each of her shoulders, as if to silence her hope. So that he didn't have to quash it bluntly.

'No, Sara, I don't think she can,' he said, with a sigh. 'She's very nice, and already I suspect she sees past all this . . . the lies, the Reich. But she's a junior reporter. She's new. She's just finding her own feet. So, no Sara. It wouldn't be right to ask her.'

Her look of disappointment, the way she stared past him and into the small parlour, where her own brother was awaiting his highlight of the day, cut into him, like a sabre into soft flesh.

'We'll be all right, Sara,' he reassured her, rubbing at the thin blouse covering her equally sparse skin. 'I'm sure of it.'

But as he turned, his own face creased with worry. Would they? Could anyone with even a ripple of Jewish blood running through their veins really be safe?

10

A Good-Natured Scrap

15th August 1938

'Here she is – reporter extraordinaire!' Rod's resounding tone spread far beyond the large, half-filled table at La Taverne. 'Watch yourselves, boys – we can only stand by as this hot-shot correspondent puts us all to shame.'

Georgie slipped in beside Rod and nudged his broad shoulder with an embarrassed coyness, but she couldn't deny being pleased at the good-humoured teasing. She snuck another glance at the back-page spread the *Chronicle* had afforded her piece, the photograph of the scrawny stable boy prominent alongside her copy; *from George Young in Berlin*. The coverage and Henry's short but sweet telegram – '*Spot on. HP*' – meant it had been worth it.

'Just a lucky break,' she said, her cheeks flushing.

'Quite the opposite,' Bill Porter replied, wiping beer froth from his moustache. 'It was a very nice twist on what will prove to be, on the day itself, a nauseous brown-nosing of the Führer's status in this sycophantic world.'

'Thanks, Bill,' she said, and Rod nodded his own admiration.

Max was sitting opposite, and she noted his look – was it bordering on a scowl? But his attention was soon elsewhere, talking to an equally engaged Simone Doucette. Utterly enamoured.

Several of the reporters peeled away to file copy – the broadcasters had late slots booked in various studios dotted around the city, and Georgie and Simone settled on sharing a cab back home, too weary to brave a late-night tram.

'Can I hitch a ride?' Max asked. 'I'll take the cab on.'

Simone was only too keen, positioning herself between Georgie and Max, urging him in for coffee as they reached the Herderstrasse apartment.

'If you're sure,' Max said. For all his aloof nature, he was ever the gentlemen, though he didn't look to Georgie for her opinion.

'Of course,' Simone breathed. 'Frida may be in too.'

Frida was lounging on the sofa in a long silk kimono and talking French into the telephone. She hung up as they came in, though didn't move to get up, and accepted a brandy that Simone offered everyone; coffee clearly only a metaphor for an invitation. When Georgie pleaded exhaustion and headed for bed, Frida implored her to stay.

'You've lived here for well over a week and we've hardly seen each other!'

'Well, all right, just one.'

From across the room, Georgie observed Max and his intent gaze on Simone as she poured the drinks and handed them out, drawing in her every fluid move, admiration worn on his sleeve. With her striking looks and breathy delivery, an accent tinged with Parisian, men flocked like moths to a flame, and Max was no exception. Frida didn't appear to notice and was keen to talk about work.

'I liked your piece, Georgie,' she said. 'The irony was very subtle – I'd struggle to phrase something like that.'

Georgie was startled, unsure how to accept praise from a woman with Frida's fearsome reputation as a hard news reporter, her bravado in rooting out stories that sold to publications worldwide. Instead, she said: 'I only hope I've not made myself persona non grata with Bruno Bauer, so early into my posting.'

'Oh no,' Frida replied coolly. 'Quite the opposite. I saw him today at the ministry and he was full of it. The stupid man wouldn't know irony if it clouted him in his oily face. You're his star, right now. It won't last, however, so just milk it while you can.' She closed her eyes and sank back further amid multiple cushions.

'I wonder why you went with a feature?' Max's steely voice cut in suddenly, Simone perched on the arm of his chair. 'Surely the whole point of a posting for a foreign correspondent is to report the news – the facts.' He looked at her directly, his face rigid with some sort of challenge: *Come on, golden girl, show us what you're made of.*

Georgie sat up, as if she'd been physically yanked by the scruff of her neck. Frida, too, opened her eyes and perked up at the prospect of a juicy dispute, a good-natured scrap.

'In times like these I think even news pages have room for healthy speculation,' Georgie began in defence. 'It's what might make our readers think, stir them to change their opinion.'

'Isn't that what the paper's editorials are for?' Max said, brow knitted and leaning forward, readying for some form of hot debate. 'It's not our job to change opinions. Only to report what we see.'

'Really? I don't agree,' Georgie said. 'You've heard of newspaper bias, surely?'

'Of course I have! I'm not blind. But if we report the facts, then we minimise any bias.' He seemed to have forgotten Simone's presence temporarily, hell bent on sparring with

George. 'Putting our own spin on it doesn't help the cause. We shouldn't get involved.'

'And how do you propose to do that?' Georgie fired back, her fatigue overridden with passion. 'Did you forget to pack your heart in your suitcase? The fact that we're human *makes* us biased, Max. Seeing others treated poorly – Jews unemployed, scraping a living, despite the Nazi glitz. It's a fact, but it involves people. We can't ignore that.'

He sat back, looking stunned at her outburst, as if regrouping his own argument. 'It's just not my style,' he muttered. 'I prefer to follow where the facts take me.'

'Yes, well, each to their own,' Georgie conceded, sizzling with irritation. *Who the hell does he think he is?*

'Music?' Simone suggested swiftly, before they could go in for round two. Max grunted, but didn't object, and Georgie only nodded – the static fizz of their sparring still bouncing in the air. The gentle jazz did temper the atmosphere, though, and the talk moved on to the bands playing in Berlin.

'We have to show you the sights, Georgie,' Frida said from the sofa. 'We'll go dancing and drinking, keep up Berlin's reputation with a healthy dose of debauchery!'

'Perhaps you can write a piece about that?' Max muttered, firing his final arrow as Simone pulled him out of the room by the hand, and Georgie was left smiling inside at poking so well at that spit again.

'You certainly touched a nerve there,' Frida said with her familiar pout. 'Well done, that woman!'

11

A Grey Butterfly

20th August 1938

When it came to socialising, Frida Borken was true to her word. Having spent her day trawling through government buildings and varying embassy introductions, walking the city until her feet ached, Georgie was ready for Berlin's nightlife in all its excess.

'What shall we drink to? The great leader and his ridiculous cronies?' Frida chinked her glass and wrinkled her nose to signal her mockery. In turn, Georgie willed the noise of the nightclub to drown out Frida's words. She was beginning to believe there really were ears everywhere, not least in her own office, where the phone line had begun to echo with a curious clicking each time she rang out.

Their indulgence was an alcoholic remedy to an entire day of pure PR – the Reich, it seemed, needed no excuse to march in front of their adored leader and afforded lucky Berliners a preamble of what could be expected in Nuremberg, though it was anything but brief. Bill Porter's assessment of the Adolf adulation was perfect: a cacophonous, military brown-nosing, with a passing appearance on the balcony of Reich Chancellery of the man himself, a few salutes – rather half-hearted, Georgie thought – but no speech. Instead, they were bored witless by Göring's puffed-up words, oozing flattery from his portly features.

In the small press box constructed along the Unter Den Linden, the front rows were given over to the German press – reporters from the Nazi-controlled *Völkischer Beobachter*, the violently anti-Semitic *Der Stürmer*, and Goebbels's own *Der Angriff*, nicely translated as 'the Attack'.

'It's a wonder they bother to bring their pencils at all,' Bill whispered in Georgie's ear, 'since Goebbels has already written the pieces they're allowed to print. He's a dab hand with that crystal ball of his, being able to forecast their news each day.'

Frida had been placed somewhere near the front of the box, and Georgie already noticed how she seemed on friendly terms with many a Nazi officer, SS in particular – and yet she was so scathing of the regime when in press company or at home. Perhaps it's what brought her the best stories, some of which Georgie knew that she wrote under a false name for protection. Being seated in the back rows, however – with Rod, Bill and more of the Adlon crowd – made Georgie feel like part of the naughty set. Amid the Nazi sycophancy, it was exactly where she wanted to be.

Bruno Bauer sat to the side of the press box, like the small child with a large bag of sweets, eyes fixed on his lookalike hero. For any foreign reporter, the crowds lining the avenue held the most fascination: some thrusting the true zeal of a Nazi salute, while others were lukewarm in their reactions, looking furtively around to check they weren't being spied on, or that their near neighbour in the crowd wasn't undercover Gestapo. What *was* in the mind of the average German then? And as the horses came by in their highly polished livery,

Georgie thought of the boy back in the stables, no doubt utterly exhausted, and the sweat-stained woman, furiously working her hot iron for Nuremberg and the Reich.

After tolerating such a spectacle all day, Frida had decided they needed fun, food and alcohol in abundance. Simone – who had ducked out of the parade – professed a headache and needed an early night. Frida was undeterred and rallied two friends from the theatre world, insisting on wining and dining at Horcher, possibly Berlin's most exclusive restaurant – 'my treat,' Frida had chimed when Georgie put up a protest. Now she was intent on dancing; expressing her pent-up energy, effervescing like the bubbles in very good champagne.

'We need to show you the Resi.' She winked at her friends.

Georgie had allowed herself to be piloted to a street just off Alexanderplatz, and into a world that she'd only ever glimpsed in the pages of a novel. She heard herself gasp as they entered the vast and legendary Residenz-Casino, eyes squinting against a blanket of tiny bulb lights above her, glimpsing a carousel and shooting gallery in one corner, a sideshow of water ballet on the other, where spray jets 'danced' to the tune of a live band. It was pure decadence, a veritable playground for adults. The air was dense with a cosmopolitan hum of conversation, floating towards the ceiling where endless glitter balls hung and turned, twisting the light this way and that.

Almost stupefied by the sight, Georgie let herself be led by Frida, who hopped towards a vast dance floor in the middle of the club and seemed instantly to bag a table on the edge. She flicked a finger at the waiter and two Martinis swiftly appeared. By then, Frida's two friends had peeled away and were waving at them from the opposite side of the dance floor, already coupled with two men.

'So, let us see who we can see.' Frida peered into the crowd, the look of a vixen on the prowl.

In contrast, Georgie could only cast about in wonder. The whole place was, at first glance, a glorified meat market, and yet vibrant enough not to appear sleazy. Each table was a mini station, furnished with a telephone on a wooden stand and a number. Brass tubing in a vast network above head height linked the tables together, with an ornate dispatch pipe hooking over the edge like the elegant neck of a swan. She watched a woman at the next table shrieking with delight as a small package arrived in the mouth of the tube and plopped onto the table – a neatly tied wrap of bonbons.

Minutes later, the phone next to her tinkled and she was soon talking to her suitor, whose eye she had caught across the floor. They waved and smiled at each other and, at the woman's urging, the man slipped into the chair next to her. *So simple,* Georgie thought. And yet, it made her feel uncomfortable too – women being picked over like an assortment of chocolates. Except, wasn't that the function of every dance floor in England too? She liked to think it was about the dancing, but in reality it was little more than a matchmaking event. Berliners were simply more open about it.

'Back in a minute,' Frida said, 'I've just seen someone I know.' She bobbed away like a firefly in the general glow. Slightly groggy with the champagne, Georgie was content to soak up the atmosphere and focus on the swirl of dancers beginning to populate the room. It was simply by chance that she spotted him in between the bodies gliding in front of her; Max sitting at a table to one side of the floor, deep in conversation. Georgie had to wait for several couples to twirl by before she had sight of his companion. Her. Not the timid woman. Simone – an unmistakable flow of her red mane, hand tucked under her chin, eyes fixed on Max.

Her poise screamed allure and not headache. But why did she feel the need to lie about it? It had been obvious from their first meeting that the two were hopelessly attracted to each other. Why would Max want to hide their liaison from the timid woman? Especially as no one knew who she was, and she seemed to have faded of late from Max's side. Was he stringing both along? Much like the wife and lover of her bureau boss, Paul Adamson. Georgie felt slightly sorry for both women. And irritated by Max's arrogance. Less than a month in the country and he was already playing the field, and yet professing loudly to being a serious journalist. No wonder he hadn't wanted her to hang around as the proverbial gooseberry.

The sudden trill of the phone next to her startled her out of her reverie, and she jumped. It rang at least six times before she gingerly picked it up.

'Hello,' said a voice in German, deep and masculine.

'Hello,' she replied.

'You look a little lonely, I wonder if you might welcome a companion.' Rapidly, Georgie scanned the tables for anyone speaking into a receiver, but the band had struck up another tune and the dance floor swarmed with bodies.

'I'm with a friend,' she stalled, eyes still skimming the crowd.

'Ah well, sorry,' he said, voice flattened. 'It was a thought, that's all.' He sounded deflated. What harm would it do? Georgie reasoned quickly. She was here to learn about Berlin and Berliners – and talk was innocent enough, even in a place like the Resi.

'I suppose we can say hello, since she's not here right now,' she found herself saying, then instantly regretting it as she put down the receiver.

The next thirty seconds dragged as Georgie squinted into the lights, scanning for a body belonging to the voice. Waitresses streamed by, while one older man seemed to be heading for her table. Was he looking at her? He strode right by and into the arms of another woman. With her head turned to one side,

Georgie's heart began to pound. She wasn't very good at this, not blessed with Simone's innate magnetism, nor a social butterfly like Frida. Speaking of which, where on earth was she?

'Hello again,' the voice came from behind her, and Georgie's head swivelled.

'Oh, hello,' she said. Anxiety and curiosity bubbled in unison. He was either here to engage her, or arrest her: unlike the majority of men, he was in uniform – SS. She'd noted a smattering of military as they'd arrived, but unlike Café Kranzler the SS weren't in abundance at the Resi. Clear bewilderment must have given her away.

'Sorry, I didn't mean to alarm you,' he said. 'May I?' and gestured at the opposite chair. Since it was clearly free, how could she say no?

He was tall and lean, yet folded his body gracefully into the chair, placing his cap on the table. He was every inch what Hitler might hold to be the perfect German: blond, with a strong jawline and full mouth, undeniably handsome. But it was his eyes that beguiled instantly; even in the gloom they were distinctive and distinguished – one iris a cat-eye green, the other a pale grey ringed with black, as if the dye inside had simply drained away to leave a void of colour. Together, they had a captivating, disconcerting effect. Truly mesmerising. She had to forcibly remove her gaze in order to focus.

'Georgie,' she said, holding out a hand to shake.

'Kasper,' he returned. 'Kasper Vortsch.'

He signalled for a waiter to bring more drinks, Georgie opting for a soda and a clear head.

'Is this your first time here?' he asked.

'Does it show? Was I really gawping so much?' She felt sure her accent would instantly expose her as an alien to Berlin, if not the whole of Germany.

'No, you look only slightly bemused perhaps.'

'I *am* here with a friend,' she added, anxious not to appear either desperate or a huntress.

'I did see her briefly,' he said. 'But if I'm honest I was glad when she left for a minute. It gave me an excuse to call.'

'And if *I'm* honest I do find this all quite strange,' Georgie said. 'Beautiful and crazy, but very odd.'

'This is Berlin.' He laughed. 'This is what normal looks like.'

Falling in with the flirtatious nature of the Resi ambience, Georgie made him guess where she was from, pleased when it took him three attempts to place her accent as British. Instead of dimming at the prospect – a near enemy – those eyes became brighter. But the next inevitable query threatened to end their conversation stone dead.

'So, why are you in Berlin?' he asked. 'A holiday?'

'I'm a writer,' she said in a split second. She didn't know why, other than – in that precise moment – she didn't want him to slink away in fear of the foreign press. Nor did she wish to be caught as an outright liar. He would find out eventually, she thought, and then he would be on his guard. For now, it was just a conversation in a nightclub. 'I'm just doing some research right now, getting the lay of the land,' she added.

'So really, you are hard at work this evening?'

'Absolutely! As you can see, it's a real toil.'

None of it was a lie. It just wasn't the full truth either. And Kasper Vortsch seemed intrigued. For once, she was enticing to a man she had never met before, and Georgina Young was charmed by the very idea.

'Do you like our city?' he said, a clear hint of pride in his voice. In her time so far, Georgie had already noted that Berliners were split in their love of their homeland, simply by allegiance; those not in favour of Hitler's politics saw the city and country in deep decline, yet pro-Nazis – the military especially – viewed the new Fatherland as a potential Utopia, blind to what the world outside saw.

'From what I've seen, yes, it's exciting,' Georgie said diplomatically, 'although I've barely been outside the city centre.'

'Well, I encourage you to see much more,' he urged. 'The forest land and lakes are beautiful, and only just a stone's throw from the Berlin itself. I think it might rival what I've heard of the British countryside.'

'I plan to,' she assured him. 'For now, I think I can safely say that here is more vibrant than dreary old London.'

It opened up a conversation that neatly skirted politics and placed them on a small patch of common ground: a comparison of clubs in both cities, good and bad coffee in either, where she learnt her German, and a lengthy explanation from Georgie as to what constituted 'fish'n'chips'.

'But why is it wrapped in newspaper?' he said, clearly perplexed.

'Do you know, I'm not really sure,' Georgie had to admit. 'The years of depression, I can only guess. Us Brits are a thrifty lot.'

The appraisal of her own country caused him to laugh and lean in over the table, shoulders close in collusion. 'Well, let me tell you a secret then – we Germans are not half as organised as we make out.' His lips were broad and spread with flirtatious enjoyment, and his eyes – alight with mischief – remained hypnotic.

'Your secret's safe with me. I won't tell anyone,' Georgie whispered back.

'Good, then you are an honorary Berliner already,' he said, sitting back and sipping his beer.

If she concentrated solely on the space above his collar, Kasper was easily a man whom Georgie might have been attracted to back home – young, open and handsome, easy with his conversation. She was relatively inexperienced when it came to love, with only a few short-lived relationships to date, but – and it was a big 'but' – if she ignored his attire, she liked what she saw. She wouldn't be the first to think it – Nazi officers had a reputation for their charming manners, whatever was buried underneath. Frida's numerous acquaintances were proof of it, and she seemed to get along well enough with them, despite her firm anti-Nazi leanings.

As if conjured by Georgie's thoughts, Frida reappeared, apologising for abandoning her flatmate but acknowledging wildly with her eyes that she had not been missed. She ordered another bottle, and this time Georgie accepted a glass, feeling it necessary to get through the rest of the evening. Frida's generally flighty manner made their three-way discourse even easier, the champagne oiling it nicely, so that when they reached the bottom of the bottle Kasper was laughing heartily at one of Frida's pert observations, even though it dared to gently mock the Führer. Another conquest for Frida, Georgie thought. His attention would inevitably slide towards her, with her quirky and enticing looks. And yet, Georgie didn't really mind, her brain mildly pickled and beginning to think about the attraction of her own bed and blissful sleep.

Kasper suddenly looked at his watch. 'I'm sorry, ladies – it's midnight and I have to be up early to serve the Reich.' He smirked a little at his own, self-important joke. 'But it has been a pleasure.'

Georgie pulled her head up to say goodbye casually, expecting his ongoing attentions to be on Frida. Instead, he caught and captured her gaze, not letting it go, his face unusually serious. 'May I see you again, Fraulein Young? Perhaps to show you some of Germany's real beauty.'

'Er, well . . . I . . .' There was a swift kick to her ankle under the table, and a sideways glance from Frida. She didn't dare look at her directly or she might have laughed out loud. And Kasper Vortsch did not deserve their petty giggles – he'd been perfectly courteous.

'Yes, I'd like that,' she found herself saying, before scribbling her new address on a card helpfully provided by the Resi.

'Until then,' he said, dipping his head and turning smartly. Georgie tracked his form towards the entrance, noting a second set of eyes on Kasper, swinging back to her as the SS man melted into the crowd. Max Spender's flinty glare was easily decipherable, decidedly unimpressed with her choice of companion.

What does he care? Georgie thought. *Or do I, for his opinion?*

Towards Frida, though, she was vocal as the band struck up again: 'What on earth have I done?'

'You've got yourself a date with an officer – a junior officer, but a very handsome one,' Frida said.

'And what happens when he finds out that I'm foreign press? He'll have read Goebbels's instructions not to fraternise with us – we're vermin in his eyes.'

'And in my experience, if he likes you it won't make a blind bit of difference what ole Joey says,' Frida said, tipping back the dregs of champagne. 'Why do you think I've got so many grey butterflies flapping around my skirt hems? And the SS are terrible gossips, the lot of them. Like old women, really. Our Kasper could well have a good story under that cap of his.'

Still, a grey mist of unease was already hovering around Georgie's ankles, threatening to rise. However innocent, a date with a Nazi rankled. But if Frida was right, Kasper might well be a means to an end. Nothing more than a good contact. After all, weren't they – the Reich, the ministry, Hitler – almost certainly watching her? Now, she could observe too. Tit-for-tat.

Georgie sunk into bed fuddled by alcohol, but also by a nagging self-doubt – uncertainties that had plagued most of her life. And then irritated that it kept her from sleep. She thought of Frida's confidence, Simone too. And Max. They seemed naturally blessed with it. *Oh, just do it, Georgie. Take a bloody chance.*

12

Girl in the Dust

There was little chance to think much of Kasper in the next week as those storm clouds of conflict began to brew anew. Unrest in the Sudetenland, a loose area of north, south and western Czechoslovakia, had been rumbling since the spring and was gaining pace. Sliced away from Austria–Hungary after the Great War in 1918, Sudeten Germans found themselves living in the newly formed Czech nation, divorced from their homeland. Twenty years on, they were agitating to be reabsorbed into Germany, and that meant reclaiming the land.

Hitler must have been rubbing his hands together at the thought of loyal Germans steering the fight, after his unopposed march into the Rhineland bordering France and Belgium, and the significant gain of Austria. Once again, the Führer could claim to be the eternal peacemaker, merely responding to his 'people's needs', all the while having an excuse to position troops dangerously close to the Czech borders. Warmongering at its most subtle. Rumours abounded that Western leaders from Britain and France were considering meeting the Führer to broker peace: only the press pack feared it would result in total capitulation to the German leader.

The *Chronicle* had requested a reporter to head into the area 'to gauge the mood'. On a brief appearance in the Taubenstrasse office, Paul Adamson begged a reprieve on the grounds that his wife was due to give birth in England any day. Cynically, Georgie might have supposed it gave him limited time to dwell in the actress's bed, though he did appear genuinely grateful when she volunteered for the trip. He looked grey and tired, and she couldn't help feeling slightly sorry for him in the moment, however complicated his private life was. Since his return from Munich, they had worked together, side by side, in the office on just a few occasions – he, too, pulled down the window blinds as they typed – and he'd been generous then in his advice; ways of courting the London desk to place stories, sidestepping those turgid Reich PR events that would end up on the waste 'spike' and never on the page. His wit was dry and caustic, but it was a wit nonetheless. And he was – without the distractions – a very good newsman.

Georgie had objected less to the planned trip as Rod Faber and Bill Porter were heading out too, in a hired car, giving them carte blanche to tour the various towns and villages and talk to Sudeten Germans. She was doubly pleased to be included, though her heart sank when she learned Max had grabbed the last space in the car. At least there would be Rod and Bill for humour and support. After several failed attempts to secure a driver, she approached Rubin Amsel and, judging by his positive reaction, the combined fee for several days' work was very acceptable.

They left early on the 25th, with a true spirit of adventure, a boot full of luggage and several bottles of good whisky; three passengers piled into the back, and they each took it in turns to ride up front with Rubin. Georgie opted for the first shift beside the driver. Once out of the city confines, the rolling countryside took shape and she realised Kasper Vortsch had not been false or boastful on that night at the Resi. Germany was beautiful; the feathered greenery of the forest, roads skirting around lake after lake, and the dotted black and white gabled homes making a Grimm's fairy tale come to life.

She stared endlessly out of the window, glimpsing people walking, working and tending their land. It had a twofold effect: she began to understand the will of the German people in protecting their own homes and a traditional way of life, and yet her heart sank too with the knowledge that Hitler was in danger of dismantling the very things ordinary Germans held sacred; marching towards war was a sure way of annihilating their entire way of life.

'Are you well, Fraulein Young?' Rubin Amsel ventured, an hour or so into the drive. 'You're very quiet, if I may say.'

'Oh, just admiring,' she replied wistfully. 'And wondering. What do you think about it, Herr Amsel? This piece of land we're heading to – some say it's rightfully part of Germany, and yet it lies 400 kilometres from Berlin. Does it really matter to Germans like you and your family? Is it *your* homeland?'

He was silent for almost a minute, and Georgie worried she'd been somehow disrespectful, pried too deeply. What he said next, his voice calm and measured, sent tremors through her.

'I'm a Jew, Fraulein Young. It no longer matters what I think. According to the Reich, my family and I are stateless. We have no home.' And yet his voice was not consumed with bitterness or hatred. 'Germans may hope for peace. I can only hope for survival.'

She turned her head and looked at his profile, eyes focused on the road: an unassuming, kindly man who could have easily been an uncle of hers, a man she felt her father would have gotten along well with, shared a day's fishing together, or chatted over a pint of beer. How and why had Rubin's family been so forcibly disengaged from a country they had been born into, and loved – perhaps until now – as much as any other Germans? It was undeniably insane to any right-minded person.

'I'm so sorry,' she said.

'Don't feel sorry for me,' Herr Amsel replied, with a brief glance at her. 'I have my family, two wonderful children, and we have faith. Perhaps more in human nature than might be wise, but we do. I'm a lucky man, Fraulein Young.'

'It's Georgie,' she replied, eager more than ever for him to feel an equal in their company. 'If you think it proper, that is.'

'Proper if we are friends,' he said. 'Georgie. So, please, call me Rubin.'

The German Sudetens were not hard to track down, and with Rubin's help at spotting the most likely watering holes, the small group arrived in the western areas late in the afternoon and worked their way through several bars, scribbling down local opinion, which sometimes switched rapidly into rants against the British and French allies for imposing the 'unreasonable' boundaries upon Germany twenty years previously. They split into two – Max coupling with Rod and his excellent German, Bill and Georgie buddying up – offering plenty of ale to keep the Sudetens sweet and talking; Bill's florid colouring and easy manner meant they fell into his confidence quickly, eager to offer their views. She was relieved, at least, in avoiding close proximity to Max and his potential disdain for her way of working.

Feeling sodden at one point with too much beer and sunshine, Georgie wandered into the local shop and engaged several women about life at home, hopes for their children and day-to-day life. She felt the words under her pen beginning to form themselves into a feature piece, pondering at the same time on what Max was making of the trip, and if his nose for hard news was twitching for something more grounded in fact. He'd been nothing short of civil to her on the trip so far, meaning Rod and Bill might never have guessed at his behaviour towards her since their arrival in Germany.

'I've got plenty for today,' Rod said as they regrouped in the car. 'Apparently, there's a hotel in the next village. I say we head there, get a decent meal and turn in for an early start towards the north. It's bound to be a long day. And hot.'

They arrived late evening at an old-style gabled hostelry, requesting three rooms – Bill and Rod to share one, Max and Rubin to bed down in another, with Georgie on her own.

'Evening,' Rod said, his big form striding up to the reception desk, ravenous for a good dinner. Rubin and Max were following up with the bags. The hotel owner perused the group, tiny pupils veiled by enormous eyebrows.

'Fine for three rooms,' he said good-naturedly, 'but we don't take Jews.' Georgie was shocked at how matter-of-fact he was, his words spoken so shamelessly as he turned to pick out the keys.

'Okay, guys, all on to the next hotel,' Rod announced, pivoting and making to usher the entire group back to the car. Given how much he had been belly-aching about his own aching, empty belly on the journey over, it was a split second, though entirely natural, reaction from Rod, driven by a deeply held belief. Despite her own hunger and fatigue, Georgie loved him all the more.

'Herr Faber,' Rubin began to protest. 'It's fine, really. I will go . . .'

'It's not fine, Herr Amsel, and it never will be,' Rod interrupted firmly, his eyes signalling to all there would be no compromise. 'We either all stay here together, or we'll bunk in a barn like the family of the good book. But bags I get the manger.'

The hotel owner flushed red under his copious hair and cast around at his almost empty restaurant. Presumably, there were plenty of available rooms upstairs. 'Well, I'm sure we can accommodate . . . just this once. For one night.'

'Perfect, one night it is,' Rod said. 'Now, what's on the menu?'

There were barely any guests to object to Rubin being part of their table, and he seemed to relax over dinner.

'So, Rubin, what did you do before all of this?' asked Rod, chewing happily on his pork knuckle. No one present needed an interpreter for 'all this': before the turmoil and madness. Before the Nazis. Before Hitler.

'I was a journalist,' Rubin said shyly.

'I knew it!' Rod exclaimed. 'I knew it. Didn't I say, Bill? Didn't I say that guy's got a nose for finding the right people?'

'You did indeed,' said Bill, fighting a piece of gristle. The two were like a well-tuned double act.

Rubin looked pleased to have been recognised as such. 'I worked on the *Berliner Tageblatt* for years before the editorial ban on Jews,' he said. 'It was a good paper, one of the best, had a very liberal stance. But now . . .'

Everyone nodded, aware that any newspaper that survived in Germany, in Berlin especially, did so at the behest and control of Joseph Goebbels, with all content heavily censored. It was either compliance or be shut down. There was no real news anymore, only what the Nazis fashioned. Hence the need for a foreign press, and the hundreds of underground pamphlets and newspapers pushing their heads up like daisies through the manure bed of propaganda.

'Do you keep your hand in?' Rod probed surreptitiously. 'Storytelling?'

'Maybe, a little.' Rubin returned Rod's wry smile. 'But it's a dangerous business. I have a family and that means being careful.'

'Of course, but you know, my paper could use a decent copy writer on occasions. No names, no by-lines. And they pay well.'

'Of course,' Rubin said, and the rest was left unsaid.

Instead, he regaled them with tales of the Berlin press, life in the early thirties, in the daring cabarets pushing at sexual boundaries, visits to the Adlon by notaries and celebrities – Germany's last Kaiser – Wilhelm the second – Albert Einstein, Charlie Chaplin and Marlene Dietrich among them.

'She was beautiful,' Rubin recalled with nostalgia and a flush to his cheeks. 'And so witty. She held us all in the palm of her hand.'

Georgie was enthralled by such talk, had always been spell-bound by the colourful recollections of reporters back home, waxing lyrical in the pub close to the *Chronicle* office, cigarette in one hand, whisky in another. She noted Max's face was alight, something of his brittle shell softened in the company. It occurred to her: maybe he was sheltering behind some type of veneer too – that his was simply more rigid, perhaps by necessity. Hers was thickened by years of fighting bias against women as journalists. His appeared more personal; he could easily lower his guard and be one of the boys, but the shield was ever ready to be pulled up at a second's notice.

'Thank you all,' Rubin said as they agreed to turn in. 'Thank you for making me feel, at least for an evening, back in the fold.'

Rod stroked his beard, flushed with confusion. For all his years and experience, his reputation as a seasoned reporter and the 'father' at the Adlon, he had a child-like quality at times – entirely without prejudice.

'But you are one of us,' he said, as if it was the simplest of universal truths, in the same way night follows day. 'Once a hack, always a hack.'

'Hear, hear – isn't that what you Brits say?' Bill chimed, with only mildly slurred speech.

'Hear bloody hear,' Max echoed.

They were up and on the road early the next morning, taking the roads to what was officially northern Czechoslovakia, though anyone without a map might have imagined it to be Germany's heartland. The chalet-style houses, the traditional German dress and signs written in Hitler's favoured Teutonic script echoed where the Sudeten's own hearts lay, demonstrated plainly by the stark warnings of 'Achtung Juden!': Jews were not welcome here either. Georgie stole a look at Rubin's face each time they passed a sign, but it remained passive. Either he no longer registered them, or he'd perfected a veiled tolerance from living under anti-Semitism for so long. Georgie didn't know which was worse.

The day settled into a pattern, arriving in a town or village, splitting into two groups of reporters while Rubin wandered with his hat cast low, sniffing out any small bars where the few Jews would be likely – or permitted – to drink. The Sudeten attitude lived up to expectations; generally mystified as to why they couldn't align themselves with Germany at will – Hitler wanted it, so did they. What was the problem? Never mind the binding word of the rest of Europe, forged in the Treaty of Versailles in 1919.

At intervals, they reconvened in the local hotel and shared what they'd gathered, each deciding on a varied tack, or news 'hook', to present to their papers. Being common knowledge, this was no scoop and it made for better reporting in pooling their material.

'I've just had a telegram from my office,' Bill Porter announced on the evening of their second day. 'I'm needed back in Berlin; someone's flying in from the US office. I can get the train back if you need to go on.'

All agreed they had more than enough to satisfy their papers and settled on driving back the next morning to the relative normality of Berlin. They ate a good meal – Georgie gradually adjusting to the dense nature of German cuisine – and while Rod and Bill put in calls to their offices, Georgie and Max gazed in silence at the debris of the dinner table. It was a familiar, awkward void, hanging like the fog back at the Ritz.

'Getting what you need from the trip?' Georgie ventured at last, if only to cut through the palpable tension.

'Hmm, it's a bit lacklustre for my liking,' he replied.

'Not enough threats and fistfights for you?' She tempered her venom with a sweet, false smile.

'No, I didn't mean that . . . I just . . .'

But Georgie was up and out of her chair and heading towards the hotel door. 'I need some air,' she growled.

Max, for his part, was not letting her have the last word, hot on her heels towards the village square.

They were both stopped in their tracks by a sense of dramatic change in the dusky air, noses instantly twitching. Something wasn't right. From the calm of the afternoon, there was a squall of noise pushing up from one corner, a crowd to accompany. It looked at first as if it might be an impromptu game, the excitement of a bet giving rise to the noise. Yet with every step taken towards the cluster of people, there was a more sinister undercurrent; cat calls edged with a steely threat. Their rancour quickly forgotten, they traded looks, slicing into the throng of bodies, Max's larger form carving a gap and Georgie sidling behind. Only on reaching the inner ring of the crowd did they see her.

She was on her knees by then, the hem of her torn dress dusty and her bare feet filthy, her face wet, though with sweat or tears Georgie couldn't tell. The girl could only have been in her late teens, Georgie guessed, but fear and shame made her look younger, her gaze boring into the ground. She looked terrified. Her vibrant red hair had been roughly shorn, sticking up in uneven tufts from her scalp, crusts of blood showing where it had clearly been yanked hard. The dark red melded with the welts on her neck. Resting on the bruises around her shoulders was a coarse string, attached to a hastily daubed sign hanging limply on her chest. 'I have offered myself to a Jew', it read. Despite the German script, Max's look said he needed no translation.

The cat calls were directed at her – a vicious and hostile condemnation not of the woman as a person, or her life, but as what she had become: a Jew lover. And she had no choice but to take it, flinching against the verbal onslaught and gobs of spit flying onto the ring, from men principally, but a handful of women too. Those housewives with a shining crown of hair but ugly, spiteful expressions, hurling insults at a woman who was once their neighbour.

In turn, she looked utterly broken. If her family were somewhere in the crowd, they too were absorbing this denunciation; perhaps they reasoned it was healthier to stay silent and scoop up her body and soul when it was over, tend her bleeding scalp and move their lives elsewhere.

It was only Max whose face mirrored Georgie's abhorrence, features flooded with total horror at the sight in front of them. Just as Georgie felt she could watch no longer, the energy drained from the mob and they peeled away, leaving the woman to slump onto her front, utterly silent. Was she playing dead, or expired from the humiliation? Georgie waited for the crowd to disperse and took a step towards the woman. She caught Max's reaction, reading it as surprise. She glared back: *We have to help.*

Approaching, Georgie was halted by a stir from the shadows, like mice scurrying from dark corners. Two older women and one man were soon upon the body, which groaned as they tenderly picked up her limp frame, one of the women looking intently into Georgie's face.

'I just . . .' Georgie began in German.

The older woman gave an urgent shake of her head, eyes wild with fear, a clear warning: *No, don't get involved. We'll see to her.*

And they were gone, back into the shadows with her, the square suddenly empty, as if nothing untoward had happened.

Back in the hotel bar, Max was visibly shaken. 'Christ, I have never seen anything like that. I never imagined . . .' He took another gulp of a much-needed brandy and winced as it went down. 'I thought I'd seen some cruel things at school – beatings and initiations. But that was . . .' he searched for the word '. . . inhuman.'

Equally, George clung to her glass, running the scene over and over in her mind. Did it really happen? Yes, it did. In a nondescript town, in the middle of a largely unseen land, away from the world's gaze, she'd witnessed an atrocity. In how many more places had it already happened, and would do so again?

Though their earlier spat had been eclipsed by the events outside, Georgie was unable to restrain her thoughts, certain this time that she wasn't merely scoring points over Max. 'What just happened – it's exactly why we need to tell the human side,' she said quietly. There was no shade of smugness in her statement, just plain fact. It was what she had always believed and was utterly convinced of now.

He looked at her, and he looked swayed. 'Whichever way we do it, it needs telling,' he murmured.

13

The Welfare Come Calling

Berlin, 27th August 1938

As Rubin slotted his key in the door he was in a good mood, the brightest he'd felt in an age. His eyes were tired from driving, but for him it had been a good trip; he was excited to tell Sara his news, that perhaps alongside the driving job, he might actually be writing again. Small pieces, yes, and not digging up stories – just rearranging words – but it was something. It wasn't until Rod Faber had suggested he might do some work for the American paper that Rubin realised how much he missed it, the camaraderie of the newspaper office, the flurry of deadlines and that tump, tump of the typewriter keys hitting the paper, tattooing your thoughts into the fibre of each blank sheet. He missed working alongside Elias especially – then, his thoughts went elsewhere, to a darker place. He painted on his home smile, for Sara, the children and Elias.

Sara was sitting in the kitchen, one dry, reddened hand propping up her chin, staring at the wall, her eyes unblinking and not even flinching until Rubin put a hand on her shoulder and kissed the top of her head. She started out of her trance, and then pasted on her own smile, for her husband's benefit.

When they'd eaten and the children were in bed, Elias too, he finally felt able to ask her, all too aware that she would try to bat it off as nothing. Equally, he wore that look on his face – the *we've been married fifteen years, I know you* expression.

'Sara?'

'We had a visit,' she said quietly, 'while you were away.'

'A visit? From who?'

'They said they were from the welfare, offering aid, but we've never had a sniff of help before. And I could tell by his shoes, he wasn't from welfare.'

Rubin caught her meaning. Even in their shirtsleeves, Gestapo had a distinctive look. A smell even. The stench.

'They asked how many people lived in the house,' she went on, chewing at the quick of her nail. 'About Elias, and why was he here. He was in the parlour and I had no chance even to move him into the bedroom, let alone the attic,' Sara rattled on, as if excusing some kind of guilt. 'Luckily, the children were here, and I pretended their uncle had come over to see them. He was sitting down at least, so it was less obvious about how he struggles to move.'

'Do you think they were satisfied? Convinced?' Rubin's face could not mask his alarm.

Sara looked up. She had aged over the last year – he would never tell her, but his beautiful, once-vibrant wife wore her anxiety these days in the creases around her face, ploughed deeper and wider with each passing day.

'I don't know,' she said. 'But if they come back again, it will be to take him. I feel sure of it. There are more rumours in the neighbourhood – anyone who's not physically fit, they're taken away, to . . . well, I don't know where. Or what.' She let out a hefty sigh, dense with despair. 'Oh, Rubin, what are we going to do?'

He didn't know. It was as simple as that. They had no family in Germany that Elias could be ghosted away to live with, hidden from prying eyes in the countryside. All their relatives were now, quite sensibly, fanned across Europe, quick to escape the Nazi scourge. If the Amsel family applied for exit visas now it would be noted, and they would be scrutinised. They had no choice but to stay put. And hope.

To lighten her mood, Rubin told Sara of his trip and the prospect of more paid work, adding to their savings tucked under the floorboard in the larder, which might buy one or two black market passports. Three if they were lucky. Sara, though, seemed cheered more by the association with yet more worthy reporters.

'Now do you think they could help us, Rubin? If they're offering work, they might help in some other way?'

'No, Sara.' He was quick to cap off her hope, his voice firm. 'I've said it before – I can't ask them. I won't. It would put them at risk. This is our problem, and we will solve it. By ourselves.' The lines in her mouth crimped with worry then, with the burden of survival. Like every family around them – the old woman downstairs, the couple with a new baby in the next block, and the German with a Jewish lover across the way. All hoping for some tiny chink of light in the clouds.

In truth, Rubin Amsel went to bed wondering how long his pride might hold out, what scenario would send him scurrying to others, cap in hand. Would it be the sight of Elias being dragged away, or his children's distress at being spat at in the street, some fellow Berliner barking 'filthy Jew!' at them, as if their very conception had been a crime? So many images came immediately to mind, but which one would break him into pieces?

14

The Eyes Have It

29th August 1938

Rod and Bill had been equally horrified at what Georgie and Max witnessed in the Sudeten, but they'd also warned against holding out too much hope of the story being published; advice gained through years of their own frustration and dealing with fickle news editors under the thumb of newspaper owners.

'My editor won't touch the story about the woman,' Georgie moaned over drinks at La Taverne, two days after their return. 'He says there's no power or proof without pictures to back it up.' She'd felt wounded by Henry's reaction, hoping her editor had more faith in her ability to paint the sheer degradation of that poor woman with words – since their return, that dusty, beaten face had coloured her dreams each and every night. It wasn't enough that she and Max had witnessed such cruelty – the world needed to know.

'Same here.' Max shrugged. 'I've been told to take a more political stance, that they don't need "colour" pieces. I wanted to tell my editor what we saw was anything but vivid, that I'd have a job injecting any colour into such a disgusting display, but he wasn't in the mood to hear it.'

They both stared into their drinks, at the disappointment of facing a stark reality and the limitations of their job. A profession that might not change the world after all. The irony that Max had recognised the value of reporting a human side, only to be told it was virtually worthless after all, wasn't lost on either of them.

'Oh dear, look at these sorry two.' Rod sidled in beside them. 'If it's any consolation, I've had scores of similar stories rejected.'

'Don't they want to show the whole picture?' Georgie said, knowing in her heart it was a naive suggestion.

'Just be grateful you aren't working for the *Daily Mail*,' chimed in Granville, the London *Times* reporter, from across the table. 'Their boss, Rothermere, is more than disinterested. He's a big fan of Adolf. The *Mail* staff are forced to spend all their time buttering up Herr Bauer for access to the great man. They've got front-row seats at Nuremberg, poor sods.'

It didn't placate Georgie. It didn't help either that she'd returned to find that Paul Adamson had finally quit the office to visit his new baby back in England, leaving only a note. It would be at least two weeks' leave and possibly more. Thanks to his long absences, she had already adjusted to her office independence. Even so, she felt more at sea than ever before, in need of a strong tether, or a good story. Or both.

One good thing – she seemed to have made peace with Max. They were far from friends, but on the Sudeten trip they seemed to have struck up an understanding of sorts, an alliance in their thinking. She witnessed the shock on his face in that hotel bar, knew for sure he possessed the emotion to be disgusted by what they'd seen, in the name of National Socialism and the Reich. They just needed a way of the print getting under the noses – and into the hearts and minds – of those beyond Berlin. Or else that storm everyone kept talking about would swiftly become a flood.

With the trip to the Sudetenland, Kasper Vortsch had slipped entirely from Georgie's mind. She was surprised to find a note from him waiting back at Frida's reminding her of their planned 'sightseeing' trip. Somehow, she imagined he'd already discovered she was press and severed all contact. But then, Frida was transparent about her profession and still the military and government attachés flocked to her door. In Kasper's case, however, Georgie suspected it was more likely his limited English meant he didn't read the foreign papers.

The note said he would call for her the next Sunday morning, for a 'day trip' to the countryside. It would be a distraction before Nuremberg, and she felt satisfied there would be no potential for intimacy, as with an evening dinner date. She reassured herself – justified it really – that this was likely a one-off; Kasper would enquire about her work as a writer and that would be the end. Meantime, she would escape Berlin for a day and dodge the endless fluttering swastikas that never quite escaped anyone's eyeline.

The days in between were routine, with the usual diktats at the ministry on dos and don'ts at Nuremberg, Herr Bauer practising his human smile. 'I'm certain he must be permanently constipated,' Rod muttered with an entirely straight face, leaving Georgie struggling to suppress her laughter.

She had also begun researching an article on the BDM, the female wing of the Hitler Youth. Much like the pre-Nuremberg article, she hoped it would be no exercise in free publicity for the Nazis; instead, when she quoted thirteen-year-old girls as 'willing to die for our beloved Führer', sitting alongside their smiling parents, British readers would surely see it as unhealthy fanaticism. Unhealthy and dangerous. And once they reached Nuremberg, she trusted her assigned photographer would capture further proof for the *Chronicle* to see, leaving them no excuse not to print.

Between the constant juggling of work, when Kasper arrived at her door Georgie was eager for some light relief. And wholly relieved to see he wasn't in uniform. He had on dark grey flannel trousers pulled in to his lean waist, a casual blue shirt pressed so as to be almost creaseless, and a black leather jacket hooked on a finger over his shoulder. His smile was as bright as the day promised to be, and those eyes . . . still intensely alluring. Politics aside, this man would surely be considered something of a catch back in England.

Frida was already up and out, and Simone was still in her room, where she often dwelled among the pillows until midday, which avoided any awkward small talk.

'I thought we would head over to the Grunewald and perhaps have a picnic in the forest,' Kasper said, gesturing to a large basket in the back of the impressive open-topped car, quick to add that he'd borrowed it from a friend: 'The Reich doesn't pay its junior attachés that well!' He gave Georgie that slightly complicit look again; quickly, it was becoming clear that he could engineer a certain self-deprecation very well, the gentle mockery of his own Reich. It was a winning part of his charm, but was it real?

Heading west out of the city, the drive was beautiful – more lines of feathered evergreen reaching up to the cloud-peppered sky, little patch pockets of houses and the odd village churning at a slow pace through life. In no time at all they'd left behind the bustle of Berlin completely. The sun was already up, and although it was breezy in the car and she'd tucked her blonde hair under a scarf, the warm wind felt glorious on her face. It didn't escape Georgie's notice that to any onlooker, they surely appeared the perfect Aryan couple out for the day, enjoying their very charmed life.

Conversation was limited due to the wind and the noise of the engine, aside from Kasper's attempts at being a tour guide, pushing out his long arm and hollering proudly: 'Eleven thousand acres of forest, and all protected.'

They pulled into a well-used picnic area, patches of grass levelled by bodies previously lying in the most popular spots, the tall branches providing a canopy to a sun that was now blazing overhead. The space, then, was almost empty but Georgie was reassured to see one or two other couples sitting near to their cars. So far Kasper had been a gentleman, but it was always wise to remember that she was a foreign woman alone, with a near stranger. And a Nazi.

'It is perfect, yes?' He was trying out his English, competent but a little stilted.

'Yes, it's beautiful.'

Kasper had left nothing to chance, providing an abundant picnic basket. The food was German but light – sausage and cheeses, plus an array of fruit she'd only seen at Café Kranzler or the Adlon, and with bread that wasn't black or dense. He'd supplied both lemonade and wine, and they chinked their glasses to a background hum of swing music, issued from the tiniest gramophone player Georgie had ever seen, compacted in a metal case half the size of the heavy black disc. Kasper beamed with pleasure as he wound up the little machine and its echoey speaker pushed out the sound. Yes, it was actually quite perfect.

They sprawled across the picnic blanket, with no sense of awkwardness. As they ate, they talked about Britain and Berlin, about their families and where they had grown up; Georgie could relate her own images of the Cotswold countryside around Stroud, in similar woodlands, eating with her friends and feeling free. And yet not once did he ask about her work. Maybe he didn't want to know, or maybe he just assumed she was from a wealthy enough family that Mummy and Daddy were bank-rolling her pretend plans to write, humouring her until the impetus fizzled. In past years, Berlin had been full of real and would-be novelists, and to him, she was perhaps one of a flock.

'So, what are your plans for life?' she said lazily. Innocently, she hoped, but still with a real curiosity, and not simply as a journalist. He had a history degree from the University of Berlin, so what was he doing in Hitler's ranks when no one had – yet – been forced to pick sides and join up?

'I want to travel, and then maybe marriage and a family,' he said, pouring out the last of the lemonade. 'I thought the military was a good starting point.'

'Always supposing there isn't . . .' Georgie started, but thought better of it.

'A war, you mean?' He flashed his white smile, as if to say: *yes, it's all right, we can talk about that.*

'Well, yes. It would put paid to a lot of plans.'

He lay back on the blanket, staring directly into the canopy of green above. His tone was relaxed, unchallenging. 'If there is, it won't be at the Führer's behest. It's the rest of Europe that seems determined to force a confrontation. Hitler is a peacemaker who only wants the best for his people.' He closed his eyes, as if what he said was simply gospel. To him, she supposed it was.

Should I argue it? Georgie reasoned. *Should I point out the treaties Hitler has already marched across – quite literally, with large jackboots – tearing up the agreements between nations after the Great War? Not to mention rearming Germany, and the creation of a formidable air force expressly forbidden by the Treaty of Versailles?*

But what good would it do? Kasper seemed nice enough

as a person, but he'd undoubtedly swallowed the propaganda pill, a regular dose since the Nazi rise to power in 1934. He was a product of the Reich. Equally, she had no evidence that he was guilty of any crime, and he was good company on a beautiful day. Hadn't Rod already taught her there were other battles more worthy of a fight?

Maybe he felt the weight of her pause, because he suddenly sat up. 'Care to dance?' A wide smile spread across his lips. Strangely, in that moment, their differences were not so much swept away as diluted – by the sunshine, the occasion, even the wine perhaps.

And so they danced, not under the sparkling Resi illuminations, but the dappling of the sun through the trees, to the tinny sounds from the gramophone. How utterly bizarre, Georgie thought and laughed inside herself. One other couple still present looked up but there was no annoyance at the intrusion. It was too nice a day for that.

Kasper gripped her hand as they circled over the grass, his other palm resting on her hip and they moulded into each other, close but not intimate, as if he were measuring the correct distance. Order at every turn. He smelled nice, of good cologne, and Georgie could only wonder at his motivations for the entire day. Did he simply want to practise his English, or be seen with a European woman? Or did he find her visibly attractive, since he'd approached her at the Resi based on looks alone? Never very confident in her own appearance, Georgie found that option quite implausible. Yet here she was: a girl from the Cotswolds in a forest somewhere in Germany, dancing with an officer of Hitler's Reich. Quite, quite mad.

As the gramophone ran out of steam and their post-lunch lethargy waned, they packed up. But Kasper wasn't done yet with his magical mystery tour – his drive took them through several villages, past Hansel and Gretel houses and farmers working in leather lederhosen. Finally, they drew into a small town with a village square. She felt a chill run down her spine, recalling events in the last traditional marketplace she'd seen. But this space was virtually empty, being a Sunday, and they found a hotel and a bar and drank a jug of very good beer, reminding Georgie of her father and how he would appreciate this brew very much.

Kasper was a master at good conversation, more so at side-stepping the issue of his profession versus hers. She knew he was an attaché, but to what, whom or where, he didn't offer. It did seem as though he was enjoying the break from Berlin and the inevitable restrictions of military barracks. Could she ever believe they were simply two people relishing the freedom of the day?

'I've enjoyed myself – very much,' he said as he drew up to Frida's flat. 'Perhaps we can do it again, dinner at some point?'

'Yes, I'd like that,' Georgie found herself saying, more surprised that he was asking for a repeat.

'I have to go away for a month or so – a very dull training course,' he said, that slight scorn again, accompanied by a smile. 'But I'll be sure to call when I'm back?'

She nodded, silently pondering if part of his time would be at Nuremberg, but given the reports of the sheer numbers expected, they were unlikely to cross paths. Hopefully not.

'Thank you for your company, Fraulein Young.' He leaned over and kissed her lightly on the cheek, a brief peck, but gentle. And as she climbed the steps to her own front door, she wondered how she felt about his touch – how she *should* feel. In truth, not as bad as she ought.

It was early evening and the flat was populated with some of Frida's theatre friends having drinks before they headed out. 'Join us?' Frida flitted by, a Martini in hand.

'No thanks,' Georgie said, 'I'm really tired.' Frida's eyebrows arched and Georgie frowned in reply.

'Had a nice day?' Max's voice came from a chair in the corner, where he was veiled by Simone's lithe form. The question was loaded – for all Frida's prowess at protecting her professional sources, she was a terrible gossip when it came to romance. And Max's tone was challenging – no hint of their new-found truce.

'Yes, a lovely time, thanks,' Georgie came back, clipped with conviction. How dare he judge her? Especially as Simone had draped herself like a blanket across Max, in a clear exhibition.

Georgie was thankful when they left en masse and the flat was silent. She made herself some tea – the British leaves her mother had packaged up and sent by post – and cast her mind back to home, rather than the previous hours. She was forced to admit to herself that she was intentionally evading the situation, having to think about the morality of a date with Kasper. No, not Kasper. An SS officer. A Nazi. Could the man be separated from the uniform? Maybe now, but perhaps not in time, not if Hitler continued on his current trajectory. And yet, was it so bad, enjoying the here and now, when the whole of Europe might soon be immersed in total conflict, and her time in Germany would forcibly come to an end?

Damn! There she was, thinking about it. Justifying it. She sighed and lay back, filling her mind instead with memories of a Cotswold summer and the taste of English strawberries on her tongue.

15

The Pantomime

No one in the press pack had the stomach for an entire week of Nazi grandiosity, and so they set off for Nuremberg a day after its opening, a small motorcade of cars, with Rod and Georgie's posse in the lead car and a new driver; Rod was fervent in his opposition to anti-Semitism, but had the good sense to know when it had the potential get Rubin in serious trouble – or worse.

Tired and desperate for a bath after a 400-kilometre drive, Georgie was unprepared for the circus facing her. The mediaeval castle town of Nuremberg had already been transformed by the thousands of Nazi flags dripping from its gabled buildings, further still by shoals of brown and black shirts moving through the narrow streets, singing and chanting, drunk on beer and rhetoric, all waiting for just one man, one true icon to worship. Georgie watched their driver's eyes widen at the increasing intimidation of the crowds as they inched slowly through, eyes fixed firmly on the road until the hotel came in sight.

Bill and Rod were veterans of Nuremberg and took it in

their stride. Max, however, stepped out of the car and echoed Georgie's reaction – a pair of rabbits in the headlights.

'And I thought an English cup final was bad enough,' he uttered as they headed through the hotel door.

It was the tip of a large iceberg. In the next days, rally upon rally was attended by the German High Command, whipping up the already converted crowds – Hess, Himmler, Goebbels and Göring as the stage stars. Hitler rationed his appearances, despite the throngs baying for his presence outside his hotel, gaggles of BDM girls shrieking for just a glimpse. He kept the early day speeches to a minimum, an expert at stoking the excitement and anticipation. And on his plinth at every event, overseeing the spectacle, Joseph Goebbels acted as the master puppeteer, smiling at his perfect pageant.

Georgie wrote copious notes and wondered how she would ever make sense of them in her own head, let alone on the page. It was like being taken to the circus as a child; overwhelmed by the display, wanting to see everything and yet always looking around corners for any leering, scary clown to jump out. As with any Nazi affair, order was paramount, but with the volume of beer consumed, tongues were inevitably loosened. It meant that, at times, she was glad Rubin wasn't present, wincing as she heard with her own ears the intense hatred aimed at Jews, ugly mouths spewing with venom and laughter. The Stormtroopers gaily burst into song at regular intervals, 'When Jewish blood spurts from my knife' sung with particular gusto. Georgie wished then her German was not quite so acute.

Each day, she and the pack filed their reports home. The Nazis were spouting the same rhetoric as in past years, Rod and Bill reported, but even they sensed a heightened zeal among the devotees, a total belief that Hitler's projections for a true, vast Fatherland could be realised. And soon.

On their last night, the rally was orchestrated as the ultimate finale and the global press were out in force. Despite their sometimes irritable relationship, Georgie sensed she and Max had again reached some understanding in Nuremberg – this time, a form of continued astonishment. They were driven close to the Zeppelin field outside of the city and Max nudged at her, half in joke. 'Hold on to your hat,' he said. 'Prepare to be blown away.'

Old Joey did not disappoint. Where the Olympic stadium in '36 had been built to house spectators, here there were 100,000 participants alone – row upon row of marching SS, Stormtroopers, Wehrmacht army, Jungvolk, with the BDM girls in their distinctive white shirts and neat, golden plaits, standard bearers and flocks of static eagles swaying in the air. Those armies of flag-making women had been busy again.

Georgie screwed up her eyes as the SS formation trooped past, wondered if Kasper was among the moving swarm below. But he would have been impossible to single out – an ant in the ranks. It was the precise symmetry that fascinated her the most; every platoon in strict formation, blocks of colour and people, yet not one straying from the lines, not a foot out of step. *People in containment, not allowed to move freely. Or think independently. That's his secret – keep them all in the box.*

Amongst the crush of spectators, there was less reserve; a continual cascade of emotion for the Reich as solemn Wagner and rousing Beethoven pumped out of the numerous speakers. Before the sun went down, Georgie eyed the crowds, the women especially as they thrust the *Heil Hitler* salute in unison, gaping in a trance of ecstasy at a huge eagle icon spiked like a dead butterfly to the back of the speaker's platform. It was where *he* would appear. Then, the sun's glow fading rapidly, Joey put his light spectacle into operation – a fan of military searchlights, scores of them, shooting from ground level into the sky, strobing to a central point and creating his 'cathedral of light'. An intense beat of drums began, almost tribal, gaining pace to charge the air with man-made electricity amid the deafening drub of noise.

Into this drove the emperor Adolf, standing and saluting, the women shrieking with delirium. If she hadn't been there, rooted in the reality of it, Georgie might have read it as fiction – verging on a horror story. *How do I ever relay this to any reader back in England?* she wondered. *Who would ever believe me?*

The Führer, though, proved himself all too human up close – small and inconsequential at first glance, his angry, hateful rhetoric was soon projecting into the air, his body rigid with animosity towards Jews, the West, Communism. Anything not purely Germanic. Flecks of his spit cast against the light from their nearby position in the press box, and yet his inner circle only gazed with outward adoration. At each pause, the crowd went wild with applause. Max turned his head towards Georgie, and she felt their fears align.

Oh Lord, his look said. *Look what's coming.*

16

Life and Oppression

Berlin, 14th September 1938

'Winded' had been the only word Georgie managed to conjure for Henry in verbalising her first experience of Nuremberg.

'I have had to tone your reports down a little,' he said on the phone days later, though with more humour than irritation. 'We've the owners to placate, and we can't be seen as biased.'

Georgie told him she understood, but in truth, she was mystified. Why weren't people overtly opposed to the events in Berlin, all over Germany? How could they all be so blinkered?

'What's the feeling in London?' she said. 'Is it making any impact?'

'On the street, few people are talking of Hitler,' Henry sighed. 'With Chamberlain set to meet him, they think a deal will be made and he'll go away satisfied, happy to get his hands on the Sudetenland.'

Georgie was sceptical, recalling the little man before her eyes just days before, combusting with righteousness. His hot, sweaty loathing for the world at large. 'I don't think he will,' she murmured, though whether her words reached across the lines to London, she couldn't tell. Henry thanked her for holding the fort so well, confessing that he didn't know when Paul Adamson would return – apparently, the baby had been born healthy, but there were issues with his family. Georgie made a mental note not to hold her breath.

In the end, it was as the reporters predicted and feared. In mid-September, and again a week later, Prime Minister Neville Chamberlain met with Hitler on the Führer's home ground of his Bavarian mountaintop retreat, the smiling diplomacy of British and French leaders masking their total submission. Hitler would get his Sudetenland without a single bullet being fired. Reading the reports, Georgie imagined Hitler as the child who'd thrown his toys out of the pram, with the rest of Europe considering whether to pick them up. The child held fast, and those around him plucked each one off the floor.

In Britain, the stand-off provoked some concern at last, with gas masks being issued in some areas, while the British fleet was briefly mobilised 'as a precaution', though it was short-lived. By the end of the month, Chamberlain had returned from Munich displaying a piece of paper in his hand, flashbulbs popping on the steps of the aircraft. There would be 'peace for our time', he pledged in the glare, claiming it as a triumph, though few at La Taverne believed it.

'Just gives Adolf more time to amass his troops,' Bill observed gloomily. 'It's a nice bit of breathing space for him, considering where to set his sights on next.' Often, Bill was like a prophet in these projections; he was a stooge most of the time to Rod's outward humour, but his reading of any situation tended to be spot-on. Everyone nodded into their own glasses.

Precarious or not, it made for exciting times in Georgie's orbit, learning each and every day – albeit in a world that seemed naive to the fact that it was sitting on a knife-edge. A razor sharp one.

*

The next few weeks signalled grassroots change in Germany – and much closer to home than the vast political stage around them. One morning in early October, Georgie opened the office door to Rubin and immediately sensed his low mood; for a man who could muster a smile to almost anything, he looked dejected.

'Rubin?' she said. 'What's wrong?'

Slowly, and almost as if it were lead, he pulled out a small and slim cardboard wallet from his pocket. 'The family, we got these today,' he murmured.

When he opened it, Georgie had to consciously ground herself, though her gasp escaped too quickly for her to stop it. There, stamped – emblazoned – alongside Rubin's photograph, was a large, red 'J'. 'J' for '*Juden*'. But also for undesirable. Unwanted. Second-class. It served to obliterate any notable element of the holder. Jew, it shouted. JEW. And nothing else.

'They took our passports,' he said, and Georgie had to look away to save him the embarrassment of his emotion. 'And with it our last remaining hope that we might get away, or at least the children.'

He wasn't looking for sympathy, never had, but Georgie could see Rubin's broad chest had been hit square on. His rights as a German citizen had long gone, but this . . . this theft had robbed him of any status, reduced his identity to a scrappy piece of card. A smudge on his proud character.

The Amsels weren't alone, all Jews being subjected to a blanket order across Germany. Strangely, there was no fanfare press conference on the subject from Herr Bauer this time, and this steady trickle of persecution throughout the Reich offices went unopposed, except in the foreign press. Only the underground pamphlets that Georgie sometimes picked up on her way across the city spoke of any resistance, but it was subtle and designed to work around the system instead of against it.

There simply weren't the numbers or the support from abroad to muster any real fight.

Rubin and his family were now, officially, aliens in their own country, and Georgie's opinion of Herr Hitler was rapidly turning from deep dislike to a burning hatred. Was it possible to remain objective in such an insidious climate?

Her answer was to reignite her 'Postcards from Berlin' series, where she could express her true feelings but use her persona to distance herself. And hope that Herr Bauer didn't see it too often.

Postcard from Berlin

Dear Readers,

While we are congratulating Mr Chamberlain and his fellow politicians on their peace pledge, we might spare a thought for those who cannot now move between nations, as Herr Hitler is so apt to do, or Mr Chamberlain hopping to and fro on his aircraft. Germany's Jews have been robbed of their passports and issued with identity cards, emblazoned not with a stamp of freedom, but a large, red 'J' - a warning rather than a celebration, a curtailment to liberty and movement.

And so while Britons are only constrained by the seas around us, the Reich's Jewish residents are constricted by borders and prejudice₁ .₁ .₁ . and simply being born. I wonder, how might this constitute the peace for our time that Mr Chamberlain so avidly champions?

Your correspondent in Berlin

Life, as they say, went on through the rest of October. Berlin was still fun, if you had a little money in your pocket, and you

112

weren't a Jew, a Romani or a Jehovah's Witness. And so long as you mouthed your support of the Nazis dutifully. Georgie noticed Rubin was becoming increasingly reserved, the worry lines over his brows more permanent, and she thought of the ID card as an insult in his pocket – hidden but never forgotten.

Yet outward persecution was also becoming more brazen every day; a prominent 'J' scrawled in chalk on the pavements outside Jewish shops as a warning. Sometimes it was '*Juden*' daubed in fiery red paint, the proprietors unsure whether to attempt removal under cover of darkness and risk the Stormtroopers' backlash. Mostly, the branding remained, cracking and fading a little when it rained, though everyone saw it as a stain, instead of the proud declaration it might have once been.

Georgie accepted an invitation from the Amsels for tea at their home that Wednesday and spent the whole of Tuesday afternoon shopping for a gift to take. She worried that foodstuffs might seem like an insult to a proud man like Rubin. Flowers for his wife, on the other hand, were too frivolous. She settled on food items that passed as treats: a box of sumptuous chocolate biscuits from Wertheim's department store – which she hoped the children especially would enjoy – and a good bottle of brandy for the adults.

Early on Wednesday afternoon, she left the office and walked north on the wide avenue of the Friedrichstrasse daubed in flags, across the river Spree, and then turned right into what had become the Jewish 'ghetto': Jews in the west of the city were increasingly 'encouraged' to swap apartments with Aryan families in the east, in the Nazis' flagrant attempt at herding. It had only been a month or two, but she felt a world away from that ill-fated exploration on her first day in Berlin, when the ghetto had appeared dark and intimidating. Her hair was no less blonde, but her confident step had changed dramatically.

Yes, the streets and the houses were a little shabbier, gardens not pristine, but the atmosphere was palpably lighter on this side of the city. People returned her wide smile, sounds of children playing wafted from balconies and shopkeepers said 'good day' as they tended their displays. Georgie noted she had not looked over her shoulder since leaving the Friedrichstrasse. Nowhere in Berlin felt entirely safe, but here seemed comfortable. Among friends.

The Amsels' home was in a nondescript block with a typical Berlin courtyard at its centre, paint peeling on the stairwell, but scrupulously clean and swept. Sara greeted her with warmth and decorum, and she'd clearly scraped every ounce of flour and butter from her larder in baking a cake. The afternoon was a joy; the children, Leon and Ester, were talkative and curious about life in Britain, practising their impressive English. Although she and Sara came from different worlds – a wife and mother versus a single, carefree woman – Georgie found they had plenty to talk about. Only the presence of Elias, quiet and watchful in the corner armchair, darkened the atmosphere a little.

'An accident,' Sara explained as they both cleared the plates in the kitchen. 'It took out most of his left side. His brain is still razor sharp, but his speech is a little slurred and he's lost his old spark.' She sighed with genuine sadness. 'He used to be such a rascal, a typical younger brother. Now, he can't work at anything physical, at least that would pay money, and he's become very withdrawn.' She looked back through the doorway, at Rubin coaxing out some words from her brother, a smile even. There was such regret in her weary eyes.

'What did he do before the accident?' Georgie asked.

'Oh, he worked on the newspaper with Rubin,' she said. 'That's how we met. He was the youngest in the office.' Here her eyes lightened with the memory. 'They used to call him

114

the "newshound".' Then a dimming of her pupils. 'We think that's how it happened – some mad chase for a story, but he won't say for sure. I think he's ashamed at what it's led to, feels himself a burden.'

Georgie looked at the sad shell of a young man. He was only a little older than Max, a whole life ahead of him and hundreds of stories that would have been channelled through his fingers. Perhaps in any other nation he would still able to work in some capacity. But in the Berlin of 1938 he was what the Nazis might term a 'weight' upon the nation.

She left with promises for them all to meet again, a walk in the Tiergarten with the children perhaps, and Georgie felt grateful to have found a place of comfort and relaxation amid a family. The irony was not lost on her – feeling at her most safe alongside a persecuted family whose future was in every way tenuous.

17

An End to the War

22nd October 1938

True to Berlin's black and white reputation, Georgie was pulling out her best dress within a week or two, in readiness for a press reception at the British Embassy, part of the endless social round intent on maintaining the fiction that diplomats and their countries were not seething enemies. Whilst she dreaded the occasions, they could often be entertaining; if she managed to escape to the sidelines, it was a worthwhile exercise in reading body language and proved very amusing.

The Adlon and La Taverne crowds were out in force, Rod in his tuxedo straining across his waist – 'bought this pre-strudel, I'm afraid,' he laughed, scooping up another glass of champagne. Frida was in Paris, and there was no sign of Max – or Simone, for that matter. Georgie mingled for a while, said her polite hellos to the British and American ambassadors, and then took her glass to a corner, hoping to be absorbed by the beautiful, high-ceilinged room and all its Weimar opulence.

It lasted all of thirty seconds. 'Evening, I've been tasked with not allowing anyone to sit in sadness alone and you're my first target. Sorry . . . candidate.' The accent was quintessentially British. And diplomatic.

'But I'm not sad, or lonely,' Georgie said quickly. She looked up at a young and willowy red-haired man, whose eyes were striking – a dazzling emerald green, underneath lengthy lashes any woman would have paid good money for. He held out a slim hand.

'Sam Blundon,' he said. 'Assistant to the Assistant Ambassador.'

'That's a lot of assistance.'

'Well, it means dogsbody really, but they couldn't very well put that in the job description.'

'Assistant is definitely better then.'

Squeezing on the couch beside her, Sam declared himself a veteran of Berlin by a year, still finding his feet, he said, but enjoying the political cat and mouse – or at least bearing witness to it. His sweet nature was evident straightaway, and Georgie considered how he had wound up in such a profession. He appeared such a gentle soul. And being a nosy reporter, she asked the question directly.

'Public school,' he said matter-of-factly, with an automatic smile at a woman passing by. 'It's like a passport to the diplomatic service – whether you like it or not. I happen to like it. Mostly.'

He was good fun and a willing partner in George's gentle mockery of the room – much like at the Resi, she gazed at couples turning on the floor to a string quartet, mentally pinching herself at being present in such company.

Sam was distracted by the subtlest of nods. 'Sorry, duty calls,' he said, standing up. 'Perhaps we can go out for a drink sometime, talk about home, or even see a film?' His smile was so eager and engaging. 'I would love to escape the embassy circle for an evening.'

'Then, let's do it,' she said. 'Give me a call at the office or leave a note at the Adlon.'

'I will. Be sure of it.'

A certain peace – that little hole of solitude even when surrounded by a hundred or so people – descended again. Until a second voice pulled her from her daydream.

'If I were to ask you for a dance, would you refuse me again?'

It was Max, dapper once again in his evening suit and a wry look on his face, somewhere between humourous and challenging. He'd left his arrogance at home this time.

'I might, might not,' she teased. 'You could try me.'

'Hmm, sounds dicey, but here goes. Miss Georgina Young' – a heavy emphasis on her full first name – 'will you do me the honour of a dance?'

'I will, since I'm actually wearing shoes that fit.'

'Well, that's a relief.'

He was a good dancer, though perhaps it was no surprise; Georgie imagined he was no stranger to a ball or two, given the circles he clearly moved in back home. 'Smooth dancing, Mr Spender. Who taught you?'

He pouted playfully at her gentle sarcasm. 'My mother,' he said. A wistful edge to his voice.

'What does she do?'

'Did. She's dead. But she did . . . well, she did dancing, and a lot of shopping,' he said, as if faint echoes were washing over him. 'I suppose you could say she was a socialite.'

'Oh. I'm sorry.'

'Sorry she was a socialite or that she's dead?' But his grin was a get-out clause for her sympathy.

'Sorry if you miss her a lot. It sounds like you do.'

'Yes. But it's all right. I have plenty of good memories.'

They turned again in silence, almost colliding with Rod, who appeared to have the dancing prowess of an octopus.

'So, no Simone tonight?' she pitched. 'I thought she would have been invited.'

He pulled back slightly, looked at her quizzically.

'We're not joined at the hip, you know.' His tone was more surprise than irritation. 'She is her own woman.'

'I know, but she likes you – that much is obvious.' *And you like her. Don't deny it.*

'Never had you down as the jealous type,' he said. 'Especially with all your suitors . . .'

'*All* my suitors! Where did you get that idea?' Georgie almost ground to a halt mid-spin.

Max propelled her on, relishing the tease. 'Well, there's our man Nazi and his expensive sports car, and your young follower this evening . . .'

'Sam? I don't think so.'

'What makes you so sure?'

'Because I'm not his type.'

'How do you know?' he pushed.

'Because I'm a woman, Max.'

'Not all the female race are blessed with God-given intuition, you know . . .'

'No, Max. I suspect it's *because* I'm a woman.' She stared hard into his eyes, pulling up her eyebrows.

'Oh. *Oh*,' he said, the penny dropping like a feather.

She filled the short silence. 'Anyway, you can talk – there's Simone, and what about that slip of a woman just after we arrived? You didn't waste your time.'

His brow wrinkled with confusion. 'You don't mean Frau Keller?' He let out a laugh loud enough to rival Rod. 'Ha! Did you imagine she was a love interest?' Now his amusement had an irritating edge.

'Well, what else would she be trailing you around for?' Georgie pressed. '*She* certainly appeared joined to your hip.'

'I'm flattered you think I'm capable of winning over women so readily . . .'

'Don't be.'

'. . . but she was my translator. I needed her.'

'Your translator!' Georgie didn't know whether to laugh or step on his toe with the sharpest point of her heel. 'And what about me? Am I covered in hairy warts or something? I offered to help you in those first few weeks – that's exactly why we were sent out together.'

He didn't flash an answer, only absorbed her wounded sentiment, appeared to be plucking at his next words carefully.

'I'm sorry, George,' he said, with what seemed like genuine remorse. 'I suppose I didn't want to be a burden, slowing you down. You seemed so . . . well, so on top of it all.'

Inside, she started. *Really, is that how he saw me?*

'Honestly, I wouldn't have minded,' she said quietly. 'And for the record, I wasn't on top of it all, if you'd bothered to look carefully. I would have welcomed the company, doing it together.'

She pulled her head back and stared at him. *There's more,* her pointed look said. She was prodding at the roasting spit again. *Out with it.*

'All right, I was embarrassed too.' He drew in a breath at the admission. 'I come from a world where the boundaries between men and women are, let's say, less fluid.'

'And what world would that be?' Except Georgie knew all too well – the life she'd seen already: university, the city, London, newspaper offices. She just wanted him to say it.

He blew out a breath, as if the admission itself was an effort. 'You don't want to know about my world. But the point is that here, I feel free of it. Despite Herr Hitler.'

He smiled. Broadly. Georgie thought he really should do it more often. Angst was definitely less attractive. The music

120

stopped and they moved to sit on chairs at the edge of the floor, the conversation halted with the music.

'*Nun, wie kommt deine Sprache voran?*' she said suddenly.

He laughed. 'Yes, my German is coming along nicely, thank you very much, Fraulein Young. I can even ask for a decent coffee, as well as a beer.'

'Well, I'm so glad your survival is now assured.' And then they were both laughing – at the same joke, in unison. It had only taken two months to achieve.

'So, truce?' he said.

'I wasn't aware we were at war.'

'Hmm, maybe a little. Let's call it a skirmish.'

'All right, a skirmish,' she agreed.

'Friends then?'

'Friends – always better than enemies. And let's face it, we might soon have a few of those.'

It had been a good evening, Georgie decided. Plenty of hand-shaking and work politics oiled by alcohol, but a minimal presence of Nazis, meaning a lighter atmosphere than so many of the functions the press were invited to. They shared a taxi back to Frida's flat, as Rubin had the night off. Max seemed suddenly tired or troubled and fell into a near silence.

'Will you be at the press conference tomorrow morning?' Georgie prompted. 'I really wish Herr Bauer wouldn't call them for such an ungodly hour.'

'Uh, no – giving that one a miss,' he said, poked out of his reserve.

She raised her eyebrows. *Friends? Remember?*

'My father's in town. I've been summoned to meet him. Dinner at the Adlon.'

'Surely it won't be that bad? And it is dinner at the Adlon.'

'And this is my father we're talking about.' He shifted and

sat up, sparked by a sudden idea. 'Come and see for yourself if you don't believe me. I can promise wonderful food.'

'Would it help?' She sensed her presence – any presence – might act as a buffer.

'Yes. A good deal. Could you bear it? You can always make your excuses early and leave if it's really awful.'

'Well, then, how can I refuse?'

'Really? You'll come?' He was like a small boy being granted access to a funfair.

'Of course. What are friends for?'

18

Reprieve

Across Berlin and away from the genteel echoes of music and diplomacy, Sara lay awake as Rubin slid into bed beside her at one a.m.; she seemed weary and aching for sleep, though listening intently for the apartment to settle. She shifted awkwardly, her back to him, and he felt the crackle of tension coming off her. Sara turned, mouth twisting into a grimace, lips tight. In the gloom, Rubin watched tears fall onto her cheeks.

'What are we going to do?' she managed, a tone of utter despair.

The images from their evening remained all too fresh in Rubin's mind. Unusually free of work, he had enjoyed a rare family dinner and time with his children, later setting out the chess pieces for his game with Elias.

They heard the commotion first in the courtyard, then moving to the stairwell: urgent shouts, frenzied barking. Rubin recognised it as Frau Vitten's noisy dog two floors below – she'd let it out as a warning. He was up in a flash, the ladder pulled from under the bed and set against the attic entrance. Elias was already alarmed, garbled sounds coming from him, his speech confused in a panic. The children, bless them, knew what to do – Leon helped Rubin lift Elias from the chair, and scooped him to the bottom of the ladder, while Ester moved to the landing with her dolls, pretending to play. Her presence outside the door might delay, if only for a few seconds.

Leon shimmied up the ladder, and with Rubin behind and Sara steadying, they attempted to push and pull Elias into the attic. He tried so hard to help, though with the deadened half of his body like a lead weight, they floundered. One leg up, and then it flopped down, all the while each trying to urge and instruct each other in a whisper, sweat forming, listening for the heavy jackboots getting closer, Frau Vitten's voice giving way to Ester's purposely loud greetings.

'Stop, stop,' Elias said in despair. 'Please stop.' Rubin shouldered his weight, lowering him to the floor. They all slumped, heavy with defeat, bracing themselves for the invasion, the cruel grasping of his frail body; Elias's face already stricken with fear and resignation combined.

But it never came. Frau Vitten's hectoring was long and loud enough that a second rumpus in another part of the building diverted the invaders below. Hearing footsteps stomp away, Rubin chanced a look down the stairwell – some plain clothes, but mostly the muddy brown uniform of the Stormtroopers, gone to snatch at some other poor target.

Their relief was welcome, though with a bitter aftertaste. It took Sara an age to settle the children, and Rubin longer in calming – and convincing – Elias. His heart had nearly broken when his brother-in-law had stared at him and said: 'Let me go. Please.' His words were indistinct, but the message clear in his sad eyes: *Don't let me be a danger. The family is safer if I surrender.*

'No! No!' Rubin had cried. And he meant it. 'You're family, Elias. We'll find a way.'

Looking at his wife now, her distress cloaking them under the eiderdown, sheer exhaustion washing over him, Rubin Amsel did not know how he might achieve it.

He put his arm around Sara's body, quelling a slight tremor in her ribs, either from the cold or fear. At least he might be able to keep her warm. The rest was anyone's guess.

19

Father, Dear Father

23rd October 1938

Max was propping up the bar as Georgie blew in from the October chill outside to the warm balm of Adlon familiarity. 'So how was the press conference?' he asked casually.

'Uh, turgid content, the same old angry hot air from Doctor Joey, puffing on about some new propaganda tool disguised as a feature film.' She yawned her distaste. 'I honestly don't know how they maintain the constant fervour – it's all so exhausting the way they bark at us. But Rod and Bill were on good form, prodding at Herr Bauer with supreme sarcasm.'

'Those two ought to be careful,' Max said. 'People have been kicked out of Germany for far less, had their press cards revoked.'

'They do it with such skill, though,' Georgie replied. 'It makes the whole thing just bearable.'

'Martini?' Max said, looking eagerly towards the bartender.

'Haven't you indulged already?' She eyed the empty glass at his elbow.

'This is my father we're meeting, and this is my way of

ensuring it's bearable,' was both his answer and his excuse. 'Two Martinis please,' he requested. 'Large ones.'

Max was perhaps justified. Montague Spender lived up to his grandiose name in every way – tall, imposing, and possessing a confidence that only comes with being born into either money or an old, established family. This assurance was transferred in his handshake, firm, uncompromising and just a little uncomfortable.

'So, Georgie – and would that be Georgina? – what do you think of Berlin?' Mr Spender began, as they settled in the Adlon restaurant, a place Georgie had not stepped foot in; despite spending so much time in the bar, the restaurant and its luxurious menu were well beyond her purse. The décor, she noted, was even more opulent than the bar and foyer.

'Strictly speaking, it is Georgina, but I prefer George or Georgie.' She plucked out a diplomatic smile. 'And I love Berlin. I feel very at home here despite the . . . well . . . the shifting sands.'

Spender senior shot a look at Max, who appeared to brace himself for inevitable embarrassment. 'Well, *Georgie*, you're a lot like my son, here, in sidestepping his full name. It's a wonder why parents go to all that trouble of naming their offspring. Eh Maximus?'

Georgie's eyebrows arched in surprise while Max's lips levelled to a thin line of resignation.

'Maximus Titus Aurelius if you want my full title,' Spender junior cut in, pre-empting his father's reveal and no doubt robbing him of the pleasure, with purpose. 'Dad's got something of an obse . . . he's very interested in Ancient Rome.'

'Not just interested, Max.' Spender senior swiped his attention to face Georgie. 'My son doesn't like to admit that his father is an author – two books on the subject, so far. Hence his name. I like to think Max will one day progress to real writing – books – once he's had his fill of journalism.'

Mr Spender switched neatly to the wine list, clearly ignorant of the hurt he'd so swiftly and expertly decanted upon his son. Max looked strangely unaffected, leaving Georgie to wonder if he'd simply become numb to it. Now, she could see the need for that second Martini. *Hold on tight, George.*

Despite the simmering acrimony between father and son, the conversation did flow, not least because the cuisine was stunning, but also down to Montague Spender's principal profession as a banker, skilled in holding court, well versed in soft-soaping and wheedling high-powered deals in expensive restaurants. That tricky question, though, was inevitable.

'Having been here a little while, Georgie, what do you make of our Herr Hitler?'

Max froze, mid-forkful, an expression of alarm skittering across his face.

'Well, I think he's undoubtedly a driven character, Mr Spender,' she ventured. 'And not unlike a good many Roman emperors in his visions. Much like in history, though, only time will tell about his methods of attaining them.'

Montague Spender let fly with a hearty laugh and Max's shoulders slumped with relief – she'd clearly passed some kind of test.

'I'm with Rothermere on this,' Max's father went on. 'I think the Führer's doing great things for the German people. We need to work with him to assure the peace in Europe. It's only a shame you're not on the *Daily Mail* staff, Max.'

Having spent the previous hour with Spender senior, this was no revelation to Georgie. The real shock was in how Max – his flesh and blood – was so unlike Spender senior, even with that initial display of detachment. Thankfully.

'You were brilliant with him,' Max said, crumpled in the back of a taxi, like a cushion with the stuffing beaten out of him.

He looked exhausted with the effort of diplomacy. 'Usually, he eats my friends alive. He must like you because he didn't suggest leaving early, though more's the pity.'

'I quite enjoyed myself,' Georgie said, mentally crossing her fingers in the white lie.

Max laughed. 'I thought we were friends – you know, honest with one another?'

'Well, the food was delicious, and I had too much to drink, so it's not all bad.' She dug him playfully in the ribs.

They were silent for a minute or so in watching the lights of Berlin move by.

Then Georgie's curiosity got the better of her. 'Has he always been like that?'

'Yes, afraid so,' Max sighed. 'I was away at boarding school most of the time, and my mother . . . she was very different. Loving. Vibrant. They were divorced by the time she died.'

'When was that?'

'I was thirteen.' He stared out of the taxi window and Georgie couldn't see his eyes, didn't want to lean over and pry. Still, she could feel the pain of a sad adolescent pulsing off him.

'It hit me like a brick,' he went on, face to the glass. 'I veered off the rails at school for a bit, which Father did not approve of – not the done thing. My saving grace was my English master. He got me to write it all down. And then I couldn't stop.' He turned towards her with a wan smile. 'And here I am.'

Georgie swallowed back the emotion in her throat, in thinking of Max so angry and alone, and then of her parents back home. They were not larger-than-life characters like Montague Spender – just quiet, hardworking people – but always supportive, despite their natural anxieties about her choice of career. She thought of her schoolteacher father being the type to have helped a boy like Max, pulling him out of an emotional hole, and she felt proud. And very, very lucky.

'He's not all bad, I suppose,' Max said, the alcohol suddenly making him ruminative. 'You may as well know, because it'll come out eventually, but he got me the post at the *Telegraph* – his "old boys" influence. I imagine he thought it would help me work it out of my system, and then I could slip nicely into an academic post and write books – something worthwhile in his eyes. Thank God my older brother has gone into banking.' He turned to look at her. *There,* his expression displayed, *you know the full me now. The fraud I am.*

Georgie thought of his reaction to her origins on the fashion pages, back in Tempelhof all those months ago; she could have been angry at his latest admission. Should have been.

'And you're still there because of you,' she said plainly. 'Your paper does not shoulder useless or even mediocre reporters. It can't afford to.' She took a breath. 'Anyway, while we're into confessionals . . .'

'Yes?' Max's curiosity was suddenly piqued.

'It's not really a confession,' she said, 'more of an explanation.'

'I'm all ears.'

'I didn't step on anyone's toes in bagging that Diana Mosley interview. . .'

'I never said you did,' he cut in.

'But you thought it, like a lot of others. I actually met her at a party – a fashion event and we just got talking.'

'Then, that's the sceptics well and truly silenced, isn't it?' He smiled. 'So we're square – like friends?'

'Yes, square. Are you coming up for coffee? Simone might be in.' In reality, Georgie hoped not – for Simone to see them arriving home a little sodden with alcohol, though given Montague Spender's fairly brusque opinions about the French, she understood exactly why Max had not invited her to dinner.

He ran both hands up and down his face, drawing on his pale skin. 'No, thanks, not tonight. I need to go home, sleep, recover from my father and wake up a new person.'

She leaned to get out of the taxi, Max grasping at her arm. 'Thanks, Georgie. A lot. I owe you one.'

'Nonsense. What are good friends for?'

The flat was empty as she let herself in, rifling through the post to find one addressed to her – ornate script, and a Berlin postmark. She opened it tentatively, since anything stamped with the Reich icon prompted caution. It wasn't unusual for the Gestapo to send out letters, or even postcards, requesting someone's 'presence' at their dreaded No. 8 Prinz-Albrecht-Strasse HQ. She tore open the envelope, and unfolded a single sheet, in German script.

Dear Fraulein Young,

My sincere apologies for not contacting you sooner, as I promised, but I have been very busy with work commitments. I so enjoyed our last day out together that I wonder if you might want to repeat it? If you are agreeable I will collect you this Friday, at 10 a.m. Please wear something warm!

Yours in faith, Kasper Vortsch (lowly officer of the Reich)

Georgie sighed, principally with relief, but also astonishment. She'd barely thought of Kasper since they parted – it had been almost two months since their day in the Grunewald, and she felt sure of slipping from his mind too. Or that he'd discovered somehow what she did. She sat in bed and reviewed her feelings – he was a potential contact, but also a curiosity for her, in knowing what made men like him tick, the inner workings of a Nazi. Since childhood, she'd been keen to unpick people, feeling relieved now that layers of Max had begun to strip away, like coatings of paint in an old house, revealing the true structure underneath. Her interest in Kasper was awakened. She heard her father whispering in her ear then: 'You're such a nosy Nellie.' He would laugh and pinch the nub of her nose with affection. 'It'll get you into trouble if you're not careful.'

It was child's play back then. She just needed to be wary of when curiosity turned perilous in this new, real world.

20

The Leaden Cloud

25th October 1938

Before Kasper, Georgie had her promised – and distinctly less formidable – meeting with Sam Blundon from the embassy, at Café Kranzler. The tables were full and they squeezed in near the window; in the background, she spied Karl circling the customers, though he didn't seem to see her among the crowd.

Away from the confines of diplomacy, Georgie found Sam funny and clever, with a healthy cynicism. Above all, he seemed intently human.

'So, tell me, what do you think of Berlin and where it's going?' she pitched as they shared a huge slab of apple cake. 'You must see both sides of the coin.'

He blew out his cheeks, and lowered his voice slightly. 'Well, it's very changed – I've been in post a year, but I did live here as a child for a few years. It was wonderful then, felt so free – skating in the winter, the lakes in the summer. The Nazis have changed that. Berliners are different now, Jew or not – they're much more guarded. Oppressed.' He took a gulp of his coffee, and switched on a light in those very green eyes. 'But I have faith the city will come through, whatever happens. Berlin has been fought over through the ages, and this is just one more battle.'

Whatever happens . . . Working in the embassy, Sam was party to whisperings in the corridors, the machinations of governments. And yet, Georgie was buoyed by his optimism, and the work he felt he could do day by day, away from the parties and receptions – helping Berliners relocate, away from Nazi oppression.

'Doesn't it get you down sometimes, seeing people forced to leave their entire lives behind?' she probed, her natural curiosity engaged.

He considered carefully. 'It helps when you take it one day, one person or family, at a time. We can't save a whole country – that's what diplomacy teaches you – but you can help some.'

'Well, I salute you,' Georgie said, holding up her cup. 'I much prefer being the agitator, on the outside looking in. And having you as an ally, of course.'

Three days later, Georgie braced herself against the chill, and what such a different encounter might bring. This time, Kasper drew up outside Frida's flat in a relatively staid staff car – mercifully there were no tiny swastikas fluttering on the lamp heads.

'So glad it's not windy,' he said, beaming as she opened the door. He issued a compliment on her general dress, most of which came from Frida's far more appropriate wardrobe: trousers and a slim-fitting sweater, a button-down jacket and her hair ready to be tucked under a cap. Even if it was borrowed, she felt stylish and comfortable. Annoyingly, she couldn't help liking that he noticed.

He wasn't in uniform as such, though dressed head to toe

in black, his leather jacket zipped up with a grey scarf around his neck and just covering the small swastika metal pin on his collar.

'Am I allowed to know where we're going?' Georgie said as they set off.

Another broad smile reflected enjoyment of the secrecy. 'I would tell you, but then I might have to kill you.' Her body stiffened, eyes surely betraying a genuine shock, however casually he said it. He let out a swift laugh at his own mischief. 'Just joking. Trust me, it's best as a surprise. If you'll allow me the indulgence.'

They headed out of the city, in the direction of neither the Grunewald nor the famous lakes at Wannsee. Soon, the countryside replaced the suburbs and Kasper kept up the conversation, asking how she'd been, if her research was going well. She gave a veiled 'yes', but didn't go into specifics, and he didn't delve any further.

'And your training, was it worthwhile?' Georgie continued their loose dance of enquiry.

'Hmm, yes and no. I can now recite the SS handbook in my sleep, but as for the application I'm not sure. Theory is always a little warped in a vacuum. Don't you think?'

Georgie wondered then if SS rules detailed methods of persecuting those whose politics they didn't agree with. Namely Jews. Or whether it was a skill picked up along the way, in purely practical sessions.

'I'm lucky enough never to have been through any formal training,' she said lightly. It wasn't a lie – her journalism had been learned mostly on the job – and it held aloft Kasper's vision of her as a dabbling writer.

'Then you are lucky indeed,' he said. 'I'm sure most of the lectures were designed as an effective sleeping draught.'

There it was again – the subtle ridicule of an organisation

he must owe some allegiance to. She felt sure no one half-heartedly joined the SS, and Georgie realised they had been driving almost half an hour without Kasper letting go of a single fact about himself or his work. Well trained indeed.

They were in open country but had been travelling for some minutes along a towering wall of evergreens, planted in a straight line and forming a dense screen. Kasper steered the car into a well-hidden gap in the greenery and onto a gravel road. Only then did it become clear what they had come to see. Georgie gasped aloud, and Kasper couldn't mask his satisfied grin – clearly, it was the reaction he'd hoped for.

The sight was beyond huge. Aside from an ocean liner, it was probably the biggest thing Georgie had ever seen with her own eyes – and yet it looked almost comical too; a bulbous grey rugby ball squatting low to the short grass, the people milling under it minuscule in comparison. Kasper pulled up alongside a monumental hangar rising out of the flat landscape.

'Isn't she gorgeous?' He dipped his head to look through the windscreen at the sleek lines of the enormous airship, pulling gently on its rope tethers.

'She's certainly impressive,' Georgie said. Gorgeous was maybe a step too far – beauty certainly in the eye of this beholder. But what were they were doing in its midst? It wasn't her idea of a date.

Kasper held the car door open for her. 'So, do you fancy a spin?' he said, his face alive with amusement.

What does he mean, a spin? Her thoughts whirled for several seconds. Until the reality hit. The corrugated metal tube posing as an aircraft had been bad enough, the take-off and the bumpy landing, but did he seriously expect her to float up in an oversized barrage balloon, full of hot air? Highly flammable hot air at that.

The *Hindenburg* disaster only the year previously had left its mark worldwide – that fateful day when Germany's largest and most famous airship came in to land in the US after a trans-Atlantic flight, the resulting fireball and a horrific loss of life caused by a spark to the combustible hydrogen gas keeping it aloft. It was reduced to a burnt-out shell in a matter of minutes, every agonising second captured on film. Almost overnight, the *Hindenburg* put paid to commercial airship travel in Germany and beyond. So what was this one doing here, and why on earth would Kasper expect her to step into it, let alone drift through Germany's airspace. Did he really imagine she would enjoy herself?

'I don't know, Kasper,' she began. 'I'm not terribly good at air travel. What about last year, the *Hin*—'

'Oh, but it's much safer now,' he cut in, tugging at her arm. 'They've sorted the problem. Some of the engineers are good friends of mine. They assure me it's totally safe. I've been up several times, and look at me.' He splayed out his hands. 'I'm still here. And I so want to show you more of Germany's beauty. This is by far the best way.'

His enthusiasm was hard to push against, and she could see Kasper might easily be offended. But that, against her life? The terror of the journey?

There were no other potential passengers lurking, and only flight engineers and ground crew hovering; no one, it seemed, travelled by airship anymore, at least not for pleasure.

'So, you can just request a trip in this?' she asked.

Kasper laughed heartily. 'Me? No, I'm not important enough for that. But they use it for weather research, some reconnais-sance. I'm friendly with some of the crew – they let me hitch a ride occasionally.'

'How long will we be . . . in there?' She stumbled for any excuse. 'I have an appointment later.'

'Half an hour perhaps,' he said. 'Just a short test flight.' His features were lit up but his tone darkly persuasive; it was clear to Georgie she would be heading into the clouds, whatever her reservations.

Still, she shot him a look. It was unequivocal. *Test* flight?

'A trial for some of the radio equipment,' he reassured her. 'The aircraft is – what is it you English say – as safe as houses?'

Having run out of reasons beyond genuine terror, Georgie found herself being led up a small set of steps, a groundswell of nausea brewing in her throat. The sheer enormity of the grey shell lurked above as they boarded, like a bloated, ashen cloud. As if the sky really might fall upon their heads.

Once in the cabin below the balloon, Georgie was encouraged to relax a little. Inside felt more stable, the same air as a solid train carriage. It was sparsely decorated – unlike the opulence of the *Hindenburg*, which had apparently afforded every luxury to its passengers – but there was a small sitting area with a table and chairs. Beyond were closed doors, presumably the control rooms and equipment. Even with her limited knowledge, Georgie had little doubt this craft was used for more than just weather research; 'surveillance' quickly came to mind.

'Here,' Kasper said, still beaming. 'I've arranged some tea.' True to his promise, a tray arrived, and Georgie accepted a hot cup with both need and pleasure. The tea calmed her and gave her something to occupy her mind beyond the prospect of crashing amid a fireball as the doors were closed. Kasper was hopping in and out of his chair like an excited child, checking progress out of the window.

'Here we go,' he said after only a few minutes, and Georgie flinched, though she noted the craft did not. She felt the rope tethers drop away to shouts of 'all clear' from the crew below, but the rise was gentle and seamless, only the view from the window marking their movement, alongside the hum of the rotors behind them. The treeline sank below the window, replaced by blue sky, and Georgie had a brief flashback to being at the funfair as a child, on the Ferris wheel – that giddy sensation of your stomach having to catch up with what's in front of your eyes.

'Come and watch.' Kasper pulled her gently by the hand towards the window, and she relented, as if her feet rested on air.

Her head did a single spin at the altitude they'd reached, but levelled at the sight below – the vast greenery nudging up against the city's suburbs, pockets of village life with ant-like people and animals below, lakes that were mere puddles with matchstick boats bobbing on the water. It was stunning in its entirety. They drifted over Berlin itself, Kasper pointing out the Brandenburg Gate and the Adlon beside it, sinking low enough to spot small clusters of people standing and looking at the moving cloud in the sky, children pointing.

'I told you I would show you more of our great country,' he murmured, his nose virtually to the glass. Unlike his politics, Kasper's pride in his own nation was unquestionable. Possibly admirable? Georgie glanced at his profile and his satisfaction. Was there a measure of innocence in there too? She felt uneasy in being wooed, though whether by Kasper or the occasion she couldn't say. What she had seen so far in Germany made her wary of the political elite, its beliefs and some of their methods. But should she tar everyone and everything with the same brush, Kasper among them? In that moment, it felt almost impossible to view the uniform, the party and the man as one embodiment.

'It is a beautiful sight' was her only conclusion.

It was over before Georgie's fear had a chance to brew into a knotty terror. The descent was gradual and nothing like the jarring decline of the aircraft into Tempelhof; they seemed to drift slowly downwards, and before she realised, the ground was coming up and a slight bounce marked their landing as the ground crew pulled in the ropes. The jolt was in her stomach as she listened out for evidence of disaster – explosions, shouts or warnings. But nothing. Finally, she, her heart and her being came back down to earth.

'See?' Kasper couldn't help pointing out. 'It's very safe now.'

They descended the steps, Kasper first and Georgie behind. Her foot caught accidentally on a loose tether and she stumbled, almost into Kasper's arms, righting herself in time.

'Are you all right?' he said with concern, before rounding on one of the crew members standing nearby, his fury instant and fleeting but ferocious, letting fly with a torrent of abuse towards the poor, blameless man. 'Are you blind? Incompetent? How could let his happen – *idiot!*'

'I'm fine, Kasper, fine,' Georgie protested, watching the man and his fellow crew shrink under the tirade. 'It was nothing. My fault.'

He stopped suddenly, grunted and stood tall, like a viper retracting its tongue. 'As long as you're not hurt.' Awkwardly, he nodded his thanks to the rest of the ground crew and marched to the car.

Georgie followed, looking back at the enormity of the craft, its dominance over people. *I went up in that,* she mused, feeling satisfied inside. Where was Max to see her now, conquering her fears?

On the drive away, Kasper's outburst sat heavily with Georgie, though he chose to ignore it, switching instantly to his charming self. When he suggested lunch, she realised how hungry the tension and adrenalin had made her. They stopped in a small village en route to the city, chancing upon a hotel bistro. Over the table, the look on his face heralded complete satisfaction.

'Why didn't you join the air force?' she asked. 'You look so at home in the air. I would imagine it to be your first choice.'

'It would be – if not for being colour blind,' he said plainly. 'Fairly crucial to be able to distinguish the ground from the sky.' He tried to hide it with a light laugh, but his disappointment was evident. 'They wouldn't even consider me.'

'Oh, I'm sorry.' And she did feel for him, though perhaps it was nature's cruel payback for such enticing eyes?

'Never mind, I'm charged with the Reich's business at ground level. And begging a lift into the sky whenever I can.'

'I have to come clean and tell you I'm fairly terrified of flying,' Georgie said.

'You do surprise me.' But the curl of his lips said not.

'However, you might have won me over just a little,' she went on. 'And i can always tell my grandchildren I went up in an airship.'

'It might creep into that book of yours,' he said. And then stopped short of mentioning her 'work' any further. Or his, for that matter. And yet somehow the conversation was never wanting, perhaps down to the mounting skills of an attaché.

They drew up outside Frida's flat late afternoon. 'Thank you,' Georgie said. 'I had a lovely day.' Oddly, she did mean it.

He came back again with a peck to her cheek, though no awkward pause in expecting an invitation inside. Georgie had to wonder at his motives: what did he want out of their liaison? She found it hard to believe it was merely her company, when – in his uniform especially – he would have had the pick of so many German women vying for his attention.

'Again, I can't promise when, but may I have the pleasure again sometime?' he said.

Was there any real reason to say no? That flash of his temper, perhaps. But she could hear Frida's voice in her ear: he was still worth cultivating.

'I'd be delighted,' Georgie said.

Back inside the flat, Frida was clearly impressed. 'A little trip in an airship,' she said. 'I'm going to have to get to know your officer Vortsch. Maybe he has a friend?'

Max was in the living room, presumably waiting for Simone to emerge from her bedroom, where she preened and pampered herself for hours.

'How's your Nazi man?' He seemed unable to prevent a caustic edge invading his tone. Georgie prickled: why was he so damned changeable? Charming one minute, judgemental the next.

'He's fine if you really want to know,' she shot back. 'Though I doubt you do.'

'A good contact to nurture?' he prodded.

'He's a *friend*,' she snapped back, tone sharp enough for Max to put up both hands in mock surrender. She turned and walked out of the room, his comments chafing but more surprised at her own revelation. She considered Rubin to be a friend. Did it mean Kasper could be one too? Two very different sides of a coin. And was it even the same coin?

21

Asking for a Friend

29th October 1938

Before Rubin had even closed their front door, Sara appeared in the hallway, her tired eyes expectant, hands wringing the dishcloth. 'Did you see her? Fraulein Young? Did you ask?'

'Yes, my love.' He was relieved to be able to give his wife something positive to hang on to at last, though whether it would bear any fruit . . .

He'd gone to the *Chronicle* office early that morning, his courage fuelled by desperation, pride relegated to somewhere deep in his boots as he faced Georgie.

'I need to talk to you, if I may,' he'd said quickly, and she reacted instantly to his already lined face, racked with fresh anxiety.

'Of course,' she'd said, ushering him to sit down.

He clutched at the hot tea she placed in front of him. Even before he'd uttered a word, he was oozing regret. 'I'm so sorry to come to you, Fraulein Young,' he began, head bowed.

'Georgie, please.'

'Sara wanted me to come and you're the only person we can think of. If there was anyone else, I wouldn't be troubling you.'

'Rubin, you don't need to apologise. Just tell me.'

So he had. About Elias, the debacle of the previous evening, and the others who – like Elias – had been labelled 'undesirables', unable to give back to the Reich. Taken away, forcibly, to Lord knows where. He couldn't stop the worry bleeding from him – the supposedly solid, dependable Rubin – almost in tears, thick fingernails scoring into his teacup.

'There was another raid in the neighbourhood last night,' he told Georgie. 'It was just lucky I was in, and between Leon and I we did actually manage to get Elias up into the attic this time, seconds before they came knocking. I thought my heart would give out, though.'

Filthy black boots had invaded Rubin's home, his family's refuge, forcing him to fend off gruff questions about the household while praying Elias was able to keep still and silent on the bare boards above their heads, explaining away his own breathlessness as a heart problem, when it was simply pure fear.

'I think we said enough to put them off the scent, but not forever,' Rubin went on. 'So far we've been lucky, but I feel it's bound to run out. And soon. I hate to put you in this position, but . . .'

'Of course, I'll help in any way I can,' Georgie cut in. 'Do you need money?'

He shook his head. 'Thank you, but no – we have some saved. What we need is help, influence,' he said. His eyes were those of a man desperate not to plead – and yet he would. Pride had no place anymore. 'If there's any way you can ask someone for a visa for Elias, and the children perhaps?'

★

144

Sara took in a large breath, the scaffold of her collarbone ever more obvious across her thinning chest. 'So can Georgie help us?'

'She'll try,' Rubin sighed. 'I know she'll do her best, but like everyone else, she can't promise anything. She has a contact to call, but we will have to keep trying other avenues. Our friends in the . . .' his voice naturally lowered '. . . well, you know. People we know.'

Sara pushed her head back, closed her eyes with a sliver of relief. It might, for a time, quieten Elias's distress, his increased agitation at being the fox to the Nazi hunt. In the meantime, they had no other choice but to carry on hoping.

22

An Actress Calls

29th October 1938

After Rubin had left, Georgie's first thought had been Sam Blundon. She knew several others at the embassy, but they were only passing acquaintances. Her friendship with Sam was new and yes, maybe it wasn't the done thing to ask so soon, but Rubin's fear was acute, a man terrified for his family. There was no room for etiquette when lives were at stake. And from what Georgie had witnessed so far of the Reich's anti-Semitic zeal, the threat to Elias was real.

Georgie put in a call to Sam's office – it was a weekend, and he was away, so all she could do was leave a request to call her urgently. At the Adlon, she asked Rod and Bill, too, though didn't advertise it amongst the entire press crowd. They each had a couple of contacts and would nudge all the more for Rubin.

'Nothing happens quickly anymore,' Rod warned. 'The embassies have queues of would-be refugees outside their doors every day. As much as we think it's urgent, Rubin's family are part of a large and needy crowd.'

'I know,' Georgie conceded. 'But at least if we all push out a plea we're not relying on a single hope.'

The wait was interrupted by yet another caller to Georgie's office two days later. She was processing press releases and sifting through the diary mid-morning when an urgent rap on the door caused her heart to lurch; Rubin's knock was distinctly different and always consistent. The blinds were half drawn, despite a brooding winter sky outside, but that feeling of being under a microscope rose sharply. Approaching the door, Georgie breathed instant relief that its misted glass did not frame the silhouette of several broad bodies – a tell-tale spectre of the Gestapo – but a single, small form. The woman's face staring back at her was unfamiliar, though streaked with concern.

'Are you Georgie Young?' Her blue eyes were rimmed with red and her make-up clearly yesterday's application, blonde hair pushed up into a beret. She was pencil thin, with a lean, almost gaunt, face. Despite this, she was beautiful, petite features and wide, full lips just touched with faint remnant of lipstick.

'Yes.' Still wary, Georgie was reluctant to throw open the door. The Gestapo came in all shapes and sizes.

'I'm Margot Moller,' the woman said. The name resonated – Georgie had surely seen or read it somewhere, and the voice was familiar. Fraulein Moller tried to smile but her lips crimped, a zipper to her distress. 'I didn't know where else to look. Paul's gone missing. I can't find him anywhere.'

For the second time in two days, Georgie was obliged to use her tea supply as some kind of panacea. 'Surely, he's still back in England,' she tried to reassure her. 'My London office says he's not due back for a while, spending time with his family.'

She sat and faced Margot, feeling sorry for this young, beguiled and misled woman having to face up to the truth;

with a new young baby, Paul Adamson had seen the error of his ways, deciding that his loyalties lay at home. 'It's not even clear whether he is coming back to Berlin,' Georgie added.

Margot set down her cup heavily, tea slopping over the side. 'But don't you see? He *was* back,' she said, lips pursed. 'He came back to Berlin three days ago. He was staying with me. And then last night he went out, said he was meeting a contact. And he hasn't come back.'

'Did he say where he was going?'

'No. And I've been to all the places I can think of, those where he sometimes drank, or met people. No one's seen him.' She blinked back tears. 'Or will admit to it in any case.'

Georgie deliberated for a minute. She didn't know anything about Paul Adamson, other than he'd been a good, but distracted, reporter. They'd had a handful of decent conversations, but only about work, and nothing about himself. Only twice had he joined the Adlon crowd, hovering on the periphery. Where would she even start to look? And had he even gone missing, or was he simply shirking his responsibilities, as he'd so far been fairly skilled at?

Margot shuffled in her chair, agitated, mentally clutching at something and clearly deliberating on letting it go.

'Is there anything else?' Georgie probed gently. 'That maybe I should know?'

'He was working on a story,' Margot said, voice quivering. 'He wouldn't say what, only that it would be big, and if anything happened to him, I should get out of Berlin. Out of Germany if possible. I've been to his apartment – it's been searched. Still ordered, things put back, but I know someone's been there. Things have been moved.' She gulped back some tea, unable to stop. 'Paul told me the number of a locker at Alexanderplatz station. I couldn't write it down, I just had to memorise it. He said if anything happened then I should go to it.'

Georgie shifted in the chair opposite. It was hard to assess what this woman was saying; whether she'd been hoodwinked by a man who was leading a double life and trying to paint himself as a mysterious investigative reporter, simply to make himself more appealing. Or whether the so-called story Paul was working on – the one Georgie had merely thought a ruse for his philandering – was actually a reality. A dangerous one.

There was only one way to find out. 'Margot, do you remember the locker number?'

They agreed to meet at Alexanderplatz station in the next hour. In the meantime, Georgie rang the London office – Henry was out but she left a message. It was important to know for sure when Paul had left England and to ask for her editor's advice; already she feared being drawn into the pages of a spy novel. There was no time to find Rubin so she took a taxi to the Adlon, hoping to catch Rod and bleed him for advice.

Max was the only member of the press in residence, sipping coffee at the bar. Clearly, she wore her concern on her sleeve.

'Georgie? What's up?'

While she was determined to maintain her independence, Margot's disclosure had already put her on the back foot. More plainly, she felt out of her depth. And she was proud but not downright stupid enough to go alone. If Paul's flat had been searched, as Margot insisted, it wasn't much of a stretch to imagine the actress was being tailed by Himmler's men.

Max, fortunately, was in a better mood that when they'd last met. He seemed intrigued, if a little sceptical of what she told him, and drank down the last of his coffee quickly. At least he wasn't outwardly dismissive.

'What do you know of this Margot woman?' he asked as they hurried towards Alexanderplatz. 'Isn't she an actress? I've seen her face on one or two posters.'

'I know almost nothing about her,' Georgie admitted, 'aside from the fact that they were having an affair. I'd heard them over the phone in the office. But Paul has always been fairly reticent, at least around me. I just put it down to the fact he was cheating on his pregnant wife and felt ashamed to be brazen about it. As for her, she seems genuinely upset. And worried.'

'That's as may be,' Max said, 'but it will also mean no exit visa for her now. If she's in Joseph Goebbels's little stable of movie starlets, the Reich will be keeping a close eye on her. Joey keeps them on a tight leash, more so if she's been liaising with an English press man.'

Georgie felt doubly sorry for Margot – kept in check by Goebbels's all-seeing eye and strung along by Paul. Naive or not, no woman deserved that.

Margot was hovering inside the station entrance at a bar, a cup of coffee in hand and looking anything but relaxed. Her body language pulsed with anxiety. Georgie noted Max scanning the area left and right; people were rushing to and fro in the direction of the platforms, but nobody appeared obviously out of place, pretending to read a newspaper with their eyes anywhere but on the print. Or had she conjured a scene from the latest Hitchcock film?

The three greeted each other with false smiles, like long-lost friends, and Georgie relied on Margot to continue the pretence – she was an actress, after all. But her body was like wood, her actions stiff.

'This is Max,' Georgie said. 'He's a friend – you can trust him.' And Margot nodded but didn't waste the effort of trying to smile.

All three took a circuitous route to the luggage lockers, Max at one point hanging back and checking any stragglers in their wake, but he caught up and signalled to go on. Margot recited the code to the left-luggage attendant and received a key, fingers shaking as she pushed it into the lock. Georgie and Max stood back, one eye each on Margot as she reached in and pulled out a single large brown envelope, sliding it into her sizeable shoulder bag. She joined them again. 'There's just one package,' she reported, 'nothing else. Shall we go to a café and have a look?'

Max scanned the station again. 'Not advisable.' His air of innocent intrigue had disappeared, replaced with gravity. 'Let's go to my office. It's private but safe. I'll go with Margot by tram and you, Georgie, follow up in a taxi, although give us twenty minutes. We'll change lines a few times. Okay?'

Georgie raised her eyebrows. His head shook minimally, though not enough for Margot to notice. *Later,* he was saying.

Georgie hovered in a café for her allotted time and sank a cup of strong coffee, much needed by then – she was beginning feel entrenched in that spy novel, and not merely a light case of murder in the style of her favoured Agatha Christie. The *Telegraph* office was only several blocks from her own, and she was the first to arrive, let in by the elderly office assistant, who only grunted and carried on working at the teletype keyboard. Georgie looked with envy at the state-of-the-art machine, able to send stories instantly across continents, unlike the distinctly less modern *Chronicle* offices, relying on phone lines, telegrams and the train mail to London. As Max and Margot arrived, flushed from the journey, the assistant was packing up and putting the cover on her machine.

'Thank you, Inga,' Max said, ushering her out of the door. Her backwards glance cast disapproval at not one but two strange women in her domain. 'I think she's trustworthy, but you can never tell these days,' Max whispered to Georgie.

Opening the envelope felt like the sinister unveiling of a booby trap device, Margot's fingers gingerly reaching in and pulling out several papers, and one or two fuzzy photographs. The papers were variously typed and handwritten, no eagle icon of the Reich at their head, but on notepaper from some kind of hospital or private clinic – the Haas Institute – an address to the south of Berlin. The typed pages were lists of names alongside a numbered code, from one to nine. At first glance, Georgie assumed it might be a nursing home, but the birth dates alongside the names were varied, aged twenty to sixty-plus. The handwritten print was a jumble of notes, with a loose spiral of scrawl circling the page.

'It's like the rough workings from inside someone's head,' Georgie murmured. She could translate the letters and words, but as to meaning, it was more like double Dutch – a blend of numbers and letters, the words 'capacity' and 'forecast' picked out. The rest appeared to be technical jargon and beyond Georgie's everyday German.

'What on earth does it mean?' Margot said in a small, disappointed voice.

'I have no idea,' Max admitted. He looked at the photographs, hand printed by an amateur – perhaps Paul himself – of two heavy-set men in overcoats leaving a building, their faces too blurred to pinpoint any features.

Georgie sighed. What they had was virtually useless in leading them to the source or the object of Paul's story. Or his whereabouts.

'I think the only thing we can do for now is alert the press crowd and get everyone to put out their feelers,' Max said.

'I'll get Henry back in London to ring the British Embassy here,' Georgie added. 'And if he doesn't turn up soon, we'll need to call the police.'

Margot looked stricken – she'd clearly hoped they would track Paul to a secret bolthole known only to the press, drunk and contrite but unharmed. And maybe that's where he was, hiding yet again from his responsibilities. But increasingly, it didn't seem likely.

Georgie did her best to reassure Margot, though she didn't believe her own empty pledges.

'We'll call as soon as we hear anything,' she said on showing her out; Margot had an audition and needed to prepare. She was a single working woman and, right then, living life as normal was her best route to remaining safe. Without Paul, she had to rely on her work entirely.

The door shut, Max switched on the radio, turning up the volume and moving in towards Georgie, heads close enough she could smell his aftershave.

'Well?' she said, eyes wide with intrigue.

'This is confusing, but equally, it doesn't look good,' he replied, fingering the pages. 'I thought I saw a familiar man arrive at the left-luggage as Margot was searching, doing a bad job of loitering. I can't be entirely sure, but I think I've seen him in the Adlon bar from time to time. Even if it is a coincidence, it's an uncomfortable one.'

They agreed to meet at La Taverne and alert the press pack, but only to Paul's disappearance and not the possible reasons behind it. Max placed the typewritten sheets in the small office safe, and Georgie folded and tucked the handwritten pages in a small compartment of her handbag. She planned to tackle them with a dictionary, possibly to ask Rubin for some help in translating. Already, it irked her that she couldn't make head nor tail of it – another puzzle to unpick.

'Sorry, but I've got some ridiculous ceremony to cover for the office,' Max said. 'Cliff's liver has finally given him a warning sign and he's in hospital, so I'm covering all the diary events.'

They looked at each other but no words were needed. Boarding the plane towards Berlin all those months ago, how could either of them imagine their baptism of fire would flare so soon?

★

Back in her own office, Georgie dialled the number for London. 'What's going on, Georgie?' Henry said, his concern evident despite the weakness of the signal. 'Paul's wife confirmed he left home five days ago, apparently to give in his notice in London and tie up a few loose ends. But we've not seen or heard from him.' He sighed heavily. 'He's always been a bit of a loose cannon, and maybe I shouldn't have tolerated it, but he always came up with the goods. He had excellent contacts.'

'Maybe too good,' Georgie muttered into the receiver.

She told Henry scant details of Paul's disappearance, though not the discovery. She'd been warned again that the phone lines in all foreign newspaper offices were no longer secure – that tell-tale clicking she'd heard from time to time being the proof. The Reich had ears everywhere, even at the Adlon, it seemed, where Bill Porter cautioned even the public telephone booths were tapped. The press used them for generalised stories, but anything mildly controversial meant going elsewhere, cabling over stories or using a courier mail service if it wasn't immediate 'hard' news.

'I'll call the British Embassy here – I know someone in the German office,' Henry went on. 'They might be able to root something out before we have to go to the police.'

Georgie was relieved at not having to ask Sam Blundon for a second favour when they spoke. What with Rubin's request, and now this, she was feeling less like a reporter and more like a detective.

'Oh, and Georgie?'

'Yes, Henry.'

'Do *not* go playing sleuth on this, all right? Let me handle it from this end.'

Christ, that's why Henry had been such a good reporter in his day – he could sniff out a story 'with legs', as the press were apt to say, even with a sea and continent between them.

'Understood,' she said, thankful he couldn't see the guilt across her face. Everything told Georgie she should leave it alone. The papers she had in her handbag were sodden with suspicion. The question was: could she?

Unable to settle to any work, she walked towards the Unter den Linden and Café Kranzler, which gave off its usual buzz of late-afternoon customers. Despite a good deal of military personnel at the tables, it was still a comfortable place for her to sit and think – the Reich couldn't put a tap on her thoughts. Yet.

She settled at the table she'd frequented over the past weeks, and where Karl the waiter had brought her coffee and asked on most occasions if she wanted extra cream on the side. She had said, 'No, thank you, not right now,' and his features hadn't flinched. Rod the wise had counselled her to use a contact sparingly, saving their services for when they were needed most.

'Afternoon, Fraulein,' Karl said dutifully. 'What can I get for you?'

Georgie's face burned, the loud, boorish voices of several Wehrmacht officers suddenly amplified. 'I'll have a coffee and a slice of strudel, with some extra cream on the side.' She smiled courteously, finding it hard to keep her face from ridiculous gesticulation. *Georgina Young, what are you playing at?*

Karl, though, was the consummate contact. 'Certainly, Fraulein,' and he floated away. Her eyes fanned Kranzler's semi-opulent room, and she was flushed with a memory of Lyons Corner House on London's Tottenham Court Road, with its flowery-themed lights and exotic indoor plants. She had gone to Lyons after her final, successful interview at the *Chronicle*, treated herself to the biggest cream cake she could find and speculated then what life as a journalist would bring. It was where the similarity ended: Kranzler was more luxurious than Lyons, and heavily populated by men of possibly the biggest threat to European peace. And here she was, engaging a contact to ferret out potentially perilous information. *That's* where life had taken her.

Karl returned several minutes later and set down her coffee, a plate of flaky strudel – which wasn't necessary for their discourse, but much wanted – and a jug of cream on the side. He tucked the bill underneath the jug, nodded and walked away.

She sipped at the coffee, itching to pluck out the small tab of paper, but forcing herself to gaze casually out of the window at the stream of people passing by, a ripple of red flags reaching into the distance. Inside, the colour scheme was the grey and green of army and SS, any one of them with grounds to arrest her based on the words written on the underside of the bill. Charge her with conspiracy, deport or imprison her. Or worse. And yet there was no going back, the crime of asking for cream on the side already committed.

The strudel eaten and her coffee drained, Georgie coolly picked up the bill and turned it over. *Schiller's bar 7 p.m.* was scribbled in pencil.

She pulled in a deep breath – *no choice but to get on with it.* She went to leave, dampening the quiver inside as she stood, when a new insult thrust at the inside of her gut. She heard him first, tucked in a corner table. One swift glance confirmed it was Kasper, with several other SS officers, holding court among three women, the type that – if she applied a crude stereotype – might be called uniform chasers: those German women enchanted by the crisp grey and black of the SS and the power it held. It wasn't so much the women's dress, or the way they styled their hair, more an eagerness in their faces. A desperation to please, to snare a man with a future in the new Germania.

Face to the floor, Georgie slunk by, careful not to attract

any attention, least of all from Kasper. But she needn't have worried – he was captivated by the company of the women, his deep laughter and the smoke from his large cigar rising above the table. Georgie found herself more relieved than envious; she did not want to be in the sights of any SS officer, 'lowly' or not. Especially now.

23

Bright Lights

2nd November 1938

Georgie considered asking Max to her evening rendezvous
with Karl, but thought better of it – one man and a woman
were able to melt more easily into a crowd. The waiter appeared
trustworthy, and it was he who'd suggested contact in a public
place. She'd never been to Schiller's but it was on a side street
just off the bright and busy clubland of Kurfürstendamm –
the centre of Berlin's twenty-four-hour reputation. Electricity
fuelling the hundreds of bright, neon lights overhead ran
through Georgie as she stepped towards the bar. It was cold
enough to see steam from her breath, hands in gloves and
pockets, but the sight of couples striding arm in arm warmed
her, their laughter tempering her anguish. *Rod trusts this man
– Karl – and so should I.* Still, each and every smiling face who
passed by could – might – be Gestapo. *Be as well to remember
it, girl.*

Schiller's was gloomy and distinctly downmarket, holding an
advantage in being badly lit, and she'd deliberately dressed in
a sober fashion, in a grey winter suit – nothing to turn heads

— and flat shoes. Subconsciously, she realised being able to run for her life was lodged at the back of her mind.

Georgie's eyes skittered over the tables and the rough clientele as she entered. Some glanced her way and turned back instantly; one or two pairs of eyes lingered too long for her liking. The room felt suddenly hot. Karl was already seated at the back of the bar, in a rough wooden booth. He leaned in to kiss her as she sat, but it was more of a play at a date. He sparked up a conversation based on her day, all smiles and enquiry, like a regular couple. When the drinks arrived and it was obvious the men sitting at the long bar were paying them no attention, Karl turned to face her.

His voice was upbeat, but low. 'And so, your cream, Fraulein?'

'The Haas Institute, over at Königstrasse, Wannsee. Do you know anything about it?'

His eyes narrowed, as if searching a dark corner of his memory. 'It doesn't come to mind,' he said. Like a good contact, he knew better than to ask why. 'Do you want me to make enquiries? Discreet, of course.'

'Please,' she said. 'Owners especially, and its purpose.'

'Very well. It may take a good few days.'

Georgie suppressed her disappointment. Finding Paul seemed urgent, but Rod had persuaded her that reliable information took time; too fast and it was likely to be either thin on detail or heavily embellished.

'Come to the Kranzler in five days. I'll let you know if I have anything then,' Karl said, draining his beer.

'One more thing,' Georgie ventured. Even then, she wasn't sure of entrusting Karl with a name, but it seemed they had nothing to lose, especially if Paul really was in danger. 'One of our correspondents is missing, since yesterday.'

Karl's face dropped in what appeared to be genuine surprise.

'Paul Adamson,' she went on. 'Have you heard anything? Did he ever come to you, or your friends?'

But Karl's face was blank. 'There are lots like me, Fraulein, simply trying to do their bit, and make a little extra for survival, in case we . . . well, you know. His name isn't familiar, but he may have had other contacts. I'll ask around.'

He nodded that their business was concluded, and they made a play of saying a friendly goodbye and promising to meet again soon.

Outside, on the brightly lit main street with its ever busy footfall, couples spilled from a cabaret or a show, perhaps choosing to ignore the grubby underbelly of Berlin just yards away. George looked on, slight envious of their normality. She would have liked to linger, innocently people-watching under the bright café awnings. But nothing in that moment about Berlin seemed innocuous, and she was suddenly exhausted – by this latest encounter, the day's revelations and events. And by what the next few days might hold.

Sinking into a bubble bath back at Frida's flat, she felt variously thankful for and guilty about such indulgence, especially in ignoring the phone when it rang several times. Doubtless, Margot Moller was not experiencing such luxury. The actress was wise to Berlin, and if she was within Joey Goebbels's beloved clique of starlets, she would know what the highest echelons of Nazi society were capable of. The gloss of the parties, the sheen of etiquette. And the ruthless reality underneath.

No, she would be feeling distinctly uneasy, alone and waiting for Paul.

24

The Red Stain

The next morning, Georgie was keen to report everything to Max as the pack convened for another press conference at the Reich Chancellery. He narrowed his eyes as she slipped into the seat beside him, and yet again she was at a loss as to how to read his mood.

'I wondered why you weren't at La Taverne,' he whispered irritably. 'I rang the flat several times, almost sent out a search party. Don't do that, Georgie.'

She was taken aback, mainly by his reaction. Yet behind his blunt words, she detected true concern. 'I'm sorry,' she said. 'I was tired and just needed to sink into a hot bath.'

'That's all very well, but in the circumstances, you might have been anywhere. You could have at least let me know.' The thin line of his mouth relayed annoyance.

In hindsight, she might have felt the same, and she apologised again, with feeling.

'So, did anyone at La Taverne have any information – about Paul?'

'No one's seen him since before he left for England,' Max said. 'He didn't socialise that much either, it seems. But everyone is asking around.' He didn't look especially hopeful.

Georgie dipped her head as the press official stood behind his lectern and coughed loudly.

'Do you think he could have come to real harm?' she whispered. Max could be gruff and sometimes distant, but he wasn't prone to exaggeration. His silence then spoke volumes.

They met with Margot after the conference, having agreed not to trust the telephone lines. She had no further news and looked even thinner, as though she hadn't slept or eaten since their last meeting.

'What about going to that clinic?' she pitched. 'I could go, pretend to be a client, or a relative.' Her face had the eagerness – and desperation – of a child.

'I've no doubt you could pull it off,' Max told her, 'but I think we need to wait for information first. Even if the Haas Institute has anything to do with Paul's disappearance, I'd be very surprised if he was actually being held there. It would be very foolish of them.' He rubbed at his chin, deep in thought. 'Perhaps now you should report him missing. It'll be low on the police's priority to begin a search, but if the *Chronicle* reports it, and the British Embassy puts in its two penn'orth, they'll be forced to do something.'

Margot nodded with a wan expression. Georgie pictured her then, sitting in the police station, some tired officer from the Kripo detective branch scribbling down her statement, and thinking what a foolish young woman she'd been to get herself involved with an unreliable British newspaperman.

Christ, Paul, where the hell are you, and what are you mixed up in?

★

There was no news over the next days; Margot either turned up at Georgie's office or sent word that Paul hadn't reappeared. As each day went by, Georgie became less and less surprised that he hadn't, and she began to fear the worst, more certain than ever that it wasn't simply a case of his philandering finally giving rise to guilt and sending him into hiding. Henry reported Paul's disappearance officially, and the British Embassy responded, putting out their tendrils of enquiry to the police, with some insistence.

Sam Blundon returned Georgie's call around midday and – with Paul's absence taking precedence in recent days – she had to pull herself back to the Amsels' plight. Rubin had been driving her around the city each day but he'd not pressed the issue. 'Can you spare some time tomorrow?' she said to Sam, then sheepishly: 'I've got a favour to ask – perhaps we could meet at Café Bristol – the pastries are on me.'

'Then how can I refuse?'

Georgie felt reassured that she would be able to promote Rubin's case when she met with Sam the next day. Before that, it was time also to check in with Karl over the Haas Institute – life was running at a rapid pace and it seemed Georgie was juggling more than several balls in the air at once. Her work was coming a poor second, so much so that Henry forwarded a short, slightly curt, telegram, asking her if Berlin had gone to sleep. In response, she fired off a 'postcard' piece, which flowed with alarming ease, on the jittery undercurrent seeping into Berliner's conversations. It was based on snippets she'd overheard – tension versus the vibrant buzz of its cafés and nightclubs; the sinister dark against Berlin's frivolous light. The nightclub content Georgie gained mostly from Frida's regular storytelling over breakfast, but the time spent in cafés was all her own.

By five o'clock she was catching the last of the teatime

custom in Kranzler's. Karl ghosted towards her table with his phantom-like ability and she ordered her customary coffee.

'Have you any cream today?' she said, struggling to maintain control of her eyebrows; this surreptitious demeanour was definitely not her forte.

'Plenty today, Madam,' he said in a flat tone, and left the bill. She flipped it over while stirring her coffee. *Tiergarten, top entrance – one hour.*

She left with plenty of time to spare, to amble from Kranzler's, up past the Adlon and under the arches of the stately Brandenburg Gate. Emerging onto the park side and towards the entrance of Berlin's 'garden of the beasts', Georgie swivelled and looked back down the entire length of the Unter den Linden. She squinted into the distance, something she hadn't done for some weeks, and realised then she'd become like many a Berliner – acclimatised. It had seeped slowly but surely into her consciousness. With her eyes narrowed, Berlin as a whole meshed to a red hue, as if the streets were awash with blood, slinking up the walls of its imposing buildings.

The mere sight created a deep knot in her chest. Paul. Rubin. His kind, welcoming family. That poor unfortunate in the street on her first days in the city. The sheared and degraded red-haired girl in the town square, persecuted only for loving another. All contributed to the Nazis' red stain. How many more to come?

Hopping from foot to foot against the cold, Georgie tried her best not to look furtive, and it was only a minute or so before Karl scooped at her elbow, his waiter's uniform covered by a long, dark overcoat.

'Let's walk in the park,' he said. Georgie hesitated – she still didn't know Karl that well, and it was dark on the paths where the gas lanterns didn't cast their light. Plenty of corners in which to fall foul. Undoubtedly, he sensed the tension in her arm. 'Don't worry, we won't be long.'

Thankfully, there were still couples along the walkways, and Karl was content to stick to the wider paths. He waited until the walkers passed before he spoke.

'The Haas Institute,' he began.

'Yes?'

'I'd steer clear,' he said firmly.

'Why?'

'Didn't you hear what I said?' he hissed this time. 'It's not good to go poking about there.'

'Is that a warning?' For a moment, she wondered if Karl was showing his true colours as a defender of the Reich, though her pure instinct said not.

His grip tightened on her arm – not sinister, more that his sentiment was honest. *Please believe me,* he was saying. 'It is a warning. But as a friend. To you and Herr Faber.'

Georgie paused, considering. 'Tell me anyway,' she said. 'Please. I'll be careful.'

He hesitated, perhaps feeling that his role was strictly information, not to consider the consequences. 'The front is a care home, elderly and the handicapped – an expensive one,' he said. 'But it's rumoured there's plenty going on backstage in the laboratories.'

'Why would a care home need a laboratory?'

'Exactly,' Karl said, and nodded 'good evening' at another couple walking by. 'You should also know that it's owned by a subsidiary company – among its directors is a cousin of Himmler's.'

Alarm rippled through Georgie's body, this time with more force. While she found Joseph Goebbels repellent at their press conferences, the sight of Himmler on the plinth at Nuremberg had seemed distinctly more sinister. Joey openly grinned his triumph, but Himmler remained in the background, quietly viewing, silently absorbing the swell of anti–Semitism. Feeding off it.

'Yes – Himmler,' Karl said, reading her unease. 'That's why you need to be careful.'

'We will, I promise.'

'I need to get back,' Karl said as they reached a side entrance to the park, emerging on the brightly lit Bellevuestrasse. Georgie unlooped her arm from his, slipping a wad of Reichsmarks into his hand as she did so.

Karl smiled weakly. 'Keep safe,' he said, turned and walked smartly away. The fact that he said it caused fresh agitation. They had information, but what would they do with it? What had Paul uncovered, and what had it led him to?

She shared her liaison with Max at La Taverne, heads together at one end of the press table. He seemed only moderately surprised, readily able to believe the clinic was a caring front for unscrupulous activities.

'What do you think we should do?' she pitched. Georgie was no investigative reporter and knew her limitations. Right then, she felt totally out of her depth.

Max blew out his cheeks. 'I think if we really want to gauge what they're about, we need to get in there, at least check it out.'

'Margot?'

He shook his head. 'She's an actress, yes, but too emotional over this, and that makes her unreliable.' He left just enough pause for Georgie's mind to calculate, raised his eyebrows only slightly.

'*Me?* You want me to go in?'

'If you're willing. But only as a prospective client,' he said. 'Your German is good. Perhaps you could be a visiting relative from overseas, needing to arrange care before you return home.'

Georgie was initially horrified, though her alarm swiftly dissolved. If they were only making enquiries and she wasn't about to ferret in corners or filing cabinets, she'd be simply getting a feel for it.

'All right, I'll do it. I'll ring for an appointment tomorrow.' She only hoped her reporter's nose was up to the job.

'We'll be careful,' Max assured her. He didn't elaborate on what they might do if the Haas Institute smacked of any illicit activity. One step at a time.

25

A Flame Under the Pot

Georgie rang the Haas Institute from a call box the next morning and spoke to a crisp-sounding receptionist, who duly made an appointment, for three days' time.

She met Sam Blundon mid-morning at the bustling Café Bristol, another favourite of Berlin's coffee and cake culture. Sam seemed refreshed from a long weekend away at a small spa town not far from the city and happy to see Georgie, though his bright eyes darkened when he heard of the Amsel family and their plight. There was concern, but no surprise.

'I'm afraid, Georgie, that they're not alone. We've got hundreds turning up at the embassy every day, claiming distant family in England – some very tenuous links – anything to get out of Berlin. And it doesn't help that Jewish passports have been suspended.'

'Rubin says he does have an uncle in the north, maybe as far as Scotland,' Georgie urged. 'He feels they would take the children, and Elias.'

Sam sighed. Heavily. He didn't look hopeful.

'I'll take their names, certainly, make some enquiries,' he said, 'but I honestly can't promise anything. A handful of benevolent charities are making moves to help children out, but the places are very limited.'

'Trying is more than enough,' Georgie said. 'The Amsels seem very afraid that Elias's infirmity makes him a specific target. Have you got wind of anything like that? Where he or others might be taken?'

Sam shook his head, dipped those long lashes towards his slab of cake. In this instance, Georgie sensed he was being unusually tight-lipped, his diplomatic training uppermost, and it didn't seem fair on him to push it. They parted with plans to link up on a trip to the cinema in two days – an English film, albeit with subtitles. More than ever, they needed the respite and a reminder of home.

She headed back to the office and put in a call to the local police – there was no news on Paul or where he'd gone. He was undoubtedly low on their list of priorities, despite the embassy's influence. She spent the afternoon drafting a third request to the Reich office for access to the Hitler Youth 'Jungvolk' for a feature – the *Chronicle* had been pleased with her piece on the female BDM and wanted more. Herr Bauer had ignored her first two requests, but Georgie was determined; even more than the blatant grandiosity of Nuremberg and its slavish women, it was the sight of young, innocent-looking boys – those who might be in the front line of war – chanting their willingness to die for their Führer that both disgusted and intrigued her. It was all she could do to repel the constant flow of propaganda.

As she went to close up the office, the phone rang.

'Hey, stranger, I hoped to catch you.' Rod's voice was upbeat. 'How about a drink at the Adlon at six? On me.'

'Perfect. Is it a special occasion, or have you had a pay rise?'

'It's my birthday,' he said, 'and I'm feeling quite happy to have survived another year in Berlin.'

'Well, in that case, I'll definitely be there!'

Georgie had just enough time to run several blocks away, to a local patisserie, and buy a box of the best strudel in Berlin. She heard the birthday crowd from the lobby of the Adlon, their laughter easily drowning out the gentle trickle of water fountains.

'Hello, you, what'll you have?' Rod was already well on the way to being squiffy, an open bottle of champagne on the bar. It was ages since she felt like having or even being bubbly; Georgie loved her job, loved Berlin, but her portion of it in the past few days wasn't joyous or light. She needed sparkle.

'A glass of fizz, please.'

Max and Simone arrived soon after, and Frida minutes later. The entire pack was present, and the next hour saw them growing in numbers and volume. Georgie sat at the bar and sipped her champagne, feeling the effects on an empty stomach, listening to stories from the veterans. One day, she thought, it might be me waxing lyrical about my adventures and near scrapes. *Is that possible? Will I survive long enough in this world?*

Adrift with daydreams and the bubbles in her glass, Georgie's swell of good cheer was soon dampened. Bill, who'd dipped out of the bar briefly and into the *Chicago Tribune* office, housed in the hotel, emerged holding a wireless print-out aloft.

'Listen up, guys,' he called out, silencing the crowd. 'Something's afoot. A German diplomat's been shot in Paris.'

Rod looked almost affronted by the news, and the rest simply confused.

'But the Paris bureaus will deal with that, surely?' someone piped up.

'Maybe.' Bill puffed out his cheeks. 'Except that he was shot by a Jew.'

His words hovered above the goodwill of the bar, the sparkle swiftly dulled; a pin had been taken to Rod's birthday bubble.

The press were well known for taking a drink and holding it, but equally skilled at sobering up quickly when a good story presented itself. Bodies began to peel away, back to their own office telephones and wire sources.

'Sorry, Rod,' Georgie said, giving him a hug as he downed the last of his glass.

'All part of the job,' he said, still with his big, bearded smile, if slightly resigned. 'If you can't stand the heat, you get out of the Berlin kitchen.' And he slid heavily off his stool, heading for the door and clutching his box of strudel.

Simone had left quickly, to make contact with her French colleagues; Frida too, almost certainly to seek out one of her SS admirers and tap into the Reich response. Georgie knew she should go too, but was rooted to her bar stool by a sudden wave of exhaustion.

'Do you think this could this turn ugly?' she asked Max as he went to leave.

'Perhaps.' He shrugged wearily, his blue eyes also pale and glazed. "A touch of *Berlin fatigue*" she'd heard others call it.

They each knew the Nazi information machine would already be in full swing; at best, the shooting was fuel for its anti-Semitic zeal, and Georgie could predict the next explosive headline from *Der Stürmer*, alongside a grotesque caricature of the devil in Jewish clothing. At worst . . . well, she didn't like to guess. Increasingly, nothing was beyond the Nazis when it came to showing their hatred. She thought of Rubin and Sara, and their faces when the news became public, more distress piled onto their mountain of angst.

Back at the office, the champagne bubbles had all but fizzled to nothing. There was a fresh telegram waiting for her:

Diplomat injured, not dead. Gauge feeling in Berlin tomorrow.
HP.

Georgie sighed true relief. The press deadline for the foreign pages of the next morning's *Chronicle* had already passed, meaning she would have time to gather opinions, rather than launching into a breathless ringing of embassies and consulates. More than ever, she wanted to slink into the flat and under her eiderdown, try to sort through the elements of her work and life, and the conundrum that Berlin had become of late. She needed to carve out space in her own head to think.

26

The Pot Simmers

8th November 1938

Georgie slept surprisingly well and woke to the early reports from Paris that seemed to put a cap on any immediate drama. The diplomat had survived the night and although the Propaganda Ministry spouted its usual scorn, outwardly blaming the Jewish population for all the world's ills, it didn't seem especially alarming. Georgie gained comment from the British ambassador, who chose his words very carefully, and then spoke to a contact within the embassy, a secretary to one of the attachés.

'It's unusually quiet,' the woman said, 'almost eerily so. Everyone came in this morning prepared to weather a political storm, but it hasn't happened.'

The press crowd gathered at the Adlon at lunchtime and reported the same. The shooter had given himself up without a fight, and it appeared then to be a case of a lone Jewish man making a stand about the way his family had been driven out of their homes, his personal fury at being treated as subhuman.

'I don't trust this reaction,' Bill said, stroking at his moustache in the way he did when something bothered him. 'The Nazis are being far too reasonable about this. I almost prefer when they are truly vile. At least we know where we are.' He spoke with a good-humoured candour, though kept his voice low, mindful of Gestapo ears.

Georgie and Max peeled away from the group, intent on planning the appointment at the Haas Institute in two days' time. So far, she'd managed to push the event to the back of her mind – the reality of walking through the doors and telling outright lies – but it was time to construct a plausible story. Mindful her accent would likely give her away as not German-born, she would pose as a visiting niece, concerned about her ageing aunt, who had always been a little 'different'. Though cared for by a wealthy family, they were all elderly themselves and the aunt needed permanent care.

'You are Hanna Seidel,' Max coached her, his face serious and close. 'You live in London and work in publishing, you are twenty-six and unmarried, but unable to have your aunt live with you because of your work.'

Georgie scanned his features as he reeled off her pseudo life. 'Have you done this before?' she said.

His brow flattened, undeterred. 'Consequence of a public-school life,' he muttered. 'You get good at taking your mind elsewhere, into other people's lives.'

Georgie felt a tweak inside her – recognised it as a pull on a heartstring. Her happy, loving childhood versus his lonesome upbringing.

'So, we all set for that?' Max said, pulling up his shoulders. 'I'll be at a café nearby. If you don't come back within forty-five minutes, I'll come in and enquire after you, pretend I'm a friend.'

Georgie's eyes widened. Was it a possibility that she might not emerge?'

'Hey, it's not likely,' he countered quickly. 'They have no reason whatsoever to suspect anything, as long as you don't probe too deeply.'

Max was right – common sense was the key. Despite his crisp exterior, she was beginning to trust him. She just needed not to overplay it at the institute. Nevertheless, it was a world away from reporting on long hems and which lace to wear.

The rest of the day dragged, and Georgie found herself not wanting to be idle or alone. There was little work as the Paris-based reporters were claiming every column inch on the foreign pages. Instead, she dropped by the theatre that Margot was rehearsing in, and they spent several hours touring bars and cafés in some of Berlin's less salubrious areas, showing a picture of Paul and asking if he'd been seen. While Margot talked, Georgie observed the faces around, the reactions, trying to sense if there was truth, lies or fear in the responses. But she could detect nothing. Paul had seemingly disappeared into the ether.

27

Boiling Point

Winter was worming its way into Berlin and the day started with a chill. The single event in the office diary was covered and Georgie dispatched it quickly, along with a second article. Opinion had switched in the previous twenty-four hours to warn of a backlash brewing against Germany's Jews, whether the diplomat survived or not, her words reflecting the palpable tension across a city and country holding its breath. There was little else to do but wait, and it put her in mind of her grandmother's favourite saying: 'A watched pot never boils'. It meant her brief planned respite with Sam Blundon was both timely and welcome.

She treated herself to a late lunch over a book, settled in the window of a café in the Southern Schöneberg district, watching the world go by until the film with Sam in a nearby cinema.

'Mind if I join you?'

Georgie looked up from her book to see Max towering over her, bearing what had lately become his familiar smile.

'Are you checking up on me already?'

'No, just passing and I saw you in the window. May I?' He sat opposite and picked up a menu. 'I did think twice about coming in – you were so engrossed in your book. But I am quite hungry.'

'Well, I'm so glad to be a convenient lunch date.'

Max forced a laugh at his own audacity. 'What are you up to this afternoon?' he said on ordering a spread of soup, bread and cheese.

'I'm meeting Sam later – from the embassy – and we're off to see *The Lady Vanishes*. It's on at the Metropol. Subtitled, but in English.'

'Oh, I've heard it's good – I love a Hitchcock.' He said nothing more, but his face bore a shadow of envy.

'Join us,' Georgie said. 'More the merrier.'

His eyes flicked upwards, eager. 'Really? I'm not being a gooseberry?'

She pursed her lips. 'No, Max, you will not be a gooseberry. Come on, let's go lose ourselves for an hour or so. Lord knows even Hitchcock might be a bit of light relief.'

They emerged from the gloom of the auditorium into the dim light of a winter evening, blinking to adjust to a varying shade of darkness. All three sensed a shift the minute they stood on the cinema steps.

At first it sounded like Christmas, a cascade of jewels tinkling as they bounced off a cold, cut surface. It was chilled on the street, though the atmosphere felt anything but festive. Expectant, Georgie watched the others hold their breath too, in tasting was what was about them. No, this was not Christmas.

Preparations for the holiday season meant there had been a suspended glow above the city centre for a week or so, with its collective lights and the lifted mood of Berliners. True enough, there was an orange hue sitting across the rooftops to their left, but its intense colour was clouded by smoke from multiple fires in view. Little puffs of white mingled with a vast tornado of black pushing its way towards what stars were still visible.

Sam turned to Georgie, perplexed. 'Has it started? Is this the war?'

To any European, it was a realistic assumption, though his eyes held alarm. Fear, even. Georgie was dumbstruck, every human sense trying to place things in order. They all knew the events of previous days had created a pressure cooker of the city. But this couldn't be the fallout, surely? The lid on the pot propelled clean off?

Max scanned back and forward, peering across the vast Nollendorfplatz, his nostrils flaring. 'I'm not sure. It's possibly a raid. But that's very sudden. There was no warning.' They'd heard nothing – no bombs pushing through the cushion of the cinema walls.

'Isn't that the point of war, though?' Sam pointed out. 'To catch people unawares?'

Georgie couldn't be sure, having never lived through a skirmish or a battle, but it wasn't how she imagined it. And yet there was an undercurrent of chaos beyond their sights.

They moved as a threesome, joining onto the larger Motzstrasse. It was then they saw it, through a sinking fug of grey mist. A draper's store was opposite, its large picture windows smashed, great shards left pointing like upturned icicles, glinting in the new, orange light. In the solitary pane left intact, a huge word in red paint – *JUDE* – surrounded by an indiscriminate daubing, spattered in anger.

As their eyes adjusted again to the fog, they saw a man in the shop doorway, on his knees, shoulders shaking – either with sorrow or coughing the dense air. A woman came at him from behind and, with great effort, hauled him up and back through the door that was just hanging on its hinges, hacked at and splintered in sheer rage. War witness or no, Georgie felt certain this was no bomb attack. This insult had been born of a hatred closer to home.

To her right and hovering at the corner, she saw two Stormtroopers in their black and brown uniforms. Unmistakable and unabashed, stock still and arms folded, looking on. She couldn't see the satisfaction on their faces, but she knew it was there. The couple having disappeared, the troopers walked calmly away.

Max, Georgie and Sam moved down the wide street and towards the billowing black sky – to where there were people, and possibly the seat of the chaos. As they neared the end of street, it was clear where the Christmas jangle had been coming from; a sickening crunch underfoot as they stepped on a shallow but vast sea of broken glass lining the pavements, shards glinting in the firelight as open sores of shopfronts pushed out flames and orange sparks.

Georgie gasped as they came upon a group of distressed onlookers, forced to watch their livelihoods burn, with no sign of the fire services or anyone else to help. She looked upwards and glimpsed shadowy heads peering from apartment windows, looking but not daring to venture out into a world suddenly turned dark and sinister; one face recoiled swiftly, perhaps sensing an eye on their cowardice, a curtain coming down on the shame.

Quickly, it became apparent the first incident they'd witnessed was not isolated. Further up the street, a fresh group of vandals in brown were at work, their fervour for destruction unabated as they aimed heavy coshes at the windowpanes, a paint pot set by for the final insult. Georgie tensed, started as if towards the small group. She felt Max's arm pull sharply on hers. 'No!

Stay back.' His eyes were bright beads in the fog. 'You can't stop this. We can do more elsewhere.'

Sam caught up and faced them, his boyish face stricken. 'I have to get back to the embassy,' he said. 'They'll need me there.' Then, seeing their troubled expressions: 'We all have our jobs to do. Don't worry, I'll go via the backstreets, be there in no time.'

'Just be careful,' Georgie said. 'I'll call you there as soon as I can.'

Sam nodded and gripped her arm tightly. 'You too. I know you need to do your work, but no story is worth risking everything.'

'Promise,' she pledged, and watched him turn tail and back up into the semi-darkness.

Max had been staring up at the sky's firestorm, perhaps trying to work out its source – he wanted to be there, Georgie knew, in the thick of it. Part of her did too.

'Let's just head towards it,' he said, glancing for her assent. 'And I think it's best if we stick together, don't you?'

'Yes, definitely.'

They half ran, half walked, dodging the piles of debris and the spitting embers from shopfront fires, emerging onto the Fasanenstrasse. The scene ahead robbed them of breath and belief; the monolithic synagogue opposite belched out huge flames from its domed roof, lapping at a night sky fogged with filthy, flying debris. It spiralled towards the fullest moon the city had seen in a long time, nature's searchlight on the montage below.

Almost mesmerised, the two hurried towards the crowds gathered before the synagogue's entrance. A man in robes – a rabbi – was running in and out of the imposing door to the burning building, bringing out statues, Torah scrolls and prayer books, anything he could carry. The heat from the flames burned their cheeks, and as they got closer, Georgie noted the rabbi's face was wet, not with sweat but strewn with tears. He sobbed as he worked. And all around him, Stormtroopers looked on, motionless, as a small army of Jews tried desperately to save as much of their sacred home as they could.

She watched Max blink repeatedly at the scene – in horror, she imagined, but almost as a shutter to his mind, committing to memory the sight that he would write up later; neither of them insensitive enough to pull out the notebooks they always carried. Besides, it was pointless taking names and details. This was an attack on a city, a people – there was no single victim – and this image would stay with them longer than any written detail.

Georgie's gaze switched to a cluster of firemen standing by, slightly apart from the Stormtroopers, yet equally inactive. Why weren't they tackling the blaze, preventing as much damage as they could? She refused to hold back then, breaking free from Max and running towards the one in charge, a soot-stained fireman already being hounded by one of his own crew.

'We need to go in, chief,' she heard the junior man shout above the roar of the fire. 'There could be people trapped inside. Why can't we go in?' His tone was just short of pleading.

'Orders, Billen, orders,' the chief snapped, his tone more of despair than irritation. His mouth set in a resigned frown. 'I've been told nobody goes in without their say-so.' He gestured towards the clutch of troopers standing alongside, arms folded, admiring their handiwork. 'I'm sorry, son, but my hands are tied.'

Max arrived at her side then, breathless amid the heat and horror.

'We can't just stand by and watch,' Georgie said. 'We have to see if we can help.'

He gave her that look she half recognised from the

Sudetenland, in front of that shaved, bloodied woman: *We're observers, we report, we don't get involved*. But this time she wouldn't accept it, answered his look with defiance. 'People could be injured, Max. Dying,' she pressed. A curt nod meant he didn't need much convincing.

He led the way towards the synagogue door, using his tall physique to weave through the crowd and guiding Georgie by the hand as the rabbi emerged again onto the pavement, blackened with smoke.

'There's someone inside,' the old man shouted above the din. 'I can hear a voice. Please help, someone please help.'

This time the fire captain leapt forward, facing up to the Stormtroopers – his gestures suggested pleading – with the crowd's intent scrutiny on the small group. After what felt like an age, the trooper nodded slowly, and the fireman instantly turned and beckoned several of his crew into the building, its bottom half billowing thick black smoke while the huge rafters above were spitting flames upwards into the air. Desperate pleas were only just audible through the tumult of destruction.

Georgie recognised several photographers from the pool they all used, buzzing like bees and snapping the devastation, the glare of their flashbulbs swallowed by dense clouds. For a second, she was sickened by their activity as voyeurs, but soon realised it's what they all were in some sense, she and Max included. And it was vital that someone should record this abuse against humanity – pictures, in this case, might be more valuable than words. So far, reports alone had not been enough to provoke any reaction from outside Germany to what Hitler was creating. Maybe the world needed to see it in stark black and white, staring at this debacle over their breakfast?

A sudden movement from the doorway caught everyone's eye. The crew staggered out carrying a limp, almost blackened woman, two firemen holding her sagging body by her arms and stockinged feet. Somehow, she had lost both of her shoes in the firestorm and amid the chaos, Georgie couldn't help but focus on the small hole in the sole of one stocking; if she ever found out, the poor woman would be mortified, Georgie thought, and then checked herself for such whimsy in amongst the turmoil. Only she knew such a detail to be true.

The crew set the woman down on the pavement and Georgie rushed forward, Max just behind. She glanced briefly at the Stormtroopers to check their reaction – they looked on blankly, perhaps knowing they couldn't stop it, not without a violent public backlash. Even so, the firefighters seemed reluctant to help further, perhaps fearful of overstepping their duties under the eye of the Reich. Georgie knew only the basics of first aid – what the hell should she do?

Instantly, Max pushed through, checking the woman's pulse, and lowering his head to her mouth, pinching her singed cheeks between one hand and blowing into her mouth; from behind, Georgie saw his own ribs draw in air to feed another breath. After two or three of his bellows breaths, the woman's body convulsed, Max pulled away and she coughed violently – her breath spewing like a sawdust of broiling charred wood, the odour of garden bonfires. The woman opened her eyes, wide with alarm, and kick-started her wheezing lungs, desperately gulping in the relatively cleaner air. Before anyone could speak, or take stock, they heard another commotion, shouts of 'ambulance', and within an instant, two men had pushed their way through the crowds, produced a stretcher and she was gone.

The pair stood in the midst of the continuing chaos, wondering what else to do, feel or say. Max wiped soot from his mouth and Georgie caught the eye of the fire chief, who winked in her direction, swiftly followed by a scowl and a nod towards the Stormtroopers, who were squinting at them through the smoke. The fireman's message seemed clear: 'Away you go, before they mark you out even more.' He reiterated with a second, sharp gesture of his head.

'We have to go,' Georgie said, tugging on Max's arm.

'But . . . there are still . . .'

'*Now.*' And there was everything in the tone of her voice.

They threaded wordlessly around the debris and slipped into an empty alleyway, eerily quiet. Max flattened himself against the wall, head against the cool of the brickwork. He breathed deeply and coughed out the remainder of the woman's singed lungs.

'What on earth was that?' Georgie panted. Trying to make sense of it caused her head to throb.

Max's eyes were bright and wide with shock, shining out from the black smudges. 'I'm not sure,' he wheezed, 'but it was one hell of a turning point. They've never been so blatant about the violence. There was no shame, no holding back.'

For a minute they were silent, absorbing the impact of Stormtroopers – Nazi-backed militia – openly vandalising, destroying and *enjoying* the power of their violence, without fear of punishment. With permission, clearly. The Wehrmacht and the SS were conspicuously absent. A horrible thought had dawned on Georgie over recent months, building progressively. Now, she felt certain of it: Hitler was unafraid. Of any one person, any race, army or country. Hadn't he already stated, in front of the entire German parliament, that his country did not fear war? Here was the proof. When the realisation hit, an arrow of ice shot through her body and she was frightened to the core. Having just witnessed the debacle of a burning Berlin, the rest of Europe had to feel the same. Surely? The world needed to know about every spitting ember and splinter of hatred Hitler had worked to contrive. And it was their job to do it.

They persuaded a taxi driver to take them through the park

as far the Brandenburg Gate, threading the streets on foot towards the Jewish quarter, noting scene upon scene of devastation.

Picking their way among the grit of glass and piles of belongings cast onto the pavements, they spotted Rod and Bill collected around a large hardware store, now a huge blaze: sad, resigned faces lit by the fire's glow. Despite the fierce crackle of wood, livelihoods and history going up in smoke, it was strangely quiet, stunned families simply looking on. They might have been at a bonfire party on Guy Fawkes Night, Georgie thought, except for the expressions of loss staring into the flames.

There was no holding off Rod's hug when he saw them both; big arms engulfing her and, for a second or so, she felt safe. 'Thank God you're okay. I was worried,' he whispered in her ear.

'How long has this been going on?' she said. 'We were in the cinema.'

'Several hours,' he said. 'We got word in the office – the diplomat in Paris died of his injuries. This is the result.'

'But where are the police and the army – to restore order?'

Rod shrugged his wide shoulders. 'You tell me. Look around – there are no fingerprints of the Nazi hierarchy on this, but it stinks of their work.' His disgust was apparent, tears brimming. 'It's the worst I've seen. What is this world coming to?'

Max pulled at Georgie's arm then, bent to shout in her ear as part of the building opposite succumbed to the flames and crashed to the ground. 'I'm heading back to the office – I need to get something over to London. Shall we go together?'

'I want to go to Rubin's first,' she replied. 'Make sure they're in one piece.'

Max shook his head. 'Going on your own is insane,' he shouted again. 'Look, come back to the office with me – you

185

can file your story via the telex, and then we'll both go to Rubin's.'

Keen though Georgie was to reach the Amsels, she could see Max was talking sense. They weaved around the backstreets, seeing less, but hearing brief snatches of triumphant chanting from groups of Stormtroopers rise and fall, drunk on power.

To his credit, Cliff Sutton had hauled himself into the *Telegraph*'s office – he looked pale and bloated, but it was clear that his profession came before Cliff's love of the bottle on a night like this. Behind the desk, he and Max quickly organised themselves to writing different angles of the story, merging press releases and comments from the chancellery now ticking through on the wire.

Already, the Reich was bent on distancing itself from the Stormtroopers and their actions: the violent reaction was not a directive from the Führer, it insisted – simply a response to the shooting that the German Government could not contain. The people had spoken with their actions. How could they restrain such a swell of opinion? At best, it was a pathetic rebuttal that sounded suspiciously like school playground wars: 'It wasn't me, Miss. *He* started it.' And the desecration wasn't limited to Berlin either. Across Germany, synagogues and shops had been attacked and burned, Jews assaulted for nothing more than their birthright – all were held responsible for the shooting of one man, it seemed.

Georgie rang her London office and warned they would be receiving her copy via telex, then got to work. Her own rage spewed onto the page – once or twice Cliff looked sideways at her, and then at Max, whose own eyes were focused entirely on his work – and she found herself slicing words to pluck out her personal animosity towards the Reich. She missed Paul – not the man himself, since she barely knew him, but as a colleague, his knowledge, to bounce around ideas and work side by side. She envied Max in that moment.

By the time they fed through each piece, it was three a.m. Henry's night editor sent through confirmation he'd received her piece and the *Telegraph* also signalled they had enough to process. Georgie's eyes were sore from the smoke and boring into the white of the page. But she wasn't tired, couldn't have slept, and Max was equally wired.

Cliff had broken open a bottle of brandy as they finished and poured out three generous measures – they all needed it then. But Georgie was anxious to get on, since Rubin and Sara still played on her mind.

Outside on the street, it was evident the night's events were calming. The cacophony had diminished to a hum, a ginger glow hovering above the city. They learned later that fire crews had finally been allowed into action, where buildings housing German citizens were under threat. A lone taxi rolled slowly over the glass-glittered streets and Max thrust a wad of Reichsmarks at the driver in persuading him to take the fare, arriving at Rubin's apartment just before four in the morning. They might have been in bed, asleep and largely unaffected by the night's events, but somehow Georgie doubted it. The whole city had been kept awake.

Lights blazed in almost all the flats, but they could see no signs of fire or wanton destruction and Georgie breathed a sigh of relief. It was short-lived, however: when they began climbing the stairs to Rubin's own apartment, open and splintered doors sparked fresh alarm. On reaching the third floor, Sara's sobs could be heard through the hallway.

'Rubin? Sara? Are you all right?' Georgie stepped over a door panel on the floor, broken like matchwood.

Rubin emerged into the hallway, his face a ghostly white, wringing his hands.

'Rubin, what's happened? Is it the children?'

He shook his head. 'No, thank God.' It was plainly not Sara – Georgie could detect her cries from inside.

'It's Elias,' he said at last, the words choking in his throat. 'They came and took Elias. I don't where.'

It was Max who moved in then, to shoulder Rubin's distress, man to man, while Georgie soaked up the tears from his wife. And they sat, and wondered – for the second time that night – what the world had come to.

28

Sweeping Up

The SS had been busy that night, and again the next morning. But being the SS, they had the sense to work methodically and efficiently in their own crackdown against undesirables, more subtle than the marauding street offensive of the Stormtroopers. As the light rose on the Berlin of 10th November 1938, the extent of Nazi hatred against Jews became clear: skeletons of businesses and lives left smoking, and the sound everywhere of glass shards being herded by brooms, like shale on a beach.

Georgie headed back towards Frida's flat around six, numbed by exhaustion and the night's tragedies. She threaded her way around families trying to piece together their lives, foraging their own homes for anything of sentimental or cash value they could. What struck her was the distinct lack of outward distress or tears; each person moved with purpose, but not bent or broken. They had a job to do, in rebuilding, and they got on with it. Something told her they had either prepared, or they'd done this before.

She and Max had sat with the Amsels until dawn broke, Sara trying to calm the children's distress while hiding her own.

'We heard the commotion outside, saw the fires,' Rubin told them, his voice flat. 'I went out to see if I could help. The whole building was awake, and there were no troops around, so I thought the family was safe.' His guilt at temporarily abandoning his family was acute. 'Sara said they came and worked quickly through the building, bashing in all the doors, demanding to see everyone. But it was clear they had targets to find – they hauled Elias out of his bed without any questions, and immediately he was gone.'

'Then you couldn't have prevented it, even by being here,' Georgie said, trying to soften his remorse. 'It would have happened anyway.'

'Yes, but Sara . . . she shouldn't have had to . . . I should have been here.' His eyes were grey and dead – the normally bright, positive Rubin, who sought to see the good side of everything, was a man defeated.

'We'll find him,' Georgie found herself promising. Then to herself: *How?* How on earth would she find a needle in a Nazi haystack?

Rubin had smiled then, weakly, but with a glimmer of hope. She couldn't let him down.

Max had left the Amsel apartment just before her to grab some sleep. Despite Cliff's appearance, the most he could hope for was that the veteran reporter would hold the fort in the office while he covered the city, mostly on foot. Trams were running, but the roads were hit and miss, the sea of glass slowing the traffic.

In the watery light of a new day, Georgie rounded the main thoroughfare into Friedrichstrasse and came upon a new sight. Now, it was not only the remnants of windowpanes being swept away; a line, twenty or so long and two deep, of men – Jews – were being led by Wehrmacht soldiers, a makeshift

Star of David hanging over one man's neck. Those bystanders with brooms stopped and looked, almost paying their respects as the men passed by, their heads bowed. Their destination was almost certainly to jail, and then to Lord knows where. But for what crime?

This sad procession confirmed to Georgie that the night had not been simply an attack but a well-planned cull. Already, she could predict the Reich's justification; these men would be marked out as agitators, sparking the riots. Jews would be the root cause, undoubtedly. The thought, coupled with a sudden, vacuous hunger, made her sick to her stomach. She was run through with fatigue, desperate to sink into her own bed, and yet her body sparked with agitation. She caught a tram that took her close to the Adlon, in the hope of finding friends equally in need of solace.

The sight of Rod at a table near the bar almost brought her to tears, and he drew her in with warmth as he always did. Bill read her mind and ordered a pot of English tea with a decent breakfast. 'You look like you need it,' he said.

'Okay, kiddo?' Rod spread a hand on her shoulder. Georgie nodded, bit down on her lip, eyes brimming, and just about holding back on what might have been a cascade.

They sat over the table, quietly digesting the night. The full scope of the damage – both human and material – wouldn't be known for several days, and even then they couldn't rely on estimations from the Reich. It was tragic and it was evil, a fact that didn't need stating, but each of them hoped the exposure on their respective pages would be the turning point for the world to wake up to Adolf Hitler's true potential.

'I would just love to be a fly on the wall in Herr Bauer's office right now,' Rod said, with his talent for lightening the moment. 'He must be wetting himself with Adolf worship. And I can't wait until he sees my paper's headline.'

The imagined picture brought a smile to all three faces, a vision of Bauer hot-footing with his unctuous fawning, his tiny moustache bristling.

'Does that mean you're going home to pack a suitcase, my friend?' Bill pitched, with a more serious edge. 'Bauer would give his back teeth to have you thrown out of the country. Though I'd prefer it if you didn't go quite yet. I feel we have a great deal more drinking to do.'

'I'm not planning on going any time soon,' Rod said. 'I've got a bit more quiet agitation in me yet.'

Energised briefly by tea and eggs, Georgie revealed the loss in Rubin's family, and they all recognised the personal cost then, of the unknown, desolate faces witnessed through the night, but also of people they knew, liked and had shared a brief past with. Their sorrow sat heavily across the table.

'I feel like I want to write about the Amsels, put the world's focus on them,' Georgie said at last, though she knew it was naive to think it would do them any favours.

'I'm afraid they would disappear into a puff of smoke – all of them,' Rod said. 'And very quickly.'

'Then I'm just going to have to find out where Elias is myself,' Georgie said, flooded with a sudden defiance. Inside she was still doubting herself: *How? And where do I even start?*

Finally, a wave of fatigue hit them all, and Rod – being her guardian angel and a wise old owl in one – packed her off in a taxi towards home. 'Grab a few hours' sleep, and we'll see you at the press briefing at four,' he said through the window. 'First to spot Bauer's nervous twitch gets a double scotch.'

He could always make her smile, yet the muscles of Georgie's mouth felt odd in doing so. More than ever, she'd felt herself come of age in just one night; there was no pretence at being a fledging reporter now. This was serious. And she had little choice but to rise to the challenge.

The apartment was deathly quiet as she let herself in – a quick peek in both bedrooms told Georgie that Simone and Frida were sleeping off whatever night they'd experienced. She left a message for Sam at the British Embassy – he was snowed under, his secretary said, inundated with requests for visas, lines of people queueing outside the building since dawn in a last bid to flee Berlin and Germany. But Sam was safe, at least.

Georgie crawled under the sheets and was asleep in seconds, a low, tinkling soundtrack to her dreams, pushing and ebbing as she woke and sank under several times. By three p.m., the flat was alive again; both Frida and Simone focused less on news and more on in-depth stories, and so their work was largely still to do in reporting on the aftermath. Frida would probably feed through to several worldwide magazines, might even have had a shot at a *Time* magazine piece. Georgie was still unsure where Simone published, yet she always seemed to be in work and have money to spend. The French popular press couldn't help but be alerted now, being Germany's immediate neighbour.

They were all present by four p.m., when Joseph Goebbels appeared on the lectern at the Ministry of Propaganda. Given his well-known hostility towards the foreign press, the atmosphere was electric before he'd uttered a word, pencils twitching alongside the irritated drumming of Joey's fingers on the wood.

It was as expected: the shooting of Herr vom Rath in Paris had been the catalyst, but the Stormtroopers were only reacting to public opinion. How could they be blamed for defending their country against the fearsome aggression of the Jews? The Reich had not ordered it but was powerless to stop the initial acts of defence. It had moved, however, to halt further damage and lives lost. Jews were the aggressors, the Reich the saviour of its people. Again.

Joey spouted it all with familiar conviction, but he couldn't have failed to note the murmurings of disbelief among his audience. To every reporter listening to his fairy-tale rhetoric, it was pure farce. Yet Goebbels remained unashamed, steadfast in his own propaganda.

Rod held up his hand during a brief pause in the diatribe. 'Can you tell us where the arrested men have been taken and what they will be charged with?' He pitched it so reasonably, and without vehemence, that Joey could not easily ignore him. Georgie glanced at Herr Bauer standing to the side and saw his eye twitch uncontrollably. Goebbels squinted and peered into the assembly, targeting his wrath. His face was thunder. The men were being held, he hissed, for their own protection, and would be questioned accordingly, in a variety of settings.

For their own protection. Georgie had heard the same phrase before – Sara had repeated as much in her worries over Elias. Why protection? And from what?

The mood at La Taverne later that evening was unusually subdued; no one had caught up fully on sleep, and each was anticipating the Reich reaction to their own publication – press timings meant the headlines wouldn't hit until the next morning. Instead they agreed to convene at the Adlon the next day as the first foreign editions came off the train.

29

The World Wakes Up?

11th November 1938

'Way to go, Rod.' Bill slapped his friend on the back and held the *New York Times* aloft, its front-page headline pulling no punches. Despite some of the US papers previously holding a conservative stance on Hitler – that perhaps he wasn't such a bad fellow at heart – almost all had reacted seriously to the night's atrocities; 'smashed', 'wrecked', 'pillaged' and 'plundered' peppered the front pages from both sides of the Atlantic.

Georgie's own *News Chronicle* headlined with: Pogrom Rages Through Germany: Hitler Turns Down Mercy Call, and she felt relieved Henry hadn't toned down her description of 'Nazi hooligans'. There was a general feeling that reporters and photographers had laid out what Germany was currently about, warts and all, in its coverage of the newly christened *Kristallnacht* – the night of broken glass. Now, it was up to the public and the politicians to react, to tell Herr Hitler this was not acceptable.

Yet the mood amongst them was anything but celebratory – more of a wake for a life gone by. Even if the world hadn't experienced their eyes smarting at the acrid burning or caught the distress in their nostrils, every press member had; Georgie felt a deep sense that something had changed. The honeymoon in Berlin was over.

It was only the next morning, after a good, full night's sleep, that she remembered missing her appointment at the Haas Institute. She rang the number from a phone booth, took a deep breath and affected a flighty voice, twittering about all the 'awful events making it slip her mind' and could she rearrange? They were suddenly very busy, the receptionist said, but they could fit her in the next week. With the continuing aftermath, Georgie was relieved to have the breathing space.

Rubin appeared for work, looking already thinner, and she signed his work sheet and sent him away to be with Sara. There was no news of Elias, he said, and little gossip of where the men had been taken. Their best hope being that the Gestapo headquarters at Prinz-Albrecht-Strasse simply couldn't accommodate such large numbers.

The entire press pack spent the next few days sweeping up the debris in print; there were embassy and ministry briefings, although Georgie used any spare time knocking tentatively on the hastily mended doors of Jewish shops and businesses, looking for a dim light inside and talking to those now contemplating leaving their life and country behind. There were no names and most of what she wrote down would never be printed, she knew, but it was important for her to hear it, as if it was slowly knitting her fabric as a reporter.

She was constantly amazed at the resilience of each family – they were wary, frightened even, of a future in Germany, and yet saddened to leave a country in which they retained some hope, while everything around them urged leaving for any kind of safety.

Despite the initial condemnation from abroad, it took four days for foreign politicians to make a real stand. President

Roosevelt recalled his US ambassador from Berlin, and the American reporters disappeared for days in their coverage. Max, too, was run off his feet. Georgie felt slightly at a loss, guilty in doing so little for the Amsels except listening to Sara's fretting and sharing endless pots of tea. It was inevitable a postcard needed to be dispatched.

Postcard from a broken Berlin,
15th November 1938

Dear England, in its green and pleasant land,

It is cold here in Germany's capital and with more than just the weather to blame; after the intense heat and fires of Kristallnacht, a chill of mistrust has descended upon Berlin - German to Jew, Jew to German. What warmth there is I found in the house of one Jewish family, formerly owners of a thriving but now ruined tailor's shop. They struggled even to boil a kettle but still brewed me tea, had little food but offered hospitality. Their four-year-old child eagerly showed me her beloved doll, pulled from the wreckage of their home in the tense hours after that endless 'crystal night'. As I admired the battered toy, I pulled a sliver of hidden glass from its stiff and singed hair, while a piece of her burnt dress disintegrated under my fingers. And yet the girl's face lit up as I returned her doll, something so precious in her life, and very possibly the only possession she will carry when her family is forced to leave this city, and the rest of their lives behind.

A muted greeting from your correspondent, in Herr Hitler's great city of the future

197

Georgie pictured the effect on Herr Bauer's twitch if he were to read it – if the *Chronicle* ever saw fit to publish it. She stopped short of imagining Goebbels's death stare if he laid eyes on the print – or her. But now, more than ever, it needed saying. She had to come out from her awning of safety and make a stand in her reporting, like Rod, Bill and the others. Even Paul, if she and Max were right about their suspicions. She just hoped she would last as long as the stalwarts.

Leaving herself no time to regret filing the postcard piece, Georgie took herself to a public call box in the nearest station and rang through the copy to London – it wasn't something for Gestapo ears. If they were to scoop her up, it wouldn't be yet.

She stopped for a coffee on the way back at Kranzler's, but there was no sign of Karl, and she hoped nothing had befallen him in the turbulence of previous days. The phone was ringing as she climbed the office stairs and she was breathless as she lunged for the receiver.

'Fraulein Young?' The voice was brusque and impatient.

'Yes?'

'You were enquiring after a missing person, your colleague Paul Adamson?'

'Yes, I was. Have you found him?' At last, there might be something to salvage from a week of chaos.

'We might have.'

'Oh, thank goodness,' Georgie sighed, her mind flipping immediately to Margot, less to his wife, whom she had never met.

The voice paused. She could hear muttering, someone's hand across the mouthpiece. He came back, voice a little less sharp. 'It's not such good news, I'm afraid. We recovered a body from the canal, and we think it might be Herr Adamson.'

30

The Crystal Ball

15th November 1938

Rod came with her to the morgue, as the one who had known Paul the longest. The police officer on the phone had hinted that identifying the body might not be straightforward.

'It looks as if he's been in there for a good few days,' he said apologetically.

Georgie had been to such places before – the juniors were sent regularly from the *Chronicle* offices to pick up the day's list of possible suicides and murders from the London morgues, what Henry gaily called 'fish fodder' for the inside pages. And strangely, it had never fazed her. But in Berlin, the smell was different, disinfectant mingling with a thin film of smoke residue. It seemed busy, people hurrying to and fro, men in white clothing pushing gurneys with sheets over bodies. Rod gave her a hard stare, and she remembered then the morgue's numbers were swelled by Kristallnacht; the early figures suggested it could be as many as a hundred dead across Germany.

In the end, there was no doubt. It was Paul. They pulled back the sheet only as far as his face, bloated and out of shape, his skin a waxen jade green. It seemed to be clear of any obvious markings or cuts to his flesh, no evidence of a beating that they could see. Despite the distension, it was certainly Paul's hair and his slightly sagging jowls, albeit puffy from the canal water. Rod nodded in unison. Georgie's heart cranked then for Paul's wife back home and his new baby, who would now never know his father. For Margot, too – she had loved him, searched for him, despite the dubious morality of their affair.

The police officer was waiting outside when they emerged.

'Have you any idea how it happened?' Georgie asked, all innocence. 'Did he simply fall in the canal and drown?' She harboured strong suspicions that he hadn't, but watched for the Kripo man's initial reaction.

He shook his head, seemed genuine. 'We're waiting for the post-mortem, but I'm not hopeful it will show anything other than an accident or death by his own hand. I understand he had family problems.'

Georgie nodded. The Kripo were worlds away from the Gestapo and may have been equally in the dark.

'Sad,' the officer went on, 'but there's a lot of it about nowadays.'

'A lot of what?'

'Suicide,' he said, almost matter-of-factly. 'We live in very strange times.' He glanced back and forth down the corridor, conscious that what he'd uttered might count as dissent. 'We'll be in touch about releasing the body, Fraulein Young.'

Georgie turned down Rod's offer of a stiff drink in favour of coffee, and they both indulged in strudel, the copious sugar equal to brandy in their book.

'Spit it out,' Rod said, after his last mouthful.

'Pardon?'

'What are you not telling me?'

Lord, will I be gifted with the same crystal ball if I'm here as many years as Rod?

'You don't seem very surprised, that's all,' he went on. 'That it was Paul.'

There was no point lying to Rod, Georgie thought, and she didn't really want to. Had it not been for the distraction of Kristallnacht, she would have told him long before.

'Max and I found something of Paul's – well, we were pointed towards it. Some papers, perhaps a story that he was working on. Something the Nazis might not have liked.' She felt relieved in spilling it, and then a slight sense of betrayal towards Max, although she didn't know why – it wasn't as if he wanted to claim the story.

Rod flicked his gaze left and right, leaned forward and lowered his naturally deep voice. 'Was it about a clinic?'

'How do you know?' Georgie's eyes were beyond her control.

'Paul and I were chatting one night at La Taverne – just the two of us. He'd had a bit too much to drink, got to telling me about his home life, and his mistress. All of a sudden he was in full-on confessional.'

The door to the café opened and a group of SS officers walked in, laughing loudly.

'Let's take this conversation elsewhere,' Rod said.

It was chilly but they blended in well with others walking arm in arm in the Tiergarten and Georgie wrapped her inadequate coat tightly across her body. Rod was still at a virtual whisper on the concrete paths, steering clear of hedges and bushes where eager ears might loiter.

'So?' Rod began.

Georgie told him the little they knew so far.

'And you're thinking of going there?' There was a tinge of the father in his voice. 'I would advise against it.'

Georgie's head snapped around. 'Why? What did Paul tell you?'

'He had a suspicion that the clinic might have something to do with a new programme – it was vague and so was he – but something to do with euthanasia. The Nazis conveniently getting rid of those who don't contribute to the Reich.'

'And did you believe it might be feasible?' She'd gone over the handwritten notes Paul had left with a dictionary – littered with words such as 'productivity' and 'wastage' though never the word 'death'. Alarmingly, it all fitted.

Rod's face was heavy with concern. 'Let's say I'm never shocked at the imagination or the reach of these people, but it is the first I've heard of it.'

'And do you think Paul could have been killed because of his suspicions?'

'Very possibly – nothing about the Nazis would surprise me anymore. Not after the other night. Please, Georgie, promise me you'll be very, very careful.'

'I will. I promise.'

In the end, there was no post-mortem on Paul's body due to 'overwork in the morgue', the police said, and any appeal seemed futile; if the Nazis had their hand in this fetid soup, no amount of badgering would change the outcome. Instead, Georgie had to plough through the red tape of getting his body flown back home. Still, she didn't relay her suspicions to Henry, wary that he might recall her back to England. A tiny part of her would have welcomed it, but a larger portion was certain she couldn't leave Berlin – or the story – behind.

31

The Good Doctor Graf

21st November 1938

The rearranged appointment at the Haas Institute came soon enough. Georgie employed every technique in pushing it to the back of her brain, but on the morning itself her stomach roiled at the prospect of any breakfast.

'Just ask the planned questions,' Max coached in a nearby café. 'It's not so much what their answers are, but how it feels in there. Look out for anything unusual.'

'I've got it.' Her mouth was already dry.

'I won't be far away,' he reiterated. 'I promise.'

They parted at the café table, and Georgie checked her outfit – a careful combination of Frida's and her own wardrobe, an amalgam of British and German styles. She even wore a hat, as befitted a wealthy young woman, which was a rarity for Georgie in past months. Still, the wide waistband on her skirt had no hope of containing the nerves running amok in her stomach as she stepped towards the imposing door of the clinic.

The reception wasn't the sterile white of a hospital, but painted in pale shades of blue, the receptionist clad in a cream singlet dress, like a trained nurse but not quite – all aimed, Georgie thought, at reflecting a clinical, professional service. And it worked. Had she been genuine, Fraulein Seidel would be reassured her money purchased excellent care.

She was shown into a side room, with easy chairs and a low table of a modern German design, clean lines and fuss-free.

'Good morning, Fraulein Seidel.' A man in a neat blue suit stepped silently through the door and offered his hand. 'I am Doctor Frederik Graf, director of the Haas Institute.'

He looked every inch a doctor even without a white coat, what with his neatly cut grey beard and round, wire-rimmed glasses. His suit and shoes looked expensive, and he had that self-assurance of the moneyed and educated classes, reminding Georgie a little of Max's father. He offered coffee, which she declined, and they got down to business. Her aunt, Georgie explained, needed care round the clock. She had never been labelled or diagnosed in childhood, but had always been beyond schooling, and the family wealthy enough to be able to protect her. Advancing age, though, had now made her behaviour 'more challenging' for untrained servants. What could the clinic offer?

Doctor Graf went through the range of services, the twenty-four-hour care in one of their 'comfortable' homes, alluding loosely to ways of containment. Reading between the lines, he meant control. Restraint.

'Am I to assume you can employ means to make my aunt at peace in her own mind?' Georgie pitched. She could barely believe she'd just said it – interrogation but with a smile. Yet strangely, it was easier than she thought, this role playing. She was almost beginning to inhabit Hanna Seidel fully – and enjoy it.

'I think it's fair to say we have the best interests of our patients at heart, particularly when they become anxious or distressed.' He smiled too, showing a mutual understanding: yes, they would use drugs to mollify.

'Well, I trust you know what you are doing,' she said. Another odd surge of confidence washed over Fraulein Seidel. 'Can I be frank, Doctor?'

He nodded, no hint of surprise.

'My aunt is not getting any younger, and her health is increasingly fragile. Our family understands there is a limit to her strength, and we all agree we don't want her to suffer unnecessarily. I'd simply like reassurance that she'll be made comfortable if that is the case.' Another weak smile, devoid of emotion and heavy with suggestion.

'You have my personal reassurance, Fraulein Seidel. We pride ourselves on our end-of-life care here.'

That, and his expression, was everything Georgie needed. They had been dancing with words, but the Haas Institute had the means and the will for ending life; he had just said as much. But how much of his admission could she use in print? She and Max would need far more proof than a spoken allusion.

They parted in the reception, Doctor Graf pledging a tour of the clinic should she want to take up their services and handing her a price pamphlet. At the last minute, the confidence Georgie possessed drained from her like a plug being pulled, and a hot flush pricked under her jacket and she willed it not to creep as far as her neck. She walked away as calmly as her nerves would permit but was almost at a run towards the café several streets away.

'Thank goodness!' Max said. 'I was just about to come in and find you.'

Over a doubly strong coffee, Georgie disclosed the essence of Doctor Graf and his work.

'Did you see any obvious signs of Reich involvement?' Max asked.

'There's the obligatory picture of Adolf in the reception, but

205

nothing else. It did occur to me that most hotels and businesses display a good deal more.'

'I wonder if they are taking pains to distance themselves,' Max replied. 'Maybe for a good reason?'

'So, where do we go from here?' Georgie asked. Alongside the press corps, she was relatively recent to political reporting, let alone the investigative type. The enjoyment of playing the actress had been fleeting, but it was not her best skill. She turned to Max for answers. He was staring into his cup for inspiration. His eyes snapped up suddenly.

'Your Nazi suitor might know something – are you still seeing him?'

'Not if I can help it, at least not after Kristallnacht,' she said firmly. There was only so much to her acting talent, and even if she did chance upon Kasper, he surely wouldn't be fooled into revealing Reich secrets, however ditsy and charming she might pretend to be. 'No, I think we'll have to find some other way. I just don't know what.'

32

A Slim Hope

23rd November 1938

Georgie's life seemed to be a round of meetings all of a sudden, with work squeezed into the gaps. The first was with Margot, who greeted the news of Paul's death like the wife she was never destined to be. She was genuinely distraught, although Georgie felt, in her heart, she must have suspected foul play.

'What will you do now, Margot?' Her family were back in Munich, and she appeared to have few friends. Acting and Paul had been her world, and with not even a funeral to attend . . .

'I've been cast in a film that's due to starting shooting in Frankfurt,' Margot sniffed. 'I was considering turning it down, but there doesn't seem much point saying no now.' It was at least an excuse to quit Berlin as Paul had initially warned her to, though Margot knew she wouldn't easily escape the Reich's reach – the film was likely to be one of Goebbels's favoured propaganda epics. If so, poor Margot would come within his orbit, and the rumours about the Minister for Propaganda and his predatory hunger for actresses were rife.

'I'll let you know if we find anything out,' Georgie said as they parted. 'About Paul's investigation.'

Margot looked faintly appalled at the suggestion. 'He's dead, Georgie – nothing can bring him back. I wouldn't want you to end up in that canal yourself. Please, forget the whole thing.'

It was surely her grief talking and, ordinarily, Georgie might have been thankful for such a reprieve. Only it wasn't just Paul's story now; if he was right, there were much wider implications. Besides, she and Max were reporters – they had the bit between their teeth.

The next day, she met with Sam Blundon for the first time since Kristallnacht, squeezed into a spare hour at lunchtime in Café Bauer, another of Berlin's grand old ladies on the opposite corner to Kranzler's. Sam rushed in, apologising for his lateness. He looked tired and beleaguered; even his youthful face appeared to have aged in the previous two weeks.

'I don't need to ask if you're busy?' Georgie said.

'It's been crazy,' Sam said, gulping at his tea. 'A constant demand for visas, statements from the diplomats, not to mention you press lot constantly requesting comment.' But his eyes were dancing as he said it.

'Sorry,' she said. 'I'll try to be less demanding.'

She waited for him to bite into his sandwich – it was Sam who'd suggested the meeting, and she hoped he would have some information on Elias.

'I don't have anything on your missing Amsel man, I'm afraid,' he said directly, and Georgie's eyes dimmed. 'But there is something else. Since that night, there are more charitable groups in England who are working on a system to move Jewish children out of Germany to safety. If your family are willing, I would at least be able to put their name forward. It is only for the children, though – there's no capacity for parents.'

George knew it would break Rubin and Sara's hearts to part with the children, but they were also selfless as parents. 'I'm certain they'll consider it,' she said. 'Thanks, Sam, you're a star.'

As much as she wanted to pick his brains about the coming and goings at the embassy, he steered the conversation away from work and politics — clearly wanting to talk of anything but.

'So, are you going home for Christmas?' Sam said. 'I can't wait to get back to my mother's roast beef and Yorkshires.'

In all honesty, Georgie hadn't thought about it, given the whirlwind of Berlin in recent weeks — Christmas seemed an untimely distraction. She was due some leave and her parents were desperate to see her safe again — their letters said as much. But she was equally loath to miss anything. She'd gotten used to living life on shifting sands, couldn't quite imagine the slow pace of life in the Cotswolds anymore.

'Maybe,' she said.

Sam eyed her from below his lashes, wiser than his looks. 'You know, even dedicated reporters take a holiday sometimes.'

It seemed he was right. At La Taverne, plans were afoot for a mass exodus for the Christmas break — Rod and Bill back across the Atlantic with most of the US and Canadian contingent, the London *Times* man to England, and others scattered across Europe. Frida was bound somewhere exotic, and yet no one seemed to question where her funds came from.

Disappointingly, and despite the graphic images from Kristallnacht, the world's wrath had not descended upon Germany and its leader; the US had made it clear — to Rod and Bill's disgust — that they would not being taking extra numbers of German-Jewish refugees, and the horrors of that night seemed diluted across the globe. There was no word on Elias, despite efforts from Rubin's underground channels, and she and Max were stumped on Paul's story. Everything had come to a standstill. And as Bill said, holding his glass aloft: 'Even the Nazis have Christmas.'

'So, will you be heading home?' Max asked across the press table.

'I would be,' Georgie sighed, 'but my parents are having to visit a sick relative at short notice and there's no room for me. What about you?'

'Not sure where home is anymore,' Max said matter-of-factly. 'My father is delayed in New York' – he flashed a look of relief – 'but he'd already booked a ski chalet near Geneva, and says I can use it. I certainly need a break from Berlin. I don't suppose you ski?'

She didn't, of course. What would a girl from the Stroud valleys be doing on a pair of skis?

'I could teach you,' he said. 'It'll be fun. The place is always well stocked with food and drink, and it's not too much of a journey on the train.'

Georgie looked sceptical, though she was sorely tempted.

'There's plenty of bedrooms if that's what you're worried about,' Max added quickly. 'You won't have to listen to me talking in my sleep. Promise.'

She looked across the table – at Simone, deep in conversation with Frida. 'Won't Simone mind?'

Max shrugged. 'She's not like that. Besides, she's going back to Paris.'

For Georgie, there was no reason not to accept – a virtually free holiday to somewhere she could never normally afford. 'One condition, though,' she said. 'You will have to explain it to my editor if I break my leg.'

'Deal.' Max sat back with a satisfied expression. 'Though I'll wager you'll be skiing like a champion by the time we come back.'

★

There was one other visit to make before the Christmas break. Sara welcomed Georgie into the Amsel apartment with as much warmth as she could muster, but the worry over Elias had taken its toll on her previously open face. Wisps of thin grey hair framed her drab complexion and her smile was carefully arranged as she made every effort for the occasion.

Alone in the kitchen, Georgie told Rubin about the possibility of safe passage for the children, watched the light in his face rise, flicker and then die; the dark realisation of losing his children too, possibly forever.

'Yes, of course, I will discuss it with Sara. And please give our thanks to your friend at the embassy.' He clasped firmly at Georgie's hand, as if it were the best ever gift. Georgie narrowly stemmed her sadness by giving out Christmas presents for the children, chosen carefully to combine luxury with practicality, pressing an envelope of Reichsmarks into Rubin's hand as she left.

'Georgie, no,' he protested, though she knew it was his pride talking.

'It's your retainer, Rubin – I don't want anyone else nabbing your services while I'm away. You're far too valuable.' It was a half-truth, but a necessary one; there was talk of Jews losing their right to drive, and she could only guess at Rubin's already fragile finances.

She'd told the Amsels of her plans to leave Berlin for Christmas, and when they assumed it would be home to England, she didn't correct them. It was partly her own shame in contemplating a frivolous holiday away from the struggles they faced daily, when they had no hope of escaping without a passport to their names. She would simply have to reconcile her guilt privately.

33

A Snowy Respite

Geneva, Switzerland, Christmas 1938

'Come on then, just push yourself off,' Max shouted from below. 'You'll be fine.' He beckoned with his hand as if it was the easiest thing in the world, like stepping onto a dance floor.

Georgie stood on what felt like the top of a mountain, actually little more than a hill for ski veterans. To her, though, looking at a panorama entirely of white, people like pinpricks below, she might have been descending Everest. It was another Georgie moment. Inside her head, she chanted. *Come on, girl, just do it. You won't die. Just do it.*

She looked at Max waiting, expectant, and dug into the crisp blanket with her ski poles, pushing herself off and diving into the frozen abyss, the cold air stinging her face, mouth tightly shut, fear and adrenalin mixing like a heady cocktail. Someone screamed like a child on a rollercoaster – was that her? – turning quickly into a squeal of delight.

The exhilaration was intoxicating, though short-lived, as she tried to swerve when approaching Max and collapsed in a heap of white spray. Yet she was laughing as Max hauled her up and helped dust her down.

'Bit of work to do on the landing,' he said drily. 'But ten out of ten for courage. You flew down there!'

Under the chill of her cheeks, Georgie glowed with achievement. It had felt like an entirely new freedom.

Back in the cosy warmth of their chalet, she groaned as her body felt the effects of three days as a virgin skier.

'I ache in muscles I didn't even know I had,' she moaned, rubbing at her thighs.

Max laughed with good humour. In fact, he'd been nothing but good-humoured since they arrived. Gone was the dour, cynical man she met at Croydon airfield, the arrogant young buck from the London Ritz, and the inconstant moodiness of their early months in Berlin. He had been charming company the minute they stepped off the train in Geneva, his face alight and smiling, and then a patient tutor with her first, wobbling attempts at standing on skis.

The chalet was large and sumptuous, entirely in line with his father's high standards – Georgie had taken a few days to justify the luxury, given what they had left behind, but both Henry and her parents reassured her beforehand that she deserved the break – she worked hard and rarely treated herself. In this case, it felt easier to believe them.

Aside from the wonderful food and the cocktails that Max was a dab hand in mixing, the best element for Georgie was in their evenings together. After a warm bath, a good meal prepared by the chalet maid, and with a drink in hand, she and Max had time to listen to the radio, reflect and talk.

'Do you think the war will come soon?' she said lazily, legs stretching over the couch, Max sprawled on the sofa opposite. After the apathy from abroad after Kristallnacht, the talk at La

Taverne had swayed towards not 'if' but 'what' would prompt a full-on conflict.

Max sighed. 'Yes, I'm afraid so, if Hitler carries on the same way. He'll just get increasingly brave – or arrogant – and the world won't be able to ignore it. Well, let's hope it won't.'

'I'm not sure whether we should welcome it,' she replied sharply from the sofa.

'I don't *welcome* war, Georgie,' he shot back. 'But we – everyone – has to make a stand against a despot. He's a bully, and he can't go unchallenged forever.' The ripple in his brow couldn't hide shadows of his own life then.

She considered his reply. 'I know we can't – shouldn't – tolerate what they're doing,' she ventured, eventually, 'but I do wonder what war really feels like, the consequences of it day-to-day. Whether you learn to live with the fear. We'll be the lucky ones, able to be pulled out, but what about everyone else – those left behind? People like the Amsels?'

Max sat up, swung his legs to the floor. 'You always think about the individual, don't you? Why is that?' Unlike their previous disputes, his voice was more enquiry than challenge.

She pushed the cool glass into her chin. 'Don't you?'

He stared into the dancing flames of the fire. 'No, I don't think so. I imagine there will be casualties, but they will be for the greater good – that it will be bloody but Hitler will be defeated.' He paused, sighed. 'God, I sound like some sort of grand army general. Or maybe even my father – you stand a loss in order to make a bigger profit in the long term.'

Now Georgie pulled herself up, drew his gaze to hers across the space. 'No, that's not true, Max. We may have different ways of reporting, and that's not a bad thing. But you did not take the easy path in life – you are here because you're a hard-working reporter and not a society darling. And you are *nothing* like your father.'

His face lit up with pleasure. 'And you, *George* Young, are well beyond frills and spills and lace,' he teased, getting up to mix another drink.

'Bloody cheek, Maximus Titus Aurelius!' She aimed a cushion at him and fell back laughing. With abandon. And strangely, without too much guilt.

34

Another Sacrifice

Berlin, Christmas 1938

Had she seen what Rubin and Sara were shielding over that Christmas of 1938, Georgie would have shouldered her guilt with more difficulty. Though not a Jewish celebration, Rubin and Sara had always tried to define it for the children; their normally meagre dinner was only made richer because of Sara's cooking skills and the small treats squirrelled away in her larder for special occasions.

Berlin was quiet, affording an opportunity to spend time as a family, leaving the chair previously occupied by Elias to appear especially empty. They lit a candle for him, and toasted his life – not knowing if it was ongoing or had come to an abrupt or brutal end.

Touchingly, Leon set out the chess set for his father, and encouraged him to play the first game since Elias was taken. While Rubin played, he glimpsed a fleeting glow in Sara – rare nowadays – in being among her children, taking solace from their laughter. Inside, he simmered with his own secret: the knowledge that soon his wife might be robbed of her only existing pleasure.

On New Year's Eve, the children in bed, he and Sara mused on the year past – and nervously on the year ahead, though the word 'war' wasn't uttered. Finally, he could contain it no longer.

'We've got a decision to make, my love. A crucial one.'

Sara's eyes were swimming before he finished telling her. 'Send them to England? But we might never see them again,' she keened. '*My babies.*'

'At the same time, it is our best chance of seeing them again – safe.' Rubin wished sometimes he could allow his heart, and not his head, do the talking. But not now. 'And they are two more mouths to feed.'

'They are not mouths, Rubin! They are our children,' Sara said defiantly.

'I know, I know, my love. But you see how hard it's become – and it will only get tighter. Surely, we owe it to Ester and Leon? A better life?'

She knew he spoke sense, but sense didn't stop the vessels in her heart from choking with fresh grief. First Elias, and now the children. When would this hellish reality end?

217

35

New Year, New Loss

Berlin and London, January 1939

It was over too soon, and although Georgie would never admit it to her parents, it was among the best Christmases she'd had. Returning to Berlin, Geneva felt like a heavenly memory that no one – not even Herr Hitler – could ever seek to steal away.

Then, the hammer blow to quash her new-found spirit. She'd lost Rubin – as a reliable driver at least. Following Kristallnacht and the accusation against all Jews, the Reich imposed not only an outrageous one-billion-marks bill for damages, but followed up on their pledge – all Jews banned from driving cars or motorcycles. In one fell swoop, a good half of the Amsels' income was wiped out. In addition, Jews were banned from key central areas of the city: concert halls, museums and public baths. Rubin said nothing, but she saw it in his face, echoed his thoughts: how many life layers were to be pared away, until there was nothing left of their liberty?

Georgie reassured him that with some careful juggling of the office expenses she could manage the retainer, find him some other employment and apply for an exemption permit allowing him to travel in and out of the city centre as a vital messenger for the bureau. 'Foreign companies are still allowed more concessions than German businesses,' she told him. Still, she watched with a heavy heart from the office window, seeing him push off on his bicycle, his shoulders rounded and carrying a dense personal load.

In brief conversations over work, Max and Georgie had agreed to prod at their contacts in trying to breathe any kind of life into Paul's suspicions. But there was work too – agency reporters had been holding the fort over the holidays and Georgie needed to tempt Henry with more stories in fighting for her own space on the foreign pages. Her first conversation with him, however, put paid to that.

'You're being recalled to London,' he said, his voice full of apology.

'What do you mean *recalled*? For how long?' Her voice was already cracking. 'Why?' Had she not done a good job? Henry always seemed pleased with her dispatches.

'They've had several people leave on the home desk and they need you to fill in. I'm not sure how long.'

'But what about here? It's a crucial time, Henry. It could all blow up at a moment's notice.'

'I know, I know. But I'm an editor, Georgie, not a manager. I don't make the decisions. They are looking for a permanent replacement for Paul, and in the meantime we'll use agency material.'

Her disappointment transmitted clearly over the phone lines. Berlin was like walking on eggshells at times, and she had enjoyed the relaxation of time away, but to lose it entirely . . .

'I'm sorry, Georgie, but the decision's made. We'll get you back there as soon as possible. As a pledge, we'll pay your Berlin rent while you're back in England.'

She couldn't refuse. While her confidence had grown, she

wasn't at the level of selling her wares as a freelancer, and at least the *Chronicle* was showing commitment to her return. The thought of seeing her parents was inviting, catching up with friends and watching films not subtitled or badly dubbed, though it was a small payback for her deflation.

She didn't hold back the tears at Zoo station, impossible with half the press corps gathered to wave her off, plus Sam. 'Bring us back some of that heavy stuff you have over there,' Bill said, prodding her to smile. 'What is it? Fudge? I'd like some Cornish fudge.'

The fact that Cornwall and London were hundreds of miles apart didn't figure to Bill, coming from the vast US Midwest, but she loved that he thought of it.

'Hey, kiddo.' Rod pulled her in for his best bear embrace. 'I'm on a strudel strike until you return, so if you have any sympathy for a poor American and his stomach, you'll come back soon.'

'Promise,' she said, wiping at her wet cheeks. It was like leaving family, and even Frida and Simone looked saddened in the background. Max stood alongside them, forcing a smile onto his stony face. As the train drew out of the station, he mimed a scribble on his hand. *I'll write,* he mouthed, and then the cluster of people receded into the distance.

Berlin, part one at least, was over.

London seemed drab by comparison, and Georgie felt frustrated by its relative inertia. No one seemed to be talking seriously of the imminent threat in Europe and what might, very swiftly, interfere dramatically with the price of milk or the train delays. War, that's what. Full-on, Europe-wide annihilation. How could they be so blind to the Nazis' badly couched cruelty?

Work was a saving grace in keeping her busy. Georgie was seconded to the *Chronicle*'s crime desk, which was pacey yet still routine by comparison. There were no personalities like Herr Bauer to laugh at, and although the other reporters were a good bunch, she longed for the close camaraderie of the Berlin' pack. She missed Rod and his hugs, Bill and his wry observations, Frida and her alternative take on life. She missed Max and his friendship. She scoured the *Telegraph* foreign pages, reading between his lines of what was really happening. She held her breath to read what seemed to be routine politics in the foreign pages, unable to bear the thought of missing out on something ground-breaking.

The *Chronicle* ran a piece on the Reich's five-year plan to enlarge their fleet of ships, easily taking it to beyond the size of the British navy by 1944 – another pledge from the Versailles Treaty the Nazis had simply discarded. Equally, they published frivolous reports on Hitler's purchase of a priceless painting, and the bizarre call from the editor of *Der Stürmer* to ban any loyal German from singing 'The Lambeth Walk'.

On the home front, there were plans for evacuation and pictures of Londoners building garden air raid shelters, yet it still seemed so half-hearted, as if the world remained convinced it would simply go away when all wished hard enough.

The weeks seeped into months – Henry had warned her it wouldn't be a short sabbatical – but London was a place to recharge. She hated the winter fogs and how they made her cough, but there was a less watchful atmosphere than in Berlin, and Georgie noted her shoulders relax as she walked the streets without an ear cocked for footsteps, not tempted to glance behind her. She managed several snatched weekends with her parents, whose anxiety was calmed by her looking so well. 'I imagined you might be grey, with all that pickled cabbage and meat.'

'Mother! It's not some out-of-the-way foreign clime, you know. There are fresh vegetables.' She didn't dare admit how much strudel was wrapped around the apples she and Rod consumed.

Max kept his promise and wrote, not quite once a week, but enough to let her know things were merely ticking over. The press crowd were all using Rubin for a variety of jobs, keeping his wages constant. Then: *'We went skating in one of the frozen-over lakes in the park, and had a lovely time – Frida is a dab hand on the ice. I missed laughing at your attempts (given what you were like on skis!). I noticed, though, that there were plenty of signs: No Jews allowed. How can one race feel that another isn't allowed to have fun?'*

Despite her own outrage and what it meant for people like Rubin, Georgie warmed at the human element pushing through Max's pen, despite his best endeavours. Politically, he wrote that the Reich office was quiet, almost worryingly so.

'The only news is that they shut down Berliner Tageblatt, which Rubin was especially sad about, but some of the reporters have got work as agency contributors on the quiet,' he wrote. He said Frida had been a little cagey and absent, but he offered no news of Simone. *'Rod has lost several inches off his waistline but is miserable, so come back soon. Please. Love and strudel, Max.'*

Life appeared to be ticking over in Berlin, spring doing its utmost to break though in London, and yet each day seemed grey to Georgie; she hovered over the wire machine on the foreign desk, eager to know if Hitler had made a sudden move, her not in the thick of it. The thought of missing something vital created a new kind of daily anxiety. So she was concerned one lunchtime to see Henry's form amble over to her desk, his face flat, giving nothing away. Was that a hint of regret that she detected in his features? Perhaps the news she dreaded – that she wouldn't be going back; they'd found someone to replace her.

'Good news,' he said at last, holding out an envelope. 'Ticket to Berlin, in four days. Train only I'm afraid.'

Georgie's hand was out in a flash, awash with relief.

'And we've decided on a replacement for Paul. How about it – George Young, Senior Bureau Correspondent?'

Henry wasn't the hugging type, so she had to be content with a warm handshake and a thousand thanks. 'You've earned it,' he said. 'Being plunged in at the deep end. Welcome back to the foreign desk fold. I look forward to lots of good copy.'

36

Home from Home

The welcoming committee was depleted on arrival in Berlin, but Georgie was thrilled to see Max as the train drew into the station. In all honesty, she was quite content on seeing him alone, wanting nothing more than a hot bath and a good cup of strong tea, courtesy of her mother's well-wrapped 'survival package'.

'We've got strict instructions to make a stop before the apartment,' Max said, refusing to reveal any more. They taxied to Café Kranzler and a cheer went up as she walked through the door – at least eight around the table, a huge platter of strudel in the middle.

'At last, I'm saved from a famine of the finest pastry!' Rod boomed and stood to cloak Georgie with his being. He looked a little trimmer but had clearly found a sweet substitute while she'd been away. And it was almost as if she'd never been away – the banter and the warmth immediate and homely, mitigated only by recent news that two British journalists had been arrested for daring to watch the expulsion of Jews, spending five long hours in the Gestapo HQ before their release.

'So, it's watch your backs, guys,' Rod said. 'Let's stick together and look out for each other. I need you lot for the sake of my sanity!'

Beyond the café windows, a sudden diatribe barked from a nearby speaker and pushed its way through the glass, a distinct, guttural German declaring the brilliance of a new Nazi enterprise. And yet it felt somehow familiar – perhaps not comforting, but strangely normal. It was good to be back.

Georgie wandered into the office afterwards to find Rubin, blinds fully down while he converted press releases into readable copy, as part of his new, diverse role, detailed as 'helper'. The lines on his face spread with acute relief at seeing her.

'How's Sara?' she asked. She had thought of writing directly to Rubin from England but stopped herself, not wanting to risk any surveillance on the family.

'She's . . . well, she's all right,' he managed, with a small shake of his head. 'There's no news on Elias. But we have managed to secure the children on the transport – they leave in five days. For England.'

'Five days!'

'Yes, it's been quick. But it's good. For them. Sara is . . . well, you can imagine. But she knows it's the right thing. We both do.' His tone was laboured and unconvincing to both of them.

She swivelled towards him, put a hand on his arm and squeezed. 'I'm so sorry, Rubin,' Georgie said at last. 'No family should have to go through what you are. I know I promised to find Elias and . . .'

'It's fine,' he said, clutching at her hand. 'You were willing at least. From what we hear, he might be in some sort of camp. There are rumours of large numbers being held.'

'Do you know where?'

'No, they're scattered across Germany. He could be anywhere. But it means if the Nazis are keeping large groups, Elias could still be alive.' He didn't allude to the conditions or if he might be suffering. 'We have to hold on to that thought, Georgie. For us, and for the children.'

Back home, Georgie opened her pile of post once in the bath, her teacup teetering on the side. Most were from family and friends, amazed at her 'glamorous' life in cosmopolitan Berlin. One, though, was in a more familiar hand, the black eagle icon of the Reich as its postmark. Kasper.

The letter was dated almost a month previously and the script was charming, as always. Could they perhaps go out again? he asked. He was back in Berlin permanently and it would be nice to 'catch up'. Georgie was perplexed. It had been months since their last contact, so why now? Her suspicions were raised, now, by any man in a Nazi uniform.

She was tempted simply to toss the note away, but Max's suggestion nagged at her – that perhaps Kasper might be gently prodded for any information, on Paul or the fate of Jewish prisoners. He could still be that vital contact, especially as they had no other leads. She'd pledged in her own mind never to see another Reich officer again, but this would be for Elias, and Rubin. Could she afford to pass up the opportunity?

Leaping on her own spontaneity, Georgie wrote a hasty reply, explaining she'd been 'back home' for a while, but yes, it would be lovely to meet. She walked to the post box and, with only a second's hesitation, pushed it in. *Oh Lord, Georgie – off we go again.*

Georgie managed to think little of it over the next week – she moved around the city independently, while Rubin spent as much time as he could with Leon and Ester before their departure to England. Travelling on the tram was like reacquainting herself with an old friend, tuning into conversations between Berliners – whispered talk on politics and the 'Jewish problem' – and what occupied their minds.

On the day of departure, she was touched to be invited to the station. Rubin, characteristically, was putting on a brave face for Sara, but Georgie could see his emotions were wound tight. It was lucky that Leon and Ester were among a crowd of children on the platform, brown paper labels tied onto their clothes, one suitcase apiece bashing at their reedy ankles. Excited chatter from some of the young ones helped to mask the parents' pent-up distress. Sara looked as if she was already dry of tears, her red-rimmed eyes a sign that she'd been crying most of the night. Somehow, she hauled a smile from the depths of her sorrow.

'Now, make sure you are polite, say please and thank you, and remember what English manners Georgie has taught you.' She busied herself tidying their hair and buttoning coats. Anything but thinking about that last touch and the enormous void their going would create.

'We'll write – all the time,' she went on. 'Mama and Papa will join you in England as soon as we can.'

The children stared, murmured, 'Yes, Mama' – Georgie couldn't imagine the swirl of confusion their young minds were facing. She had to turn away as the train shunted out of the station, hands waving furiously from open windows, tears rolling onto the platform, until the last puff of steam was out of sight.

'It is better this way, isn't it?' Sara sobbed into her husband's coat. 'We've done the right thing, haven't we?'

Rubin's pained expression met with Georgie's over Sara's hair. Grave. Bereft. He nodded. 'Yes, we have, my love. We have.'

227

37

True Colours

Since the dawning of the new year, rumours had been circulating among the press that Hitler was planning something big – they just didn't know what. Perhaps blindsided by the huge investment into the German navy, everyone was surprised when the attack came on land. Each had written of Hitler dipping his toe into Czechoslovakian lands to the north-west, the Führer claiming once again that his troops were merely 'protecting' Poles in the area and reclaiming the land for Poland, like the venerable neighbour he was.

And then the blow. Czechoslovakia was severed in one fell swoop, sliced in two as a pro-German Slovak Republic emerged overnight. Hitler had his troops poised to march into the remaining half the very next day, with little opposition from the winded Czechs; the Reich's 'Protectorate of Bohemia and Moravia' was instantly created. So much for Chamberlain's 'peace for our time', Georgie thought disdainfully.

It was a busy few days workwise, as the shock news

dominated the front pages of British newspapers, with in-depth analysis on the inside pages; Georgie's head was spinning with politics and quotes, liaising with the Czech bureau as Hitler's staccato victory speech rang out from Prague's ancient castle.

Days later, the Führer returned to Berlin and Joey G pulled out all the stops for his 'triumphant' homecoming parade. Arriving back into the office, having endured the sickening spectacle, Georgie found herself virtually dry of inspiration. How much more of an example did the world need before this man and his dangerous ego were properly challenged?

In frustration, she rolled a single sheet into her typewriter and willed her words to spill.

```
                              Postcard from Berlin,
                                18th March 1939


Dear British public,
    Spring marches in Germany's capital with yet
another parade, an endless line of inch-perfect foot
stomping and unified raising of palms to welcome
the Führer back from his pillage. If he weren't so
decidedly German, we foreigners might easily mistake
him for a Viking raider returned with his spoils.
The pomp and bluster of such occasions are all too
familiar, but now - with a successful stranglehold
over the former Czechoslovakia - Berlin smoulders:
flaming bowls of oil line the Führer's procession,
casting an eerie glow while searchlights play into
the sky.
    But this is no longer a carnival. We might be
reminded of Adolf Hitler's public pledge on seizing
```

the Sudetenland last year, that it represented 'the
last territorial demand I have to make in Europe'.

After tonight, I feel sure the world has not
seen the spectacle of the Führer's finale yet.

Auf Wiedersehen, your correspondent in Berlin

Georgie sat back and blew out a sigh, looked out into the
lights of Berlin. She'd forgotten to draw the blinds and the
unease of being watched lingered, but she couldn't motivate
herself to act. She needed sleep but wanted company more
and, as if someone had been watching or even reading her
thoughts, the phone rang.

'*Chronicle* office,' she said wearily. It was often Henry at this
time.

'Oh, I can't tell whether you need alcohol or coffee,' said
the voice at the other end. Not Henry but Max.

'Either,' she said. 'You offering?'

'I'll stand you both at La Taverne. See you in twenty minutes?'

'You're on.' The promise of good company who might share
her flattened mood was motivation enough.

It was already eleven and the restaurant was almost empty,
so too the press table, and the place had a dejected air. But
Georgie rallied on seeing Max come through the door, alone.
She loved the others, but the prospect of a combined moan
– one to one – was exactly what she needed then.

'So, how's living on a knife-edge been for you today?' Max
put down two large brandies with coffee alongside.

Georgie blew out her cheeks. 'I thought I might scream having
to watch that blasted parade,' she said, keeping her voice low.
'The arrogance of the high command sickens me. They look
more and more like playground bullies with their smug smiles.'

'A very apt description,' Max said. 'You should consider a
career as a writer.'

'Ha ha.' She frowned. 'Seriously, though, where is it going to end, Max? How much more proof does everyone need?'

'I hear you, but it seems others don't. All we can do is continue to bleed our souls onto the keyboard and hope it works.'

They sat nursing their brandy for a minute.

'Oh, I forgot,' Georgie said. 'Kasper got in touch.'

Max cocked his head quizzically.

'My Nazi man, as you like to call him. He's proposed another date.'

'And?' Max had one eyebrow raised.

'I said yes. If he still thinks I'm some sort of rich-girl socialite, I might glean something from him. About Paul or Elias. I think it's worth a try.'

'Are you sure about this?' Max's expression was a world away from a few months previously. Worry lines ran through his brow.

'Well, you've changed your tune,' she grumbled. 'It was you who suggested it last time.'

'Things have changed, Georgie.'

'Yes, they have,' she snapped, suddenly irked. 'It's become far more important to find out what happened to them both.' Why *was* he so changeable, just when she thought they'd come to a perfect point in their friendship?

'Well, it's up to you. Just make sure you let me know when and where,' he said, downing the last of his brandy. Georgie bit her tongue, tempted to deliver a glib reply about not needing a bodyguard and yes, it *was* her decision. But she was simply too tired to fall out with Max, who might – after all – only be watching out for her. As friends often did.

The foreign press coverage after the Czech invasion put a new strain on relations with the Propaganda Ministry; Herr Bauer had a face like thunder whenever he came across Rod in particular, whose reporting was so cleverly worded as to make it seem unbiased and yet condemned the regime entirely. Either by association, or because her postcards had begun to be more frequent, Georgie also received a slice of his cold civility.

'I was sorry to hear about your colleague, Herr Adamson,' Bauer managed. Of course, he wasn't. And it was entirely possible he knew how Paul had come to meet his death. 'Is your publication planning to replace him?' A minuscule portion of his teeth came into view.

'Thankfully, they have.' Georgie smiled, feeling very smug inside. 'It's me, Herr Bauer. I'm the new bureau chief.' Currently the head of only one, but the mini-Hitler didn't need to know that yet.

The teeth disappeared, his lips set together. 'Congratulations, Fraulein. I'm glad to say we already see more of you than your former bureau chief.' But, of course, he wasn't, not after the last *Postcard* and the missives of support in the *Chronicle*'s letters page.

He nodded and clipped away.

'I swear he's adopted Hitler's awkward shuffle,' Rod whispered. 'It's uncanny. I bet you he's touting for the job of the Führer's double – would gladly stand in the way of a bullet for his leader, deluded asshole that he is.'

'Careful, Rod, you really are going to get into trouble one of these days.' Georgie scanned the walls for where the nearest listening device might be.

'Oh yes, but won't it be worth it?' He smiled, linking arms.

'Not if the SS get hold of you it won't. You might wish you'd succumbed to strudel poisoning then.'

'An equally lovely way to go. Come on, Kranzler's is waiting.'

They sat at their usual table, and Georgie noted Rod eyeing the room.

'Looking for someone?' she asked.

'No, I just haven't seen Karl around here for some time. Have you?'

'Actually, no. Not since before I left for London.'

Rod looked unusually worried. He leaned in to stir his coffee, inviting Georgie to join in a cosy tête-à-tête. 'I asked him to make a few enquiries about a story I was working on,' he murmured. 'He did, but that was three weeks ago. I hope he hasn't fallen foul.'

These days, it was entirely possible – more uniforms on the streets, more SS in sight. And who knows how many more Gestapo lurking in the shadows.

38

Empty Nest

20th March 1939

He heard Sara's key turn in the lock only seconds before she called out: 'It's me, anyone home?' Rubin noted she still did it each day, as if by some miracle another voice would call out that they were present – one of the children, or even Elias. Habit surely, or perhaps simply his wife trying to maintain her sanity.

'I'm home,' he sang out, 'in the parlour. Come and see what I've got for you.'

Her face was quizzical as she came in, perhaps a little brighter in past days, now they'd had a letter from each of the children. It had been only a short note, but enough to know they were safe in London, waiting for a more permanent home, and together as they hoped. The tears that day, at least, had been of relief.

'Don't tell me you've found fruit? Or real coffee?' Her face was expectant, fell a little when Rubin admitted that no, he hadn't, and handed her a small, soft package instead.

'Oh, Rubin, it's beautiful,' she cooed over the delicate silk scarf, patterned with fish in fashionable blues and greens, wrapping its softness around the scant flesh of her neck and palming the fibres against her cheek. 'But where did you get it? How can we afford this?'

He smiled, tapped the side of his nose playfully. 'Oh, I do know a few people.'

Rubin did know a good many tradesmen, but none who bartered in this level of finery. He'd already wrestled with himself on coming clean, but decided Sara need not know that he'd simply found it on the pavement near to the *Chronicle* office. He'd scanned the pavement for any shoppers who might have dropped the finely wrapped parcel from Wertheim's, but no one it seemed had lost a package. If Sara knew the truth, she might be offended, mortified at wearing something picked off the street. And yet she deserved it – she'd had no new clothes for years now. If Rubin could have bought it for her, to raise a smile, he would have. And she needed a distraction – not to think about the huge, echoey void in their tiny apartment, not to have to look at the children's empty beds and finger the toys they'd left behind, the family photograph she touched each and every time she passed. If, for just a minute she could feel like any other woman, spoiled on occasion, he would swallow the guilt of deception.

'Oh, one more piece of news,' Rubin called as Sara went to put on the coffee pot.

'Yes? Any word?' She was quick to hope again.

He moved into the kitchen, lowered his voice. 'No word, but a meeting's been called – seems that the Gestapo has ears, but so has the resistance. We might know something soon.'

Sara's smile was short-lived. 'Rubin, promise me you'll be careful – where you go, who you meet.'

'I will, Sara, but I'm certain that unless we take some chances, we'll never know anything. About Elias, or any of them.'

'I understand, but I couldn't bear it if . . .' and Rubin moved to her, knowing the delicate silk could never stem her tide of sorrow.

39

The Temple

The political lull in the first months of 1939 gave way to furious activity, as Hitler set his sights on further acquisitions. He marched brazenly into the Lithuanian territory of Memel, claiming it was Germany's by rights, and then – as if collecting properties on a Monopoly board – turned his attention to Danzig, a tiny free city state in the most northern part of the Polish 'corridor' sandwiched between Germany and East Prussia. No one doubted the Führer's greedy eye was focused on its thriving port and coastline into the Baltic rather than the freedom of German Danzigers.

Two days later, it became plain that the ongoing tussle over Danzig was also a distraction; Germany and the USSR signed a pact, agreeing on how they would split the big prize: Poland.

Finally, the world's politicians stirred, and by the end of March, Britain and France had made a verbal stand at least, reassuring Poland they would support its right to defend independence, though they stopped short of any details. The foreign press was incensed, and yet the sheer adrenalin drove them on, running from Reich briefings to embassy statements, pushing heads together at the Adlon and then winding down at La Taverne over pasta and beer, Rod holding court and trying, at the same time, to keep tabs on his increasing frustration with the Reich, the world and humanity.

'Is he all right?' Georgie whispered to Bill one evening. 'He seems so wound up.'

Bill sighed, nodded. 'I've known Rod a long time, but he's never been like this. I'll have another word, get him to calm down. Even this place has ears.'

Georgie looked around the otherwise relaxed restaurant, with not a uniform in sight. But yes, Bill was right. Nowhere in Berlin was beyond the long arm of the Gestapo.

In the midst, Kasper had replied in his typically ornate but unrushed fashion. He suggested an evening date, and although Georgie's gut twisted a little at the intimacy, it did mean a public place. He proposed meeting at the fashionable Ciro bar, moving on to a reception. Her mouth went dry at the prospect of a Nazi social gathering, brimming with pro-Führer personnel. But her ears would be on full alert, and if she proved convincing, Kasper's trust was further gained. *It's work, Georgie. It's essential.*

On the appointed evening, she was not surprised to see Max and Simone already ensconced at the Ciro at a corner table looking towards the bar, the French woman casually consenting to be part of their plan. Max looked the part – dapper in his evening suit with a cocktail to hand, and Georgie had a fleeting reminder of that night at the Ritz, his arrogant approach and her flighty rebuff. Strange how she was intensely relieved to see him now, even with Simone at his side. Georgie had never quite warmed to Simone in the same way as she had to Frida; Simone's cool exterior sometimes seemed chilly. Frida was intensely intelligent and ambitious, but she was also fun, flighty and easy company. Simone was her opposite – aloof and, at the Ciro, also irritatingly beautiful.

The bar was busy, both the people and the chic surroundings oozing luxury; it attracted a moneyed, multilingual crowd eager to hear jazz tunes amid the Arabesque décor, with a chattery blend of German, French, English and American accents. Georgie was disappointed not to find Kasper at the bar already; she'd never felt comfortable striding into a London pub on her own, despite the numerous press gatherings over a pint.

She took in a breath, pushed back her shoulders and flashed a brief glance at Max, who caught her eye without a flicker, though she might have seen the briefest of nods.

Come on, George, play the game.

She was at least appropriately attired; back at the flat, she'd raided Frida's wardrobe and gained all-round approval. The emerald cocktail dress fitted like a glove, everyone said, the silk hugging Georgie's small waist and draping over her wider hips as if it was made for her. Frida – the hardy journalist who could drink a man under the table and still beat him to a story – had teased at Georgie's blonde hair, pinning and curling as she imparted tips on how to flatter a Reich officer without fawning. Still, she didn't question why Georgie had chosen to make such an effort for what was increasingly becoming the enemy. Nor did she ever expect to be quizzed herself.

Cloaked in a new confidence, Georgie walked to the bar with every ounce of poise she could muster and perched on one of the stools. The barman was there in a flash.

'Vodka Martini please.' The first sip was a honey tonic on her tongue, and she surveyed the Ciro scene; the beautifully dressed women with their aura of true assurance, throwing back their heads with laughter and casually blowing smoke into the air. Their enchanted male companions had either been born into money or eased into its comfort very quickly. Looking about, Georgie knew her limited acting ability needed to reflect this; previous dates with Kasper had seemed like fun. Now, there was much more at stake.

'Georgie, you look lovely.' Kasper was upon her in a flash, picked up her hand and kissed it as he bored into her with those magnetic eyes. This was new, and it rankled; she'd heard from one of the other reporters this was often how Hitler himself greeted women, using his eyes to draw people in. The Führer's were apparently button-black up close, where Kasper's were eternally alluring. She smiled with appreciation at Officer Vortsch, because that was her job now.

'Thank you,' she said. She didn't afford him the same compliment – he was in uniform, though pressed and crisp. And perhaps adorned with one or two more silver insignia, though she couldn't be sure. He ordered a cocktail, and they sat gossiping about the crowd, Kasper pointing out several of the women as film stars attached to one of the city's picture studios.

'So, you've been away, back to England?' he said.

'Yes, my mother wasn't well, and it was a chance to catch up with some friends.' She'd progressed to an outright fabrication of facts. What else could she do?

'I'm sorry to hear about your mother. But you came back – that must mean you prefer it to London?'

'Absolutely,' she said, relieved to speak a sliver of truth. 'London is so drab compared to Berlin. And, of course, I need to be here for my work.'

She studied his face, for his features to shift – to suspicion, or disbelief. But it reflected little more than a feigned uninterest.

'Yes,' he said. 'Is your writing going well?'

'Yes and no. It's a love story and I'm struggling with the main characters right now.'

'Well, I hope that tonight Berlin can afford you some inspiration.'

It was a stock, throwaway comment, since he wasn't really listening – those disarming eyes were on her, but his ears tuned in elsewhere, and Georgie felt confident her false life was holding fast; to Kasper she remained a daddy's girl straight out of finishing school, biding her time until she landed herself a husband.

He encouraged her to drink up. 'I have a car waiting,' he said. She turned and made a lengthy play of putting on her jacket, catching half a glance from Max as he and Simone hastily finished their drinks. Their loose strategy meant Max shadowing her as far and as close as possible. Beyond that, she and her acting skills were flying solo.

Kasper had obviously gone up in the world – or the hierarchy. A large Mercedes stood idling outside the Ciro, with a uniformed driver, but it was Kasper who opened the door for Georgie. Inside, a mingled smell of expensive leather, cologne and whisky.

'So, where are we going?' Georgie asked in her most upbeat voice. With or without Max as a tail, it would help her nerves to know their destination.

'It's a surprise,' Kasper said, with his former boyishness. 'I promise good food, though, and lively company. I hope you've not eaten.'

She hadn't – her nerves had seen to that – but if there was more alcohol to consume in the spirit of the evening, she would definitely need something in her stomach.

They headed north. Georgie could tell that much but the streetlights whizzed by in a flash, petering out as they seemed to be leaving the city confines behind. She wanted desperately to swivel her head round and check if there were headlights following, though it would be impossible to know if it was Max and Simone tailing. Once on the road out of the city, there were no landmarks for Georgie to navigate by and she gave up. Her stomach pinched with a strange mix of mild nausea and preordained fate, though she was surprised that it was not panic. *What will be will be.* At least Max would know at whose hand she had perished. He would find out. Being Max, he wouldn't let it lie, she could be certain. Her parents would have answers.

'We've been driving for a long while – I hope this food is well worth it,' she said in a flighty voice.

'Oh yes, it will be.' Kasper smiled, though not with any hint of malevolence. For now, he wore that eager-to-please expression she'd seen before.

It changed, rapidly, as the car came to a sudden halt. Georgie had noticed houses becoming more frequent, as if they were driving up to or through a small village – a sign flashed by: Orenia . . . Orana . . . ? But she couldn't make it out fully. The door was opened by the driver and Kasper stepped out, his demeanour switching over a split second. Gone was the excited boy of their balloon adventure or the expectant face from minutes before. Even from the back, she saw his body stiffen and his right hand launch into the night air – he had become Officer Vortsch. He was immediately saluted by a waiting officer returning the 'Heil Hitler' with enthusiasm.

There was neither sight nor sound of any other cars following, and Georgie hoped Max wasn't fool enough to follow this closely. Equally, she wished he was somewhere nearby, close enough that he could scoop her up if she wanted – needed – to make a break on foot.

They'd pulled up in front of a low building in a grandiose chalet style, with steps leading up to an imposing front door, Kasper putting out his hand to lead Georgie upwards. Her roaming eyes saw the building was freestanding with little else around, making the high wall opposite seem strangely out of place. Yet she had a sensation, even in the darkness, that they weren't entirely adrift, a distinct feeling of people and buildings nearby. At least the hope of it. It was eerily quiet, but with an underlying hum of a presence and a sour odour, nothing to assault anyone's nostrils but enough to make hers twitch.

Kasper's face was back to gleeful anticipation. 'Please, come on in,' he said. 'I want you to meet everyone.'

There was small vestibule where a tall, thin man in a white waiter's uniform took her coat, and Kasper led her formally into a spacious room with a large dining table down one side, several easy chairs arranged in a loose semi-circle on the opposite side around a fireplace. It was more comfortable and sumptuous than any officer's mess Georgie had seen – the furnishings chintzy and expensive, artwork on the walls, like a living room of the wealthy middle classes.

Most of the easy chairs were occupied by uniformed officers – all SS – drinking and smoking, with several women in evening dress perched on the arm of the chair and, in one case, sat on the lap of an officer, his hand straying noticeably upwards on her thigh. Georgie smiled, though her facial muscles already ached with the effort.

'*Hallo, alle zusammen!*' Kasper announced loudly to the room. 'I'd like you to meet Fraulein Georgie Young. She's a writer, from England.' Kasper's hand was in the small of Georgie's back and he piloted her firmly towards the group, his face flushed with pride.

It hit her squarely then: what she was to him, why she was there, in a roomful of SS officers, in the middle of God knows what and God knows where. *He's presenting me,* she realised.

I'm his trophy.

Hitler had his own clutch of female devotees – she recalled the staring, hypnotised features of women at Nuremberg in their slavish worship of the Führer. And only recently the *Daily Mirror* had run a full-page article on the inexplicable devotion of British debutante Unity Mitford towards Hitler – she the sister of Diana Mosley and the daughter of an English lord, no less. Behind his charm and his smile, Kasper was ambitious. Georgie could see it clearly then. Hitler had his aristocratic disciple, and now Kasper had his own German-loving Brit to parade before his peers. What a coup for the up-and-coming attaché.

She felt sickened. And stupid – beguiled by a bogus charm. Though she'd never been entirely convinced of her attraction, Georgie had felt Kasper at least enjoyed her company. Possibly he had, but tonight her status as an English woman wooed by the Reich's charm was the prize he wanted to display.

And now, Georgie girl, you have to play it to perfection.

The conversation as they sat down to dinner – six couples in total – was light at first, on the clubs in Berlin and films, some of the women grilling Georgie about English fashions, and she thanked her early training in making her cover more convincing. The dinner was heavy German fare of sumptuous meats and richly flavoured vegetables, which the men tore into and the women picked at like birds. The waiters who served them in succession were all painfully thin under their white jackets, cheeks sallow, eyes flat behind fixed expressions. They worked silently, never speaking as they served.

Out of the corner of her eye, she glimpsed one of them practically salivating as he dished out potatoes, pressing his lips as if he was trying to prevent his tongue going rogue and licking his own flesh. He caught her looking and sliced his eyes away instantly, bracing himself for her reprimand. She was in character – all she could do was look away. Georgie knew that plenty of families, Jews especially, were scratching for money to buy food but this seemed extreme. They looked malnourished. Where were they from? Next to several of the officers, whose uniforms strained under the pressure of their bulk, they were mere shadows. The food became instantly bitter on her tongue.

'That's enough! Get out!' One of the officers sparked fury as a wine glass toppled in front of him. He raised his arm in anger, causing another waiter to flinch and cower, his expression now flooded with fear.

They all crept out silently, the officer muttering after them. 'If they can't do a simple job, what's the point in having servants?' He stuffed more pork knuckle into his mouth. 'Fucking idiot Jews, the lot of them.'

The insult was disgusting, though mild compared to the abuse she'd heard at Nuremberg and the grotesque language of *Der Stürmer*. What shocked Georgie was how the table laughed openly and heartily – Kasper included. Fuelled by the wine he was sinking in gulps, his voice grew louder and more boorish by the mouthful.

The waiters were ordered back in, but only to replenish the endless flow of alcohol, and Georgie had to put a hand over her glass more than once, and slip in water when she could. The women, too, went from tipsy to slurring their words, the general conversation morphing from light to grey and then decidedly dark.

'Do you know, we've driven a good portion out of Berlin already, slinking back to their holes in the ground,' the fattest officer boasted. 'I'll be a happy man when not one single filthy Jew is left in this city. The Führer will see us right.'

'Except who will shine our shoes and shovel our shit?' another one pitched in, to more peals of laughter from the table.

'Good point – we'll keep a few just for that,' Kasper joined in.

'Well, you'll soon need one just for your shoes where you're going, eh Vortsch?' the fat one replied with a wink. 'An up-and-coming attaché to Schenk– in Himmler's eyeline too. You'll need to be well turned out for the inner circle.' Kasper feigned embarrassment and blushes, but Georgie saw that he was secretly delighted, while the rest snickered their amusement between forkfuls of meat.

She breathed deeply to keep down the food hovering in her gullet and excused herself to go to the bathroom. Inside the cubicle, she pushed back her head, hoping gravity would discourage the tears eager to spill from her lids. She was out of her depth, surrounded by the filth of these people, one of whom she had badly misjudged from the outset. It had backfired, and now she was stuck.

When would this hideous evening end? And how?

Taking a deep breath, Georgie pinched at her cheeks and practised a full smile in the mirror. It fell instantly as she emerged and almost collided with one of the waiters passing. He stopped and gave way immediately, muttering 'sorry', his face stricken and body bent double in submission.

'No, really, it's fine,' she stammered. *I'm not one of them,* she wanted to scream at him. But he'd scampered away in a flash, and Georgie was left feeling grubby, tarred with the same ignorant, dirty brush as those around the table.

'All right, my English rose?' Kasper slurred at her as she joined the group, now in the semi-circle of chairs. He pulled lightly at her fingers, although he didn't – thankfully – tug hard or try to direct her onto his lap, and she slipped into a chair next to him. He was decidedly drunk, those eyes swimming with inebriation, clearly content that he had already shown off his prize and impressed.

'To the Führer!' one shouted, raising his glass and they all followed suit, brandy slopping on the floor. One of the waiters was on his knees in a flash, mopping near to Georgie's feet, the wet rag nudging at her shoes; instinct made her start to pull away with deep discomfort at this man's servility. Part of her wanted to get down on the floor with him and help. Out of one corner, though, she saw Kasper's look through his fog of alcohol – an expectant glint in his eye. Georgie made a swift shooing motion, as if mildly irritated at the intrusion on her space. Was it enough to play the game?

Thankfully, Kasper's scrutiny was neatly distracted by a junior officer who appeared and opened a curtain against the wall, revealing a projector. He pulled down a screen over the fireplace and Georgie's heart sank at the prospect. A cheer went up among the group as the lights were dimmed and the grainy images started up. At first, Georgie imagined it might be a film featuring one of the women, one having proudly boasted she was 'in films'. The alternative, however, was worse; scene upon scene of various celebrations featuring the Reich's principal star, barking his venom into the microphone, interspersed with snapshots of the Führer 'at play', surrounded by women thrusting their children to be touched as if he were a new messiah.

Unable to stomach the sight, Georgie scanned the room as the black and white images flickered across the attendant faces – they had gone from rowdy to entranced, utterly spellbound.

Still, she couldn't fathom Hitler's apparent magnetism. Could it be because she wasn't German, and hadn't lived through the humiliation of the post-war world, their country forcibly reshaped after 1918 by the Treaty of Versailles? Most Germans voiced that they'd felt scolded like naughty children; Hitler had since reinstated their pride. Even so, what he preached was – to Georgie – pure evil. To anyone, German or not. It was merely one man's hatred against another. And so why was this room, and entire stadiums of people, so taken in?

As if he were reading her mind, Kasper turned his head slowly and leered at her. 'See, I bet the English wish they had someone like our great leader, instead of Chamberlain, a silly little man with an umbrella? What do you say?'

What could she do but say nothing and smile meekly? Inside, the heavy food churned and Georgie wished for nothing more than the clock hands to spin at a faster pace.

The film seemed endless, but it did at least have a soporific effect on the group; the fat one was soon asleep as Adolf's appeal gave way to the alcohol. Once the film ended, Kasper moved lazily to his feet and barked an order for the car. Some of the officers managed to stand and bid them goodbye, but the fat one was slumped in the chair, tongue lolling, and his escort lay across his ample chest, both snoring. Kasper appeared not to notice.

Outside, Georgie looked back at the building where she'd spent an intolerable evening; its appearance took on new meaning then − the shape not of a chalet but a small temple, not unlike something out of Ancient Rome. A symbol of power. It struck her that the dissolute behaviour inside had mimicked rich Romans with slaves at their beck and call, eating to excess and lolling about, togas replaced with SS uniforms. To Georgie, everything about it was depraved and corrupt.

In the car, Kasper struggled to keep awake. 'I trust you had a nice evening?' he slurred.

There was no point in speaking the truth − it would never change them as people and Kasper was too drunk to appreciate sarcasm.

'Enlightening,' Georgie managed, but he was dozing off even as she said it. She looked at him slumped against the leather seat, hair dishevelled, and the collar of his uniform loosened and askew; no longer the charming young officer she had met at the Resi, the one she imagined might be different. Was she such a bad judge of character? Either his Resi persona had been a convincing front or Kasper had changed with his speedy ascent; comments at the dinner made Georgie think it was the latter. Still, she was clear on not wanting anything more to do with it

– or him. This was her last date with Officer Vortsch. She would have to get the information she needed some other way.

The driver drew up outside Frida's flat and Kasper stirred enough to say goodbye, pull up her hand and kiss it lightly. The stench of alcohol oozed from his breath and every pore.

'Until next time,' he said, with that mismatched leer of the very drunk, his eyes unable to focus. He pawed at her, made to grab her hand but she was too quick and he sluggish with inebriation. She was up and out of her seat, mumbled a goodbye and almost ran up the steps of Frida's flat. She wanted a bath, to strip off her clothes and scrub at the filth sticking to her skin, to stop the Nazi infection seeping in.

'Thank God you're back!' Max met her in the hallway as she closed the door, his face a mixture of relief and alarm. Georgie glanced at her watch – it was gone midnight. He came towards her and for a minute she thought he might want to hug her. Did she stiffen? She didn't mean to, and he put a hand on her arm instead. 'We've been really worried.'

Simone was in the living room, and poured Georgie the brandy she so badly needed then.

'Sorry, George,' Max said with true apology. 'I'm not used to driving in Berlin and we lost you on the outskirts as you drove north. Where on earth did you end up?'

Miserably, Georgie recounted her disastrous date. Even Simone, with her cool manner, looked perturbed. 'Sounds terrible,' she said.

'That is me and Nazi officers well and truly finished,' Georgie said, throwing her head back on the cushions. 'I didn't find out anything useful, except how deluded some people can be. And I think I knew that already.'

Simone floated off to bed in her spectral manner, and Max made to leave. She caught him staring at her, an odd look on his face. 'What?' she said.

249

'Nothing. I'm just glad you're safe.' He touched her shoulder as he walked towards the door, but seemed to consider what he said next. 'For what it's worth, you look very nice in that dress.'

'Well, I also feel very grubby,' she said, heaving herself off the sofa. 'I need a good soak and to fall into my bed.'

40

A Fond Farewell

It was either coincidence or good timing, but Rubin was already in the office as Georgie arrived the next morning. He stood sharply as she walked in and seemed almost to dance on the spot.

'Rubin, is anything wrong?'

'We've heard from him, Georgie – we've had word from Elias.' Mercifully, his eyes were bright and his expression upbeat.

Rubin pushed a sheaf of crumpled papers in front of her, though she struggled at first to make out any sense from the scrawl and the jumble of tiny illustrations dotted around the page.

'I'm sorry but I can't quite . . .' she said.

Rubin took the pages back. 'Elias's writing was always bad at the best of times, and now it's worse.' But his voice smacked of happy nostalgia. 'This came through a contact of mine, mixed with other letters smuggled out. They're in Sachsenhausen. In one of the camps.'

Georgie read the relief on Rubin's face that his brother-in-law was alive at least, but the word 'camp' caught on his tongue.

'Elias describes it like a prison,' Rubin went on. 'It's very overcrowded and there's pitiful food – he talks of being hungry all the time. And there are punishment blocks.' He took a breath. 'He's among a lot of Jews, Romanies and Sinti too. But he seems to have found a job in the infirmary, fetching and carrying – a sympathetic doctor maybe. That will thankfully keep him from failing at the really physical work.'

'If it's a prison, have they been charged with anything?' Instantly, Georgie knew the question to be naive. Rubin gave a sideways look: *Being Jewish, that's the crime.*

'Who did these drawings?' she asked, after a brief silence.

'These? Oh, that's Elias – he was always doodling at work.'

There were faces in amongst the scrawl: tiny caricatures and scratched line drawings of men at work, one portrait directly face on. A chill sliced through Georgie's being. She recognised it – not the identity, but that sallow look, scrawny, wanton and fearful. From only the previous evening. The waiter's hollowed eyes looked back at her through Elias's pen.

'Where is Sachsenhausen? Is it near to Berlin?' The rippling inside her was gathering force.

'Yes, it's just north of Berlin, near Oranienburg. Thirty or so kilometres away.' The fact there was prison wall between Rubin and his family didn't seem to faze him – Elias at least felt within arm's reach.

Georgie flooded hot and then cold. She'd been there, in darkness, somewhere near the camp at least. Clearly, the 'temple' was an officer's rest area – for the camp. And she had felt the presence of people nearby, imagining that they were German citizens, happily tucked into their homes – not inmates. The food had stuck in her throat at the time, and now – despite ample time for digestion – it felt ready to purge fully.

What could she do? And what should she tell Rubin about

her close encounter? Nothing yet, she decided, not before talking it over with Max.

'What can we do, Rubin? Who should we go to about Elias?' she said instead, though it seemed futile – if the Reich wanted to imprison people for being Jewish, that's what they did. The lines of men being led away after Kristallnacht proved that. How could they campaign for Elias's release, one amongst thousands?

He shrugged. 'I don't know that we can, Georgie. I'm loath to apply for a visitor's pass, if there is such a thing, since we're not supposed to know where he is. He says that they have an occasional passage for letters like this to get out. I suppose we just have to wait – and hope.'

Georgie's heart bled for him then. Rubin spent his life hoping – for his children's safety and happiness in England, that his wife's spiralling sadness would get no worse, for her brother to stay alive. Always, he dredged optimism from somewhere. In turn, Georgie hoped the world would not let him down.

'Just let me know if there's anything we can do,' she said. It was a meek comment, but needed saying. Independently, she knew what she might have to do, and the dread washed over her. The previous evening, she had vowed to leave the rising, wretched world of Kasper Vortsch behind for good. Only now, maybe that wasn't possible?

Georgie longed to tell Max, but he was away on a 'tour' of Germany, gauging grassroots opinion of the latest developments – that both Britain and France had pledged to defend Poland if that's where Hitler set his next sights. Increasingly, it looked a possibility. But for Georgie, the days were to drag until Max's return.

'You were there, actually in Sachsenhausen? Are you sure?' Max struggled to keep his shock under wraps as they walked towards the Adlon, a weak sun pushing beyond the light cloud. Berlin had climbed out of its post-winter slump and was now firmly into its spring step, the sound of birdsong increasing as they came close to the Tiergarten, sometimes even screening out the tinny lamppost speakers bleating their ceaseless propaganda.

'I wasn't in the camp itself – and no, I'm not entirely sure, but it all seems to add up,' she said. 'The distance we drove and the sign I saw.'

'God, how do you feel about that?' Max said.

'Soiled. But you know, if Elias is there, and I'm in Kasper's favour . . .'

Max stopped abruptly, swivelled on his feet and looked at her with something approaching horror. 'Georgie, don't even think about it.'

'But, Max, I was so close. I have to try. For Rubin, and Sara.'

He carried on walking, annoyance in his long strides, and she had to half run to keep up.

'What are you so irritated about? This is not some story, Max – I'm not going to scoop you, if that's what you're worried about.'

He came to a standstill again, fury on his features that she had never seen before. 'What do you think I am, George? I'm not worried about a *story*. I'm worried about you. It's dangerous. *He* is dangerous. It's not a game.' He marched off again towards the Adlon and Georgie felt her naivety as a sudden, cold shame. Max was right. Kasper's innocence was long gone and he was inching his way into Heinrich Himmler's inner circle, the man generally considered to be the quiet one among the Führer's cronies. His malevolence, however, was not to be underestimated. Even Rod reserved a special distaste for Himmler: 'A healthy fear', he called it.

They walked on in silence, Georgie learning over the months to let Max simmer rather than keep jabbing at the argument.

He would come round. He had to. It was impossible to stand by and do nothing.

The Adlon bar was crowded but not buzzing. There was a sombre air, and for a minute, Georgie thought war had broken out, or that someone close to the circle had died. Max's bureau boss, Cliff, perhaps?

Rod immediately drew her into the crowd, hugged longer and squeezed harder than he normally did. 'They finally got me, kiddo,' he said, holding up a piece of paper. She saw the eagle icon of the Reich first, but the words swam before her eyes.

Rod Faber . . . guilty of transgressions against the Third Reich . . . work permit revoked . . . to leave by . . .

'No! Rod, surely not?'

'Afraid so – my time as a debauched Berliner is at an end.' He was smiling but everyone present could see it was to cover up the real emotions couched under his greying beard.

'But how . . . how can they accuse you?' Georgie was all disbelief. This was a nightmare: Rod – her rock, her strudel mate. She couldn't imagine life without him.

'Bauer got his way. They finally caught me on the envelope plant.'

'The what?'

'It's an old Gestapo trick, but tried and tested,' Bill explained. 'Someone drops off an unmarked envelope at your apartment, packed with incriminating evidence that 'proves' you are working with enemies of the Reich, and the Gestapo pitches up a little while later to do a thorough search. Bingo! You're caught red-handed.'

'They tried it several times, only I got wise quite quickly,' added Rod. 'I had my housekeeper sneak out the back and bring any suspicious packages to the office, where I burnt them tout suite. Those lovely guys in leather coats couldn't figure out why they kept missing their own evidence. I must admit it was quite satisfying watching them sweat as they searched in vain.'

'So what happened this time?' Georgie said.

'My housekeeper was sick and sent another woman in her place. Just my luck it was the day Mr Nazi mailman came to call.'

'Can't you fight it?' Max ventured. The veins in his neck were standing to attention. He was less emotionally attached to Rod, but had an unswerving loyalty to the press pack. Any attack on journalists spiked his anger, and he'd already railed at the Nazi curbing of US radio broadcasts in recent days.

'My paper's already tried that,' Rod said. 'But the exit order is signed by our Joey. Herr Goebbels, it seems, has had enough of my wit.'

'Oh, Rod.' Try as she might, Georgie couldn't help the tears spilling onto her cheeks.

'Hey, hey,' he said, pulling her in for another hug. 'Don't be sad. I will demand regular strudel updates and I'm only going as far as Paris for the time being. It seems the French don't mind having me. Come see me there and we'll check out the patisseries. And the bars.'

She pulled away, wiping away the tears and her embarrassment. Along with Max, she was the newest recruit to the pack, and yet she and Rod had hit it off immediately, thanks to his almost pastoral care; she clearly reminded him of his daughter in the way he looked out for her.

She managed a smile. 'Be careful what you promise, Rod Faber. I *will* be coming to Paris, so don't eat all the pastries before I get there.'

'Yes, Ma'am.'

★

The Reich were impatient for Rod's departure and his leaving 'celebration' – as he insisted on calling it – was a riotous night at La Taverne the next evening. The proprietor, Herr Lehmann, donated two insanely large bottles of champagne and schnapps, and no one left with a clear head. Rod held court at the table, telling tales that were often so bizarre they might have been tall, except Bill was on hand to confirm their content as the honest truth.

'You're only leaving so you can miss our dear Führer's fiftieth birthday party,' one radioman shouted from the across the table.

'Too true,' Rod admitted, 'though I daresay what I might write about that would get me kicked out of Germany anyway!'

Rod held his glass high and made his farewell speech, voice wobbling with emotion more than the spirits inside him. 'I challenge all you glorious hacks with a task,' he concluded. 'And that is to make the lives of our dear Nazi friends as difficult as possible in their pursuit of propaganda. Long live the press hounds!' Georgie joined in the resounding cheer as she glimpsed Bill's features grow dark, the sadness at losing his best friend outweighing her own.

With thick heads and heavy hearts, a small group spent Rod's next, remaining day in various cafés, downing coffee and strudel and looking at their watches, hoping the hands would turn slowly until his evening train. The appointed time arrived all too soon, and Georgie was in two minds about saying goodbye at the station, certain she would never manage to keep her emotions in check.

'Come on,' Max chivvied. 'You'll regret it if you don't go. And Rod needs the help – he's got that much strudel stashed in his suitcase.'

The Reich had dictated his leaving should be swift and quiet, alongside Herr Bauer's whispered warnings against a 'spectacle'. Thankfully, it fell on deaf ears. The platform at Zoo station was packed with forty or so noisy journalists, one of whom had set up his portable radio broadcast equipment in direct protest at the recent curb; he was giving a running commentary while Rod basked in the demonstration of dissent. Gestapo men were unashamedly taking photographs of anyone in the group, and in a cheeky retort, some of the journalists formed a line and posed for them. Rod stood beaming his approval.

'Please don't hug me too much,' Georgie begged, as the train let off steam and prepared to leave. 'You might just squeeze all the tears out of me.'

'Understood, kiddo.' He gripped her hand tightly instead. 'It's not goodbye, nor *auf wiedersehen*, merely *à bientôt*. I'll see you in Paris.' He winked and climbed into the carriage.

She wasn't alone in the tears; Bill's moustache was distinctly wet, along with Frida's cheeks and – unusually – Simone too. 'End of an era,' Bill muttered. 'I shall miss the old bastard.'

41

Making Plans

Georgie felt the void left by Rod acutely over the next week or so; the very knowledge that he'd been nearby, or propping up the Adlon bar, always made the world seem at less of a spin. His absence cast a gloomy shadow, and although his replacement was a competent reporter who slotted in well, it wasn't her beloved Rod.

The foreign news focus had switched briefly to Italy, where Mussolini – in an effort to play alongside the big boys and show his fascist might – had invaded Albania with little resistance. There seemed to be a dictator's pattern forming. Hitler, for his part – and with no hint of irony – accused Britain of trying to encircle Germany with anti-Nazi feeling: the oppressor claiming to be the victim to his own people, the warmonger painted as peacemaker. *Very clever propaganda,* thought Georgie, darkly. *Well done, Joey.*

One bright spot was the reaction to Rod's station farewell; Herr Bauer's glare at the weekly briefing was enough to know they had touched a nerve and there were nudges all round as they sat like reprimanded children in front of his lectern.

Unusually for the Nazi Party, who were never shy about voicing their animosity, Bauer's actual comments were disguised. 'The party hopes press reactions will remain unbiased' was one comment, to derisory sniggers from the reporters. When had the Nazis ever been impartial about anything?

The questions from the floor – delivered with a deliberate, innocent air – prodded at the regime's hypocrisy, until Bauer's blustering became so obvious that he barked, 'No more questions' and flounced off. One up to Rod Faber and the pack.

Georgie arrived home from the briefing to a letter, addressed with familiar script; had it not been for the Amsels' plight, she would have gladly tossed it in the bin without opening it. Frida was lying on the sofa with a book as Georgie slumped on the chair opposite, releasing a heavy sigh.

'More from your SS boy?' Frida said. She would have noted the Reich icon pulsing like a beacon on the post pile.

'Sadly, yes.'

'Not the charmer you thought he was?' Frida lay her book down and sat up, puppy eyes wide with interest.

'How did you guess?'

'Because,' Frida said, with too much sagacity for her age, 'they all lose the initial appeal over time. Did he get hellishly drunk on the third date?'

'Yes. How did you know that?' Georgie hadn't spoken to Frida in detail since before she had left that night, though Simone might well have told her.

'Bitter experience. The Nazis are a shrewd bunch for sure, but they haven't yet figured out that making alcohol freely available to their officers always backfires in the end.' She grinned with her copious, red lips. 'On the other hand, it's a bonus for those of us who want to wheedle out a few choice snippets. It tends to loosen their tongues. And makes them slow when you have to dodge their roaming hands.'

Frida had either been a fly on the wall in Kasper's car, or she was describing a typical scenario – no doubt her source of many hot tips from inside the Reich. More and more, it became apparent that Kasper was no different to the swathe of arrogant young bucks in the grey and black uniform; enticed by power, kudos and everything that went with it – wine, women and song. It was undeniably time she used him properly too. Fair's fair: if she was his trophy, Kasper could be her unwitting mole.

His short note was full of apology, not about his chosen venue or the behaviour of the company, but 'indulging too much to pay you due attention'. Would she allow him to make it up to her?

'He's apologising for getting drunk,' Georgie said to Frida, who had gone back to her book.

'They always do,' she muttered from behind the page. 'Don't expect any different the next time. If you're going to repeat the occasion, make sure it's for a very good reason.'

Georgie thought of Rubin's face on reading Elias's letter. The hope etched in his aged features that his brother-in-law would survive. It was reason enough. Wasn't it?

The next afternoon, Max put his chin into both hands, elbows on the table at Café Bauer. 'So, you think you might be able to get him to talk? Ply him with drink and say, "Hey, Kasper, what about doing me a favour and letting one of those chaps go?"'

Georgie creased her brow. 'You don't have to be so sarcastic,' she snapped. 'I am just trying to help.'

Max's face softened, and his hand reached out for hers as she stared out beyond the window; in the breeze, the flags had become a river of red.

'I know you are, but we have to be realistic, and make sure you're safe.'

'We?' She pulled back her hand. 'I thought you didn't want anything to do with this.'

'Oh, don't be so dramatic.' He almost laughed. 'Of course I'm going to be with you, and a better tail this time. But it has to be worthwhile, doesn't it? We – *you* – need to have a plan, or a script, to turn the conversation around to Sachsenhausen and the inmates. And you might have to turn on the charm quite a bit.'

Georgie felt sick at the very prospect. Having initially thought Kasper attractive, she now realised his beauty was truly skin deep. And very close to the surface. Even his eyes had taken on a devilish air in her mind. Only her deep fondness for the Amsels and concern for their future mitigated the idea of him physically fawning over her.

'Well, I'll just have to put on my best act, won't I?'

Max looked at her, lips flattened in that 'okay-if-you-say-so' way. Ironically, and with the world around them increasingly precarious, Georgie felt he had become more relaxed and open in recent weeks. He was no longer the angry and angst-filled Max of old, and it was a welcome transformation. He was proving a true and valued friend.

42

The Birthday Boy

15th April 1939

Despite her keenness for it to be over and done with, Kasper was put on hold for several weeks as there was plenty to keep everyone occupied. Georgie had penned a reply, hoping he wouldn't detect a reluctance in her tone, and said she would be 'delighted' for him to make amends. A day later, his reply arrived – he was tied up with preparations for the Führer's birthday celebrations and couldn't meet until the first week of May. Although it felt like fending off the inevitable, the reprieve brought a sense of relief.

The preparations for a grown man's birthday were exhaustive; a city already adorned with emblems and banners became entirely shrouded in black, white and crimson, and soon every lamppost, statue and government building projected the great leader's image as he reached his half century.

'I remember my fiftieth,' the *Times*' chief correspondent bemoaned at La Taverne one evening. 'We went down the pub and had a good drink, and my wife made me a birthday cake. I was quite content with that. Isn't this all a bit like a children's party – my balloons are bigger than yours type of thing?'

'But you're not the leader of what might become the free world, if he has his way,' the *Daily Express* man piped up. 'I'm not sure a pint and a slice will suffice.'

'Did someone say "free world"?' a voice butted in, and the table threw up a burst of laughter in derision. Humour, even when couched in the dark truth, had become their currency, their way to soldier on.

The birthday of 20th April was predictable and pompous – a seemingly ceaseless, four-hour parade aimed at showing the world what military strength Germany had amassed, perpetual cheering and estimates of a million Germans gathered to see their Führer soaking up the adulation. Georgie looked on as Hitler stood, half-smiling (though it was difficult to assess under *that* moustache), and found herself missing most of his speech; there was something about his guttural ranting that made her brain immediately switch off. She borrowed notes off a fellow reporter and then realised she could have easily written her piece without them, given it was the self-same invective as his previous speeches, steeped in vitriol.

'You'd think he might lighten up a bit on his birthday,' Max had whispered in her ear.

'No such luck.' Georgie couldn't help wondering what Rod would have thought of it, and his subsequent, acidic report in the *New York Times*. Typing up her observations meant curbing her own opinions, or risk being on the same exit train out of Berlin. There was no need, however, for such restraint in a postcard, and she felt every need to write it, whether Henry saw fit to print it or not.

Dear Englanders

Speeches are a particular speciality of Herr
Hitler; give Germany's leader a pulpit, a lectern
or even a soapbox and he will avail you of all he
thinks, in glorious detail. We in Berlin are treated
frequently to the Nazi view on the Jewish population,
Germany's rights to all manner of lands, and the
evils of its neigbouring nations. The Führer is
free with his speech. Sadly, others do not have
that luxury – only whispered in cafés and bars, and
curtailed in the street.

And now in the press, it seems: a pillar of our
correspondents' circle only recently ousted from the
city he loves. His crime? Simply telling the truth,
German warts and all, with his own honest pen. Should
we stand by and watch Hitler use more than words
in pursuit of his vision? See him progress to using
the cosh perhaps, or the military hardware he loves
to boast of? Or worse? Very soon, Europe will have
to decide.

Farewell from the 'free' world of Berlin

Georgie pulled the sheet from her typewriter, narrowed her
eyes at her own audacity and laughed to herself. It was the most
political she'd ever dared to be; even if it never saw the light of
day, it made her feel better. 'What the hell,' she said to the empty
air of the office. 'Stick that in your pipe and smoke it, Herr Bauer.'

Days later, Hitler was on the podium again, this time on his
home territory of the Reichstag parliament, where he all but
tore up the Anglo-German Naval agreement of old, and the
German–Polish Non-Aggression Pact. Sitting in the press box,
which was surrounded by fat-necked politicians, Georgie had

a sudden image of each treaty or pledge as bottles lined up on a wall, the Nazis picking them off one by one, using their best sniper. The atmosphere on each occasion was dark and tenuous, as if the world might spill over into conflict any minute, the consequences chewed over at the Adlon and La Taverne.

In the light of day, however, the tension always seemed to dissipate. The military was increasingly present on Berlin's streets, in shops, bars and cafés, Gestapo potentially in every crevice. Paul was dead, Rod expelled and Elias imprisoned. And yet life went on, with many of the reporters taking short sabbaticals to recharge their batteries, either in the Alps, or the safety of Geneva and Paris.

It was like watching a storm brewing from across the deep Gloucestershire valleys back home – willing it to divert, and yet knowing that those black clouds had to dispense their load somewhere. Who, in the end, would get well and truly soaked by this caustic storm?

She said as much over coffee to Sam, who had rapidly become a barometer and her sounding board of reason in their regular café rendezvous. He saw it from the British perspective, forced by his role to protect borders from an influx of refugees, yet not blind to the lines of desperate families queuing to escape Germany's oppression.

'I've said it before, Georgie – you just can't help everyone,' he urged. 'If one or two get out alive and free, then their families carry on and thrive. You have to be content with that.'

'But why can't the outside world see what's coming?' she lamented. 'It's so obvious.'

'They do,' Sam replied, with his look of knowing – and access to embassy communications.

'Then why don't they do something?' She lowered her voice to barely a whisper. 'Stop him?'

'Probably because – like the rest of us – they are terrified of what lighting the touch paper will do.'

43

The Right Thing

Sara sank her head into her hands, solace in the dark of her own skin; space to absorb this latest bombshell.

'Don't you see, Sara? I have to go. I have to do my bit, take part.' Rubin's normal persuasiveness verged on pleading.

'But what if something happens to you? It's dangerous!' Her voiced muffled by flesh, then clearer as her head snapped up, dejected. 'I thought it was enough you went to the meetings, but this . . . I couldn't bear losing you, Rubin. Not after everyone else.'

'But you won't, I promise,' he said, pulling her head into the crook of his arm, her hair coarse and dusty from her factory job, filthy and exhausting work but which she did without complaint. 'I'll be careful, my love. I'll come back to you. *For* you.'

He rubbed his thumb on her cheek, knew he would find tears to brush away. 'But the underground, they've worked so hard to create this route, and it's my place to help. It's not just for Elias. It's for so many others. And you know how important the letters are for us, don't you?'

'Yes, yes,' she sniffed. 'And I'm proud of you, Rubin. I am. But I'm also afraid. That's normal, isn't it?'

'Yes, Sara, it is,' he murmured. Though Rubin Amsel wasn't quite sure what 'afraid' meant any longer; blended so expertly these days with terror, defeat, despondency and death. It was just another word. Feeling had become a luxury he couldn't afford.

44

A Welcome Breath

Despite an ever-present shroud of threat, the first few days of May settled into a lull. It seemed the perfect time for Georgie to recharge herself, especially when Kasper sent apologies for another delay in their meeting, causing irritation then relief. His deferral provided the opportunity to exit Berlin for a few days.

As the train crawled out of Zoo station, she felt the tension seep from her shoulders, replaced with an expectation of light over dark. Rod greeted her in his own special way, showing her the sights of Paris in a whirlwind week. They ate pastries, and a lot else besides – what would her mother think of her sampling snails? Rod introduced her to the bars he favoured and the friends within. He seemed content, and undeniably more relaxed than he had been in those final few weeks.

'I'd lived with the rise of the Nazis for so many years I suppose I didn't notice the tension creeping up alongside,' he said. 'Now I'm relatively free of it, I realise how Berlin has become such a pressure cooker.'

'Waiting to explode?' Georgie raised her eyebrows.

'I'm afraid it's inevitable, kiddo.' He stared into the froth of his coffee. 'Just make sure you have an escape route ready. Please.'

'Surely foreign correspondents will be protected?' she ventured. 'We'll still have reporting rights, war or not.'

'Probably,' Rod said. 'But if you think life in Germany is oppressive now, imagine how it will be when Hitler has carte blanche to ride roughshod over everyone. Goebbels and Bauer too. The question is: will you want to be there?'

Their conversation was timely; sitting in a café over newspapers and croissants, they learned six Britons had been expelled from Germany in some tit-for-tat political scrap, the chief correspondent on the *Daily Express* among them. Another empty spot at La Taverne.

Hitler was increasingly pushing for control of Danzig city, and British fascist devotee Oswald Mosley had marched in London with 3,000 disciples in tow. The smattering of tables nudging the wide Parisian boulevard seemed a world away, spring sunshine lighting the sky and the mood. Couples were holding hands, friends talking with animation, and only a few military uniforms darkened the tone. This was how the majority of Europe, to the west of Germany at least, was living life. Unencumbered. And while Georgie was loving it, this precious contact with Rod, she couldn't help thinking the approaching storm should be met with some preparation.

Why wasn't the rest of the world truly afraid? Did everyone have to live directly under Hitler's tyranny to realise his vile capabilities?

Leaving the beauty and freedom of Paris was a wrench, and seeing Rod's form disappear as the train pulled away from the platform made her heart twist with sadness. At the other end, however, the familiarity of Berlin proved a strange comfort –

the smell of bratwurst and the coffee stalls at the station. Yes, that added odour of mistrust too, but she had missed it all the same.

Rubin was there to meet her, helping with her luggage into a taxi. 'Herr Max has asked that I take you home – he wants to talk to you about something.' He paused, coughed slightly and clarified. '*We* want to talk to you.'

'Do you now?' Georgie replied, though she was more intrigued than annoyed at the presumption. And she could never be irritated at Rubin.

She was unable to be cross with Max either, waiting at Frida's with a beautifully prepared dinner, plus cocktails. She eyed him suspiciously at first. 'Who did this?' she asked, gesturing to the table.

'I did.' He looked slightly affronted. 'I can cook, you know. I'm not a total Neanderthal.'

'Never said you were.' Though she couldn't disguise her sheepish presumption. Was it all for her and Rubin?

'Where are Frida and Simone?' Georgie looked around the empty flat.

'At the cinema,' he said. 'German film – way beyond my language skills. Besides, Rubin and I have got a proposition for you.'

'So, go on, I'm all ears.' She sat down and eyed the food hungrily.

Max and Rubin exchanged looks and Max nodded. 'We're going to make a trip to Sachsenhausen,' the older man said.

The transport of letters from Elias and others had been via a small underground resistance group, made up mainly of Jews, and Rubin admitted to being among the circle for some time.

'I couldn't tell you before because I was afraid of the implications for you,' he went on. 'That you might be put in a position to cover up for me.'

'So why tell us now?'

'Basically, I was very nosy and wheedled it out of him,' Max cut in.

The conduit for the letters was a night-time drop from a junior guard, paid handsomely for his services, and it was Rubin's turn to pick up the package.

'And I've volunteered us as drivers and look-outs,' Max added, though Georgie guessed at a second motive – her being able to confirm it as the site of her evening with Kasper.

It didn't sound like much like a fun excursion to Georgie. Did she want to revisit memories from that dreadful evening? Definitely not. And yet, the temptation was too good. She would have been furious with Max if he had gone without telling her – and he knew it. He had read her perfectly, prodding her weak spot in helping the Amsels. Max, surely, was driven by excitement and subterfuge. And if she was entirely honest, duty was not her sole motivator either.

'All right,' she said. 'When do we go?'

45

The Temple Revisited

Oranienburg and Berlin, 28th May 1939

The town of Oranienburg seemed different in the evening dusk; a small collection of squat stoical German houses gathered around the archetypal town square and train station. Georgie's eyes darted back and forth the entire journey, attempting to prod at her memory. But nothing emerged; it had been dark during her last journey and her attention then focused firmly on Kasper and his amusement, with little hope of logging any landmarks.

Max drove the borrowed car, its licence plate carefully doctored to give a false identification, skirting the town and parking up in a residential street.

'Is this it?' Georgie queried. There was nothing to indicate a camp was nearby, the sole movement a lone cat padding across the road. She had no visual clues, only a faint prickling in her nostrils.

'Beyond the next street,' Rubin said. He was virtually twitching under his jacket, eyes fixed on the space ahead. 'We're early, and we need to wait until it's dark.'

Max was quiet in the front with Rubin, his breathing measured. They all knew how it should play out: they would park a little way from the camp entrance and Rubin skirt the perimeter on foot – he had a roughly drawn map in his pocket passed on from the last collector – with Max hovering not far behind, a link in case Georgie needed to make an audible signal to both of them from the car. It was a sign with only one meaning: *We need to leave! Quickly!*

The package would have been buried under the fence some time during that day – if they were lucky – and Rubin would retrieve it. It sounded simple enough, but they couldn't yet see the look-out posts raised high on wooden platforms, overlooking the fence. Or the guards with guns cocked and ready.

The minutes crawled by, air inside the car becoming thick and stale. Two women with small dogs walked down the road, their eyes flicking towards the car as they talked. Suspicion rained upon everyone in Germany, it seemed – the Nazis had skilfully made potential spies of everyone, creating so much mistrust among people who would otherwise be neighbours.

Rubin kept his head still, like a child, and, from the front seat, Max muttered, through clenched teeth. 'Just smile at them, George. Nothing too cheesy, just a friendly nod.' George felt her skills as an actress reaching their zenith as she tipped up her chin in greeting and tried to look nothing like a woman on a highly suspect quest. The women returned her look but didn't smile, walking on without a backward glance.

Finally, the dark descended and Rubin looked at his watch. 'Three minutes,' he said, peering at the pencilled map for the last time. Max started the car and drove around the corner to a parallel street. This road was wider with no houses, but it was the cobbled surface under the wheels that stabbed at Georgie's memory, in rumbling slowly towards the temple with Kasper. She peered into the gloom but saw very little, aside from a high, rough-brick barrier looming in the darkness. So, the divide she'd seen then *had* been a wall, to barricade people in – to unlawful imprisonment. How comforting her naivety had been then. And how much more would she have wanted to escape the temple if she'd known the stark truth?

'If I'm not back within ten minutes, just leave. Both of you.' Rubin's steely voice sliced the atmosphere. He turned towards Georgie and his face had never looked so determined.

'But . . .' she started.

'No buts,' he said firmly. 'I mean it. You should not be caught. Max?'

'Understood. Ten minutes, from now.' He looked at his watch and they both opened the door.

'Okay, George?' Max checked as she slid into the driver's seat. He smiled through the car window, but it was so obviously fuelled by adrenalin and not the reassurance she wanted.

'Yes, fine.' But she wasn't. Of course. Why would she be? She was a reporter, a virtual cub despite her new title as senior bureau chief. Just yards from a Nazi-run camp, where unspeakable acts were being perpetrated on people guilty only of being born into one sub-stratum or another. The world really had tipped upside down very, very quickly. All she could do was watch as their bodies were swallowed by the gloom.

If the minutes had dragged in waiting for darkness, now the seconds moved at a snail's pace, each rustled leaf or squeak of wildlife piquing her attention. She opened the window, allowing her ears to tune in to the night sounds, and stem the slow grind of nausea inside her guts. *Concentrate, George. Concentrate.*

Five minutes in, she heard the growl of an engine starting ahead, felt herself sinking automatically down in the driver's seat when headlights sparked into life. Was it coming from outside the temple? Were they that close? She froze as the yellowy orbs became larger and brighter, almost blinding, and a car rolled slowly alongside over the cobbles. It was stupid but instinctive: she turned her head sideways and looked at the car's occupants, saw the Reich flag flutter just before she glimpsed the lone body in the back seat, lit by something inside. Owlish glasses and a stern man's face glanced in return, though not with any great recognition, merely curiosity. He – anyone – would have been thinking: what is that woman doing here? Parked up, in the darkness, alone. Or speculated she wasn't alone, perhaps a man beneath her, skulking out of sight. Georgie didn't care then what anyone thought of her reputation, only that they dismissed her as idling, innocently or not.

There was something in the man's face, though, that tweaked at her memory while the car's back lights receded into the distance, a shadow of the familiar. He wasn't in uniform – even with a brief glimpse there was no glint of pips or epaulettes – so unlikely to be an officer from that awful night. Clearly, it was her imagination running riot, fuelled by anxiety at the minutes ticking by to seven and then eight. Where was Max? He was supposed to be hovering on the edge of the small brush of trees, eyes on the car and ears towards Rubin. But there was no sign. Should she get out, peer into the sparse wooded area? And do what?

The hands on her watch began to speed up. Nine . . . nine and half minutes. Her neck pulsed with a sudden, intense heat. She sparked the engine into life. Her father had taught her to drive, insisting it was a life skill everyone should have; she was rusty, though, and hadn't admitted as much to Max. Georgie winced as the gear cranked noisily into forward and then reverse, turning the car around in several back and forward moves, bobbling slowly over the stones and wary of the attention of any more late-night walkers.

Even in the shadows, her watch registered ten minutes and

she stuck fast, with no intention of abandoning them both. Her eyes were fixed on the rear-view mirror for any sign, the window rolled down for any twitch of the undergrowth. Tick, tick . . . the seconds crept towards eleven minutes. *Come on! Where are you?* She willed their arrival with every bone and muscle in her body.

The assault on her ears seemed to come from everywhere; a swaying light in the mirror with shouts in her left ear to accompany, and in her right, more shouts, closer and moving swiftly. Urgent. Desperate.

'. . . un, Rubin . . . run!' She caught only half of the words, but it was undoubtedly Max's cry, his breathless pleas spraying backwards into the darkness. Georgie swivelled her head to see him emerge from the bushes near to the wall, stop and say again – 'Come on! Nearly there' – making scooping motions with his hand, as if to reel in Rubin like a large fish.

Her foot was brushing the accelerator in readiness. Rusty or not, that was instinctive.

Finally, out of the blackness there was a second body emerging – the slower, slightly more solid frame of Rubin from between the foliage, Max stretching to pull at his arm and dragging him towards the car door. The glow behind them was not headlights, as she first feared, but several torches, their beams swinging in the blackness and catching the back of the car. But they were moving closer, along with the sound of boots clattering on the cobbles, the smack of their soles more pronounced with every second.

'Halt! halt!' voices ordered loudly as they sprinted towards the car.

Intent on the lights in the mirror, Georgie felt the weight of Max thud into the back of car, followed by a second heft that she took to be Rubin.

'Drive! *DRIVE!*' Max shouted and her foot slammed down

on the pedal, the car juddering and almost bunny-hopping across the road surface, wheels screeching and a smell of burning oil flooding the air as Georgie willed the engine to work even faster. The shouts receded into the background and Georgie allowed herself a gulp of air – her first for what seemed like an age – only to have it snatched back as there was a crack behind and something hard ricocheted off the metal body of the car with such force that it could only have been a bullet.

'Are you both all right?' Georgie cried, driving as fast as she dared, unsure of which direction, but away from the town and buildings and towards the black and anonymous countryside. Behind them, the torchlights became pinpricks in the mirror. Only then did Georgie begin to breathe properly, her heart still at a fierce gallop, slamming her chest wall until it hurt.

'Rubin?' questioned Max, as they slowed to a normal driving pace. The older man had uttered nothing since they'd leapt into the car.

'Yes, I'm fine . . . fine.' He was still panting, with exertion or fear it was difficult to tell, but Georgie relaxed a little. Despite being short of breath, he sounded like the Rubin she knew.

'Max, where's this coming from? Are you hurt?' Then, it was Rubin's voice in a mild panic. She daren't take her eyes off the road, but Georgie could hear the two righting themselves in the back seat, one hauling the other onto the leather seat and a distinct groan.

'There's a lot of blood,' Rubin said.

A fresh injection of panic speared her heart. 'Max? *Max?*' Silence. 'Rubin, what's wrong with him?'

She drew into a small lay-by between some trees, pitch dark around them and no lights visible for at least a couple of miles – the last of which had felt an eternity until it was safe to stop. They managed to stem the bleeding with Georgie's scarf and by the weak light of a fading torch, she looked at the wound on Max's lower leg as he lay on the back seat.

'How bad is it?' He grimaced, a delayed dread and pain taking hold.

Georgie was no nurse, but neither was she squeamish. She looked hard at the four-inch gash, flesh red and raw underneath. It was deep. Almost certainly, it needed stitching and cleaning well to avoid infection. It wasn't hard to guess that Max had been torn on barbed wire, his own adrenalin acting as a powerful analgesic until they had made it into the car.

'We need to get you to a hospital,' Georgie said. Each flashed a look – the same, shared thought: *How do we explain this?*

Rubin took over the driving until they reached the more populated city boundary, while Georgie applied an even pressure on the wound, Max's leg on her lap in the back seat.

'I'm really sorry if I've got blood on your skirt,' he said, head back and teeth set together.

'Oh, this old thing,' she played along, 'it's just a rag.' The fact that it had cost her half a weekly wage in Wertheim's was not worth saying. To have Max there at all, in the back of the car and not lying on those cobbles outside a Nazi camp, was compensation enough.

'Here we are,' Rubin announced, drawing up in a darkened suburban street, no hospital in sight. Max limped into the house with help, disappearing into a room with a grey-haired man, whom Rubin addressed as 'doctor'.

'He's a good man,' he told Georgie. 'And discreet.'

They were silent for a while, staring at the paintings on the parlour wall, the man's wife supplying them with tea, a sympathetic smile but asking no questions; one who knew the value of necessary ignorance. The tea was hot and strong, acting like an antidote to everything that had happened. With each sip, Georgie's heart was persuaded back into its rightful cavity. The more she went over each moment, the more surreal it seemed – a high-speed chase, being shot at. It meant something, and more than her being terrified. It meant that the Reich did not want anyone near their camp, witnessing what they were doing. It followed that they might not be ashamed, still be righteous as Nazis in their beliefs, but they knew the world at large would view their methods differently. Outsiders would think it wrong. Morally so.

'It's a long way from protective custody, isn't it?' Georgie murmured, turning to Rubin. She remembered writing a story in the days after Kristallnacht, reporting on Goebbels's insistence that Jews would not be allowed to emigrate, imprisoned instead. She felt confused then: emigration was an easy way for the Nazis to rid themselves of a race they loathed. Only not the most permanent. And it was that conclusion which created a fresh dread.

'Yes, it is,' Rubin replied, and he pulled a package wrapped in filthy material from inside his jacket – the object of their mission, a treasure trove of communication. They sifted through the bundle: snippets of letters on scraps of paper, empty packets and even ragged patches of material addressed to a whole host of families; drawings and doodles – detailed or drawn in haste – simple lines depicting a prisoner laid over some kind of trestle, a guard and whip being employed. No animation was needed in reflecting the plain, abject cruelty. The various scrawled messages were not letters of love, though the words tried to give some cheer: 'We'll be out of here soon, I feel sure', 'Don't worry about your papa'. Mostly, it aimed at simple information – this is what it's like. The subtext for Georgie and possibly for Rubin, given the sad expression as he read, was far more chilling. *This is only the beginning of what they can do.*

Max emerged from across the hallway, wincing with each step. The doctor handed him a small package. 'One or two twice a day, until it starts to ease,' he said. 'Rubin will bring you back when it's safe, and I'll remove the stitches.'

'Thank you. I really appreciate it.' He was clearly in pain, but more relieved not to have an official German doctor quizzing him about a ragged tear to his flesh.

Georgie drove them back to Frida's flat, insisting on Max staying the night, on the sofa if necessary. She was tempted to offer Simone's bed, but still wasn't sure of their relationship and how far it extended. And he didn't ask. Rubin said he would chance returning the car quickly under cover of darkness, strip the registration plates and get back to Sara.

'We'll meet in the office in the morning?' he said. They all needed to unpick what had happened and what, if anything, they would do next.

Never seeing herself as a natural nursemaid, Georgie had a sudden urge to make cocoa from her package of English goods – it was her mother's natural panacea when anyone fell ill at home. She perched on one end of the sofa as Max lay with his leg raised on the cushions, and handed him a steaming cup.

He sipped, closed his eyes and breathed deeply. 'Nurse Young, now that is very good cocoa,' he announced.

'Less of the nurse, please. And when did you ever have cocoa at home?' It was surely not sophisticated enough to be a regular in the Spender house?

He raised his head, looked faintly insulted, but only sighed. 'We had it in the infirmary at school,' he said. 'Matron Taylor put in extra milk for her "sicklings", and sometimes she would sneak in a hug as she gave it to you. I loved her madly – we all did. The infirmary was full to bursting with not very sick boys.' He smiled at the memory; in Georgie it sparked only sadness for him and those poor boys, missing their mothers, when hers was ever present. And eternally loving.

'Well, that was certainly what you'd call a night,' he added after a pause. Georgie nodded into her own cup. Nothing more to be said, not until the morning. She was suddenly so tired that even the memory of their near capture might not keep her awake. Draining her cocoa, she pulled herself from the sofa and held out her hand for Max's cup. For a second, her mind was elsewhere, focused on some piece of life trivia, and that's when it struck her.

'I've got it!' she cried. 'I know who he is.'

'Who?' Max was roused from the soporific effects of cocoa.

'The man in the car. It's been driving me mad all evening. I was sure I knew him from somewhere. It's just come to me.'

'Who?' Max repeated, with slight irritation. 'What the hell are you talking about?'

46

A Doctor's Appointment

Berlin, 29th May 1939

'Doctor Graf,' she announced to Rubin at the office the next morning. 'It was the doctor from the Haas Institute driving away from the camp last night.'

She and Max had discussed it the previous evening, and again at breakfast – whether or not to mention it to Rubin, a fact that could only increase his worry and anxiety without any real explanation. Doctor Graf may have been a visiting physician to Sachsenhausen, or attending a social event, as Georgie had done. But it didn't seem likely. The fact she and Max had been led to him via Paul Adamson and his beliefs about wrongdoing at the institute made his presence suspicious at best. Georgie recalled their conversation on her visit to the clinic: 'We pride ourselves on end-of-life care,' Doctor Graf had said. His subtext then had been abundantly clear. One tiny step further was euthanasia.

All three looked from one face to another, sharing thoughts again, Rubin's features twisted as he absorbed this latest blow to his family's existence. The Nazis were capable, certainly, but

283

would they really do that? Killing for no reason other than infirmity, or what they saw as 'defects'? Georgie watched him nod subconsciously to himself.

'I think we need to look at our Doctor Graf again,' Max said. 'Don't you?'

All three felt a sense of urgency over Elias's predicament, but it was frustrated by the demands of work and Max's injury. His leg was clearly painful and took longer than expected to fully heal, his limp explained away to all – even those at the Adlon – as 'a damn fool fall down the stairs'. Georgie was unsure whether he'd told Simone the truth, but she said nothing when they met in the flat over breakfast or dinner. The scar on his leg remained a deep purple welt, though he joked, 'It's the only war wound I'm ever likely to see.'

With spectacularly bad timing, Henry requested Georgie do her own tour of several German cities, this time gauging opinion from any Italian connections she could discover, Germany and Italy having recently signed their own military alliance, known as the 'Pact of Steel'. And while it was good to get out of Berlin again, what she did find among small pockets of Italian sympathisers was predictably brash and frankly dull. Among Germans, by contrast, Mussolini was seen as a pompous, blustering figurehead – their own version of the much-mocked Göring – and he was viewed as a weak link, not equal to the power of Hitler. It felt to Georgie like pedestrian journalism at best, and nothing like the mystery waiting back in Berlin.

She returned to find it was Rubin who'd made the most progress. In his spare hours between newspaper work, he'd been able to keep a watch on Doctor Graf's house; it didn't take much to discover a medic's home address, a large house on the edge of Lake Wannsee. Judging by the number of servants passing in and out, business at the Haas clinic was thriving. Rubin learned that Dr Graf was a creature of habit; he left at the same time every day, lunched at one of three different restaurants, and returned home by train to his wife between eight and nine every evening. His routine was predictable, including his twice-weekly visit to a small basement club amid the nightlife centre of Kurfürstendamm which – when he hovered around the back entrance – Rubin discovered was anything but upstanding. The good doctor had his peculiarities too.

'We'll have to get someone inside that club and engage him in conversation,' Max said on regrouping in Rubin's flat. Georgie's paranoia over her office walls sprouting ears meant she felt uncomfortable talking at the bureau. And as much as they hated it, and railed against it personally, Berlin had all but shut down to Jews in public – even in permitted venues, the trio attracted unwanted attention. Being the kindest of souls, Rubin eased their guilt by suggesting his own home when Sara was at work. 'I doubt the Gestapo are looking at us now – we have nothing left to give,' he half-joked as he served up coffee, not intending to pull at their heartstrings, though his forbearance depressed Georgie further – and stoked her fury against the Reich.

'There's a fair chance Graf would recognise me from the clinic,' Georgie said with secret relief. 'Besides, I'm not enough of an actress to pull off the persona of a club girl.'

At the word 'actress', Max shifted with optimism. 'Will Margot be back from Frankfurt?' he ventured.

'Possibly,' Georgie said. 'Shall I give her a call?'

'Do you think she'd do it?

In the end, Margot was both – returned from Frankfurt and willing to help. 'I worked the clubs as a budding actress,' she said. 'I know exactly what these fine professional men want from a place like that.'

285

Max started, eyes wide with shock. 'No, Margot, you don't have to . . .'

'Don't worry, you rarely have to go that far,' Margot assured him. 'You take them to a certain point – it's the tease they so often enjoy. Then they can pretend to themselves and their wives that they're not actually being unfaithful. Poor sops.'

Her expression, however, was anything but sympathetic. Time and distance had not healed her sorrow over Paul's death; it was evident that if she could help flush out his killers then she would do almost anything. For such a young woman, Margot appeared to have a real measure on life, possessing a confidence Georgie often craved for herself. Still, for all her beauty and talent, Fraulein Moller cut a lonely figure. Her pain at losing Paul remained raw.

It was two weeks later that Georgie found herself in the driver's seat again, the mid-June sunshine and vivid memories of her last time behind a wheel prickling against her skin. At least Rubin was sitting beside her, sharing the anxiety of the wait. Max had casually meandered into the club off Kurfürstendamm an hour previously, at around four o'clock, followed by Margot several minutes later. She'd dressed perfectly for the part – the make-up and clothes of a good-time girl, available and happy to please. She glanced backwards on entering the basement club and Georgie caught a well-disguised wink. A short time after, they watched Doctor Graf slipping down the stairs, work briefcase in hand. Right on time.

Then, that interminable wait again. Over an hour later, he emerged – with Margot on his arm, an inebriated smile on his lips, and the briefcase swinging by his side. Max was thirty seconds behind them, but at the top step, Georgie could see the strain on his leg was slowing his pace in trailing the couple.

She started the engine and followed at a discreet pace, the agreed plan being that Margot's charms would persuade Doctor Graf to take their celebrations to a hotel only a couple of blocks down. In advance, and under a false name, Max had booked a second-floor room facing onto the street. If Margot felt in any jeopardy, she would open the window and lean out, making a prearranged signal.

Georgie and Rubin watched Doctor Graf – now very unsteady on his feet – negotiate the hotel steps with Margot's help, Max following to observe inside the lobby. The rest, then, was up to the actress and her talents.

More waiting. The itch inside her own skin convinced Georgie she didn't possess the patience or courage for this kind of subterfuge. Rubin kept up the conversation, both with their eyes fixed on the hotel window. Why was it taking so long? More to the point, what were they doing in there? And what was Margot having to relinquish?

It was another hour later when her slight form emerged through the hotel entrance and onto the dusky street, looking neither dishevelled nor distressed. She was alone, Max appearing in her wake and crossing the street towards the car, slipping into the back seat. Margot kept on walking, tipping her head to signal meeting a little way up the road. She climbed into the car several streets away and Georgie drove another few minutes, parking up in a wide avenue between the Tiergarten and the zoo, the boughs and sprouting leaves a convenient canopy to their discussion.

'So?' Max could hardly contain himself.

Margot did look fairly pleased with herself, and – to Georgie – not as if she'd been exploited in any way.

'He's definitely well in with the Nazi command,' Margot began, wiping at her bright lipstick with a tissue. Maybe she felt grubbier than she appeared, both inside and out. 'Once he had some alcohol inside him, he couldn't wait to tell me how important he was to Himmler and his "vital plan".'

'Plan? What vital plan?' Max's voice was sharp, almost interrogating.

But Margot only looked back at him, narrowed her eyes. 'It wasn't that easy to get details, you know, especially as he got more and more drunk. I did gather it had to do with his skills as a doctor. He kept muttering about "the end being the solution to all the problems", it being the beginning, or something like that.'

Georgie and Max traded looks. Dark looks. Rubin was staring sideways through the passenger window but Georgie didn't like to guess at his expression, or his thinking. If Doctor Graf was willing to end the lives of innocent old ladies, how much thought would he spare for Jewish prisoners? Beatings and 'accidental' deaths in custody, among the Gestapo especially, were commonplace. But could there really be an agenda, a strategic and precise plan? Despite what they knew of the Nazis and their methods, it still seemed unthinkable.

'Did you get a look in his briefcase?' Max pressed, though with little hope of a positive answer.

Here Margot spread her lips, plucked out and held up a hair pin holding her style in place. 'Of course,' she said triumphantly. 'He was out cold as I left him, but I only had a minute or so as one of the maids began knocking on the door. I found a lot of clinic paperwork – typed lists of clients, I imagine. There were a couple of handwritten sheets filled with mathematical formulas – I had no hope of understanding those. And one note, talking about "plans we must finalise with your help". I didn't understand what it all meant but I did recognise the signature.'

'Yes?' Now Max was on the edge of his seat, Georgie not far behind.

'Kasper Vortsch,' she pronounced.

In one scarring jolt of her heart, Georgie's head spun, and her entire blood supply seemed to drain into the car's leather seat.

'Now he *is* a Nazi,' Margot went on, oblivious. 'Some new attaché that's risen up through the ranks very quickly. Himmler has taken a real shine to him.'

'How do you know this man?' Since Georgie had been struck dumb, Max was quick with the questions.

'Oh, the usual parties – Goebbels loves to pepper his gatherings with his starlets. And like most of them, this Kasper does love a pretty girl.' She looked disdainful then, perhaps ashamed at being lumped in with the stable of actresses used by Goebbels as glorified hostesses. Everyone in the car knew Margot was better than that, both at her job, and as a person.

'Have you ever spoken to him?' Georgie crawled out of her silent state. She felt sick again at her former naivety over Kasper.

'Only a little,' Margot said. 'He's very charming, but they all are, at first. He soon got bored of me and made a beeline for another actress – there's one who's half-English. According to the other girls, he's got a thing about English women.'

'Why?' Max posed. It was a pertinent question, with England fast becoming the Nazi Party's principal enemy.

'Sees them as something of a challenge, I assume. A trophy. Hitler has his own Unity Mitford, and what's good for the Führer . . .'

There it was – that word again. *Trophy*. What little blood supply Georgie had left washed away entirely, her veins set with ice. Max shot her a look of concern.

'Georgie?' he murmured, his fingers crawling to place a hand on her shoulder only to feel how rigid it was.

'I'm fine,' she managed. 'Um, we need to get Margot home. Make sure she's safe. Then we'll head back to Frida's?'

They convened around the kitchen table, Max instinctively adding brandy to their coffee. With the alcohol kick–starting her blood supply, Georgie opened the discussion. 'As much as I already loathe the idea, I think meeting Kasper one last time is essential, perhaps the only way to find out any valuable information.'

Rubin had been silent for the entire journey back to Margot's and onwards to Frida's. Now, he came out of his shell.

'No, Georgie! Absolutely not!' he said firmly, climbing to his feet, the chair scraping noisily behind. His normally soft features were set firm, eyes glinting under the harsh kitchen light. In a flash, he had become the father protecting a daughter no longer under his roof. 'I've not said anything before, but now I can't watch you putting yourself at such a risk. For what? Possibly a small titbit of information. It's not worth it.' He stopped, checked himself and sat down. His voice was suddenly small. 'However much we know, whatever we find out, it won't get Elias out of there.'

Georgie was silent for a moment, stunned at his outburst. Then, it was her turn. It brewed from nowhere, but the torrent was unstoppable; fury not aimed directly at Rubin, but at all those men dictating what she could or couldn't do in the world, for years now. Poor Rubin – suddenly he was that sneering editor back in London who questioned her very existence on the news desk, the countless others who always assumed she was the secretary, capable only of typing up someone else's opinions. And, if she was honest, Max in his first incarnation at the London Ritz. It made her hackles stand at a full ninety degrees, her eyes blaze and her temper flare. Years of frustration bubbled to the surface.

'I will not have anyone tell me what's good for me,' she blazed. 'I am fully aware of the dangers, but that's for me to decide, and no one else. It's *my* life. And *my* fate, if it comes to it.'

The two men at the table almost bent to the wind of her wrath, eyes wide.

Speech over, she sipped the non-existent dregs of her coffee, just for something to do in the hole that had been sucked out of the kitchen. Max and Rubin each took a breath.

'I'm sorry,' Rubin muttered, sad eyes on her. 'It's just that I – Sara and I – we care for you. Our children are safe, thanks to you, and I want the same for your parents.' She believed him, wanted to hug Rubin tightly like she would her own father – for his kindness, and to draw on him for her own courage too. Instead, she put a hand on his, squeezed his big, rough knuckles with affection.

'I understand,' Georgie said, a sudden and inconvenient lump growing in her throat. 'And I'm not angry with either of you. But we have one opportunity left to find the root of a solid story – something Max and I can get out there, for the public to see. Hitler has, by degrees, broken law upon law, treaty upon treaty. But he's never been exposed as a murderer. If we can show it, prove it, who knows what the world might think of him then? It has to be worth a try.'

The only discussion then was how and when to engineer it. It would be for Georgie to write a reminder to Kasper – a jaunty 'how are you? Let's meet soon' type of note – and see what came of it. There was every chance he was too busy with his new spiral of success to see her, the hope being that his vanity outweighed the demands of his diary.

In the meantime, they pored over the messages from Elias, some of which Rubin had shielded from Sara out of concern for her already fractured heart. The resulting guilt he purged on the two reporters; as much as Georgie hated women being kept in the dark, for any reason, she understood Rubin's motives. He was willing to own the anxiety, as a means of protecting his beloved wife from the pain of her own imagination.

In his scrawl, Elias vividly painted conditions in the camp. In his first message smuggled out, he'd described how the prisoners were categorised with triangles sewn onto their shabby clothes – yellow for Jew, red for political prisoner, green for criminal, pink for homosexual. Elias had both red and yellow, the red inverted triangle placed over the yellow to create the shape of a star and presumably for his role as a former journalist. It was cramped in all the huts, he added, the death rate high from disease; over the winter temperatures had fallen to below zero, and daily he helped the medics in amputating prisoners' frozen limbs. While horrific, being in the infirmary kept him employed, and more than likely alive. The fate of the amputees – from infection or disability – he didn't elaborate on.

Now, Elias's second dispatch was ever darker. The three-tier bunks in the long wooden huts teemed with lice, he wrote, food was a watery soup of old turnips and potatoes infested with weevils, reflected in the lines of bony and haggard faces. The punishments were illustrated in sketches – that trestle table with a prisoner's bare back uppermost and SS guards ready to wield the whip. Beside it, he'd scribbled '25 lashes'. In another, he'd drawn a collection of prisoners squatting under the sun, hands stretched out – Georgie felt the burn on her thighs at having to hold such a pose even for a few minutes in gym classes. There was an arrow pointing and 'three hours' beside it, along with its given name: 'Saxon greeting'. Exercise morphed into torture. It made her visibly wince.

'Is there any way we can get this into a story? Into the wider world?' Rubin asked out of desperation. Facing them, his heart was breaking.

Max and Georgie swapped looks. They would try, of course they would. But each knew that both the *Chronicle* and the *Telegraph* needed more than doodles or scribblings as evidence for running such an inflammatory piece, accusing the Nazis of outright torture in such a political climate. In her 'postcards', Georgie had hinted heavily at the oppression in Berlin, but always played carefully with her words.

The *Chronicle* especially liked photo spreads as a way of drawing in their readers – but how on earth would they smuggle a camera in and out of the camp? Asking Herr Bauer for access was futile; even if he agreed, any press trip would be sanitised, prisoners scrubbed and smiling, on their best behaviour. Rubin understood their caution – with his previous experience, he knew any self-respecting editor would demand proof before going out on a limb. But as a man, and a brother-in-law, he clutched at every straw he could.

47

Weaving the Truth

20th June 1939

The reaction was as they thought. Over the phone line to London, Henry was sympathetic but not encouraging. 'I can't go to the editor without strong evidence, and you know that the features pages will demand pictures.' He paused. 'Sadly, I think the British public will view it as unpalatable,' he added.

'It *is* unpalatable, Henry!' Georgie almost shouted into the phone, looking around her for anyone listening. She was in a public booth in a small hotel off Friedrichstrasse, not chancing a call from the office – the sensation of being watched had intensified the closer they hurtled towards war.

'Look, I'm sorry, George,' Henry placated her. 'But there is plenty for you to do. All eyes are on Hitler now. On Germany.'

'Yes, they are. So what about my replacement?' If she had some help in covering the routine diary jobs, she could focus more on the story that felt far more important.

'We're still working on it,' Henry sighed. 'We're using a lot of resources in Europe – Prague, Paris, Warsaw. We're spread thin. I'm sorry.'

She knew Henry meant it. As a man who'd covered the Great War in France from the trenches, he valued reporters on the ground, seeing events with their own eyes. Shame he didn't hold the purse strings.

George flopped onto the chair in the hotel bar with a heavy sigh. The city heat was rising, and she was hot with nature and frustration.

'No luck?' Max pushed a cold glass of beer towards her.

'They want it pinned down before they consider publishing,' she said. 'Something concrete.'

'Same here,' he said. 'No one wants to know unless the facts are watertight. My editor says it could easily start a new war rather than stop one in its tracks.'

'They could be right.' She took a long gulp of the beer – tart and strong, so much better than warm London ale. It sank into her stomach and delivered a spark. Georgie sat upright. 'Well, we'll just have to get that proof from our Herr Vortsch, won't we? By hook or by crook.'

Max didn't move. He eyed her from across the bar, brow puckered.

'Max, you know it's the only avenue we have left, unless we want to break into the Haas clinic in the dead of night. And I for one don't want to end up as a guest of the Gestapo.'

'Nor do I. But I don't like the thought of . . .'

'Like I've said before, not your decision. Besides, Kasper's already replied – and he seems keen for another date.' The attaché's usual upbeat reply had arrived a week earlier, saying yes, he was sorry for any delay and that he owed her a 'very good night out' for his prior behaviours. He planned yet another 'surprise' – which swiftly became another source of anxiety that Georgie had neatly pushed to the back of her mind.

She looked pointedly at Max and drained her beer. 'Come on, we've got work to do. The very least we can do is try and knock this Sachsenhausen piece into shape. If they want "concrete", let's give it to them.'

'Yes, Sergeant Major. Reporting for reporting duty.'

They did try – sitting side by side in Max's office with the titbits of prisoners' messages, pooling them into one person's narrative, the experience of an unnamed captive 'direct from inside a Nazi concentration camp'. The drama wasn't false, just a tool to attract press and reader attention, to put the human spotlight on what was happening behind those high walls and the Nazi shield of diplomacy. The hard, harrowing facts were entirely true.

And Henry was true to his word – he fought for the half-page in the *Chronicle*, the insider 'exclusive' from their correspondent, about the conditions and the assault on humanity. The Adlon crowd were full of praise, Rubin awash with gratitude. But like everything else they'd reported so far, Georgie could only wonder at the response. Would it make any real difference?

48

A Hot Date

Sweat pooled at the base of her neck, slinking uncomfortably down her back, and Georgie almost convinced herself it was the stifling heat of a Berlin summer creating her inner furnace. Almost. Every window in Frida's flat had been flung open, shades pulled down where the late-afternoon sun beat through mercilessly, but it remained a sauna. Georgie pulled the plug on the cool water of her bath, flapping the towel around her body to beat away the moisture forming as fast as she dried. This was a cruel trick from Mother Nature, she thought irritably – the temperature and her evening's destination. How on earth was she to contend with both?

She lay on the sofa in her lightest cotton robe, picked up a magazine as a makeshift fan and shut her eyes. In the past week, she'd tried to play down her date with Kasper, to Rubin, and to Max especially. But as the day loomed closer, her nerves had reared and triumphed; she'd been more short-tempered around the flat, even rejecting drinks at La Taverne in favour of a good book – the whimsy of Dickens being light years away from the Berlin outside her door, rumbling towards personal and worldwide conflict.

Now, the day had come and the plan – if they could call it that – was in place. Max and Rubin would be tailing in another anonymised car, to wherever she and Kasper spent the evening. Georgie's part was to persuade Kasper back to Frida's flat after his inevitable slide into drunkenness, steering the conversation around to his work. It was a scheme of sorts. The flat would be empty, aside from Max listening from the confines of Frida's room, nearest to the living room.

'You mean, you're going to leap to my aid, as if I'm some kind of damsel in distress?' she had only half-joked. It wasn't how Georgie chose to picture herself, and yet when she thought of Kasper and his capabilities, she was grateful Max planned to be there.

'I've never thought of you as either a damsel, or distressed,' he'd replied, throwing her a weak smile. 'I just want you to be all right.'

'Then let's hope I've absorbed a little of Margot's talent. It will save you the bother of shining your armour.'

Georgie finally climbed into her dress at half past six, before Kasper's allotted arrival at seven. She spent a while in the mirror applying her make-up, perfecting more of an 'English' look – slightly more conservative on the lipstick, using slides to tease her hair into a style from a magazine her mother had sent. 'Will that do?' She blew out her cheeks into the mirror's reflection, hoping the result was subtle rather than contrived. The angst she could do little about, praying it would fall away as the evening got into full swing. *Please let us go somewhere public* – the echo playing over and over inside her head. She flinched when she heard a loud ringing, realising quickly it was not the doorbell, but a sudden ring of the phone.

'All okay?' Max's voice had a slightly breathless quality.

'Yes, fine. Just waiting. Where are you?' She had a sudden panic that he and Rubin weren't already stationed outside the flat.

'I'm in a booth around the corner, three minutes away. Just checking in.'

'Good. Thanks.'

He paused. 'And I wanted to say good luck.'

The butterflies in her gut were still dormant, readying for flight, but the fact he said it grounded them a minute or so longer. A tiny respite.

'Thanks,' she said. Then desperate to lighten the moment: 'I'll see you on the other side?'

'You can be sure of it,' he replied and hung up.

The butterflies took full and furious flight at a resounding knock on the door. *Deep breaths, Georgie. Don't think about it. Just do it.*

Kasper was all smiles, a large posy of creamy white roses set against the lead grey of his uniform and the black of his highly polished boots. In his other hand, he clutched a sizeable leather wallet, the type used to hold letters and bound with a leather strap.

'Evening, Fraulein Young, a little something for you,' he said, offering the bouquet.

'Oh, they're beautiful.' She beamed, turning to lead him into the living room. *I'm still his English rose.* 'I'll just put these into some water. Would you like a drink? A Martini, perhaps?'

'Thank you, but no,' he said, perching on the sofa, the wallet held firmly against his body. 'I'm determined not to repeat my behaviour of old – I'm afraid I drank rather too much on our last meeting.' He oozed a new confidence, seeming to have aged or matured – gone was the boyish look, his jaw was more pronounced and his chest broader. He had grown into his rank.

'I don't know,' she trilled, panic rising inside at the prospect of a sober Kasper throughout the evening. 'You were a perfect gentleman. I'm quite partial to a tipple. Surely, you won't make me drink alone?'

'Well, perhaps when we're having dinner. Shall we go?'

They stepped into a gleaming staff car, the door opened by a well-dressed driver – at each meeting he seemed to be afforded a newer and better vehicle – and Georgie glimpsed Rubin's car a short way down the street. Awash with trepidation, yes – but she was not alone. They slid into the back seat, Kasper moving the leather file to one side and edging closer to Georgie, cosier than his manners had ever allowed before.

'Surely not another balloon ride tonight, or a trip out into the countryside – not in this heat?' She was pumping for any indication, while driving flirtation into her voice. Kasper smiled, clearly pleased at her allusion to their previous dates. Perhaps fuelled by it, he placed a hand on Georgie's thigh, looking directly for her reaction. She giggled and slid her own hand on his. A bead of sweat broke free from the nape of her neck and crawled downward, though the icicles inside held firm.

Kasper was in an ebullient mood, talking openly about his new position as a senior attaché to Major Schenk and how he was enjoying some travel.

She gasped, eyes wide. 'You've been abroad? Anywhere nice?' She reminded herself then not to go overboard with the flirtation. It wasn't 'in character' for what Kasper already knew of her. *And you are no Mata Hari, girl.*

'Nothing too exotic at the moment,' he said. 'I've been lucky enough to see a lot of our beautiful country, with one or two trips across the borders.'

And what borders are those? Georgie mused bitterly. *The moveable ones, that the Nazis shift on a whim?* But her smile remained fixed, her attention centred entirely on Kasper.

Flicking her gaze out of the window at opportune moments, Georgie tracked the route; it was still light so she was able to log the city's landmarks as they skirted the scorched green of the Tiergarten. But there was no need – the driver pulled up within a short time, in one of Berlin's elegant districts and just a stone's throw from La Taverne.

'It's not in the least original but I wondered if you wouldn't mind our evening to be here?' Kasper said, and he looked up at the ornate stature of the Hotel Eden, its shape like the prow of an ocean liner amid Berlin's stoical architecture. 'I have an early morning meeting and so a trip out of the city is not possible tonight.'

Georgie's delight was not entirely forced – the Eden was among Berlin's most fashionable of hotels, and she'd never had money or reason to set foot through its doors. Its clientele was famously cosmopolitan, a blend of European socialites and wealthy Americans attracted by the live band music and the aptly named American Bar. The Eden was also notorious for its exquisite afternoon tea in the palm court, after which guests could play a round of mini golf on the terrace. Alongside the Resi, it was a rival playground for the rich.

'It's perfect, Kasper.' Georgie beamed. 'Is there music tonight? Can we dance?'

Her obvious pleasure blended with relief that her prayers had been answered – the Eden was very public and its cocktails famously strong. And she was unlikely to meet anyone from press circles. They might – just might – pull this off.

Georgie eyed Kasper as he climbed from the car, still clutching his leather wallet, and she caught a glimpse of Rubin and Max parked on the opposite side of the street. She chanced a smile in their direction: *everything's fine.* She expected Kasper might hand the folder to his driver for safe keeping, but he clasped it firmly in one hand. She glanced at it, cautiously:

There's something in there. Something I would like to see.

Kasper guided her inside, head up and shoulders back, his free palm planted into her back. He was showboating for sure; she was his date, his Aryan – though non-German – catch, and he was a man to be reckoned with. It was there in every stride he took, in the way he guided her to the American Bar, the stance that sent the waiter scurrying to find a good table. And still, he kept the wallet with him, never out of sight, declining to check it into the cloakroom, or even the hotel safe when the maître d' offered up the service.

The place was buzzing – a mist of cigarette smoke and fusion of languages hung above the tables, some uniforms of SS and high-ranking Wehrmacht, with the silken dance music of Oskar Joost and his band in the background. Outside, military vehicles patrolled the streets and distrust clogged the air, but up on high at Hotel Eden, life appeared to be untouched. Before she could even begin to relax, Georgie scanned the bar for anyone she might know, or who was likely to approach and introduce themselves – thankfully, most of her acquaintances were too poor to frequent the Eden. Kasper's, though, were not – before they could sit, he toured several tables, either saluting or shaking hands and introducing Georgie as 'Fraulein Young, from England', the wallet tucked under his arm and that hand always securely on her. Possession, it said firmly. My own English devotee.

They were on table number four and heading towards another when Georgie spotted him, emerging from the gents and pulling at the cuffs of his shirt. By now, she had his face marked in her memory – his clipped beard and owlish glasses: Doctor Graf. She watched his face lift up and look towards Kasper, dawning with recognition and a smile, his body starting towards them. In a flash, Georgie turned her own face away, wriggled herself free from Kasper's hold and leaned into his ear, her face sideways. 'Do you mind if I visit the ladies?'

'By all means,' he said, and the hand fell away.

The short walk seemed endless, heart pounding in her throat, and she almost stumbled over someone's handbag, reddened at attracting undue attention to herself. *Did he see my face?* He might not even remember her as Hanna Seidel, but Georgie reasoned Doctor Graf was not a medical man without possession of a good memory. She couldn't take that chance.

On her way back, she hovered in the foyer facing the bar, face peeking over her compact mirror. Then, a stroke of luck as she watched Doctor Graf say his warm goodbyes to Kasper and walk towards the exit. A sigh, and a flush of blissful relief.

Kasper was sitting at their table as she arrived back, eyes on the menu. With such an atmosphere, it wasn't hard to persuade him into an aperitif, and then wine with their dinner. Georgie checked her own consumption and, when he went to the bathroom (taking the wallet with him), she poured her wine into his glass, replacing her own with water.

Much like their first meeting at the Resi, the tableaux around them eased the conversation – they locked heads good-naturedly over German versus English sport, and Kasper delighted in letting slip what he knew about the clientele and their indiscretions, indicating with his eyes at those considered friends of Germany, and those who might not be for much longer. Georgie giggled in the right places, never quite offering an opinion, maintaining the illusion of agreement. Kasper was a mine of information, but didn't once reveal his sources; it wasn't a leap to imagine he had friends in the Gestapo, some of whom might be tapping their feet to the band at that moment.

Kasper leaned in conspiratorially, his spirited breath warm on her cheek, and Georgie's heart froze; surely, he would ask for it now? Her allegiance, which side she was on, what she thought of the Führer. Did she adore the great man, like the honourable Miss Mitford? And how on earth would she sidestep that?

And yet, he didn't. He only asked about her family, and she spent a good ten minutes scratching in her memory for what she'd already told him in the Grunewald on their first outing, an entire age away. She embellished her carefully spun tale of minor aristocracy, somewhere in the Cotswolds, and the Scottish countryside, where in reality she'd only spent family holidays in a tiny cottage, describing the urge of simply 'having' to break away to become her own person and write. And for the first time, he asked some detail about her writing; on the spot, she weaved a romance steeped in history, where the man gets his girl and the girl is only too delighted.

Whether it was the second bottle of wine, or just that she was very convincing, Kasper seemed enthralled – to the point where Georgie had to invent a second arm of the family, an eccentric aunt in Paris, and a second twist to her fantastical novel.

'Shall we dance?' she ventured, having run out of her own yarn.

It was essentially a test – to see what he did with the leather folio and how unsteady he might be on his feet. The wallet stayed visible on the table, but only after Kasper called over a waiter and instructed him to guard it at all times. His feet were wandering, but so was his eye – back to the table each time they twirled and turned. Drunk or not, Kasper Vortsch was intent on that wallet. And he was not nearly drunk enough yet, Georgie decided. She needed to up her game; Mata Hari it might have to be.

With one more cocktail downed – hers only sipped at – it was Georgie's cue to lean in, close enough to smell his cologne. 'What say we drive back to my place. Have a nightcap?' Her tone signalled everything he desired, even though it sickened her inside, while she thought of Margot Moller and the sacrifices she'd had to make in her life.

'Better make it coffee for me,' he said. 'Remember, I have that early meeting.'

Her heart plummeted, but she forced a winning smile. 'Coffee it is. Let's go.'

Outside the Eden, they waited a few minutes for the car to be brought to the front, Kasper holding her arm and leaning in, as much for his own benefit as hers. Those once enticing eyes were drifting lazily, up and down her dress and into the curves of her chest. Georgie squinted nervously into the gloom, to where Rubin was parked. She raised her hand in a prearranged gesture, looping a lock of hair over her ear – their signal that she and Kasper would be headed directly back to Frida's. She watched as Rubin's headlights lit up and the car moved off.

Kasper was subdued on the journey back, stifling a yawn and then apologising by planting his hand on her thigh again. He was beginning to slow his words, had clearly drunk a good amount over the entire evening, but they made it back to Frida's with little more than small talk. His hand stayed fixed on her flesh, head beginning to droop on Georgie's shoulder, but with the wallet on the seat beside him, safe under his thigh.

She spied Rubin's parked car as they arrived at Frida's flat; the sudden halt of their own engine brought Kasper to attention, and for a minute Georgie thought he might shy away from joining her inside – it would mean the evening was a disaster, nothing more to show than her deeply scarred nerves and some Nazi tittle-tattle. She had to get him up into the flat, leaving her no choice but to step up the allure.

'Come on, I'm not nearly tired enough to go to sleep,' she teased, fingering his collar and brushing his jawline. 'I'd like one more dance, just the two of us. Please, Kasper. How about it?' She forced a wanton, child-like plea, close into his face.

It worked. Despite his fatigue, Kasper's manners responded,

and he diligently collected his folder and raised himself from the seat, dismissing the driver.

Georgie sensed Max's hidden presence the minute she walked through the door, and noisily piloted Kasper into the living room, where he flopped onto the sofa, tucking the wallet under his thigh again. Frida's door was shut, and as she passed by Georgie called backwards down the hallway: 'I'll just get this coffee on. Don't you fall asleep on me now!' *Please fall asleep on me. A deep, deep slumber. Please.*

Kasper returned a light groan. There was a coffee pot ready to go on the stove, a bottle of brandy on the kitchen table, with a small envelope next to it. Inside were two white tablets and a note in Max's hand: *for emergencies – sleeping tablets.*

Christ! Was he suggesting she drug Kasper? A Nazi officer on the rise, one who had Himmler's ear and very possibly Hitler's too? Maybe Max had pre-empted a scenario where Kasper stepped over the mark and Georgie needed a swift antidote to his desires.

'Make mine good and strong,' Kasper's voice came down the hallway. His body was already stirring from the alcohol and the prospect of any flirtatious loose talk rapidly receding. Georgie's mind raced, thinking of every avenue aside from those tablets sitting in full view. There was nothing – he would taste brandy in his coffee for sure. It had to be the tablets. She poured the thick, strong coffee, making sure her own cup was distinct, and stirred both tablets into Kasper's. Guilt swilled in motion with the spoon. *Georgie, what are you doing?*

Kasper was only too eager to drink down the coffee in needing to reverse his fatigue, while Georgie masked her fresh anxiety fizzing inside.

'What about that dance?' His mouth was a hungry leer, his face sporting renewed hope. And why wouldn't he? He had wined and dined her throughout the evening. Georgie had invited – insisted – he come in for a drink and . . . as an officer of the Reich it was the return he would expect.

'Of course.' She put on a record as he rose from the sofa with only a slight falter. Lord, how long would this take? She'd never taken a sleeping tablet herself, didn't know their strength or whether the effect would be instant. She was exhausted with the effort of keeping herself in character – and still the wallet lay there. She had no idea if it contained anything relevant but there was no doubt of its importance, to Kasper at least.

They danced close – too close for her comfort – and Kasper's hands wandered slowly across her back and downwards. Her skin crawled with unease, and she felt sure he would feel her heart crashing against her chest wall. Inside her head, she was screaming. Nothing about this scenario felt good.

After a few minutes, his feet slowed to barely a shuffle and his body leaned heavily against hers.

'Kasper?' she tested quietly. 'Are you all right?'

'Yeess . . .' It was a definite slur, and his head lolled against her cheek, seconds before his legs fell away and she had to shoulder his entire weight, while manoeuvring his limp body backwards onto the sofa. His eyelids were at half mast, those unsettling eyes still on her, but she saw no other signs of consciousness.

'Kasper, Kasper . . .' She tapped at his cheek to be sure, lifting a hand, which flopped heavily onto his lap. He was out cold. But for how long?

Georgie picked up the leather wallet and half-ran towards Frida's room, startling Max as she careered through the door. 'What's happening? Something wrong?'

'He's asleep – unconscious – but I don't know for how long. Do you?'

'No, I got the tablets from a friend, no details.' She glared at his lack of knowledge – Max was usually a stringent fact checker. But there was no time to lay blame now.

Georgie was breathless with panic, even though she could hear Kasper's snores from the living room. 'He's had this file practically glued to his side all evening – we need to check it, and quickly. You go through it, and I'll keep watch.'

Inside, Max found twenty or so sheets, some typed on Reich notepaper, others handwritten with numbers and letters beside them.

'That's Kasper's writing,' Georgie confirmed, her head switching back and forth down the hallway. At first glance, all appeared to be lists of some sort, or notes ready to be grouped.

'There's just too many for me to read and make notes,' Max said. 'And my memory isn't that good.'

'So, what do we do?' Chancing on Kasper's file had been pure luck – even so, Georgie couldn't contemplate replacing the sheets without proper scrutiny, not after everything they'd risked.

Max was silent, thoughts churning. Suddenly, his eyes lit up. 'Simone has a small camera, in her room. She put film in it a few days ago – I saw her do it. It's in her bedside drawer. Can you get it?'

Georgie hopped into the corridor and a second's glance told her Kasper was still sleeping like the proverbial baby. She scrabbled in the bedside drawer and was back a minute later.

Max positioned a lamp on the floor and laid each sheet next to it. 'I'm no photographer, so let's just hope this comes out,' he muttered as the shutter clicked over each page.

It took less than ten minutes but felt like several years off Georgie's life; her mouth was dry, head spinning with alcohol and adrenalin. She just wanted to be somewhere else – in La Taverne with the crowd, or better still, propping up the Adlon bar with Rod and Bill, Max teasing from nearby with a glass of beer in his hand. Instead, he was next to her, on his knees, committing Lord knows what kind of subterfuge, espionage, or theft. Probably all three. With her, simply a girl from the Cotswolds.

'That's done,' he said at last, sliding the sheets back in. Georgie tiptoed out from the room, and gently placed the file back alongside Kasper, whose head was on his chest, eyes mercifully closed, in a deep sleep.

She padded on her stockinged feet back to Frida's room. 'What do I do now?' she whispered urgently. 'I don't want him on the sofa all night.'

'Can't we just let him sleep it off?'

'No! Frida will be back eventually — if anyone can, she'll smell a rat. Besides, we're not supposed to know he's had a sleeping draught. Anybody who collapsed so suddenly might well be ill — it will look more convincing if we call for some help.'

Max nodded. 'All right, search his pockets, see if there's a number for his barracks, or his driver.'

Kasper twitched slightly and groaned as Georgie picked through his pockets gently. A tiny notebook in his breast pocket had a list of names and numbers — Georgie recognised one as Hans, the evening's driver. She was half-tempted to hand the notebook to Max for more copying, but Kasper began muttering in his sleep and it would be pushing their already extended luck.

The voice on the end of the line was stark and military, but at the right location. 'We'll send a car directly,' he said, as if her request was customary. The young driver was entirely unfazed on arrival, giving Georgie a look that said drunken retrievals were commonplace, if not with Kasper exclusively, then among other SS officers. 'He might be ill,' she said dutifully. 'He simply collapsed. Maybe he needs a doctor?'

The driver looked doubtful, gently manoeuvred Kasper – wincing at the alcoholic vapour on his breath – and shouldered his weight. 'Thank you, Fraulein,' he said. 'I'll see he gets help.'

After watching them disappear down the steps, Georgie closed the door, pressing her back into its cool wood and sinking to the floor. The lengthy breath escaping her lips left her body entirely depleted. She felt grimy with dried sweat and the film of an unseen moral filth. She craved a bath, and yet had nothing left – not even the energy to crawl into the living room. She heard Frida's door handle turn slowly, and the void fill with Max's form. She felt him test the air.

'It's okay, they've gone,' she croaked.

He walked quickly towards her, face awash with concern. 'Georgie? What's wrong?'

She willed her mouth to produce a weak smile. 'Nothing that a bloody large slice of strudel won't fix.'

It was midnight and Georgie was drained but wired from the coffee, Max hopping with his own stock of adrenalin. They had no strudel, but he produced plates of bacon and eggs – it brought on a pang of nostalgia for them both, of home and late-night university life, the British cure for all ills in the form of fried food.

Frida arrived and sloped straight off to bed, giving them both a strange sideways look but clearly too drunk and exhausted to question. Georgie would have to fend off her particular method of interrogation later. It left her and Max to chew over the evening.

'What on earth did we just do?' she said, trying to believe her own version of events.

'We won't know until we get those pictures developed.'

'No, I mean, what did we do to get them? I'm pretty sure none of that was in our journalism training. At least not mine.'

It cultivated a laugh, at least. 'It might not be strictly legal either.'

'Oh Lord, what if Henry ever finds out about this?'

'He'll either sack you or put you up for an award,' Max said. 'I'm sure we're not the first journalists to step over a line.'

'But it's my first line,' she moaned.

'Then congratulations,' he said. 'And very probably the first of many. Besides, George, these are bad people, and this is war.'

'Not yet it isn't.'

He gave her a knowing frown. 'Elias is at war; Rubin, Sara and everyone in their neighbourhood too. Every day. That's why we did it. You know that, Georgie.'

She nodded wearily. 'Then let's hope we've got some ammunition out if it. For everyone's sakes.'

49

An Unwelcome Discovery

9th August 1939

Unlike the evening itself, Georgie was not on tenterhooks for any serious repercussions over her Kasper date, especially when his note arrived the very next day, with a second bouquet. She tried to ignore the fact that white lilies were often sent at funerals.

> *Dear Georgie,*
> *My sincere apologies for my ungentlemanly behaviour a second time. I think maybe I ate or drank something to upset me. But there are no excuses, and my thanks to you for summoning help. I am well now, thanks to your diligence.*
> *Your willingness permitting, I would like to dance with you again. Unfortunately, I will be away on Reich business for several weeks, but I will contact you on my return in the hope of seeing you again.*
> *Yours ever, Kasper (upholder of the Reich, if not his own manners!)*

Georgie threw the note away, determined that somehow she would wheedle her way out of another date. Minutes later, she plucked it out of the bin and burned it in the ashtray, feeling that shadow of paranoia hovering.

She and Max had to wait for news of what treasure they'd captured on film. It was too risky to entrust the developing to any photographic shop, and Max's German friend – an amateur photographer and a known anti-Nazi – said he would need a couple of days. It would have been an agonising wait, except for the three-way game of tennis between Germany, France and Britain gaining momentum, meaning they were both criss-crossing Berlin with real work.

Rubin wasn't aware of the precise activities with Kasper in the flat, and so far they'd played it down; Georgie was guilty at their deceit, justifying it to herself that it still might not bear any fruit for Elias anyway. Even so, Rubin was quiet and preoccupied, much like any German watching his city and country slipping towards war.

She and Max met in a small café-bar in Charlottenburg, one that had the good fortune of being unpopular with Nazis. They kept up the pretence of a loved-up couple exchanging sweet nothings and – amid the surrounding chatter – the mixed clientele would never have guessed at their true conversation.

'Your German is much improved.' Georgie's smile was teasing.

'So rude!' He kept up the look of allure. 'I'll have you know I ordered a full meal in German the other night, and not once did the waitress ask me to repeat myself.'

'And were you pointing to the menu at the time?'

He frowned good-humouredly. 'Smug, Georgie Young – that's what you are. Just you wait until we're in Paris and I am regaling you with my fluent French tones.'

'We're going to Paris, are we?' She was amused, lightened, if only for a few minutes, and even with the heavy approach of troopers outside. Where once the conversation might have halted on hearing the trudge of jackboots advancing, now the café dwellers simply raised their voices as they passed by. The echoes of war had already become part of the German soundtrack.

He lowered his face, words spoken into the tabletop. 'Well, when we get kicked out of Germany for crimes against the Reich, I – for one – am not going back to dreary old London.' His eyes went up suddenly; to an older man who walked in and swept by, bumping his chair and muttering 'sorry', then shuffling up to the bar.

'Same again?' Max offered and stood up.

The two men exchanged several words of greeting at the bar, as strangers often do, and Max brought the drinks back to the table, then disappeared in the direction of the toilets. The man followed him a minute later. The café clientele carried on oblivious while Georgie looked on, in semi-disbelief. This really was a scene out of a film noir, something the Gestapo would delight on discovering. She felt uneasy, and yet strangely excited, at the same time knowing that she would never make it as a spy – the charade was just too exhausting.

Max returned after a short time, and they picked up their pseudo love talk, sipping and smiling for a good quarter of an hour, while the man sat alone at the bar.

'Shall we get dinner?' Max said at last, and they walked out into the late-afternoon sunshine, he reaching for her hand to complete the façade. He was undoubtedly better at the ploy, but his hands were as sweaty as hers, with the heat and their joint purpose. Still, Georgie was surprised that it didn't feel odd, or uncomfortable, their fingers meeting. And that felt odd too, an unexpected popping inside her chest.

'Back to mine?' he said, nudging into her shoulder.

She guessed he had some sort of envelope tucked under his jacket – the weather was hot enough that some men were in shirtsleeves, but enough wore suits for him not to stand out. He was sweating under his light jacket, and she could feel his muscles trying not to hold the precious envelope into his body too forcefully, sensed the effort in his fingers of appearing happy-go-lucky.

They took a tram to Max's apartment in the Wilmersdorf district, going one extra stop when they both sensed one traveller looking a little too long and hard, Max taking Georgie's hand and hopping off suddenly, leaving the startled observer on the tram. To be certain, they took a small detour through a local park, checking they had no other tail. Max lived in a large, unassuming residential block, with an entrance that led into a leafy courtyard, though scorched brown with the summer sun. Georgie had never visited before, and he led her by the hand up a stairwell onto the second floor. For such a large building, there were few people around, only an older woman who appeared at the landing door opposite, a white cat weaving around her ankles.

'Evening, Frau Sommer,' Max trilled, employing his best, charmed smile.

'Evening.' She jerked up her chin to Max, and frowned at Georgie. Was she surprised to see a woman, or just someone who wasn't Simone? The cat mewed noisily, and Frau Sommer shushed it inside without a backward glance.

'Is she all right?' Georgie whispered.

'I think so – moans endlessly about the Nazis. At least from what I can catch – she talks very fast. I just smile and nod, comment on the weather.'

Checking left and right, Max stopped short of putting his key in the door. Instead, he reached up to swipe away what appeared to be thin air, but was actually a piece of sewing thread hitched across the doorjamb. Satisfied it was intact, he unlocked the door.

'Expecting company?' Georgie said. Maybe she wasn't being careful enough herself. Did they have cause to be wary?

'Never underestimate those lovely boys in the Gestapo,' he said, 'especially after what happened to Rod.'

The apartment was not what she expected for a man living alone. It was certainly big enough to share, but it was also tidy – the living room had no debris from the kitchen, or shirts hung over the chairs. Nor the ashtray full of cigarettes that was a feature at Frida's, or the remnants from her wardrobe draped across the floor. Although stuffy from heat, it had a pleasant smell to it. She wondered, too, how many times Simone had been there, felt her eyes scouting for any exotic residue. Any perfume odour? And then she told herself firmly to stop.

'The perfect bachelor pad,' she said. 'Do you like living alone?'

'I love it,' he said. 'After sharing a dorm with twenty other boys and then rooms at university, I am a blissfully happy lone tenant.' Despite the heat outside, he was already pulling the curtains on the closed windows, creating an oven effect. He took off his jacket at last to reveal sweat patches on his shirt, puffing out his cheeks with relief.

He slapped a large envelope on the coffee table. 'Let's see what we've got,' Max said decisively.

They each took ten sheets to scrutinise. The quality wasn't good, as some frames had been enlarged, blurring the script.

'There's a letter here written from Major Schenk to Doctor Graf,' Max added. 'It's a bit difficult to read but seems to be talking about finalising their "initiative" and commencing in the very near future – at Sachsenhausen.'

He looked at Georgie, face drawn. Neither was naive enough to think Doctor Graf was bent on improvements to the camp's medical care; his speciality as a doctor lay elsewhere. Paul really had been onto something big.

'I've also got a list of names,' he went on, 'with some sort of code by them – an "A" or a "D". What do you think that means?'

'Same type of thing here,' Georgie agreed, 'though some are handwritten by Kasper.'

Any file compiled by the Nazis had to be worrying for those listed, and this was proof of Kasper's involvement in the Reich's unsavoury politics, his position as a true follower laid bare on paper.

'The names are all Jewish from what I can tell,' Georgie said. Her mind calculated for a minute, arriving at an unhealthy conclusion. 'Do you think "D" might mean deportation, and "A" is for arrest?'

Max looked up, his heat-flushed face suddenly drained. Ghostly white.

'What? Max? What have you found?'

His sigh was long and his voice thin. 'I really hope you're wrong, George, because if you're not, we really are in trouble.'

'Look at it! It's there in black and white,' Max urged. 'You can't deny it. We need to do something. And quickly.' He blew out his cheeks in frustration, hopping from foot to foot.

They'd taken a taxi across the city, straight to the Amsels' and found only Rubin at home.

The older man was in denial, despite the shake of his fingers as he held the photographic sheet in his own living room and read his own name next to his brother-in-law's. And his wife's. The letter next to it meant the Nazis would not be helping the Amsels leave Germany with their possessions and dignity intact, in a timely fashion. It was 'A' for arrest. And a guess as to what else might follow. If the Amsels were to avoid it, they would need to flee. Quickly.

'How do I tell Sara, persuade her to leave Elias, and our

home?' Rubin's already lined face was creased with anguish. 'Can you be sure this is what it means?'

Max peeled away with exasperation towards the kitchen, but Georgie's voice was measured, hopefully persuasive. 'No, but do you really want to take that chance? It's the best guess we have. The fact that you're even on that list – in their sights – is not good news. You know that, Rubin. Especially when they've come once before for Elias.' She gripped his hand, while his large fingers curled around hers for reassurance, some grounding that his entire world hadn't been pulled from under him. Again.

Georgie knew only too well that Rubin had seen families torn apart over the past year, people he'd known for decades. He didn't need reminding of the report in her own paper just a month or so previously warning that 24,000 Jews would be deported or thrown into concentration camps; he could visualise the scene where he and Sara were led away from their home, separated from each other, possibly for eternity. Second only to the scenario of Sara being forced to break the bond with her own brother – their survival or his? Either way, the choice for him – for them both – was agonising. Again.

'How soon do you think we need to go?' Rubin sounded defeated.

Realistically, there was no way of knowing; the lists could have been in Kasper's possession for some time – a couple were dated the week before. It was anyone's guess how quickly they would be acted on, but the mood on the streets and the pace at which Europe appeared to be hurtling towards war instilled a sense of urgency in Georgie and Max. Every day was another risk taken, more time for Rubin and Sara's names to be circulated. Already a heavy presence of border guards at Berlin's main stations made travel difficult, eyes crawling over passports and identity cards.

'I know someone who might be able to get us forged papers

– we've been saving for some time,' Rubin said. 'But it'll take a few days at least.'

'You can't stay here – just in case,' Max said. 'You and Sara can have my apartment. The *Times* reporter is out of town for a few days and I have his keys – I'll bunk there.'

'Tonight we'll take our chances,' Rubin said, voice measured and calm. His stance, too, was unmoving. 'Sara is at a neighbour's. I'll break it to her myself when she comes in. But we need one last night in our home.'

They left the Amsels' apartment with a minor relief that Rubin had agreed to leave – and that they only had a single night of unease to get through. The days after they would tackle later.

'I don't know about you, but I'm starving,' Max said. 'With all that, we missed dinner, and I would love nothing more than a plate of Frau Lehmann's pasta. And some decent conversation.'

It was ten p.m., and one half of Georgie was exhausted, with another day of intense work promised. But like Max, she was too restless to head home and chose company over sleep.

The press table at La Taverne was almost full – the more news to report, the more it seemed the pack needed to restore and refuel with their own kind, chewing over the good food and the world at large. Unusually, Sam Blundon was there with another reporter, pleased to see them both. Georgie gave him scant details of their most recent discovery; he pressed his lips together and said, diplomatically: 'Get them out if you can. And as soon as you can – the walls are closing in.' Clearly, he couldn't say any more, but the raise of his red eyebrows endorsed the urgency.

The talk, as usual, was on Hitler's continued pawing at areas of Poland and its effect on Berliners – jittery in some quarters, assured of victory in others – and the news that correspondents in neighbouring Warsaw had been issued with gas masks.

English papers were full of conjecture, but progress from the politicians on all sides was slow. Only Hitler appeared to sit poised, like a coiled snake awaiting its prey, despite rumours elsewhere that he was already moving troops into position.

Bill blew in within half an hour, face as red as his hair, and he slapped a day-old copy of his own paper on the table and announced: 'Well, I have the story of the day, folks! It's a complete disaster, and sure-fire proof we will be at war very soon.'

Alarmed faces looked up. 'What to gods have you unearthed?' someone said. 'Is Hitler moving now?'

'Hitler?!' Bill huffed, his face solemn. 'No, not him. Although he's surely to blame for this bloody rationing. It's worse that that – there's no damn oranges at the Adlon. Not a single orange fruit to juice in the entire building. A travesty. Give me war any day.'

50

Departure

10th August 1939

The daylight hours until Rubin and Sara could be moved might have dragged, if it weren't for the demands of news gathering: a constant toing and froing from chancellery to embassy, ping-pong comment gained from ambassadors and the Reich mouthpieces, either Bauer in his official capacity or muttered in corridors via Goebbels's carefully planted 'sources'. Sitting at her desk in the late afternoon, it felt to Georgie like unpicking a giant mass of impossibly tangled wool, only to arrive at a hole in the middle where the truth was supposed to be. Whatever words people uttered, it was their body language, facial expressions and general pessimism that pointed to the inevitable – that British and American reporters would soon be on the 'other side'. The enemy.

The heat made it impossible to keep the office windows closed, the constant growl of military engines and the trump-trump of troops rising up from the main streets, adding to general feeling that Berlin city was on the move, those shifting grains of sand below an ever-changing tide.

At last, darkness descended and offered Rubin and Sara's cloak of safety. There was no great removal; they slipped from their apartment building with one piece of luggage each, lives reduced to a single suitcase. Georgie's heart reeled for Sara, having to leave behind memories of family life, discarding precious trinkets in favour of more valuable objects they could trade for their passage onward. She looked pale and wan as she climbed into the back seat of the car, yet was quick to voice her gratitude. 'Thank you' for being wrenched from everything that was rightfully hers, theirs, as native Germans. The injustice sat heavy among them all they drove towards Max's home.

The transition appeared easy, as few people in Max's neighbourhood were out late; the sound of their lives pushed out through open windows – dinner talk and a tinny chatter of the radio – and the Amsels stepped noiselessly towards their temporary home. Georgie was relieved when Frau Sommer did not make an appearance at her door, sniffing out anything untoward.

Georgie made tea while Max settled them into the house. It was agreed they would not leave the apartment, at least until the false papers arrived – Max would bring home groceries, to keep up his pretence of living there. There was no telephone, so they worked out a system of signals in case of any alarms, either in the windows or near to the front door. There was a young lad Max had befriended, a Jewish boy of ten or so called Aron, whom he would use to pass messages – Aron's father owned a pawnbroker's a few blocks down, with a telephone. The old man had nodded his understanding to Max. The plan was for the Amsels to use their papers to drive as far as they could towards a small border town, taking their chances where the sentry posts were poorly staffed. Then into France, and eventually towards England, armed with letters of introduction from Max and Georgie, and one Sam Blundon had pledged.

No one dared imagine the dream scenario where they would be reunited with Ester and Leon, and the joy that would bring. One thing at a time.

The days following were a whirlwind of reporting, blended with the static of summer heat; real life and politics on parallel rail tracks and moving at different speeds. People plodded slowly along the scorching pavements, while the world spun on its axis at an alarming rate: Göring and Heydrich – head of the security service – had joined Hitler at his Bavarian mountain retreat, still plotting Danzig's 'peaceful and unconditional' return to Germany. In Britain, the *Chronicle* published a helpful visual guide for readers on British war planes likely to be flying over the English countryside. And yet, to Georgie, there still seemed that widespread illusion it would never actually happen. It was like putting a low flame under a large pot of soup and only ever expecting it to simmer. Except the heat was being turned up. And they'd already seen how it could boil.

Each day, Aron was sent on foot to see check if the papers were ready, returning with a simple message: 'Tomorrow.' Forgers, it seemed, were in hot demand. By the fifth day, Aron brought back the message they craved: 'They're ready.' Max insisted the young boy wasn't to collect the papers; he'd never forgive himself if Aron was stopped and couldn't outrun any suspicious guards, those with guns especially. The next morning, Georgie made his excuses at a ministry press conference, as Max crossed the city by tram. They planned to meet in Kranzler's after the pick-up, keeping up a pretence of normality until it was safe to deliver the papers to the Amsels.

The press conference overran by half an hour, and Georgie walked rapidly in the heat towards Kranzler's. The tables under the awning were full, but there was no sign of Max, and he wasn't inside either. She scanned over the green and grey uniforms, beads of sweat forming, imagination running riot.

With forced smiles, she ordered a cool drink and strudel – nothing out of the ordinary. And then she waited. Agonisingly.

Max blew in almost forty minutes after the agreed time, all smiles himself and weaving through the tables of uniforms. Did he not have the papers? He looked far too relaxed.

He sat opposite, virtually expressionless.

'You're late?' Georgie's eyebrows were fully arched.

'Blasted army vehicle broken down, right across a tram line,' he said.

'All good, though?'

'Perfect.' He smiled. 'Any strudel for me?'

He's too good at this by half.

They should have known it was too simple; those more experienced at this kind of deception would have been wary of its ease. Only when Max spotted Aron's bobbing form outside Kranzler's window, peering in like some form of Dickensian waif, did he feel a spike of alarm. Outside, he exchanged words with the boy, who'd courted danger just by coming into the city centre. Max's form visibly stiffened. He walked back in, maintaining what composure he could, pulling out a bill of Reichsmarks as he approached. 'We have to go,' he said. This time, his smile wasn't in the least convincing.

Outside, he hailed a taxi with urgency. 'Aron says there's a search party in my neighbourhood, going house to house. It might just be routine, but I don't think we can take any chances.'

The taxi seemed to take an age, and they remained tight-lipped in the back, Max's knee bouncing up and down, jittery with anxiety. Georgie pushed out a hand to quell his nerves, though she understood his disquiet – it was his apartment the Amsels would be discovered in. For the Nazis, a clear case of guilt by association.

They spied the troops as the taxi drew up, not so much swarming, but stealthily working their way through the next apartment block like worker ants. There was no sign of Rubin or Sara, or a general unease that anyone had been hauled away, and the troops hadn't yet reached Max's block. A few dog walkers slowed up as they moved past, but no one dared to stop and stare for long.

Max grabbed Georgie's hand as he would a wife or girlfriend, and they headed towards the centre of his own building. The sun beat down on the courtyard, the flap of washing on a line breaking an eerie, deserted silence. Even those with nothing to hide had retreated indoors, windows firmly shut.

Max took the stairs two at a time and Georgie ran behind. He checked the thread was still in place and put the key in the door – only he and Georgie had keys, and the Amsels wouldn't have been alarmed by the sound. Frau Sommer's door opposite was shut, although Georgie thought she might have seen the curtain twitch. Or was that her over-egged imagination?

Rubin and Sara had already heard the search party – both suitcases were on the bed, ready to go.

'Should we just leave, pretend we're out for a walk?' Rubin suggested. 'Try and sneak back in later.'

Max shook his head. 'Too risky.' His brain seemed to be calculating. 'I'll run to the pawnbroker's and use the phone. Do you have the number of your garage – the one that supplies your cars?'

Rubin nodded.

'Good, then we'll just have to move things forward. Georgie, you take a taxi and collect the car. Meantime, we'll move to the basement, where the rubbish is kept. I've seen the troops do this before – they generally start at the top and move down. Hopefully, it will buy us some time.'

It seemed the only thing to do. There was no telling how zealous the search would be; if the troops were targeting only known addresses, or crashing through random doors and grasping any deceit. The only certainty was that any enquiry would not be polite.

Georgie moved as if in a dream, wanting to half run out onto the main street, where taxis trawled more regularly for business. But she was conscious of keeping a bounce to her step, at the same time naturally slowed by the heat of the day – just a woman out walking. She passed a trooper outside the next building standing sentry and he returned her smile. 'Good day, Fraulein.' He nodded, and she was struck that – if stripped of his uniform – he would resemble any young man across Europe. It was already a waste, whether war followed or not: a young German hunting down his own countrymen. So futile.

Georgie flagged a taxi, praying the traffic was not too heavy. Twenty minutes later, she was driving away a car that promised to be returned later that day, silently absolving herself of the lie. It was necessary and, if needed, she and Max would find some way of repaying the garage owner. The drive was hot and sluggish, fumes pushing their way into the open windows, and she had to refrain from using the horn to avoid undue attention. 'Go on, go on,' she hissed at drivers in front. 'Keep moving!'

The troops had just arrived in Max's block, scampering like ants in a line towards the courtyard. Georgie parked outside the adjacent block and waited for their uniforms to be absorbed by the building, unlocked the boot, and walked as confidently as she could towards the basement stairs at the side of the building. She hummed a tune as she neared, hopped down the few stairs to a closed door and rapped three times in quick succession. Amid the heat, gloom and unbearable stench of festering rubbish, Sara looked terrified, her eyes white and wide. Georgie reported only one sentry had been left outside, and the car was parked a little way down the street.

'Max and I will walk out down the street with the cases,' she said. 'If we're stopped, we have our press cards – it's easy to say we're going on a work trip.'

'Once we reach the car, we'll go, just Sara and I,' Rubin said. His mind was set again – no more risks for his friends.

'No,' Max said. In the darkness, his voice projected equal determination. 'You two can travel in the back, out of sight, Georgie and I in the front. We'll get you just beyond the city confines, and then we'll say goodbye.'

Shouts from above meant Rubin had no time to argue. Georgie and Max took a case each and, checking the way was clear, strode out into the sunshine, a show of laughter as they walked towards the car. Max started the engine, while Georgie returned to collect the Amsels, casually casting her eyes at the windows above, hoping any Nazi sympathisers were being kept busy. With the Amsels in tow, the distance was only a few hundred yards, but each step felt like wading through a sticky bog. The car in sight, she could see Max's wide eyes willing them to keep a steady pace, and yet hurry at the same time. A sudden shout from above induced Georgie to almost stop and snap up her head, but she reeled the instinct back in, forced herself to plough on. Only Max's image through the car window kept her moving.

She opened the back door and the Amsels poured themselves in, shrinking onto their knees behind the front seat. Georgie covered them with a blanket, while they melted into the car's dusty floor; she could only guess at the heat and humidity underneath, fear in the total blackness under the covering.

'Let's go,' Georgie said through another faux smile.

Max drove the route dictated by Rubin, his voice relayed via Georgie from under the blanket, streets he recalled were less likely to have checkpoints, bypassing government buildings with a military presence. Then, their worst nightmare – halted at an impromptu roadblock, an officer walking the line of traffic, scrutinising some papers and waving on others randomly.

Despite the open windows, the stench of sweat trickled into Georgie's nostrils; she could smell her own trepidation.

The Wehrmacht officer approached. Georgie smiled automatically, though not convincingly enough, it seemed. He smiled back, lips together in that ominous Nazi style, eyes tacking their faces, his own nostrils twitching, sniffing out duplicity.

'Heading out of town?'

Georgie handed him her press papers. 'Far too hot for us,' she trilled. 'Going for a swim in the lakes.' *Don't look in the back, please don't look in the back.*

51

Blind Panic

In the car's rear, amid the blistering, blind hellhole of the musty blanket, Rubin and Sara suspended life and lungs. Muffled by the scratchy, dank fibres, they could pick out every other word of the officer's gruff tone, but it was unequivocal. Heavy with underlying threat, his suspicion was rife. He was looking for his day's prize of fugitives and intent on finding them.

Both were crouched like rolled-up beetles, head to head, squeezed by the seats, flesh broiling, backs aching, muscles in rigor mortis. Somehow, Rubin unfurled a finger, crawled the filthy floor and silently found his wife's single digit, also probing for touch – a pulse of terror, then hope traded between them. Instantly, it sent him years back, to the first time he'd set eyes on Ester, in Sara's arms only minutes after the birth – her tiny newborn fingers pushing out like tendrils into the air, gauging her new world. Oh, and what a world it was now.

Sara's finger responded now as Ester's had done then, curling around his for extra surety – that if they were discovered, the blanket pulled back, their deceit exposed, nothing would ever rob them of this intimacy – not a prison cell, or the Gestapo's torture. Not even death.

For a few seconds, Rubin's resolve seemed unbreakable, but in the next moment he thought of no life, then worse – an existence without Sara, and his faith almost crumbled. It took every effort – and the sudden shouts of Wehrmacht beyond the car's thin casing – to keep his breath and sobs from escaping.

52

A Hard Parting

The officer's eyes flicked away, narrowed and crawled over the papers. Tick, tock, tick. Georgie felt her lungs squeeze, hot blood static – her congealed heart went out to Rubin and Sara in their back-seat sauna. Then, a shout from along the line: 'Move it along! Quick!'

The officer reacted sharply, waving them on, breath and sweat spores freed inside the car. Seconds later, a large, open-topped Nazi staff car swept by, Wehrmacht hands saluting the superior SS.

Max turned his head and his look said it all: *Oh, the irony – saved by the SS.*

Georgie's laughter was driven more by hysterics than true humour: that was too, too close.

Dusk was approaching and the heat receding a little when Max pulled into a lay-by north of the city, half a mile after passing a local train station. The Amsels had unfolded themselves gradually as the population fanned out the further north they drove, and they allowed themselves the relief of laughter at the close call. None of them wanted to calculate how many more Rubin and Sara might face before they crossed the border to any semblance of safety. If they got that far.

Rubin dusted himself off at the roadside, Sara fiddling with the cases. All four were putting off the inevitable. Finally, Georgie could not endure the delay, the unavoidable hurt.

'Come on, you need to go,' she said, in a mother hen fashion. Rubin's eyes were already brimming, Sara's mouth pinched with sadness. Lord knows the conversation between husband and wife in persuading her to leave her brother, her country and – besides her children – her entire belongings in the world.

Despite her grubbiness, Georgie threw herself at Rubin in a Rod-style hug. 'We'll see you in England,' she said into his ear, willing herself to believe her conviction. 'All of us will have some very warm English beer. I won't let you escape that pleasure.'

'I look forward to it – my Berlin girl,' he said, and broke away before his tears turned to glue. Max dispensed with the formal handshakes – he embraced Rubin in a way he might never have done with his own father. Sara, too, held tight with every muscle, muttering her endless gratitude. Each was fending off the thought that this might be their last sight of each other, all together.

Georgie couldn't look back. She daren't. It might have broken her. They heard the engine start and the car draw away, and Max – knowing her – tugged at her hand in the direction of the train station.

'Come on, we have to get that train home. And if they don't have a cold beer at the station bar, then I might just have a little boy tantrum.'

The hole left by the Amsels was lessened by the thought they might have a chance. But the lack of news was agonising for Georgie; the mileage to the border was easily covered, but their route would be necessarily winding, and reports of their progress a long way off.

Work, however, kept her occupied: the days were frantic and Henry's demands increased to not one or two but three major stories per day. Help had not arrived in the Berlin office, diverted instead to Warsaw, where editors predicted the epicentre of war might initially be. Georgie and Max were both working long hours and there was no hope of investigating or exposing the link between Kasper, Doctor Graf and Sachsenhausen, and yet it seemed more urgent, with war just around the corner.

Around the table at La Taverne, later and later into the evening, there was no longer any talk of 'if' there would be a war, merely how soon it would be. Days? Weeks? Hitler was steadfast in his claims on Poland as a right for the German people, the rest of Europe desperately trying to postpone the slide into conflict, as if teetering on the edge of a very steep and mud-filled gully, knowing a messy fall was imminent but treading carefully anyway.

Berlin's streets choked with fumes from the throaty exhausts of military vehicles, though – much like the creeping crimson of the flags – everyone seemed to adjust very quickly, sidestepping lines of troop carriers and getting on with their day. Once again, Georgie reflected on Hitler's consummate skill in making the abnormal mould into everyday life. The British papers at home, by contrast, reported a frenzied preparation as only the British knew how, a mild panic whipped up by speculation.

Georgie and Max managed little time to talk privately, only a veiled shaking of the head at La Taverne, meaning 'no news yet'. Simone had made a reappearance after several weeks largely absent from the flat and was at Max's side again, though Georgie sensed their body language was decidedly cooler. Elsewhere, Rubin's garage owner was a sympathetic non-Jew but still had to be persuaded not to report the borrowed car as stolen. He was out of pocket to the tune of one vehicle, after all, and could have made life very difficult for them both, proving – thankfully – there were plenty of Berliners who had not swallowed Hitler's hatred entirely. *There is some hope for us, after all,* Georgie mused.

53

A Visitor

23rd August 1939

Georgie was alone in the office, frantic to make her deadline but enjoying the solitude and the clatter of her typewriter drowning out the military din floating up from the street. Still, any knock on the door startled her and she spent precious seconds assessing if the bodies loomed large and grey. It was merely a slight lad bearing a telegram.

4km north Saarbrucken, French border. Au Revoir. Merci.

Georgie checked the origin of the telegram – a French mark. Could she believe it? Dare she? That it was from the Amsels – that they had made it across the border and were letting her know where they'd left the car? She checked her map of Germany. Yes, Saarbrucken was a town nudged on the border. It was everything she and Max had hoped for, and yet she couldn't quite believe it to be true. She needed him to agree, to rubber stamp that feeling of joy.

She pushed out the remaining words of her story in pure

excitement and ran to Max's office, where he would surely be filing his own copy. Like her, he read the same line again and again, turned the paper over several times in disbelief, and – finally, finally – endorsed her hopes.

'I think they've done it,' he whispered to avoid the ears of his German admin worker. Max gripped Georgie's hand, his face bathed in delight. 'I think they really might make it all the way.'

'Celebrations tonight at La Taverne?' she suggested.

Max's face fell. 'Hmm, wouldn't be so sure of the mood there. Bill's been on the phone – he's livid. Some radio commentators, Americans, were turned away from Tempelhof today, met by the Gestapo and hustled back on the plane. He thinks it's just a taste of things to come. We might have to become very inventive.'

It was a blow for the press, but nothing could dampen Georgie's mood as she sauntered back to her own office. She swung the door open, humming 'Greensleeves' to herself – and stopped in her tracks. Stunned into silence.

His back was to her, sitting in her office chair. He didn't swing around immediately, giving her enough time to appreciate just what his presence meant. Here. Waiting for her.

'Kasper?' she said. Her surprise was genuine, the reaction pathetic, a croak of alarm rising in her throat. He swivelled, brow raised, those unnerving eyes bright with the joy of his coup, lips pressed together in a thin, half-smile. Lazily, he picked up an envelope addressed to her.

'George Young, Chief Bureau Correspondent, *News Chronicle*,' he read aloud. 'You are a writer, then?'

'I am.' Her mouth was dry. Parched. She forced the next words out. 'Truly. You made a presumption that many men have in the past, and I didn't disabuse you.' Her eyes crawled the office – no SS or Gestapo hiding in the walls that she could see.

He rocked his head from side to side, humouring her. 'Hmm, I'd call it creative with the truth. Wouldn't you?'

'And would it have made a difference?' she ventured. 'Didn't we have a nice time all the same?' She was blathering, saying anything that came to mind.

Now, his eyes dimmed. Darkened. The green became muddy, the grey ashen. 'You know it would have, Fraulein Young, hence your little white lie. That our liaison might not go down so well: Himmler's boy – yes, that's what I am, for now – in league with British press. I'm certain, too, that you're aware I have a weakness for the company of English women, but don't flatter yourself. You were never the only one.'

The twist in her gut was not from vanity – Georgie only too pleased not to be in Kasper's sights anymore – but his manner. Cold. Switched. She'd expected the Nazi in him to multiply. Here it was – he was – showing her the full transition.

He pulled up, stood up swiftly, switched on his light again. 'No matter, I'm not here about my wounded pride. I'm looking for someone – a man I *know* to be an employee of yours: Rubin Amsel. He appears to have left Berlin with his wife, inexplicably and quickly. Would you know anything about that?'

He didn't for a minute expect her help. It was his game now. Kasper was too senior even then to be a common Jew-catcher trolling the streets; the entire visit had been only to inform and bait her.

'No, I haven't seen Herr Amsel in a while. He was a messenger for me, that's all, paid on a retainer by the paper. I haven't needed his services for a few weeks.'

He didn't push her lie, only changed tack: 'Do you want to know why we want to find him?' Kasper stepped closer, cheek to cheek, the combination of cologne and sweat on his collar. She could hear his breath. *This close, can he smell my dread?*

Fury overcame fear then. 'I suspect because he's Jewish,' Georgie said calmly. 'As I understand it, that's a crime now.'

He stopped, stared at her, exuding hatred for her mettle, as a woman and a non–Nazi. His look swapped to pitying, and Georgie read it plainly: *You don't know the half of it,* he was thinking. *I feel sorry for your kind. You non-believers.*

'You'll excuse me if I don't engage you for another date,' he said instead, approaching the door. 'It's simply not appropriate.'

'I understand entirely,' she said. Relief was inching within sight at his departure. Only then did she really see how much Kasper had gleaned from his superiors in recent months, the skill in timing the glancing but fatal blow.

'I'm interested to see what your friend Max Spender has to say about the Amsels,' he said pointedly, as he reached the door. 'I think I'll ask him.'

Breath stopped in her, choking back pointless words of protest. But Kasper wasn't finished.

'Oh, and one more thing,' he oozed. 'What I said about Germans not being so organised . . .'

She cocked her head at the memory, their innocent banter all those months ago at the Resi.

'I lied, Fraulein Young. We in the Nazi Party are extremely organised. Which makes us not only determined but very efficient when we want something done.'

One parting glint to those eyes and he was gone, with the swagger of a gothic vampire character in a bad film, only the swish of his cape absent.

Georgie was on the phone as she heard Kasper descend the stairs. 'Pick up, Max, pick up. Please. Please.' He had to be there, had been only half an hour before, the office woman too. *Please, Max.*

But there was only the ringing tone, endless and echoey, into her ear.

'Bill, Bill?' Georgie banged on the door of the *Chicago Tribune* office, tucked on the ground floor of the Adlon. The bar was absent of any press in the late afternoon, and she'd already hurried to Kranzler's, eyes surfing over the crowd. Nothing but the ever-confident tones of SS and Wehrmacht officers. La Taverne wasn't a realistic option at that time of day, but she'd rung all the same – the Lehmanns hadn't seen Max. It was the same at Frida's flat – no answer, and as much as she didn't relish the image, she couldn't see Max and Simone taking to her bed with so much happening out there in the wider world.

'What's up?' Bill Porter emerged, blinking, from the gloom of his office. He hadn't seen Max since a morning press briefing. 'He's probably following up on a story,' he added, though concern dawned when Georgie relayed her encounter with Kasper. 'Oh shit. That's not so good.'

It was what she feared, but not what she wanted to hear. Anxiety multiplied.

'You go to his flat, check if he's been there, and I'll head to his office,' Bill said. 'If he's not back, I'll put in a call to London and find out what time he last filed any copy. Meet here in an hour, okay?'

Anguish was an efficient fuel as Georgie took a taxi to Max's building. The street was quiet, no search parties this time, only a curious cat winding around her legs, though it disappeared smartly as Frau Sommer's own feline stamped its territory with a loud meow. This time, the curtains definitely twitched. Maybe she wasn't the innocuous neighbour Max had supposed.

The thread in the doorjamb was absent, and Georgie prayed it was Max's own doing. She rapped on the door, pushed her ear to the wood. Nothing. Was he asleep? Unlikely, even with the frantic pace of work in past days. Another knock, then she fumbled in her bag for the key.

'Max? Max, are you here? It's George.' Her voice echoed in the empty flat. But someone had been there. It was moderately untidy, a few clothes lain across the bed and the sofa, a single sheet of paper poking from a drawer. Having witnessed Max's pristine way of living, it was clear the flat had been searched. A scuffle? That was harder to tell. A small ruck in the mat in front of the hearth was possibly innocent. But maybe not.

Panic began to swell in her chest, and Georgie worked to cap it off before it could overwhelm her. It would not help find Max. Instead, she forced herself to circle slowly in the living room, eyes crawling over every small thing she'd noted, on that first visit and the length of the Amsels' stay. But there was nothing too out of the ordinary, nothing to say he was in direct danger. Yet . . .

Max, where the hell are you?

Georgie ran from the address, hailed another taxi and headed back to the Adlon. In days of old, she would have called on Rubin and Rod for help. And Max himself, of course. Now, it was Bill – cynical but reliable Bill – that she went to.

He was in the bar, shaking his head as she approached. 'Not been at his office since the afternoon. Apparently, he left soon after you did.'

'Anyone come to see him after me?'

'Not according to the fierce Fraulein at the *Telegraph* offices. She's a bundle of laughs by the way.'

Georgie twisted her fingers with worry. Kasper's face loomed again, the smirk of satisfaction at making her squirm, payback for her deceit. Using Max as bait. Bill didn't know the whole story and she felt too sick to relay it now.

'Too early for a drink?' he said. They had nowhere else to look, aside from the whole of Berlin. They could only wait, for Max, or some signal from the Gestapo.

'No,' Georgie said resolutely. 'Definitely not.'

It was six o'clock when he waltzed in casually, as they were bent over the bar, Georgie's imagination still running riot.

'Hello there, didn't expect to see you two here this early,' Max said, dropping his bag and hopping onto a stool. Georgie didn't know whether to laugh, cry or scold him for causing such heartache, choosing merely to frown at him.

'What? What have I done?' he cried in all innocence.

'You didn't get a visit from the SS?' Georgie quizzed. 'From Kasper?'

'Not unless he's hiding around the corner, or under the chair here.' He made a play at searching, then realised it was a bad move when Georgie's scowl became thunderous.

'Don't joke, Max. It's serious. Your flat has been searched. I've been worried sick.'

'And there's me thinking you don't care.' But this further attempt at humour wasn't working.

Bill got off his stool, wincing at the storm about to break. 'I'm off, leave you two to sort this one out.' He slunk back to his office.

'So, what do we do now?' Georgie pitched, her tempest abating after relaying the details of Kasper's visit. 'He still may come for you. You should have seen his face. Underneath that smug exterior, he was livid. Furious at how I'd deceived him.'

'As press we are protected – not fully but to a certain extent,' Max argued. 'It sounds to me like he's enjoying the threat. Bluffing with menaces. But I will be careful.'

'Just please don't go anywhere alone. Make sure you're in crowds, around people.'

'Yes, squadron leader.' He made a mock British salute. 'But, you know, I am a big boy now.'

'You are bloody infuriating, I *do* know that.' The thunder had moved on, clouds breaking to reveal blue sky. Calmer.

'So I've been told.'

With Georgie's certainty that his flat had been searched, Max agreed not to return home that night. An early press conference had been called at the Reich Chancellery, and with a large, late gathering at La Taverne, he and Georgie headed back with Frida to her flat. Simone sent word she was 'on a story', and Georgie felt relieved to avoid the embarrassment of the sleeping arrangements.

They ambled slowly back towards Frida's, enjoying the late, light evening, despite the rumble of the city in the distance.

'You needn't have worried, you know,' Max said suddenly, breaking their own, contented silence.

'About Kasper? But he's dang—'

'No,' he cut in. 'I didn't mean that. About Simone, it being awkward at the flat.'

How on earth did he know what I was thinking?

'We're not an item anymore,' he added. 'And it's fine. Really.'

'Oh, I'm sorry,' Georgie said. Though deep down she found she wasn't.

'Why sorry?' he shot back.

'Well, because she seemed to like you, and you appeared to like her. A lot.'

'Maybe,' Max said. 'A bit of fascination on both sides, I think. But there is actually someone else . . .'

Her head turned, needing to gauge his look, to read his features – stopped short by a throaty roar overhead, which forced both heads to snap up and watch as a fat queen bee of a troop carrier droned low across the Berlin sky. The thunderous noise – the sound of war – prompted Max to grab her hand, squeezing it tight. She flicked again to face him. What was that look? *Dammit, why couldn't she read him?*

'Hey, you two! Hurry up – I've got a new cocktail just mixed.' It was Frida hanging out of her window onto the street and waving, Max's hand instantly relaxing and breaking the hold.

'Great timing,' he said jauntily, though Georgie couldn't tell if it was sarcasm or disappointment in his voice.

54

Plucked

The pack was out in force the next morning, amid rumours that Britain was about to make a strong pledge of support to Poland in the event of a German attack. Words were firm on both sides, though no one dared to make the first move. If it happened, the only result would be all-out war. The biggest story, but the outcome they all dreaded.

Max had slept on the sofa, leaving Frida's early to check in at his office and arrive at the briefing on time. Exhausted, Georgie slept through her alarm and was shaken awake by Frida, the two of them scrabbling to make it in time. Imminent conflict or not, Herr Bauer still reserved fierce disapproval for latecomers, his expression as if he'd sucked on the very lemons that were no longer available in the shops.

Things were different again on the streets; in recent weeks aircraft had flown over Berlin at odd times of the day, moving between airfields. Now, as both women ran towards the chancellery, there was a permanent buzzing above their heads, swarms in formation hovering high in the sky. Some Berliners gazed upwards, but most looked resigned to what was simply the newest backdrop to their lives.

Press numbers were swollen and the room packed, Georgie sliding into a seat at the back. She could see Max up front, next to the *Times* correspondent and a group of radio hacks from the BBC and NBC. The rest were French, Italian and Eastern European reporters, some Scandinavian. With so much political bartering in recent days, everyone wanted the story, and with the windows fully open, the hum of air traffic pushed its way through. Herr Bauer stood like a schoolmaster at the front, fiddling with papers and fingering his minuscule moustache.

'He must be having kittens at this attendance,' Georgie whispered to Frida, and they both giggled at his officious façade.

The levity was short-lived, not only with the start of the briefing, but also by a frantic signalling from Bill, who was peering through a crack in the door. He beckoned Georgie towards him with an expression of near desperation.

'What's going on?' she whispered.

'It's a set-up,' he said hoarsely, eyes wide with alarm.

'What do you mean?' His tone was giving her goose bumps.

'They have a warrant – for Max's arrest. I just heard via a source. That's why I'm late. It's signed by Himmler and Goebbels.'

When, what, where and how? – the four key questions a reporter asks of any story. Now they flooded Georgie's mind, in a pressing need. The when and where elements were crucial – they had to warn Max immediately.

Georgie edged back into the room, shuffling past a quizzical Frida. Bill had begun inching quietly around the opposite side of the crowd unnoticed, easier said than done as his presence caused several reporters to look up and nod in recognition. The man speaking at the lectern was a junior press officer, giving out minor details in a dull monotone before Goebbels took to his stage. Max remained four rows beyond Georgie, his head bobbing as he scribbled down words. She was tantalisingly close and had to stop herself catching his attention with an urgent whisper. She looked up at where Bill stood, saw his head snap to something behind. Why wasn't he focused on Max?

Half a second later the noise registered; a loud scuffling of bodies near the door, barging past a clutch of standing reporters. Four heavily built men, all in suits despite the rising heat of the room. They marched up to where Max was sitting, and Georgie could see from the cock of his head that he was more confused than alarmed.

'Max Spender?' one said, though it was a statement, not a question.

'Yes?' Still only curious.

'I have a warrant for your arrest. Please come with us.'

The room gasped, stood and burst into a cacophony of noise and opposition. 'No, no! You can't do that! He's press!' But they – presumably Gestapo – were deaf to the pleas and bent to take physical possession of Max.

His voice was lost, head disappearing from Georgie's view as she fought desperately to reach him. Then, the swathe of bodies shuffled towards the door and she was caught in the tide, fighting to weave her way through to him. She skirted the edge, close to the wall and made some ground; Max's height meant finally she could follow his head nearing the door. Georgie spied a gap, ducked under several bodies and pushed herself out into the hallway, like breaking the surf of a drowning wave. She scooped in the air and space, scanning quickly. Being nearer to the door, Bill had already made it to Max and they were exchanging words as the prisoner was hustled away. She ran forward, lunged and was held back firmly by one of the Gestapo men. Max turned and caught sight of her.

'Georgie, it'll be fine,' he assured her, though his eyes said not. 'Call my paper, and the embassy. I'll see you soon.' And being Max, he tried to smile.

Then he was gone. The hallway was empty, the press room in disarray and Herr Bauer called an easy halt to the proceedings, with no hint of disappointing Joey Goebbels waiting in the wings, because the Minister for Propaganda had never been there at all. As planned. Meticulously. The briefing was a bluff; a carefully scripted scene, ready for Max to exit stage left, serving as a warning to all around him. Georgie cast around the empty hallway – Kasper was nowhere to be seen, but his fingerprints lay all over this page.

Bill approached and did his best to mimic Rod's reassuring embrace. Georgie wanted it to last forever, lost in the human touch amid this nightmare, but they needed to act.

'I'll call his London editor,' Bill said. 'You go to the embassy – easier for you to do that as you're a Brit. Meet back at my office in an hour?'

She could barely nod. The shock had taken hold. The consequences of her initial flirtation, her vanity at being flattered by Kasper's charms, her dangerous manipulation of him. What if something happened to Max as a result?

'Georgie? Georgie, come on. No time for thinking too much,' Bill urged. Both hands were on her shoulders, just short of shaking. 'We need to just do it. Let's go.'

'All right, one hour.'

Frida ran up behind Georgie then, pulled on her shoulder. 'I'll see what I can find out,' she promised, 'pull in a few favours.' Undoubtedly, she meant amongst her Nazi acquaintances, but Georgie didn't care so long as it helped Max.

The grandiose buildings were a blur on the short walk to the British Embassy on Wilhelmstrasse; a combination of her press card, the tears beginning to prick at her eyeballs and a wobbling voice got her into Sam Blundon's office immediately. Being a good friend, he made her sit, supplied tea and brandy. She'd seen arrests before, God knows she knew of the lengths Nazis stooped to when it came to Jews, had even identified Paul's bloated, murdered body. But this was Max. Her Max. The uncontrollable shake in her hand made her realise what a friend he'd become; they'd worked, laughed, shared bad reporter jokes, beers and pastries. She realised then how much of an ally he was, a voice of reason, a comfort that this world they'd entered together would not spin out of control, and them with it. She had felt in her gut that they needed to tell the story to the world, but Max's steadfast agreement in that pursuit gave her more courage, sealed up the holes where her confidence was lacking. She'd even forgiven him for his behaviour at the Ritz.

This was Sam's world now and he stepped up. 'Since Max is a British citizen, I can ask officially as to the purpose of his arrest. I'll request to see him, but if the charges are related to espionage in any way — and you know they can make it so — then it's not likely they'll let me.'

Georgie looked dejected. Guilt was seeping through the pores of her skin, and she came clean about Kasper — her courting of him, and the reasons, Max's involvement, the Amsels' stay at his apartment.

'Ah, that makes it more difficult because it's become personal for this Vortsch character,' Sam said. 'I think the most we can hope for is that they deport Max. And quickly.'

Georgie's soul plummeted to depths she'd never imagined. She felt so helpless, with Max undoubtedly at Gestapo HQ; the same emotions Rubin and Sara had felt on Elias's arrest, and every day since. And it was horrifying. Max was no more special than any person whose rights had been stomped over by the Nazis in their polished jackboots and gilded conceit.

And yet, to her he was. Deep inside, her heart ached. It was painful. Physically. She felt blindsided – by the situation and this alien feeling.

Christ, Georgie! No wallowing allowed. Just get on with it.

Back at the Adlon, Bill had spoken to the *Telegraph*'s London office; Max wasn't the first reporter on their books to be arrested, though the first on the brink of a war. The editor pledged to tug on every string they had in the British Government, old boy circles and the lords if necessary. Max's father would use his influence too. But it might take time.

'How much time?' Georgie cried. She felt control was fast deserting her.

'A few days maybe,' Bill said.

'And in the meantime, in there? Bill, you and I both know what happens at Gestapo HQ.'

'We can't think about it,' he urged. Commanded almost. 'It's likely they will make him sit and stew, use him only as an example – for the press to behave.'

Georgie nodded. She had to believe him. She had no choice. And she had to make herself *not* think about Paul and his desolate, violent end, lying on that cold slab.

If the days after the Amsels' escape had been agonising, this wait was torturous. The core of Georgie's thinking was with Max, but her job still demanded focus and the world on their doorstep twisted every hour. The news they'd all been waiting for came through the next day – a female journalist new to Berlin had dug out her scoop, a sure sighting of German tank divisions on the Polish border, ready to move. It was the confirmation everyone needed that the snake was ready to strike. Not even the Germans tried to pretend they were on military exercise. War could be only days away, and while high-ranking British and French diplomats hoped for an eleventh-hour reprieve, no one truly believed it would happen. The world would be forced to wake up – and quickly.

In response, the British Embassy issued a recommendation for all correspondents to leave immediately, which sailed over Georgie's head. Not without Max. Others stood firm, the Americans included, and they convened earlier than usual at La Taverne – there was no point in writing anything, as communications in and out of Berlin had been suspended all day, both telephone and telegraph. The US radio reporters, who usually broadcast late, sat twitching with stories tumbling around their heads. Georgie could only shake her head at the queries over Max.

'All they'll say is the charges relate to spying,' she relayed to the table.

'Bastards,' someone piped up. 'It's a fit-up. They wouldn't know a free press if it smacked them in the gills.'

Bill wasn't tipsy, as he sometimes could be at this hour, merely belligerent. 'Well, let's show these bastards we won't be beaten,' he rallied. 'Let's report our little asses off.' To which there was an almighty cheer and the mood lifted for a few seconds. Then all eyes fell on Frida as she came through the door.

She walked over and pushed her mouth into Georgie's ear. 'Let's go to the ladies.'

Checking each stall was empty, Frida lit a cigarette and took a long drag, stunningly beautiful with her defiant look.

'My source tells me Max will be deported, thanks to some pressure from your English side, but probably not for a few days.'

Georgie sagged with a mixture of relief and sadness. 'And is he all right? Do you have any details on that?'

'Not much, it's only what my source has heard. Knowing the Gestapo, he might have a few bumps and bruises – just for show,' she said. 'They can't let their reputation falter.'

'One more thing,' Frida added, raising her sculpted eyebrows. 'Simone has gone.'

'Where? What does that mean?' Georgie pressed. Frida was enigmatic at the best of times, but did she think Simone might have been involved? The same Simone who visibly draped herself over Max, and genuinely seemed to like him.

'I don't know.' Frida took another drag on her cigarette. 'She disappears on stories all time, and I don't usually worry, but this feels different. She's been acting oddly recently, and something tells me she's gone for good.' She tossed the cigarette into the toilet. 'Just goes to show you can't trust anyone, doesn't it?'

55

Discovery and Dread

29th August 1939

Sleep over the next four nights was fleeting and fitful for Georgie, awash with dreams of screeching car tyres and rerunning the escape from Sachsenhausen, this time with Kasper barring their way, self-satisfied and with that malevolent grin that only dreams can bring.

She hauled herself to the office each day, reporting on the introduction of formal German rationing; no oranges, but also limited food in general, and on soap, shoes and coal too. And if nothing else had so far signalled war, the Nazis had called off the annual Nuremberg rally, planned for early September. They would be otherwise occupied, they were telling the world.

Sam phoned as she was contemplating a timely postcard. 'I've seen him,' he said.

Georgie's breath stalled. 'And?'

'He's fine,' Sam sighed. 'Relatively fine for Gestapo HQ – a few bruises, but I've seen worse.'

'And how is he in himself? Holding up?' She could barely force herself to ask.

This time, Sam's voice relaxed. 'He is well, Georgie. He asked me to say hello, let you know he's being a big boy, whatever that means.'

Breath reinstated. Heart reduced to merely a clatter.

'They're talking about Thursday for release – and immediate deportation,' Sam added.

'That's two days! We could be at war tomorrow.' It felt that close. 'What will happen then? If we're at war, the embassy won't have any leverage. They could just leave him in there.' The heart hammering became fast and noisy again.

Sam's sigh was heavy in the receiver. 'As is too often the case these days, we just have to hope.'

```
                                Postcard from Berlin


Dear News Chronicle Readers,
    It's a lottery as to what will reach you first
- this missive or the news that Europe is at war.
I suspect it may be the latter, given Germany's
current preparations. With food and goods rationing,
Berliners have become foragers in their own city,
whilst grocery trucks criss-cross the city, packed
with their new cargo of troops. The hot, summer
air is sticky with speculation, the footfall of
ordinary people deadened by a resignation that this
is life, for the foreseeable future at least.
    Farewell from a country still at peace, but for
how long we wonder?
    Your correspondent in Berlin
```

Georgie headed home through the warm, sultry evening, choosing to walk through the Tiergarten and admire its beauty – in the back of her mind, she thought it might be her last opportunity, so unsure was the world underfoot. But away from the park's greenery, military exhaust fumes had made the Berlin she'd come to love feel suddenly fuggy and dirty. Previously loyal citizens looked dejected, as if rationing was the blow that finally robbed wind from their sails. Certainly, the flags were flat, with not a breath of air causing the crimson to fly. She'd already passed by the chancellery and noted only a small crowd outside – tiny by Nazi standards – who could barely raise a combined voice under the dull whine of aircraft. Even the strudel at Kranzler's, so far unaffected by rationing, couldn't lift her spirits, and she left to share a rare pot of tea with Bill at the Adlon, glad when he didn't attempt to say 'chin up'.

The day before Max's deportation, Georgie's mind churned endlessly, split between the continued shunting of tension on the war front and this personal dilemma. Her focus should have been entirely on work, with so much at stake, but she couldn't stop her mind from wandering. Nothing in Berlin was right any longer, but there was some element – she couldn't pinpoint exactly – which felt very wrong.

Frida had gleaned one final nugget of information from inside No. 8 Prinz-Albrecht-Strasse – that Max would be moved at eleven a.m. the next day, from the front entrance. Once again, it was a Nazi sideshow, insisting to the world's press that they would tolerate neither impudence nor humanity from the reporters present at their invitation. Hitler's perfect control mechanism – fear and threat.

'To the airport, or the station?' Georgie quizzed.

'That I don't know,' Frida said. 'If it is by train, they'll surely escort him to the border and makes sure he stays on.'

Georgie filed her copy for the day and headed to Max's apartment. One thought had sprung to mind in the early hours of sleep evasion: she could at least try to pass him some clothes on the steps. There was a good chance his editor would divert him only as far as Paris, and he would need some clothes other than those he stood up in.

Both Frau Sommer and her cat had the good grace not to appear at the window, and Georgie let herself into the flat, seemingly untouched since her last visit. She found a bag and looked through drawers for essentials and personal trinkets. It felt intrusive, but she reasoned that if there was a precious photograph left behind, of his mother especially, Max would want it. She found one tucked under his passport, lingering for a moment over the informal, tender picture of a mother and her fresh-faced son, smiling together, her arm affectionately around him, chin resting on the top of his hair.

At the same time, a thought cranked into motion. Why was the passport there? Max would need it to travel on. The Nazis were all too aware, would have seized it in their search, surely?

The realisation came slowly, landing finally like a boxer's killer punch. And that feeling was beyond painful – a burning, searing brand of dread at his true destination: Max wouldn't need a passport where he was going.

Oh, Kasper, what a clever little Nazi you've been.

56

Farewells

31st August 1939

Diplomatic notes had been passed back and forward for days across the channel, with British Ambassador Nevile Henderson acting as the all-important messenger in the tit-for-tat politics. Only this was no longer a playground spat between silly boys, the reported content of each message – no side seemingly prepared to give any ground – serving to whip up the tension. It felt to the world as if every avenue had been exhausted, and Hitler was standing firm, so too Chamberlain at last. The broil of a storm above Berlin couldn't feel any more tense; the air smacked of certain conflict. In Georgie's dry mouth, there was little spit to remove a metallic taste of terror mixed with determination.

She sat in front of Gestapo HQ with a bag of Max's belongings, a small holdall of her own on the car seat beside her, fear neatly tucked inside her stomach. Her resolve she wore freely like a scarf blowing in a good breeze. They would not do this. To him or her. Not without a fight.

Georgie's scheme was based on opportunity and not much

else. And she'd told nobody, to avoid their guilt by implication. She'd hired a car early that morning, locked up the office and set off. The wait was, as usual, agonising. At one point, her heart jolted when she imagined seeing Kasper walk up the steps but shrank again when it proved to be another young officer with the same SS swagger.

True to the source, at eleven o'clock a group appeared on the steps. There was no attempt to hide the prisoner, and Georgie was relieved to see Max free of handcuffs. He didn't appear to be limping or struggling to walk either, talking to the men around him with no sign of rancour. But then he would, if he imagined heading towards a train or a plane to safety. Their treachery caused Georgie's anger to swell.

The car moved off, Max in the back with a Gestapo man, another in the front alongside the driver. She followed behind. Now, she had to wait and pray for the right opportunity, whenever and wherever it fell.

They drove south-west out of the city, and Max must have assumed – in his blissful ignorance – they were headed for Zoo station and the train to Paris. Georgie willed herself to stay calm behind the wheel, keeping as much of a distance as she dared without losing sight. Soon, they had passed the road towards the station and were veering north instead – perhaps rounding the city towards Sachsenhausen? The Gestapo car slowed at a newly created checkpoint and Georgie's head throbbed in time with the engine. Was this it? Her only chance? Once they were clear of the city, there might be no other. She grabbed the two holdalls and pulled what courage she had from somewhere inside. Almost on autopilot, she stepped from her car, turning off the engine. Walking towards the Gestapo car, Georgie quickened her stride, willing it to fuel her resolve like some kind of dynamo, injecting her with enough nerve for the plan only just formulating in her head.

Come on, time to give Margot the actress a run for her money.

'It's you!' she screamed, pointing at the Gestapo man, who'd left the car and was talking to the checkpoint guard. He wheeled round at the sudden volume, hand immediately going to his waistband inside his jacket, then dropped it when he realised the noise was coming from a woman.

'What do you mean it's me?' he came back angrily. He was tall and broad, muscles evident under his shirt, and Georgie had to rely on sheer fury to keep her legs moving forward.

She pointed accusingly again. 'You, you bastard!'

She turned towards others in the car, the guards and two cars in the line behind them – anyone within earshot. '*He* assaulted me. He got me drunk and took advantage. What would the Führer say of that – defiling a woman? A wife, and a mother?' Georgie took another leap: 'What would *your* wife say about that, eh?

She'd hit a nerve. The man winced visibly and Georgie leapt on it. 'I bet she'd like to hear all about it, wouldn't she? I know where you live, I could go and pay her a visit. Would you like that?' She grinned like a woman possessed, the face of someone crazy enough to do just that.

She was making it up as she went along, but the man shrank as if facing a tornado, up against the verbal power of this harridan, lips curled in rage, finger jabbing like a bayonet. The driver and the other Gestapo man got out of the car to try and calm Georgie, but she twisted away from their grip, forging forward. She glimpsed Max's face pressed up against the car window, knew he'd seen her and trusted he understood.

Georgie couldn't stop, didn't dare wind down yet. 'Yes, you, Hans, I'm talking to you,' she poked, nearer to him.

He shrank again. 'But my name isn't Hans,' he said weakly. 'You're mistaken. It's not me.' He looked embarrassed and fearful at the scene she was causing.

357

'Well, *Hans*, or whatever your name is, I am going straight to the Kripo. I will find your superior, and I will make sure everyone knows what a disgusting bastard you are.' Her voice was already hoarse and she struggled to keep up the volume.

They would have laughed it off in any other situation – the idea of such accusations sticking to any man, but in the moment they just wanted to shut her up. Passers-by were starting to slow and look, cars backing up in the line.

'Hey, we can talk about this, just come in here,' 'Hans' said, gesturing towards the small wooden guard hut. The others had congregated by it, one sparking up a cigarette.

Now or never, Georgie. You might die, but just do it.

She dropped her shoulders, made as if to consider the offer of negotiation, backing several steps nearer to the Gestapo car. The group of men shrank back in response, hackles down, scene over, silly woman placated. Then Georgie spun on one foot, leapt towards the door and dropped herself into the driver's seat like a stone, pitching the bags beside her. The men froze with disbelief as she crunched the idling car into gear, reversing wildly and whipped the steering wheel around, clipping the barrier as she swerved off in the direction of what looked like a road. Any road.

Engine roaring, she seemed to have the element of surprise; the men would be scrambling to find another car to give chase in, the guard's military truck or the one she had abandoned, but she calculated having at least a minute head start.

Max was silent, perhaps with shock. Breathless, his voice finally came from the back. 'I can't see them, not yet.' Her foot was to the floor, the engine straining loudly, gravel spitting under the tyres, knuckles white again on the steering wheel.

She daren't look in the mirror, relying on Max. 'They're behind, I can just see them,' he said.

'I can't go any faster,' she cried.

After an age: 'Hang on! They're slowing, I think they've stopped.' His voice rose in celebration of Lady Luck. 'I think they've got a bloody flat tyre!'

She didn't chance it – drove out as far and as fast as she could for another twenty minutes, into open countryside, until the petrol gauge winked that the tank was nearing empty.

'Bloody hell, Georgie, what have you done?' Max said as she dared to slow. His tone suggested she'd been extreme, in perhaps only delaying his deportation.

'You weren't going to the station or the airport,' she stated plainly, eyes fixed on the road. 'They don't have your passport. Never intended to get it.'

'Christ. Really? They were bloody convincing.'

'That's their job, Max. They're very good at it, in case you hadn't noticed.'

They parked up at the entrance to a dilapidated farm, found a map in the glove compartment and were trying to work out where they were and what to do, when an old man, likely a farmer, walked towards them.

'We're just lost, all right?' Georgie whispered as the man came near. She switched on a smile.

'Can I help?' he said. His accent wasn't German; if Georgie wasn't mistaken, it was Polish. And possibly Jewish.

They made a play of being lost, but as the farmer scanned the car out of the corner of his eye and the unusual registration plates, his face hinted suspicion.

They'd had opportunity, now they needed more luck. In abundance.

'We're not Gestapo,' Georgie announced suddenly, pulling out her press card, to Max's wild stare of disbelief. It was their only hope, in explaining away the Gestapo vehicle.

Luck was on their side still. The farmer *was* a Jew, married to a German. And a firm anti-Nazi. They pushed the car into his barn and covered it with tarpaulin. He called over two muscular young men working nearby. 'They'll have that stripped down to spare parts within the hour,' he said with a satisfied smile.

The farmer and his wife offered a bed for the night, but they declined – again, all too aware of the danger of guilt by association. At the table, Max wolfed down what was offered, Georgie searching his face for signs of the Gestapo's work. There were several bruises on both cheeks – she pictured the delivery of that hand swipe that acts as an aperitif to more violence – and one purple swelling where the flesh of his neck met his collarbone. Her heart pinched, though Max only radiated delight at tasting good food and freedom. Perhaps his school upbringing had made him tougher than she gave him credit for?

They both spent time with a bowl of hot water, washing off the morning's grime, and Georgie got busy with her compact on Max's face.

'Ever considered a new career as a make-up artist?' he quipped.

'I might have to,' she shot back. 'Question is, what are you going to do?'

'I'm quite good at making cocktails. Any future in that, do you think?'

By three p.m., they were in the back of the farmer's covered truck, rattling over the bumpy roads, lying on a bed of potatoes and turnips. The last flight out of Tempelhof to Europe was at five p.m. And they had to be on it, Max calculating that trains were more risky – they could be stopped and searched at a whole number of points. They hoped the Gestapo would rely on them making for a border by car, the airport being far too dicey to contemplate. And, in truth, it was. But once they were up in the air and out of the German airspace, they would be out of Gestapo clutches.

Only the airport to get through.

They lay in silence for a while, listening to the farmer's tuneful whistle as he bumped along. Although neither relished it, there was enough produce in the back for a decent turnip burial in the event of a search.

'I think you'd look good with a turnip for a hat,' Max said at last.

'And potatoes for earrings?' She giggled. A dose of relief, exhaustion and adrenalin had injected a real absurdity.

'You would be the queen of the fashion pages for sure.'

'Don't you mean the fashion scribe?' she teased.

'No, definitely not that. You are George Young, hard-nosed news reporter. And my saviour.'

She shrugged. 'All in a day's work, Max Spender, investigator extraordinaire.'

'Shame we'll probably be unemployed. I think I've burnt my final boat with the *Telegraph*.'

'Henry won't be too pleased either. Perhaps we can simply sail away somewhere exotic and avoid the war,' she said, weaving dreams in her head. 'What do you say?'

'Yes. Gladly.' Now there was no humour in his voice. Only solemnity.

She squinted in the gloom. Trying to read his features and his mood, for the hundredth time since that first meeting at the Ritz. Failing again.

'Max?'

His hand crawled spider-like, little finger locking into hers. She didn't flinch or pull away. His flesh was hot, along with the day. But it was something more. An energy.

'Marry me,' he murmured.

Her laughter was lost as they hit a pothole and the truck bounced dramatically. 'What?'

'Marry me. Please, Georgie Young. Bloody amazing, brave,

talented woman. Marry me, and we'll blaze a trail across the world as the best journo team it's ever seen.'

She was silenced by his look of utter . . . she still couldn't tell what. 'But why?'

'Because I love you.'

'But . . . what . . . since when?' The woman of words suddenly had little of sense inside her.

'Oh aeons,' he said with fervour.

'Please don't tell me it was love at first sight, Max Spender, because that will not wash.'

He laughed then. 'No, definitely not at the Ritz. Sarcastic, belligerent, too clever by half – that's what I thought then.' She went to speak but he cut in: 'And yes, I was arrogant and prejudiced and way too full of myself.'

'And now?' she quizzed. This declaration of love was a novelty to her, and she craved more.

'I'm full of you, or I want to be. I think you're amazing, Georgie. There is no one else I'd rather be rescued by.'

Silence, more bumping, turnips tumbling. What else could make this day the oddest one possible?

He looked concerned by her silence. 'George? Could you even consider it?'

Could she? Had that tight pinch of her heart at the thought in him in Gestapo clutches been something more than concern for a friend? Her drive that very day to risk everything – her future, liberty and the job she loved? Possibly, her life. The sharp nip on seeing him with Simone time and again? That squeeze of his hand the night before he was arrested?

'I thought you said there was someone else,' she murmured, still unable to fully believe this wild confession.

'It's you, Georgie,' he sighed. 'It has been for ages.'

He paused, brow wrinkled. 'When I was in that cell, you

362

were the only person I thought of consistently, the only one I couldn't bear to think of not seeing again.'

'Really?'

'Yes, *really*.' He cast around the inner gloom of the truck, wriggled a metal wire from the side of a box, and bent it into a shape. 'Georgina Young – you are the only woman I can imagine being beside me as we travel the globe. I think, and I hope, you feel the same. So will you bloody well marry me?'

She filled her lungs with a breath. On the run in the middle of Germany, amid the earthy smell of vegetables filling her nostrils and hurtling towards Lord knows what fate, there was only one answer. 'Yes, Maximus Titus Aurelius Spender. I bloody well will.'

He pushed the rough metal ring on her finger and leaned over to kiss her – his lips were soft, as she'd imagined, not dry or dusty. Had she ever conceived this moment? Yes, obviously she had, in some shady corner of her heart. Eyes closed, they moulded, each pushed further into supple flesh by riding the bumps like a wave. The pleasure was clipped short with a sharp jostle of the truck, but long enough to make her entire being shiver. For once, not with anxiety or fear, but bliss. Pure bliss.

'Perfect,' he said, his smile wide and white under the tarpaulin. 'No escaping me now.'

'We just have to slip out from under the Nazis' noses and not get caught or killed.'

'All in a day's work for the best duo in Berlin.'

The farmer left them on a small back lane, half a mile from the airport, with a wave of good luck. Georgie dusted herself down and tried to look as if she was a legitimate traveller, pushing her hair under the brim of a hat and applying more make-up than she normally wore, while Max pulled a clean shirt from the bag Georgie had packed, hiding his purple bruise under the collar. They were undoubtedly *persona non grata* in Germany – but they didn't have to look like desperate escapees.

They talked tactics on the short walk to the airport; both favoured a brazen approach through the main entrance, rather than skulking around the perimeter where guards were sure to be plentiful. They'd stopped at a phone booth on the way, and Georgie called in one last favour, which might prove helpful, if it worked.

Tempelhof was changed since their arrival just over a year before. Military outnumbered civilian staff, po-faced and armed at each entrance, while the noise overhead, a constant buzz of planes in and out, signalled the increase in air traffic. Max grabbed Georgie's hand as they approached the main terminal doors, squeezing it tight. 'Time to show me some more of those excellent acting skills,' he said, beaming like a new groom.

Georgie recalled the women at the Ciro bar, threw back her head and made a faux laugh in character. 'Watch and learn, Spender. Watch and learn.'

There was a short queue to gain entrance, the guards checking papers meticulously. Assuming the SS had circulated an all ports warning for them both, they still hoped Tempelhof was lower down the list. They hung back a little, waiting for the right moment. An older woman up ahead proved a convenient stooge, rifling in an enormous carpet bag for her passport, the young guard close to rolling his eyes. 'I have it in here somewhere,' she muttered. 'I'm sure I packed it.'

'Now!' Max murmured under his breath, yanking Georgie's hand towards the front of the queue and breaking into a run.

'We're going to miss it, darling, if we don't hurry!' Georgie projected in her best upmarket German accent. 'Our honeymoon is ruined!' Her face contorted into a dramatic twist of distress as they came upon the guard directly. He looked terrified at the thought of it spilling into tears, presenting him with two tricky situations.

'Can we . . . can we? Thank you . . .' Max bustled past the old woman, rattling on, his own glance at the guard appealing to an unspoken masculine need: 'Please help me not to disappoint my new wife.'

With continued grumbles from the old woman, the guard paused for a second, then waved them on hurriedly. They slipped inside the door, striding towards the ticket desk.

'One down,' Max mumbled through his teeth.

'Several more to go,' Georgie said.

The ticket desk mercifully had no queue, attended by a young and attractive woman; Max's turn to switch on his charm as Georgie hung back. 'I wonder if you might be my angel of mercy today,' he began, and her expression instantly softened. He gestured towards Georgie, looking mournful to his rear. 'My fiancée and I have been to visit her parents in Berlin, but now my own mother is very ill in London, and we need to get back as soon as possible.' The muscles in his face rippled. 'She might not have much time left. I wonder if you can help? I mean, if you're at all able. I'd be so grateful.'

The woman's heavily made-up face twisted with empathy at Max's plight. 'I'm sure we can, sir. The five p.m. flight via Paris has one seat available . . .' She looked past his shoulder to Georgie. 'Perhaps your fiancée can take a later flight?'

Georgie's face fell again with false misery, though her pulse rising towards the lofty ceiling was genuine enough. 'Oh, Maxy,' she whimpered pathetically. 'You won't go without me, will you? You can't leave me – I couldn't bear it.'

Max had already pulled out a wad of Reichsmarks with the flourish of the truly wealthy, the notes he and Georgie had pooled, and the woman's face spread with alarm.

'Let me see . . .' she blustered, scanning her seating plan.

'I'm sure we can work something out. Make an exception for your mother.'

'Could you?' Max's smile oozed gratitude. 'It would mean the world to us – and to her.'

'No luggage?' she questioned.

'Just our hand luggage.' Max thought on his feet. 'The rest will follow on. No time to pack properly.'

Handing over their passports prompted fresh beads of sweat to prickle across Georgie's body. They both combed the woman's features for signs of suspicion, if her eyes strayed to a list of 'wanted' or undesirables. Georgie could hardly believe it when she simply passed over two tickets and wished them a good flight. 'You just have time for a quick drink in the bar before departure,' she said cheerily, and Max clasped her manicured hand in appreciation.

'You are definitely my angel,' he said.

They turned tail with relief. 'Well, that was award-winning, Mr Olivier,' Georgie said as they walked resolutely away. 'Remind me never to believe a word you say in an argument.'

'Touché, Fraulein Young,' he came back, squeezing her fingers again. 'And we're not there yet. We're still on the charm offensive.'

As much as they both desired – needed – a drink, each hovered in the men's and women's bathrooms, counting down the long minutes until they could reunite and board. Every passing second on Georgie's watch felt increasingly sluggish, her energy at the pretence waning, buoyed only by nature's concoction of innate drive and sheer terror. If they were caught, there was no explaining it away, not even as bone fide press. It would be their war and possibly life over in a flash.

She looked at her hastily primped face in the bathroom mirror and almost didn't recognise the Georgie looking back. Entering Germany, she had been a fresh-faced and eager guest, albeit naive. Now she was experienced and weary, possibly cynical – and a fugitive. How did that happen?

They emerged at boarding time, linked hands and walked with bogus confidence towards the gate.

'We wish you a pleasant flight,' the steward said on checking the tickets. Pushing out onto the concrete beside the runway felt like escape from a hot and humid prison; even the warm wind of aircraft engines was a blessed respite as the late, low sun beat down. Still, each step towards the waiting plane was a milestone, not least because Max's clammy hand pulsed into hers with his pace. One step closer, one more. There was an urgent, rhythmic throb in her ears, her heart beating time, and Georgie desperately worked to screen it out. She wanted to hear everything, be on full alert. She needed to know if the Gestapo were a hot breath on their collars, to be ready. Though no shouts of 'Halt! Halt!' behind them. Not yet.

They reached the aircraft steps and Max virtually hauled her up each one and inside, his head dipping to watch through the windows as they found their seats at the back of the plane. Strapped in, they willed the doors to be secured and the engines to choke and rumble in readiness. Max broke his gaze away for a second and gave Georgie a weak smile. *Nearly there.*

Dare she think it? Risk a smile in return?

Then a dip in the roar of the metal around them, a head-to-head conversation up ahead between the stewards, furtive glances towards the back of the plane. Towards them. On them. Bodies moving in their direction with no portal or hope of escape. Out of the window, a car swerved into view and drew up on the runway, SS bodies streaming out, striding confidently towards the plane.

So nearly there.

Georgie braced herself for the doors opening, SS ravens coming to pluck at their prey, the indignity of being hauled back from near freedom. But nothing. More mutterings up ahead and she strained to see out of the window; the familiar form of red hair and a slight frame by the steps, talking, negotiating, his body language near to arguing, certainly insisting. Sam Blundon. A friend responding to her call, and now a saviour. Her own angel of mercy.

It seemed like an age – again. Rivers of perspiration flowed between her and Max, trading looks of hope and defeat. But something Sam said or produced appeared to have an effect. With what seemed like a fit of temper, the SS man threw up his arms and returned to his car, slamming the door shut. Sam squinted into the windows, scanning for their faces, and Georgie waved furiously. Did he see her? Was that him waving back?

But they were already beginning to taxi away. Air dared to move again within, Max equally unbelieving as his eyes mirrored hers: more good fortune smiling down.

She shifted in her seat and something inside her jacket crinkled; an envelope hastily lifted from the post pile as she left Frida's that morning. It was the distraction she needed to inch away the next minutes – and the familiar script made her heart flip.

Dear Georgie,

I hope this finds you as well as we are – Sara and I, and the children. Yes! The dream I didn't dare think of has happened, reunited in London, and now in your beautiful hometown. My only regret is that you weren't there to witness it – the sight of Sara's heart instantly mended, sinews sewn with threads of love (you can see how my news language has deserted me!).

For this old man it was . . . how to describe the feeling of their healthy, innocent limbs in mine, drawing in the smell of their hair? It was as if each child's birth occurred all over

*again. To you and Max, and all who aided, thank you, thank
you, thank you. I am sitting next to your father as I write,
sipping at a warm pint of English beer – there is one waiting
at the bar for you. Hurry home if you can, my lovely, brave
Georgie.*

Regards always, Rubin Amsel

A hot ball of emotion rose in her throat as the plane finally
lifted from the ground, and Georgie thought she might start
to cry. The letter was the best news. But was she also sad? Yes
and no. Regret for those lost or left behind with slim chance
of escape – Margot, Karl and Elias, of course, unable to save
him from a tenuous future in Sachsenhausen. And so many
other Jews in Berlin and beyond. Paul's killer – she was certain
he'd been a victim of the Reich – left unpunished, with Doctor
Graf allowed to work his deathly skills. Kasper too. They'd
failed in exposing Paul's story and Hitler's murderous intent.

Perhaps Sam was right – you had to be satisfied with small
triumphs, those like the Amsels. She mourned the loss of the
press pack too; Berlin had been her baptism of fire, a chance
to prove herself. But it would undoubtedly become a battle-
ground of wills, correspondents already stifled, and it could
only get worse with Britain and Germany at loggerheads. There
were other places to report on war, always assuming she and
Max still had jobs. Not forgetting Georgie Young had also
gained a life partner, contemplating a future with the man still
gripping her hand, the man she surely loved, but had not dared
admit a growing attraction to, even to herself.

She turned to his weary face, his eyes closed with exhaustion,
and thought how far they'd both come since that hot and
heady night at the Ritz. Grown up. Big girls and boys now.
Men and women of the press.

Below, the airstrip reflected a different Germany, a country already at war; lines of military craft sitting like black moths ready to swarm, the crimson flags – swollen since her arrival – flapping a red-rag call to arms. As they climbed higher, propelled forward, the landscape altered, and German airspace was left behind – perhaps forever, Georgie pondered. A crackle came over the tannoy: 'Good evening, ladies and gentlemen, we hope you enjoyed your stay in our beautiful city of Berlin.'

There was a reception committee of one waiting at Paris airport, thanks to the wonderful Sam getting a crucial call out. But his stature, the length of those big arms and his huge smile equalled any crowd.

'Welcome back to Paris, kiddo,' Rod said, pulling both into his orbit. 'You made it out then?'

'No choice but to leave,' Georgie said. 'They threatened to run out of strudel.'

'Damn travesty,' Rod cried. 'But let me tell you, I have discovered the best patisserie, and they make the most gorgeous little cream clouds of ecstasy . . .'

57

The Inevitable

Three days later, the expected arrived, though where Georgie and Max heard the news was anything but predictable – in the balm of a breeze and with a border between them and Berlin.

Rod's expression was intent, his beard resting on his knuckle, as the café owner tuned in to the BBC World Service, and the customers fell into a hush.

Prime Minister Neville Chamberlain's voice seemed weak, and – to Georgie – already tinged with defeat. 'I have to tell you now—' a sudden gust caused the leaves to tremble and flutter, muffling his words '—and that consequently this country is at war with Germany.'

The rest was merely details – the words had been said. The storm had come, clouds set to rain their brimstone and fire. Max gripped Georgie's hand, pressing the makeshift ring into her flesh. 'Well,' he said with a smile, 'we'd better get to work then.'

Epilogue

Postcard from Paris,
3rd September 1939

Dear islanders across the channel,

In Paris, there is still sunshine, a breeze rippling the awnings above the street cafés, as French and English citizens huddle around their radio sets. When the announcement came from Mr Chamberlain, that much-awaited declaration signalling we are now at war with Germany, there were mixed feelings of fear, stoicism and relief: that Hitler should be stopped, that his jackboots and his ego can no longer ride roughshod over nations he simply plucks at will to be his own.

Do we relish war? No. Do we fear it? Maybe. Can we win it? The verdict here is uncertain. The conviction, however, is that we can only go forward, to push back a tyranny that is purely and simply wrong, that bullies can never to be allowed to triumph.

If truth be told, we are certain only that the enemy we face is one worthy of our efforts, and that the time is ripe for us as allied nations to stand tall and fight for freedom.

Your Berlin Girl, signing off

News Chronicle, 6th September 1939, p.6

NEWS CHRONICLE REPORTER IS WED –

our very own 'Postcards from Berlin' author marries fellow reporter

News has reached the *Chronicle* office of a happy event as Britain readies for the consequences of Herr Hitler's invasion of Poland. A former Berlin correspondent of this paper, Miss Georgina Young – who writes in these pages under the name of George Young – was married to the *Daily Telegraph*'s former Berlin reporter, Mr Max Spender, in Paris yesterday. Also present were Mr Rod Faber, chief correspondent of the *New York Times*, formerly expelled from Germany under the Nazi regime, the *Chicago Tribune*'s Mr Bill Porter, and Mr Samuel Blundon, a British Embassy assistant recently arrived in the city, as the diplomatic service in Berlin is hastily reduced.

The happy couple met in Berlin over a year they both describe as 'full of adventure, and a steep learning curve'. However, they will not be setting off on honeymoon just yet. After a celebratory afternoon tea at the Paris Ritz hotel, the couple will travel to new postings in Europe, where they will continue reporting for the *News Chronicle* and the *Daily Telegraph*.

AFTER THE EVACUATION:

Our correspondent George Young reports on a seaside town left empty after the Allies' dramatic flight from French shores

Dunkirk is desolate, its population distended briefly by the hungry and the desperate, now a graveyard of war ephemera, streets emptied like a British seaside town in deep winter. The human cost of the evacuation has largely been removed, and what remains now is the debris of conflict scattered across the wide sands; a French warship beached like a mighty killer whale, its belly exposed with the steel skin cut cleanly in two by German bombs, carcasses of loyal horses left behind, their flanks still shiny, gulls pecking and filling their bellies.

Only a handful of local beachcombers dare to scavenge what they can. And the smell – a mix of human habitation and acrid cordite overpowering the salt spray scent. There's near silence, save for the gulls and the gentle engine throb of our vessel, one of the last to leave the French shore. Desolation hits every sense as we bob our way over the waves, Dunkirk left with the promise of fresh occupation only a little way behind – German tanks and troops ready to reinvade as the flotilla of British boats recedes across the Channel to safety, to regroup and reignite the battle for Europe.

Time magazine, 24th April 1945

The efficient but 'forgotten' camp of death

By George Young. Pictures by Max Spender

A short distance from the singed rubble of Berlin city lies another catastrophe of this war, small in comparison, and hidden behind a nine-foot stone wall. Even in liberty, Sachsenhausen remains one of the lesser-known Nazi concentration camps, compared with the shocking images of Auschwitz and Bergen-Belsen. Lesser known, maybe, though the suffering is no less hard to observe, as the physical wreckage of human cruelty is laid before the first wave of press observers: an odd shoe cast aside, a shorn piece of striped material common to inmates, evidence of lives lived and lost, blended with the stench of death and torture.

Those few souls left behind sport skin-and-bone faces, pinched and ghostly, eyes glazed, hoping but also daring themselves not to hope, weak smiles still questioning whether freedom has truly arrived.

I was here, briefly, before war broke out; I saw only the granite wall, knew something of the suffering beyond that barrier, but seeing really is believing.

Since its opening in 1936, Sachsenhausen has been exploited by the Nazis as a prototype, a working blueprint to practise their architecture, hone their skills for degradation, and their experiments for more efficient annihilation elsewhere. As such, it was a testament to production and variety: the Nazis' largest currency-counterfeiting operation was placed here in the war, so too a vast brick factory to construct Hitler's utopian ideal, a lengthy track for exhaustive testing of military footwear, not to mention the avid development of fatal mustard gas by medical experts. A camp relatively small and hidden, nicely within Berlin's reach, but so, so deadly.

The prisoners, too, were a mix: German political, Jews, Romani, Jehovah's Witnesses, homosexuals, the so-called 'work shy', mental 'defectives', British commando agents, Special Operations Executive prisoners – all were incarcerated, and many died here. In all 30,000, another 30,000 forced on a vast route march in the days before Soviet troops arrived to liberate, as the Nazis fled and scattered their dirty spoils. It is the legacy of that barely human existence that we see now.

The smell forces into our nostrils, sour and hostile, the sights beyond belief – barracks designed to corral humans and laid out in a fan shape, meticulously designed so that machine gun posts were afforded a bird's eye view, picking off stray targets in the gravel strip known as the 'Death Zone'. In its relative abandonment, it is a stretch to imagine everyday life in Sachsenhausen; the torture and the abject cruelty, but also the humour, the tenacity and zest for life that carried some through to freedom.

It may never be the name that sticks in our minds, not one to mark in the global consciousness, but Sachsenhausen is no less worthy of our attention – and our pity. This correspondent will surely not forget.

Der Bund newspaper, 13th March 1946, p.17

DOCTOR'S DEATH IS RULED SUICIDE – SUSPICIONS OF NAZI LINKS DIE WITH HIM

The death of a former German doctor, found in his home three weeks ago, has formally been ruled as suicide by the Swiss coroner, *our correspondent writes*.

Doctor Frederik Graf, sixty-five, was found at home by his wife, Lieda, after a bout of reported depression. Beside his body, she told the Coroner's Court in Berne, there was a one-word note stating: '*Sorry*'. Asked what he might be apologising for, Lieda Graf shook her head and became overcome with emotion.

Doctor Graf made a name for himself in his native Berlin at the Haas Institute, a clinic renowned for its elderly care, though rumours of links with the Nazi hierarchy have dogged him since the war's end. He arrived in Berne – some say fled – from Berlin in February 1945, and took up a hospital post in general medicine, but retired through ill-health soon after. He is survived by his wife. His only children, two sons, were both were killed in the D-Day battles in France.

The Daily Mirror, 23rd December 1947, p.10

Nazi chief caught out by his 'unusual' eyes

The last day of the month-long Auschwitz trial in Krakow took an unusual turn yesterday with a late guilty verdict for one concentration camp officer, thanks to an unusual eyewitness report – on spotting a distinctive pair of eyes.

The trial of sub-camp commandant Kasper Vortsch – in the dock alongside forty other guards and officers at one of the Nazis' principal death camps – was set to collapse due to a lack of evidence. Vortsch, thirty-four, consistently claimed a case of mistaken identity.

But when former prisoner Egon Cussel saw a picture in the local press, he recognised Vortsch immediately as 'the one with those eyes'.

'I was in Sachsenhausen camp in the early years of the war, and he used to visit the officers' mess all the time,' Mr Cussel told the court. 'They made us wait on the tables, serving up platefuls of food, while we had only weak turnip soup to live on. He had a charming smile, but after dinner, he would make us watch prisoners having to stand for hours in an agonising squat until they fell and were beaten. I watched those green and grey eyes light up as they suffered.'

On giving his damning evidence, Mr Cussel went on: 'My brother, Felix, made it out of Auschwitz, and he told me about an officer with these unusual eyes being a "particularly cruel bastard", watching men squat until they dropped. And I knew instantly who he was talking of. Sadly, Felix died a month after his release. That's why I'm here now.'

Vortsch was sentenced to twenty years imprisonment for his part in hundreds of deaths at Auschwitz and made no plea for mitigation.

Kindertransport child graduates from Oxford with first-class degree

One of the first children included in the operation to save Jews from the tyranny of Nazi Germany has graduated from Oxford University with a first-class degree in English.

Ester Amsel, now twenty-one, was among the first wave of children sent to England via 'Kindertransport', with her brother, Leon, then twelve. Ester was only nine years old when she faced saying goodbye to her parents at the train station in Berlin, unaware that she might never see them again.

'I remember it to this day,' she said. 'My mother was trying not to cry, telling me to mind my English manners. I realise now how hard it must have been for our parents to send us. But thank goodness they did.'

Ester's parents, Rubin and Sara, were lucky enough to escape Germany's anti-Semitic oppression only weeks before war broke out, with the help of two British correspondents working in Berlin, former *Daily Telegraph* reporter Max Spender, and Georgie 'George' Young, who reported for this paper at the time. The now married couple had to effect a last-minute escape just days before Hitler's tanks rolled into Poland, and both were present in Oxford to see Ester graduate from Somerville College with honours. Brother Leon now has his own engineering company in Bristol.

'We're delighted to see Ester and Leon thriving,' Georgie Young told the *News Chronicle*. 'The Amsels were typical of so many families in Germany at the time, living under threat, and it could have been so different but for Kindertransport. It ensured the futures of children like Ester and Leon.'

Once reunited in London, the Amsel family settled in the Cotswold town of Stroud, where Mr Amsel – a former journalist in Berlin – is a reporter on the *Gloucester Citizen* newspaper.

'We left behind so much,' he said. 'My wife's brother, Elias, sadly did not survive the Sachsenhausen concentration camp beyond 1944, but we're endlessly thankful as a family to have avoided what many did not. We love England and think of it as our home now. I don't even mind the warm beer!'

Ester now plans to follow in her father's footsteps as a reporter, using 'Georgie' Young as her role model in a bid to become a female overseas correspondent.

Radio Times Listings, March 1972
4 p.m., Radio 4

'The women who courted and reported Berlin'

Renowned war correspondent Georgie Young investigates the lives of three former acquaintances, Frida Borken and Simone Doucette – both fellow reporters in Hitler's pre-war Germany – and actress Margot Moller; all three known resistance agents across Europe. Were these three glamorous women working for governments, the press and the German film industry in unison?

Simone died on a French resistance mission in 1943 and was soon exposed as a double agent for the Nazis. Margot Moller found fame in Joseph Goebbels's renowned stable of starlets, was later a key informant for the Allies and shot for treason by the Reich. And Frida Borken – a one-time contributor to *Time* magazine – has not been seen in peacetime. Young, who knew all three women in pre-war Berlin, asks: Was or is Frida an heiress who simply melted into the shadows? If so, where is she now?

The Guardian, 12th October 1994, p.3

Celebrated war correspondent writes her last lines

The Fleet Street of old has turned out in force for the memorial to award-winning journalist Georgina Young, who died last week at the age of eighty-two, writing her last lines only hours before her death.

Hundreds attended St Bride's, the journalists' church in central London, for the much-loved correspondent, who for years went under the by-line of 'George' to offset prejudice against female reporters. She was apparently working on an article about the irritations of old age when she fell victim to a sudden stroke, leading to her death. 'It's so typical of my mother that she was scratching in her notebook right up until the last, insisting that I type it up properly!' her son, Elias, said in one of many fond eulogies.

The Cotswold-born reporter started life on the fashion pages of the now-defunct *News Chronicle*, rising to the newsroom and then opting for a posting in Berlin in the year before war broke out. She met her husband and long-time work partner, reporter Max Spender, in Berlin, the two having to quit Hitler's Germany promptly after helping a Jewish family to escape the city, a year they later described as 'a fairy tale and horror story in one'.

They continued freelancing as a couple throughout the war, covering Dunkirk, the French and Dutch occupations and D-Day, Georgie being among the few women to land alongside the invasion forces. Often, they reported in war zones with their press colleague, Pulitzer prize-winner Rod Faber, and remained friends until his death at the age of eighty-five.

During the war, Max discovered a talent for photography, and their words and picture essays were seen in *Time* and *Life* magazines, a stream of Sunday supplements and worldwide publications. Both received multiple single and joint awards for their work, although Max later joked that his shrapnel wound from France in 1943 'is the only talisman I don't have to share with my wife!'

Georgie chronicled their adventures as roving reporters in her memoir 'Postcards from my Life', and continued working after the birth of their two children, Elias and Margot, though in what she described as 'weekend war reporting'. They specialised in snapshot news features, flying into conflict areas difficult to reach, bringing human stories to light from Korea, Vietnam and Cambodia. She described one of her best moments as seeing the Berlin Wall pulled down to 'free a city I can't help being in love with'. She and Max worked tirelessly together until his death two years ago from heart failure.

'It's all about the humanity,' Georgie told Radio 4's Desert Island Discs in 1990. 'Behind every picture, every word, there is a person, even if it seems to be a very dry political story – it affects someone. I love words, I love to use them to speak out, but at the end of the day, all I've ever wanted my words to do is tell the truth about people.'

It is only fitting, then, that we leave the last word to a woman credited with such skill in weaving them, in the introduction to her memoir:

POSTCARDS FROM MY LIFE

It's odd because when I think of that time, it's always in pictures. My life has been dominated for decades by words on a page, and yet I view the memories as if I'm looking through a magnifying glass at a tiny reel of film, stopping and slowing, juddering in the places where the adrenalin spikes in reaction to near disasters or heart-stopping moments. And when I recall it in detail, there were a good many of those. Then, it jumps ahead, to new scenes, people and places. Sometimes other countries.

But my first foray in Berlin – that time when the world held its breath in fear of a maelstrom of a war – I remember it with fondness. It was my apprenticeship to conflict, and yet oddly exciting. I was enticed. Hungry, fuelling a lifelong appetite pushing forevermore to be satisfied. So, yes, that time was precious. It was the beginning of war – and me, in so many ways. Part of me, I think, will always be that Berlin girl.

George Young, February 1978

Acknowledgements

As ever, I am indebted to so many people in helping me wrestle this book into being, not least since I made the monumental break (for me at least) from midwifery to full-time writing, halfway through this book. Having said that, all my colleagues at Stroud Maternity figure hugely as my 'chivvying' support network, sharing much-needed walks, wine and whingeing; Gez, Kirsty, Annie, Sammi, Sarah, Isobel and Kelly – especially good at the walking (and wine). Hayley, Micki and Idris, too, for their coffee meets and wise words.

More thanks I extend to fellow writers: Loraine Fergusson (LP Fergusson in print) – ever present as the common-sense tsar in the mad world of books – and Avon stablemate Lorna Cook, whom I have been prevented from meeting face-to-face by lockdown, but that doesn't stop us nattering endlessly on Zoom or social media. Katie Fforde – you're a constant support just by being a Stroudie legend.

Thanks also to Fiona Vandenburgh-Harwood, who not only had a beautiful homebirth and allowed me to be there, but also speaks German perfectly and is generous with translations.

My family I include in that buffer between the angst of

writing and needing to make the dinner – Simon, Harry, Finn and Mum – bringing me back to earth very quickly. Basil, the muse mutt, too – always keen for his tea.

I thank yet again my wonderful editor at Avon – Molly Walker-Sharp – always there with a positive comment and a chirpy email, ensuring a much easier journey for me, plus the entire team at Avon and HarperCollins worldwide. Without them, my books wouldn't be anything, anywhere. I'm still terrible at IT, so please grant me ongoing forgiveness.

Thanks also to my lovely agent, Broo Doherty at DHH Literary Agency – supportive, tenacious and very ready to absorb the sometimes dour bleatings of a sometimes wobbly writer. You must have been an agony aunt in a former life.

As ever, I couldn't have done this without my own vital sustenance of coffee; the chaps at Coffee #1 in Stroud and their ability to make mine 'just so', along with their chat and humour, and the new Felt Café in Brimscombe with its wonderful writers' vibe.

And readers: where would we be without you? More than ever, in these strange times, I have been reliant on books to take me to worlds away from my own, only too glad to be among the many still buying, absorbing and inhaling the language of others. Thank you for reading my own humble scratchings.

Germany, 1944. Anke Hoff is assigned as midwife to one of Hitler's inner circle. If she refuses, her family will die.

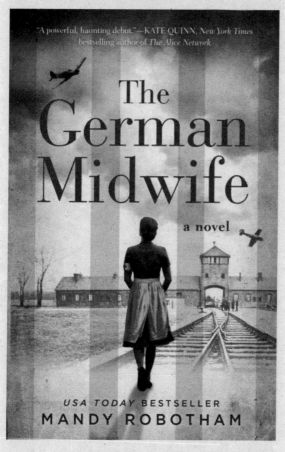

"A powerful, haunting debut."—KATE QUINN, *New York Times* bestselling author of *The Alice Network*

The
German
Midwife

a novel

USA TODAY BESTSELLER
MANDY ROBOTHAM

A gritty tale of courage, betrayal and love in the most unlikely of places, for readers of *The Tattooist of Auschwitz* and *The Alice Network*.

The world is at war, and Stella Jilani
is leading a double life.

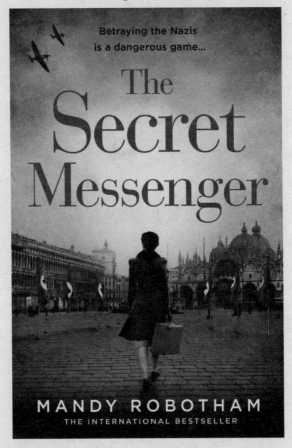

Betraying the Nazis
is a dangerous game...

The
Secret
Messenger

MANDY ROBOTHAM
THE INTERNATIONAL BESTSELLER

Set between German-occupied 1940s Venice
and modern-day London, this is a fascinating
tale of the bravery of everyday women in the
darkest corners of WWII.